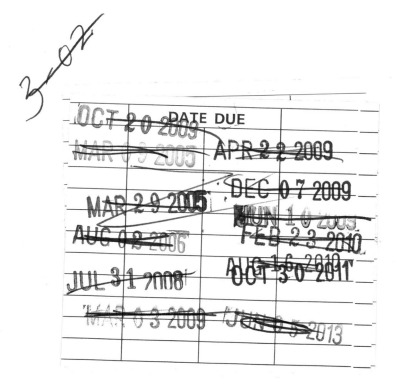

GABRIEL'S WOMAN

GABRIEL'S WOMAN

ROBIN SCHONE

BRAVA

KENSINGTON PUBLISHING CORP.
http://www.kensingtonbooks.com

3 - 02   19.00

BRAVA BOOKS are published by

Kensington Publishing Corp.
850 Third Avenue
New York, NY 10022

All Kensington titles, imprints and distributed lines are available at special quantity discounts for bulk purchases for sales promotion, premiums, fund-raising, educational or institutional use.

Special book excerpts or customized printings can also be created to fit specific needs. For details, write or phone the office of the Kensington Special Sales Manager: Kensington Publishing Corp., 850 Third Avenue, New York, NY 10022. Attn. Special Sales Department. Phone: 1-800-221-2647.

Kensington and the K logo Reg. U.S. Pat. & TM Off.
Brava Books and the B logo are trademarks of the Kensington Publishing Corp.

ISBN 1-57566-698-7

First Kensington Trade Paperback Printing: September 2001
10 9 8 7 6 5 4 3 2 1

Printed in the United States of America

GABRIEL'S WOMAN

Chapter

1

Gabriel knew the woman in the lusterless cloak.
He knew her because he had once been her.

Cold. Hungry.

The perfect prey and the perfect predator.

She came to kill an angel.

She wouldn't live to see the dawn.

Jumbled voices spiraled upward on ribbons of yellow fog and gray smoke. Men in black dress coats and white waistcoats and women in shimmering gowns and winking jewels shifted inside a flickering maze of candlelit tables: standing, sitting; leaning back in Honduras mahogany chairs, slanting forward over white silk tablecloths.

They did not know they were bait, the English ton who sought pleasure and the London whores who sought their wealth.

They did not know that a woman stalked them; Gabriel's body throbbed with knowledge.

Of pleasure; of wealth.

Of life; of death.

By reopening the House of Gabriel—a tavern where every carnal desire could be satisfied—he invited both patrons and prostitutes.

Sex and murder.

White flame shot upward.

Twenty feet below him, a man snared his gaze.

A man whose hair was as dark as Gabriel's was fair.

A man with violet eyes instead of silver.

His right cheek was pitted with shadow.

Twenty-seven years of memories arced between them. Images of war-hungry France instead of winter-shrouded England; of two half-starved thirteen-year-old boys instead of two forty-year-old men in tailored black dress coats and white waistcoats.

My two angels, the madame who had plucked them off a Paris street had said. *A dark one, for the women. A fair one, for the men.*

She had trained them to be whores, and they had excelled at it; she had taught them the eighth deadly sin, and they had broken it.

The flare of candle flame dimmed, abruptly recalling Gabriel to the pistol that weighted his left hand.

Michael, the scarred angel had come to protect Gabriel, the untouchable angel.

Revenge would not be possible without him.

Without him there would be no need for revenge.

The woman would die because a dark-haired angel lived.

And loved.

A pulse tattooed a relentless rhythm against the rosewood grip: *men*, women; *pain*, pleasure; *life*, death.

The Adams revolver was equipped with a double-action lock: manual cocking for accuracy, self-cocking for rapid fire.

He could manually cock the revolver.

He could release the trigger in a single, precise shot.

One bullet would kill Michael.

One bullet would stop the twenty-nine-year-old cycle of death.

Gabriel did not cock the revolver.

He could not kill Michael.

The second man had sent a woman to do the job Gabriel had failed to do six months earlier.

A sharp report ricocheted down his spine.

The woman halted on the edge of candlelight, Michael in her sight.

Out of the corner of his right eye, Gabriel saw a waiter in a short black cloak and white waistcoat bend over, straighten with a white silk napkin. Immediately below Gabriel, two waiters inched closer to Michael.

Their hands remained at their sides: they were not prepared to shoot a woman.

Four tables over, a waiter poured champagne from a newly uncorked bottle, crystal glinting, liquid sparkling.

Of the second man, there still was no sign. But he was down there, a chameleon in a black dress coat and white waistcoat. Disguised as a patron or a prostitute. Leaning back in a Honduras mahogany chair or slanting forward over a white silk tablecloth.

Hard. Erect.

Turgid with the heat of sex and the thrill of murder.

Time slowed to the beat of Gabriel's heart.

The cloaked woman brought her arms forward and clasped a dull, dark object between her hands.

A blue-plated pistol did not reflect light. Gabriel knew that because his own pistol was blue-plated.

The thundering roar of sexual parley dimmed.

Her head was concealed by the fold of a dark hood: Gabriel could not see her features.

Regret knifed through him.

For the men and women who had died; for the men and women who would die.

For the woman below who was about to die.

Perfect prey and perfect predator.

Gabriel aimed at the pale blur of her face.

At the same time a clear, feminine voice rang out: "I offer you my virginity, gentlemen."

Gabriel froze.

The woman dressed like a streetwalker; she spoke like a well-bred woman.

One by one the tons' genteel guffaws and the prostitutes' practiced titters died.

Silk whispered. Candle flames fluttered.

Uncertainty immobilized his waiters.

Duty dictated they expel the woman in her cheap black cloak; experience warned them it was too late: she had attracted the attention of rich patrons.

Virgin flesh was prime produce.

The waiters would not interfere.

"The man who tenders the highest bid shall possess their reward this very night," she continued in a clarion voice, hands still, body poised, death just a bullet away. "Shall we start at one hundred and five pounds?"

One hundred and five pounds tumbled through the fog and the smoke.

On London streets a maidenhead—whether real or manufactured—sold for five pounds, not *one hundred and five.*

Sudden recall smashed through Gabriel's consciousness: of a French *maison de rendezvous* instead of an English night house; of a woman in luxurious purple satin instead of a woman in a dark, worn cloak.

Twenty-seven years ago the *madame* had sold his virginity for two thousand, six hundred and sixty-four francs.

One hundred and five English pounds were equivalent to two thousand, six hundred and sixty-four French francs.

The woman could only have gotten her information from two men: Michael or the second man.

Gabriel did not doubt for one moment from which of the two she had gained her knowledge.

He manually cocked the revolver with his thumb.

" 'Ere now!" Malice unveiled a female prostitute's Cockney origins. "Ain't no fish bladder worth one 'undred five pounds, dearie!"

Light and shadow jittered in a burst of masculine and feminine laughter.

The cloaked woman did not laugh.

Did the second man?

Did he train a revolver on Michael while Gabriel aimed his pistol at the woman, or did the cloaked woman slowly squeeze the trigger of a gun through her reticule, unaware of her fate?

Had the woman come to kill an angel . . . or had she come to distract one?

"I assure you, madam," the woman coolly returned, "my maidenhead does not come from a fishmonger. I am indeed a virgin."

It was possible.

Circumstances forced chaste, educated women out onto the streets, just as it did gay, uneducated ones.

It was of no consequence.

A weapon wielded by a virgin was just as deadly as one wielded by a streetwalker.

Curved metal cradled Gabriel's middle finger.

"Then remove the cloak, girl, and show us what you're selling," Lord James Ward Hunt, earl of Goulburn and home secretary, crudely challenged.

Gabriel did not spare him a glance.

In the candlelight, the man's greased hair shone like black oil.

Shadow turned red into black.

The woman's blood would shine like the home secretary's hair.

"I see no reason to exhibit myself, sir," the cloaked woman calmly rejoined. "It is not my body that is of value, but my virginity."

Shock halted the remaindering snickers.

Whores desiring purchase did not refuse to show their wares.

Gabriel knew that because he had been a whore for over twelve years.

Dressing. Undressing.

Enticing. Seducing.

Sex had seemed a small price to pay for food and shoes and a bed to sleep in. In the beginning.

In the end he had fucked merely to prove that he wasn't the whore he had been trained to be.

The second man had proved him wrong.

"By jove, she's got bottom!" Gabriel focused on the woman instead of the newly elected parliament member who spoke. "I'll give you twenty pounds, eh, what?"

"A woman's virginity is her dowry," the cloaked woman said

evenly, body turning away from Michael toward the parliament member. The change of position revealed the dark object she clutched: it was a reticule, not a weapon. "Is that all that a woman's maidenhead is worth to you, sir? Twenty pounds? Would you sell your daughter—or sister—so cheaply in marriage?"

Disapproval turned the tide of masculine interest.

Male or female, prostitutes did not compare their worth to those of the *ton*.

No matter how high of a price their flesh commanded.

Trilling laughter sliced through the candlelit darkness.

An English gentleman and a London prostitute climbed up the plush red-carpeted stairs that edged the saloon, black coattails flapping, bustled silk gown sashaying.

They had reached an agreement while sipping vintage champagne; their flesh would seal the bargain in an upstairs bedroom.

Gabriel's body coiled to fire the Adams revolver while the heat and the scent and the sound and the sight of men with women squeezed his testicles.

Gabriel did not fear for his own death this night.

That would come later.

Watching Michael die would be his punishment; death would be his reward.

For the pain, *for the pleasure* . . .

"I will give you one hundred and five pounds, mademoiselle, for your . . . innocence," volunteered a silky, masculine voice.

Electric awareness tightened Gabriel's scalp.

When he had last heard that voice, it had spoken fluid French instead of clipped English. There was no mistaking who it belonged to: the second man had bid on the cloaked woman.

Black and white movement slashed through his peripheral vision.

Gabriel's head reflexively snapped toward his right, heart pounding, left hand steady, the waiting over.

A man in a black dress coat leaned across a white silk tablecloth. Blue and orange fire flared between a blunt cigar and a tapered candle. Gray hair shone in the dual play of light, disappeared in a wreath of smoke.

He was not the man who had bid one hundred and five pounds.

He was not the man whom Gabriel would kill or be killed by.

A distant *bong* penetrated the wood, the glass, the throbbing sexuality and the pending death that the House of Gabriel was built from: Big Ben announced one hour, two, three . . .

"I bid one hundred and twenty-five pounds."

A balding pate shone like a gibbous moon above gleaming gold studs.

"I bid one hundred and fifty pounds."

Teardrops of fire ricocheted off crystal and glinted off dark hair.

"Mein Got." Baron Strathgar shouted from the middle of the saloon. His round face was dark from alcohol, his German accent heavy with excitement. "I bid two hundred pounds."

The feel of Michael's keen alertness squeezed Gabriel's chest while the second man's anticipation fisted inside his stomach.

Low murmurs rose to a dull cacophony, the sound of two hundred voices raised in conjecture.

An auction had never taken place in the House of Gabriel. Yet one did now.

Men did not pledge two hundred pounds to pierce a woman's hymen. Yet Strathgar just had.

Gabriel prepared for the next bid.

Watching.

Waiting.

Remembering . . .

. . . Reading the name Gabriel for the first time, printed by Michael while they waited for day to turn into night.

. . . Writing his first word, *Michael,* practicing the script inbetween the women who purchased a dark-haired boy and the men who purchased him.

Wondering . . .

. . . When the need for sex would die and he would stop throbbing with what he could never have.

. . . Why he could not forget a woman's benediction: that he find a woman to give him pleasure. *To make up for everything he endured.*

The waiting ended with a flurry of motion.

Scooting back his Honduras mahogany chair, the German baron rose to claim his prize.

"I will give you five hundred pounds."

Strathgar halted mid-stand.

The gray-haired man had bid.

Gabriel's gaze glanced off the back of the gray-haired man, leaped over the blond-haired woman who sat across from him, and settled on the man at the table behind them.

The back of his hair was so black that it glinted with blue highlights.

Gabriel did not need to see his irises to know their color: he saw them every time he closed his eyes to sleep.

Suddenly the saloon came alive with masculine speculation and feminine spite.

A bid for five hundred pounds had been placed on the cloaked woman. Every male patron determined to have her.

Jangled voices called out in rapid succession: "Five hundred twenty-five pounds." "Five hundred seventy-five pounds." "Six hundred pounds." "Six hundred fifty pounds." "Seven hundred pounds . . ."

An internal snick cut through the uproar, a door opening. Light slashed the darkness, the end approaching.

One man halted two feet behind him; from twenty feet below him, Michael pinned his gaze.

"One thousand pounds," scraped across Gabriel's too tightly drawn skin.

It came from the second man.

Stunned incredulity washed over the saloon.

Only two whores had ever commanded that high a fee. Michel des Anges—Michael of the Angels, a man named for his ability to bring women to orgasm—and the man who for the last twenty-seven years had been known only as Gabriel.

Gabriel, the whore.

Gabriel, the proprietor.

Gabriel, the untouchable angel.

Sputtering candlelight dimmed the comprehension that flowed across Michael's face: he realized that the second man had twice bid.

But did he recognize his voice? Gabriel wondered.

He aimed the Adams revolver at hair that was so black it glinted blue.

Would Michael recognize the second man's features after a bullet entered the back of his head and exited through his face?

"Monsieur." The man behind Gabriel did not step closer— Gaston had been in Gabriel's employ too long to make that mistake. "Monsieur, he has come, just as you said he would."

Everyone who worked for Gabriel knew to expect the second man. It was why he had rebuilt the House of Gabriel, to lure him with sex . . . murder.

Michael.

Gabriel.

But they didn't know what he looked like.

They didn't know what he smelled like.

They couldn't feel him, as Gabriel felt him, a cancer that devoured hope and despair, love and hatred.

"How do you know that he is here, Gaston?" he asked neutrally, pistol unwavering.

"He wrote *un* message for you, monsieur."

Gaston spoke with a native French accent.

Michael spoke French like a Frenchman, yet he was English.

Gabriel spoke English like an Englishman, yet he was French.

He did not know from what country the second man came. Gabriel had killed the only man who could tell him.

It did not matter. It was not necessary to know a man's nationality in order to kill him.

Gabriel squeezed the trigger . . .

The gray-haired man suddenly stood up, body shielding the second man. He assisted the blond-haired woman to her feet.

She stood taller than the gray-haired man, elegant as only a successful prostitute can be. Diamonds sparkled at her neck and ears. Fog and smoke twined about her hair—hair that was almost as fair as Gabriel's.

It dawned on Gabriel that he had seen the gray-haired man and blond-haired woman before. But where?

"When did he give this message to you, Gaston?" he asked shortly.

The second man had bribed his two doormen, else the woman would never have been allowed entrance.

The House of Gabriel did not cater to the destitute.

He wondered if the second man had also bribed his manager.

And knew it was all too possible.

Every man and woman inside his house had a price.

They would not be in Gabriel's employment if they did not.

The gray-haired man and blond-haired woman unhurriedly wound through the candlelit tables. A trail of gray smoke followed them.

The cloaked woman remained statue-still. Untouched by the danger that crackled around her.

"A waiter picked the message up off the floor," Gaston said stiffly, hurt by Gabriel's unspoken suspicion. "It is written on *une serviette.*"

An image of a waiter leaning over and straightening with a napkin in his hand flashed through Gabriel's mind's eye.

His flesh crawled with sudden apprehension.

The waiter had not been near the man with the blue-black hair.

He wanted to pull the trigger.

He wanted to kill the second man.

He wanted the cleansing finality of death.

Gabriel did not pull the trigger.

Instead, he watched the gray-haired man. He watched the blond-haired woman.

He watched the pair pause at the exit.

Behind Gabriel, Gaston tensely waited. Below Gabriel, the blond-haired woman gracefully turned, pale silk gown swirling.

The gray-haired man stepped through the doorway.

The moment he disappeared from sight, Gabriel remembered who he was: he was a member of the Hundred Guineas Club, an establishment that catered exclusively to homosexual men who assumed female personas.

The blond-haired woman netted Gabriel's gaze.

Recognition slammed through him.

They were not the eyes of a woman who stared up at him; they were the eyes of the second man.

Disguised as a prostitute instead of a patron.

A woman instead of a man.

Realization followed recognition.

The second man had not brought the cloaked woman to kill Michael, the dark-haired angel: he had brought the cloaked woman for Gabriel, the fair-haired angel.

Smiling, the second man blew a taunting kiss and stepped back. Out of Gabriel reach.

Out of Gabriel's house.

While Gabriel watched. Unable to stop him.

As he had been unable to stop him when chained in an attic while he taught Gabriel what the French madam had not been able to.

Rage tightened his muscles.

He had set a trap, only to be trapped himself.

The second man would not kill Michael tonight, but he would kill. He would leave no one alive who could identify him.

No one save the cloaked woman . . . *if* Gabriel took her.

"What does the note say?" Gabriel asked tautly.

"*Il dite* . . ." Gaston cleared his throat. "It says: 'Gabriel, I quote to you from Shakespeare, a man who no doubt would have been inspired by both your beauty and your expertise: "All the world's a stage, and all the men and women merely players."

'You have set a delightful stage, *mon ange*, now I bring you a woman. A leading actress, if you will. *Laissez le jeu commencer.*' "

Directly beneath Gabriel, Michael perused the saloon in search of the second man.

His innocence knotted Gabriel's stomach.

Michael had only ever wanted a woman to love.

Gabriel had only ever wanted to be like Michael.

A man with passion; a man with innocence.

A man with a soul.

The cloaked woman stood alone, seemingly impervious to the furor she had created.

Fear feathered Gabriel's flesh.

I bring you a woman, reverberated inside his ears. It was followed by *Laissez le jeu commencer.*

London streets were cramped with streetwalkers; women slept on the steps of poorhouses.

Yet the second man had chosen this woman.

She was a virgin. Or she was a whore.

She had been hired to kill Gabriel. Or she had been hired to be killed by Gabriel.

She was the last living link to the second man.

There was nothing Gabriel wouldn't do to catch him.

And he knew it.

"I bid two thousand pounds for the woman," rang out over the volley of noise below him.

The voice belonged to Gabriel.

He felt the impact of two hundred pairs of eyes.

Gabriel had not been with a woman in fourteen years, eight months, two weeks and six days.

The patrons knew it .

The prostitutes knew it.

The man who would save him knew it.

The man who would kill two angels knew it.

The woman's face was shrouded in darkness.

Gabriel did not know what she knew. *Yet.*

But he would.

Before the night was over, he would know everything there was to know about her.

He hoped, for her sake, that she was an assassin.

It would be far better for her if she were.

If Gabriel did not kill her, the second man would.

It would be a far, far worse death than that which Gabriel would deliver.

Laissez le jeu commencer.

Let the play begin.

Chapter

2

Passion.

Victoria gazed into silver eyes and understood why respectable men and women came to the House of Gabriel.

They came to experience passion.

She had come to escape it.

"You may leave us, Gaston."

The silky masculine voice pierced fog. Smoke. Wool. Flesh. *Bones.*

A whisper grated across Victoria's skin, the sound of a door closing. Sealing her inside a library instead of the bedchamber she had expected.

It would not alter the outcome of the night.

Victoria knew that a man did not need a bed in order to couple with a woman: a doorway or an alley often sufficed.

Above her, an electric chandelier pummeled her with light; in front of her, a silver-veined, black marble-topped desk and a pale blue leather Queen Anne chair stood between her and the blond-haired man.

Her hood blocked her peripheral vision; it did not blind her to the danger that crackled around her.

It did not shield her from the fact that she had sold her body to the highest bidder.

He did not move, this man who had purchased her virginity, a Greek statue garbed in a tailored, black-silk dress coat and a white waistcoat, pale blond hair shining like spun silver.

A sharp pang stabbed through her chest.

He was so beautiful it hurt her to look at him.

Victoria tore her gaze away from his, heart racing, thoughts chasing.

She had seen him before: the high cheekbones, the sculpted mouth, eyes that saw through the most basic desire . . .

His left hand rested palm down on top of the black marble, pale fingers long, slender, short nails buffed to a polished sheen. A mound of white silk abutted his little finger.

Victoria had no illusions about what men did to women. The hand that caressed them could also hurt them. Disfigure them.

Kill them.

Her gaze snapped upward.

Silver eyes were waiting for hers.

Victoria's stomach clenched.

From hunger, she told herself.

And knew that she lied.

She was afraid.

But she could not afford to be afraid.

"You bid two thousand pounds for my virginity," she said bluntly.

"I bid two thousand pounds," he agreed neutrally, silver eyes inscrutable.

But a woman's virginity is not worth two thousand pounds, Victoria wanted to cry.

She did not.

"I am not experienced in these matters." She gripped her knitted wool reticule; her ring finger slipped through a loose purl. "How is it that you intend to pay me?"

"That is entirely up to you, mademoiselle."

Mademoiselle.

The waiter who had brought her to the man behind the black-marble-topped desk had called her mademoiselle. He had spoken with an unmistakable French accent.

The man who had bid one hundred and five pounds and then one thousand pounds had also called her mademoiselle. He had spoken with an unmistakable English accent.

Like this man.

A compulsive need to know the nationality of the man who would take her virginity overcame her.

Victoria swallowed it.

Prostitutes did not question their patrons. And by her actions this night, she'd left the rank of unemployed governess and become a prostitute.

Deliberately, she reached up and shoved back her hood.

Electricity bolted through the air.

Victoria froze, hands suspended.

The man's little finger that had bridged the mounded white silk was now buried underneath it.

She had not seen him move, but he had.

"Take off your cloak."

The order was cold, clipped.

Her gaze shot upward.

His face and eyes were devoid of desire.

The last six months had taught Victoria that men did not need to desire a woman in order to possess her. Some men took pleasure in power while others took pleasure in pain.

Perspiration pooled beneath her breasts, crawled down her stomach.

What did this man take pleasure in, she wondered: power . . . or pain?

Why would a man—a man who could surely have anyone whom he desired—pay two thousand pounds for a woman's virginity?

His silver gaze did not waver; the long, pale fingers did not move away from the silk cloth.

Soon he would touch her with those fingers, Victoria thought with a growing sense of unreality. He would knead her breasts and probe her vulva.

Or perhaps not.

Perhaps he would take her leaning against the wall or bending over the marble desk with no preliminary kisses. No caresses. Their only contact through their genitals.

The woman inside Victoria screamed for her to flee.

The pragmatist inside her warned she had nowhere to run.

An ember sparked, underscoring her decision.

Whatever happened this night, with this man, was *her* choice. She would not back down.

Clumsily, she released the wooden buttons on her wool cloak, lips firming with resolve, reticule swinging. Slipping her left arm free, she transferred the reticule to her left hand, and slipped the cloak off her right shoulder. Carefully, she draped the moth-eaten wool over her left forearm as if it bore some value.

It did not.

In the last six months she had sold everything she possessed.

And it *still* had not been enough.

The silver-eyed man briefly glanced down at the hem of her brown wool dress. Dark lashes gouged even darker shadows into his cheeks.

She knew what he saw.

The skirt puddled around her feet. Victoria had sold her bustle two months past.

Slowly, he raised his eyelids, face an alabaster mask.

Victoria saw herself as he must see her. Her face was gaunt from cold and fear and hunger, her dark brown hair dull from no cleansing agent other than icy water.

She was not beautiful, but she had not offered him beauty; she had offered him her maidenhood.

Victoria squared her shoulders.

"What is your name, mademoiselle?" he asked pleasantly, impersonally. As if they met at a ball instead of a tavern of ill repute.

Various names floated through Victoria's thoughts: Chastity. Prudence.

None were applicable.

A chaste, prudent woman would not now be in her predicament.

"Mary," she lied.

And knew he was aware that she lied.

"Put your cloak and reticule on the chair."

Victoria sucked her lips against her teeth to quell a rising tide of anger. He could yet reject her, this elegant man who was surrounded by beauty and comfort. And not once would he think about the hell his rejection would condemn her to.

To her left, gold glittered on a wall of embossed leather books. Overhead, a crystal chandelier radiated heat. To her right, blue and orange flames danced inside a black marble fireplace.

For one blinding second she hated the silver-haired, silver-eyed man for the wealth that he possessed and the masculinity that he had been born with. She had been reduced to *this*—selling her virginity—solely because of her sex and the power a woman's subjugation gave men.

Victoria stepped forward and draped the ragged wool cloak over the back of the pale blue leather chair that was her sole means of protection. Reluctantly she dropped the reticule onto the cushion, deriding her unwillingness to part with it—the only valuable article she had left was her hymen.

And soon it, too, would be gone.

Sharpness abruptly spiked his voice. "Move away from the chair."

Glancing up, Victoria was pinned by frigid silver eyes.

Her heart leaped up inside her throat.

The anger simmering inside her forced it back down.

She *would not* be a victim.

Not of this man.

Not of the man who had systematically destroyed her life simply because he wanted for free what the silver-haired man was willing to buy.

Victoria deliberately stepped to the side of the chair.

"Shall I remove my dress?" she asked brashly, heartbeat drumming inside her ears, her temples, her breasts. "Or shall I merely hitch up my skirt and lean against a wall?"

"Do you often hitch up your skirt, mademoiselle?" he asked politely, silver eyes intent.

Victoria's head snapped back. "I am not a whore," she said tightly.

But for whose benefit?

Shadow shimmered inside his eyes, silver turning to gray. "You auctioned off your body, mademoiselle. I assure you, that makes you a whore."

"And you purchased my body, sir," she lashed back. "What does that make you?"

"A whore, mademoiselle," he said flatly, pale face a beautiful mask. "Are you wet as well as hard?"

Shock rocketed through Victoria.

Surely he had not said what she thought he had said.

"I beg your pardon?"

"Your nipples are hard, mademoiselle. I merely wondered if you were also wet with your desire."

Victoria held her hands at her sides, suddenly, acutely aware of the wool that abraded her nipples with each breath, each exhalation. The maroon carpet, high white ceiling and pale blue enameled walls silenced the sounds of the patrons and prostitutes who coupled beyond them; they did not obstruct the images his words forcibly conjured.

Of men and women.

Embracing.

Kissing.

Touching.

Naked bodies writhing.

Giving pleasure. Taking pleasure.

Engaging in all the sexual acts that respectable women did not desire to engage in. Or so she had wanted to believe.

The last six months had taught her differently.

"My nipples are hard," she said shortly, "because it is cold outside."

"But it is not cold in here. Fear, mademoiselle, is a powerful aphrodisiac. Are you afraid?"

"I am a virgin, sir." She stiffened her spine; her nipples stabbed her wool bodice. "I have never before taken a man into my body. Yes, I am apprehensive."

"How old are you?"

Victoria's heart skipped a beat. Did she look older or younger than her years? she wondered.

Should she lie or tell the truth?

What did a man such as he want in a woman?

"I am thirty-four years old," she said finally, reluctantly.

"You are not a young girl."

"Nor are you a young boy, sir," she retaliated.

Victoria clamped her lips together, too late, her words echoed between them.

"No, I am not a boy, mademoiselle," he said imperturbably. "But I am very curious as to why you, at your age, decided to part with your virginity this night, at the House of Gabriel."

Hunger.

Desperation.

But a man such as he would not want to hear about poverty.

Victoria attempted to be coy. "Perhaps because I knew that you would be here tonight. You are very beautiful, you know. A woman's first time should be with a man such as you."

The compliment fell flat. Victoria was not a coy person.

"I could hurt you," he said gently.

There was nothing gentle in his gaze.

"I am well aware of what a man can do to a woman."

"I could kill you, mademoiselle."

Victoria's heart slammed against her ribs.

"Are you that large, sir?" she asked politely.

Wanting to flee.

Wanting to fight.

Wanting the night to be over with so she could piece together the remnants of her life.

"Yes, mademoiselle, I am large," he said deliberately, silvery gray eyes watchful. "I measure over nine inches long. Why didn't you take off your cloak in the saloon?"

Burning wood popped.

Over nine inches stabbed between her thighs.

The image of a man's member—dark veins bulging, crimson crown protruding—flashed before Victoria's eyes. It was superimposed by an image of Lord James Ward Hunt, earl of Goulburn, home secretary. . . . *Remove the cloak, girl, and show us what you're selling.*

On Sundays the home secretary dined with her father; throughout the week he reviled abandoned women—the "frail sisterhood"—before the House of Lords in an ongoing effort to cleanse London streets of prostitution.

She wondered if her father knew of his friend's nighttime activities.

She wondered if her father shared them.

Nothing was as she had thought it to be six months earlier: not so-called respectable men and women, not the denizens who roamed London streets, certainly not Victoria.

All her life she had hidden from desire; now she could not escape it.

"I saw no benefit in flaunting my person in public," Victoria said woodenly. "It is my virginity that is of value, not my appearance."

"Were you afraid that men might not find you attractive?"

She was afraid that men might recognize her.

"I did not offer beauty," she said defensively. And bit her lips at being drawn into an emotional response.

Ladies did not publicly demonstrate emotion. Prostitutes, like governesses, were not expected to possess them, let alone give way to them.

A former lady, governess, and now a practicing prostitute, Victoria possessed emotions. But she didn't *want* to possess them.

"You do not think you are beautiful?" he asked lightly, silver eyes probing, face and fingers starkly elegant, the first framed by a short white collar and matching bow tie, the latter by silver-veined black marble.

"No, I do not," Victoria said tensely. Honestly.

Women forfeited their lives to their parents, their husbands, their children.

There was no beauty in subjugation.

"Yet you think that you are worth two thousand pounds."

"I asked for one hundred and five pounds, sir," she riposted. "It was *you* who bid two thousand."

"Money is important to you," he probed. Voice. *Eyes*.

Victoria gritted her teeth. "Money buys coal. Food. Shelter. Yes, money is important to me, as it is to all of us."

The money he had spent renting this room for one hour would keep her in comfort for several weeks.

"Exactly what would you do for money, mademoiselle?"

A chill ran up Victoria's spine; it was chased by heat.

Was he asking her what sexual acts she would perform?

"I will do anything you wish."

"You would let me hurt you."

It was not a question.

Her heart skipped a beat, raced to catch up. "I would prefer that you did not."

"When is the last time you ate?"

Anger knifed through Victoria.

He was playing with her. *Simply because he could.*

"I am not here to discuss my appetite, sir."

"But you *are* hungry."

Her stomach roiled in assent.

"No," Victoria lied. "I am not hungry."

"But you know what it is like to be hungry."

She would *not* admit weakness to this man whose beauty called to every feminine instinct she had ever tried to suppress.

"I have missed an occasional meal, yes."

Victoria had finished the crust of a quarter loaf of bread three days past.

"Would you kill for money, mademoiselle?"

Streetwalkers sometimes robbed and killed the clients whom they serviced.

Did he think she was a streetwalker?

A jagged fingernail penetrated her right palm. "I may prostitute myself this night, sir, but I am not a thief nor am I a murderess. You need have no fear of me."

"You have never before killed a man?" he persisted.

"No," she said adamantly. But Victoria had wanted to.

Watching her meager savings dwindle day by day, she had wanted to hurt the man who was responsible, as she had been hurt by his actions.

"Would you beg me, mademoiselle?"

The coldness fusing Victoria's vertebrae settled in the center of her chest.

"No," she said clearly. Decisively. Gaze holding his. "No, I will not beg you." She would not beg any man.

A burning log dropped inside the fireplace. Sparks shot up the chimney.

"Take off your dress."

Victoria's stomach growled, a betraying reminder of her mortality.

If he took her, she could die.

If he did not take her, she *would* die.

Of cold. Of hunger.

Or perhaps she would be killed for her cloak and shoes so that someone else might survive the London streets another night, another week, another month.

Feeling as if she were outside her body, Victoria raised her hands to her bodice. She watched her actions through silver eyes.

Fingers that were red and chapped released one button, two, three . . . Pale skin shone through the widening gap of the brown wool bodice. The base of her throat . . . the valley between her breasts . . . the curve of her abdomen, concave rather than rounded . . .

Taking a deep breath, Victoria shrugged. Harsh wool cascaded down her back, her hips, puddled around her feet.

There was no chemise, no corset, no petticoats to hide behind.

They, too, had been sold on St. Giles Street.

She squared her shoulders, more aware of the baggy silk drawers that rode her hips and the wool stockings that sagged about her knees and the half boots that rubbed her ankles than she was of her own breath.

Forcibly she blanked her mind.

Heat licked at her skin while the coldness of his gaze roved over her body. Shoulders. Breasts. The silk drawers covering the apex of her thighs.

Back up to her shoulders, her breasts.

He lingered over her nipples.

They *were* hard.

From the cold, she told herself.

And knew that she lied once again.

Victoria wanted to feel a man's hands on her body.

She wanted to feel *this* man's hands on her body.

She wanted to end once and for all the virginity that was both a woman's prized possession and the instrument of her downfall.

Purposefully, Victoria reached for the waistband of her frayed silk drawers. Then they, too, were gone, lost inside the circle of her wool dress.

Goose bumps spread over her bare buttocks.

She did not have to follow his gaze to know at what he stared: the hair between her thighs was curly as the hair on top of her head was not.

Heat followed the track of his gaze.

No man had ever seen Victoria naked.

No doubt this man had seen hundreds of naked women.

Women whose skin was soft and whose hips were full and supple. Women whose ribs did not stick out like the whalebones sewn inside a corset.

Women who knew what to expect from a man such as he.

Victoria hurriedly leaned over to untie the makeshift garter belt circling her right thigh, back stretching, breasts dangling—

"Stand up."

She jerked upright at the harshness of the command.

Pale color suffused the man's cheeks. It hardened rather than softened the chiseled perfection of his face.

The air pulsated around him. Or perhaps it was the veins inside Victoria's eyes that pulsated.

The silver-eyed, silver-haired man was not as removed as he pretended to be.

She was not as removed as she pretended to be.

"Step out of the circle of your clothes."

Stomach somersaulting, Victoria awkwardly stepped out of the wool drawers and the collapsed fortress of her dress. The twin strings holding her stockings in place bit into her flexing skin, right knee, left knee. Her feet sank into the bog that the plush maroon carpet had become.

"Take down your hair."

His voice was still harsh; the words were not quite as clipped as before. English with a trace of French.

Victoria's breasts throbbed in time to the pounding inside her chest. Fleetingly she wondered if he could see her heartbeat.

Lifting her arms, she searched for a hairpin, senses sharpening, breasts jutting, stomach tightening—

"Turn around."

Victoria stilled, heart pounding, *pounding.* "I beg your pardon?"

"Turn around and take your hair down with your back facing me."

With her back toward him, she would not be able to protect herself.

She had not been able to protect herself six months earlier, laced inside a corset hiding behind her virtue.

Victoria turned around.

A pale blue leather divan monopolized the far wall. Above it, a blue sea lapped an orange sunset.

Vaguely Victoria recognized the painting as being from the school of Impressionists, creators of dancing light and shimmering color.

Carefully, she released the hairpins; behind her, the man's gaze was a palpable touch.

On her buttocks. On the nape of her neck. Her shoulders. Back to her buttocks.

In the painting a shadowy man leaned over a small boat; he rowed across the canvas of a dying sun and rippling water.

No one would ever know his name.

Perhaps he had no name. Perhaps he was a figment of the artist's imagination.

A man who had no life outside of the painting.

Inexplicable emotion welled up inside Victoria: humiliation, excitement; anger, fear.

Her hair plunged down her back, a thick, heavy blanket that hid her nakedness and tickled the valley between her buttocks.

It did not stop the coming reality.

"Now turn around and face me."

Hairpins biting into Victoria's right palm, she slowly turned around.

The warmth of the room was not reflected inside the silver eyes that watched her.

This was it, she thought—this was the moment when she would lose the last vestige of her girlhood.

This was what the last six months had built up to. That the frenzied bidding below had led to.

The future yawned before her.

She did not know what lay beyond this moment, this night.

She did not know who she would awaken to the next day—to Victoria the woman or Victoria the prostitute.

The fear Victoria had held at bay during the auction swelled over her in a black wave of pure, unadulterated panic.

She had lied when she told herself that a woman who sold her body retained control—Victoria was not in control: the silver-eyed man was.

And he knew it.

"I do not know your name," she blurted out, hair a heavy anvil that weighted her body.

"Do you not, mademoiselle?" he asked softly, seductively.

Victoria opened her mouth to reply that she could not possibly know his name: women such as she did not move in the same circles as men such as he.

"Do you find me desirable?" she asked instead.

Tomorrow she would be horrified, remembering her question. But not now.

No man had ever told her she was desirable.

For eighteen years she had plainly dressed her hair and her body in order to avoid a man's attentions lest she lose her position.

Only to lose it anyway,

Her position. Her independence.

Her self-respect.

She was giving this man her virginity, no matter that he was paying for it.

She *needed to hear* that he found her desirable.

She needed to know that a woman possessed value in her sex as well as her virtue.

The overhead chandelier flickered and flamed inside silver eyes, a mirror to the bleakness inside her own soul.

Victoria's heartbeat counted the passing seconds. . . .

If he denigrated her . . .

"Yes, I find you desirable," he said finally.

And he lied.

Pain swiftly blossomed into anger. "No, you do not," Victoria rashly countered.

He wanted what the other man wanted: a piece of flesh instead of a woman.

The silver lights glittering inside his eyes stilled. "How do you know what I feel, mademoiselle?"

Blood drummed inside Victoria's breasts and thighs, spurring her on. "If you desired me, sir, you would not sit there and stare at me as if I were infested with vermin. I am as clean as you are."

As *worthy* as he was.

The stillness surrounding him expanded until it sucked up the very air.

"Why would I bid upon you if I didn't desire you?" he asked softly.

"You did not see me," Victoria pointed out, trying to rein in her galloping emotions, failing. *She had not asked for this.* "How can you desire what you cannot see?"

How could she yearn for what she had not experienced?

But she had.

She had secretly dreamed that a man would love the woman that she was and not the paragon of virtue that she had modeled herself after. And now that dream was gone.

No man would ever love her: men did not love whores.

The man before her sat statue-still, gaze unblinking. Had he ever loved? Been loved? . . .

"Why do you think I bid on you if I do not want you?" he asked, voice a beguiling caress.

There was no tenderness in his eyes.

But Victoria wanted tenderness to be there. She wanted him to *care . . .*

She would not be the same after this night, and she needed someone to mourn the old Victoria Childers and welcome the new.

"Some men believe that the pox can be cured by taking a virgin," she stated baldly, wanting to provoke some emotion—some response—out of this man who had never known a day's hunger in his life.

She succeeded.

His silver eyes narrowed. "I do not have the pox, mademoiselle."

Victoria did not retreat from the threat inside his voice and eyes.

"Nor do I, sir," she said stridently.

Danger shimmered in the air.

"What do you want, mademoiselle?" he asked softly.

She wanted what any woman wanted.

"I want a man to want me instead of my virginity," Victoria said rawly.

"You want me to desire you rather than your virginity?" he reiterated, as if the thought that a woman would want to be desired for herself rather than her innocence had never, ever occurred to him.

The time for lying had passed. "Yes. I do."

Light. Shadow.

Silver. Gray.

Victoria refused to look away from his eyes that alternately reflected light and darkness, silver fire and gray steel.

This was the woman she was. This was the woman she had always been. . . .

"And how would you have me show my desire?" he asked, gaze holding hers, *swallowing* hers . . .

Victoria thought of the man who had demonstrated his desire by having her dismissed from her position.

"You paid two thousand pounds for the privilege of touching my person," she said, heart cramming her throat.

"You want me to touch you?" he asked in that soft, seductive voice that was neither soft nor seductive but danger pure and simple.

"I do not want to be taken like a woman on the street."

The truth rang out harshly over the roar of the fire and the blood thrumming inside Victoria's ears.

For one disorienting moment the pain she felt shone in his eyes.

Immediately, the pain was gone.

From his eyes, but not from hers.

"Yet you came here, selling your virginity"—there was no emotion in his voice, no life in his eyes—"like a woman on the street."

Victoria would not cower from the truth. "Yes."

"How do you want to be taken, mademoiselle?" he asked abruptly.

With passion. With tenderness.

But they both knew she had sold that right.

Victoria's breasts shimmered with the force of her heartbeat. A steel pin pierced her palm.

"With respect," she said tautly. "I want to be taken with respect . . . *because* I am a woman."

Not because she was a virgin. She wanted to be respected because she was a woman. *Because* she was not pure.

The gathering tension squeezed the air out of Victoria's lungs.

" 'All the world's a stage, and all the men and women merely players,' " he recited unexpectedly. Watching her. Silver gaze sharper than the steel pin pricking her palm. "Are you a devotee of Shakespeare, mademoiselle?"

Victoria blinked at the sudden change of conversation. It did not slow down the race of her heart.

"I am not particularly fond of that particular play by Mr. Shakespeare, no," she managed.

"Which play is that?"

"As You Like It," Victoria said . "The play you just quoted from."

The air vibrated—a door opening somewhere in the building, perhaps. Or closing.

"Do you enjoy the stage?" he asked in that tantalizingly seductive voice that no man had a right to possess.

It danced on her skin like St. Elmo's Fire.

Teasing. Tantalizing.

Taunting her with what she could not have.

She forcibly concentrated on his question and not her need and her nakedness.

Victoria had only once been to a play.

"Yes," she said. "I enjoy the stage."

Again there was that subtle vibration—a chord of response.

But to what?

"Come here, mademoiselle."

The soft command did not lessen the pressure constricting Victoria's chest.

Now he would take her. Fully dressed, while she wore sagging stockings and worn half boots.

Leaning against the wall or bent over the desk.

Like a whore.

Victoria realized how ridiculous she must look—a former governess who possessed no elegance and whose sole redeeming value was her hymen. How comical he must have thought her, demanding respect when her clothes would be sneered at by the lowest of drudges.

"My shoes—" she stalled.

"Leave them on."

"That is not . . . ." Victoria's voice trailed off.

"Dignified, mademoiselle?" he offered, mouth twisting cynically.

The knowledge of other nights and other women was indelibly etched on his face.

How many times had he gone through this ritual? she wondered.

How many skittish virgins had he calmed?

"I was going to suggest . . . practical," Victoria replied, fighting for control.

She did not know this woman who stood unabashedly naked in front of a stranger, who cried out her pain and her need—she scared Victoria as much as the silver-eyed man.

"I assure you, mademoiselle, your shoes will not get in the way," he said cryptically.

The thick carpet sucked at Victoria's feet; she waded forward, pelvis jutting.

Her thighs rubbed together; the friction dancing on her swollen nether lips glittered in his eyes.

He knew of the desire his beauty created, those eyes said. He knew of the moisture that leaked from her vagina and the heat that beaded her nipples.

He knew more about Victoria in the short time they had spent together than any other person she had ever known.

Victoria's left heel turned.

Hair swinging like a pendulum, face burning with embarrassment, she righted herself.

The silver-eyed man showed neither approbation nor derision, marble made into flesh. He swiveled in his chair, wood creaking, physically following her progress, expression inscrutable.

Victoria halted, hemmed in by his body and the desk. Behind her, the wooden fire crackled busily, unaffected by the pending loss of a woman's innocence.

He smelled of expensive soap; underneath that she breathed the faint aroma of tobacco and perfume that had pervaded the downstairs saloon.

The top of his head was level with her breasts; the toes of her worn shoes were scant inches away from the toes of his suede-and-black-patent boots.

The advantage of height was no advantage at all. Victoria had no doubt whatsoever who was the strongest. The quickest.

The most dangerous.

He stared at her breasts for long seconds, at her nipple that peeped through the mane of hair hanging over her right shoulder. His lashes were long. Thick. Dark as chimney soot. They cast dark, jagged shadows on his pale, flawless skin.

Only now he was not so pale. Dusky pink edged his high cheekbones.

Victoria could feel her nipples lengthening, hardening underneath his gaze.

Slowly, his lashes lifted. Silver eyes riveted hers.

"I don't *want* to want . . ." she whispered fiercely, feeling ineffably vulnerable.

She had never wanted to want . . . a man' s touch, a man's kisses, a man' s passion . . .

The thin prick of his pupils dilated, silver metamorphosing into black. "Desire is a part of all of us, mademoiselle."

Victoria's throat inexplicably tightened. "You do not seem . . . afflicted . . . by these desires."

Regret skidded across his face, was swallowed by the blackness of his pupils. "Desire is not considered to be an affliction by some."

But it was by him, Victoria all at once realized.

This man fought his needs, as she fought hers. Afraid to want, unable to stop either the fear or the desire.

"Is that why you came to the House of Gabriel tonight . . . to find a woman who does not deny her needs?" she asked hesitantly.

A pulse pounded deep inside her vagina, once, twice, thrice; a matching pulse ticked inside his cheek, once, twice, *thrice* . . .

"How far will you carry this game, mademoiselle?" he asked in a curiously harsh voice.

"It is not a game when a woman gives her virginity to a man," Victoria replied unevenly.

"What if I want more than your virginity?"

Flyaway strands of hair aureoled his head, creating a silver halo. She realized where she had seen this man before: she had seen his likeness inside stained-glass windows. He had the face of an angel.

An angel who brought salvation with one hand and destruction with the other.

Tears pricked her eyelids. "That's all I have."

"You have seen men with women."

The images Victoria had seen over the last six months—of hurried couplings and open gropings—was reflected in his eyes.

"Yes," she said.

There was nothing she had not seen these last six months.

"Then you know there are many ways that men want women."

Heat and coldness raced up and down Victoria's spine.

This was blunt speaking, indeed.

"Yes."

"Have you ever taken a man into your mouth, mademoiselle?"

The warm breath laving her skin was suddenly ice-cold against the scalding heat that crawled down her neck and chest. "No."

Light and shadow glimmered inside his eyes. "But you would do this . . . for me?"

Victoria fought a lifetime of inhibitions. "Yes."

For this one night . . .

With this one man . . .

"Do you speak French?"

"*Un petit peu,*" she admitted. *A little.*

Enough to teach grammar to children. But he would not want to know her prior profession. After this night neither would ever see the other again.

The prick of the steel pins inside her right palm arced up her arm.

"The French have an expression called *empétarder,*" he said, marble skin glowing like candle-warmed alabaster. "Are you familiar with it?"

"*Pétarader* means to . . . to backfire," Victoria said shakily.

Breasts swollen. Nipples hard.

"*Empétarder* is an antonym," he murmured, gauging her reaction.

"It is used purely in a sexual content, meaning to receive something through the back."

Through the . . . back.

Victoria's breath caught in her throat.

Her comprehension shone in his dilated pupils.

"Would you grant me access there, mademoiselle?" he asked deliberately, provocatively. "Would you share your body with me . . . in whatever way I asked?"

Victoria's instinctive response was to recoil.

No.

The darkness inside his gaze would not let her recoil.

"Yes. If that is what you wish."

"But would you take pleasure in such a possession?"

"I . . ." *Don't know.* Victoria swallowed; her breasts bobbed with the motion; breasts he had yet to touch. "Pleasure is always preferable to pain."

"There is always pain in pleasure, mademoiselle," he said in a strangely remote voice. "The French sometimes refer to an orgasm as *la petite mort*, the little death. Would you share your pain . . . as well as your pleasure?"

The little death . . .

There was no *little* death on the streets of London; every one of them was fatal.

"I would try," she said.

"You would let me hold you when both of our bodies are dripping with sweat and the scent of our sex fills our lungs," he said, a statement rather than a question.

His words were electrifying.

"No one has ever held me," Victoria confessed unbidden. No one save a child . . .

But Victoria did not want to think about that. Not tonight.

"But you would let *me* hold you," he persisted.

Dripping with sweat. The scent of their sex filling their lungs.

She took a deep breath, smelling the faint, clean, masculine scent that was uniquely his. "Yes."

Victoria would let him hold her.

"And you would hold me."

The barrenness inside his eyes squeezed her heart. He did not believe a woman would want to hold him.

Or perhaps he did not believe a *whore* would want to hold him.

"Yes," Victoria said.

"Because I would give you two thousand pounds," he prodded.

"Yes," Victoria lied.

It was not for two thousand pounds that she would share her body with him: this man had touched her with his words if not his body.

A tiny warning bell rang inside Victoria's head. It chimed that it was the height of presumption for a woman such as she—a woman who had no experience—to assume that a man such as he yearned for intimacy.

Victoria ignored the warning.

His hair was longer than fashion prescribed; it curled over his collar.

Feeling curiously weak yet infinitely powerful in her femininity, she reached out a trembling hand to touch a spun silver curl.

There was no warning, no protest of wood to signal that he moved, but suddenly the distance between them spanned far more than the inches that separated their bodies.

"Get dressed, mademoiselle," he said flatly. "And tell me the name of the man who hired you."

Chapter

3

Get dressed, reverberated inside Victoria's ears. It was followed by, *And tell me the name of the man who hired you.*

Abruptly she became aware of the fireplace that warmed her buttocks and her breasts that all at once felt like blocks of ice.

Heavy.

Cumbersome.

Undesirable.

She did not understand the blond-haired man's dismissal. She did not need to.

Rejection was rejection in any language, whether it be verbal or physical.

Holding on to her pain, Victoria stepped back.

Her left heel turned.

She wildly grabbed . . . the white cloth.

Hairpins rained down on top of black marble.

Slamming heavily into the desk, she stared down through twin streamers of dark, lifeless hair at a pistol. The grip was carved out of rosewood, body a dull blue-back. It was the same color as her father's hair, she noted numbly. And then there was only the dull blue-black metal visible, wood swallowed up by long, elegant fingers.

Head snapping back, Victoria dropped the napkin. At the same time she pushed away from the desk.

Light bled into the man's pupils until the black of his pupils were two tiny pinpricks and his irises turned into molten silver.

There was no passion inside them. No compassion.

No evidence of the intimate words he had spoken.

Immediately an image of her corpse clothed only in sagging stockings and worn half boots popped into her mind.

She did not want her corpse to be found dressed in sagging stockings and worn half boots and her hair tangled about her.

Words pushed up inside her throat; she swallowed them. She had said she would not beg. And she would not.

"Are you going to kill me?" Victoria asked evenly.

Creaking wood was her answer.

The silver-eyed man lithely stood up; at the same time he slid the pistol underneath the right lapel of his dress coat into a holster that hung underneath his arm, a flash of brown leather that was immediately swallowed by the fall of his coat. Turning, he rounded the black-marble-topped desk and strode across the plush maroon carpet, black coattails smoothly flapping, *left,* right, *left,* right. He scooped up her clothes, taut buttocks straining against black silk trousers.

Silk and wool slapped her chest.

Victoria reflexively caught her clothes.

He was as elegant from the back as he was from the front.

But it wasn't his back that now confronted her.

Cold gray eyes dismissed her nakedness and her worth as a woman, virgin or otherwise. "Should I kill you?" he asked imperturbably.

It seemed as if she had lived with the threat of death all her life.

Victoria trembled—legs, hands, *stomach.*

Not for the life of her would she give him the satisfaction of showing her fear.

Raising her arms, she defiantly jerked worn wool over her head, arms tangling with silk, clearing. Leaning forward, she stepped into her drawers. Hours passed, fastening the two tiny buttons on the waistband of her silk drawers. Days passed, fastening the wooden buttons lining the bodice of her wool dress.

His silver-gray eyes were waiting for hers.

"I am a virgin," she said evenly. "And I do not have a"—six months earlier she would not have known the word by which men who lived off the revenue a woman's flesh brought were called—"pimp."

Silver ice glittered inside his eyes. "I am fully aware of your virginal status, mademoiselle."

Victoria sucked in air; it did not still the pounding of her heart.

The desire that only moments earlier had tightened her breasts and pooled moisture between her thighs continued to pound and throb, a beast that had yet to realize it had died.

Victoria took a calming breath; it did not calm her. "Then I am afraid I do not understand what it is that you want to know."

"I want to know why you are here."

"I thought that was obvious, surely," she returned, blood throbbing, heart pounding.

"A man sent you here, mademoiselle. I want his name."

"No man sent me," she repeated. At least not directly.

But she would not be here if it were not for a man.

"Then a woman sent you."

"I was not sent here by a woman."

His voice sharpened. "Who gave you money to bribe the doormen?"

She would *not* panic.

"I did not bribe the doormen."

"My house is not a common pub, mademoiselle." His gaze was implacable. "How did you get past my doormen, if you did not bribe them?"

My house. *My* doormen.

Dread premonition mingled with Victoria's fear and anger and throbbing desire. "Are you the proprietor of this night house?"

His silver eyes did not reveal so much as a flicker of emotion. "I am Gabriel."

Gabriel. The House of Gabriel.

Dear Lord. Victoria had said she had come to the House of Gabriel in the hopes that he would be there.

A woman's first time should be with a man such as you, she had said.

Did he think she had deliberately crashed his house in order to gain his interest?

"Are you French?" she asked impulsively. And wondered if the last six months had addled her brains.

What difference did it make what his nationality was?

A Frenchman could shoot a woman as easily as an Englishman.

"I am French," he agreed coolly. "One last time, mademoiselle. How did you get past my two doormen?"

Victoria remembered the two men who had guarded the entranceway: one had possessed hair that glinted like spun gold instead of the spun silver that the hair of the man who stood before her shone like; the other doorman had had hair that gleamed like rich mahogany wood.

Their beauty paled in comparison with that of their employer.

"I told them I was in need of a protector," she said shortly. Wondering if he would believe her.

Wondering why he wouldn't believe her.

"And they let you in?" he asked caustically, silver eyes glinting a warning.

Victoria squared her shoulders. "I am not in the habit of lying, sir."

"Are you not?"

There was no mistaking the cynicism in his voice.

What is your name, mademoiselle?

Mary, rang inside her ears.

"No," Victoria affirmed, "I am not."

"The street price for a woman's virginity is five pounds."

She clung to her pride. It was a far more comfortable emotion than fear. "I am fully aware of what a woman's virginity is worth."

Her reputation. Her position.

Her life . . .

"Then why did you ask for one hundred and five pounds?"

Because she had not expected to receive it.

"You do not think that a woman's virginity is worth that sum, sir?" she challenged.

"I believe that women—and men—are worth far more than one hundred and five pounds," he replied enigmatically.

It was not the answer Victoria had expected.

"Because you enjoy deflowering women," she said scornfully.

"No, mademoiselle, because *I* was sold for one hundred and five pounds. But you already knew that, didn't you?"

Words echoed inside her ears.

You auctioned off your body, mademoiselle. I assure you, that makes you a whore.

And you purchased my body, sir. What does that make you?

A whore . . .

Victoria suddenly realized where she had seen his eyes: she had seen them while scouring the streets of London in search of respectable work. Homeless people possessed that same flat gaze. Men, women and children whose daily fare was hunger, cold and hopelessness.

Men, women and children who routinely whored, stole and killed that they might live while others died around them.

Her heart pounded against her ribs.

"Who are you?" she whispered.

"I told you who I am: I am Gabriel."

Proprietor.

Whore.

But not of his choosing.

None of it his choosing.

Poverty deprived men—as well as women—of choice.

"I'm sorry," Victoria said. And instantly knew that it was the wrong thing to say.

This man who had survived impossible odds would not welcome pity.

He did not.

Silently he blocked her exit, black silk trousers brushing the pale blue leather arm of the Queen Anne chair.

"Why are you sorry, mademoiselle?" he asked so softly she had to strain to hear him.

Victoria refused to back away, either metaphorically or literally. "I am sorry that you were sold against your will."

"But it was not against my will, mademoiselle," he countered silkily. "Or did the man forget to tell you that?"

"We do what we must to survive." Victoria ignored his reference to "the man." "It is not a matter of will."

His nostrils faintly flared. "And did you do what you must do this night?"

Victoria firmed her lips. "Yes, I did what I must tonight."

"You agreed to come to my house and auction off your virginity."

Anger flashed through her; she tamped it down. "I did not agree, but yes, I came to your house tonight for that purpose."

"So you are an unwilling accomplice," he goaded.

"I am not an accomplice."

"But you are here because of a man."

Yes.

Victoria stiffened her spine, wool abrading her still-swollen nipples. "I told you, I do not know this man to whom you are referring."

"Then who did refer you to my house, mademoiselle?"

"A prosti"—no, Victoria would not call the woman who had befriended her a prostitute; women—and men—did what they must to survive—"a friend advised me that your clientele would be more . . . generous than a man on the street."

"And this friend"—he purposely imitated her hesitation—"is it a man or a woman?"

Victoria wanted to protest that it was none of his business: reason warned her not to.

The thin wire running up between her shoulders tightened.

She did not like being manipulated.

"A woman," Victoria said curtly.

"Did this woman tell you that you should open the bidding at one hundred and five pounds?"

Victoria refused to glance away from the heart-stopping intensity inside his gaze.

"I am sorry you feel that I mocked you by offering . . . by starting the bidding with one hundred and five pounds." Victoria forced the apology out of her throat. "I assure you, neither my friend nor I knew about your circumstances; indeed, I did not know that you existed prior to this night."

The silver-haired, silver-eyed man was not impressed with either her apology or her ignorance.

"Answer my question, mademoiselle."

"Yes," Victoria snapped, "it was my friend who suggested that I start with that sum."

His gaze narrowed. "How tall is your friend?"

"Shorter than I." Victoria drew herself up to her full height of five feet eight inches. "If you will excuse me, sir, I will take my leave."

He did not step out of her way. "You cannot leave, mademoiselle."

Victoria's heart skipped a beat. "I beg your pardon?"

The polite phrase was a discordant ring. Three times now she had begged his pardon.

"You are well-spoken," he sidetracked, hand reaching, finger unerringly finding a wrinkle in the pale leather arm pad.

The wrinkle had a small island in it.

It dawned on Victoria that it resembled a woman's vulva, lips gaping, vagina a darker depression . . .

She jerked her head up.

"Proper speech is required in a governess," Victoria said stiffly. And realized she had unwittingly confided her former occupation.

She bit her bottom lip.

The silver glint inside his eyes acknowledged her lapse.

"How long have you been a governess?" he asked easily.

Victoria was not fooled by his sudden easy manner.

The man who called himself Gabriel was like a cat. A large, beautiful, deadly cat who played with its prey one second and ripped its throat out the next.

Victoria defiantly tilted her chin. "I hardly think that is any concern of yours, sir."

"But it is, mademoiselle." His voice was a silky purr. "You sold yourself to me for two thousand pounds."

Her heart skipped a beat.

"I sold my virginity to you," Victoria protested sharply. "I did not sell myself."

And he did not want her virginity. Let alone the woman who possessed it.

Dark lashes shielded his eyes. Victoria instinctively followed his gaze.

Gently he caressed the blue leather wrinkle. "How long have you been out of a position?"

An image of her naked body, legs splayed for easy access, flashed through her mind. It was chased by a picture of a long slender finger caressing her . . .

Her gaze snapped up from his caressing finger. Hot blood flooded her cheeks. "Six months."

His silver gaze snared hers. "How long were you a governess?" he repeated.

He would repeat the question until she answered, Victoria realized.

"Eighteen years," she bit out.

"You became a governess at sixteen?"

Victoria glanced down at his hand, away from the memories that had determined her profession.

A long finger gently prodded the dark depression of leather.

"Yes." Sharp sensation stabbed up between her thighs. "I became a governess at sixteen."

"And after eighteen years, you have just now realized that prostitution pays more than being a governess?" Gabriel asked idly.

Victoria glanced up.

There was nothing idle about the silver gaze that captured hers. *Yes,* rose to her lips.

"I was dismissed from my post," came out of her mouth instead.

Victoria had been dismissed without a reference, she did not need to add. The knowledge was inside his eyes.

Society did not trust their children with governesses who were dismissed without a reference. Nor did employers hire inexperienced governesses for menial positions when rural laborers migrated to London by the flock.

There were many women in Victoria's situation. It did not make it any easier to bear.

"The whore who sent you here"—shadow lurked inside his eyes, memories, perhaps, of his own past—"you believe she is your friend."

Victoria did not hesitate. "Yes."

"You would protect her from me."

Dolly had stopped a man from raping her when no one else had lifted a finger. She had talked to Victoria. Confided in her. Advised her when Victoria had needed advice.

She had been a friend when Victoria desperately needed friendship.

"Yes." Victoria squared her shoulders. "Yes, I would protect her if it were within my power."

Without warning, the long white finger that had been idly worrying the blue leather wrinkle slid over the padded arm of the chair and hooked the wool laces of her reticule.

For a second Victoria stared at the flawless beauty of his hand and the squat, graceless purse he plucked from the chair.

The full impact of his action struck her.

He had her reticule.

Everything Victoria possessed was in that reticule. He had no *right*. She rushed forward to reclaim her property. Her life. *Her dignity*.

Reaching into the wooden rim, he pulled out a small piece of tightly folded brown paper. "What is this?"

Victoria halted, remembering the pistol concealed inside his dress coat. "It is a . . . a remedy to prevent conception. Please give me my reticule."

He did not relinquish the reticule. "Your friend . . . did she give you this contraceptive?"

There were men who believed it their right to indiscriminately impregnate women merely because they were male and women were female.

Surely he was not one of them?

"Yes, my *friend* gave it to me." She imperiously held out her hand. "Please return my reticule."

Looping the twin wool laces over his wrist, he unwrapped the paper, reticule swinging, paper crinkling, dark eyelashes shadowing his cheeks. Two white tablets spilled into the palm of his right hand.

Slowly he raised dark lashes. "Did your friend tell you what this is?"

Victoria's silence spoke louder than words.

"It is corrosive sublimate, mademoiselle." His silver eyes were relentless. "Did your friend tell you how to administer the tablets?"

"You seem well informed about the product, sir," Victoria returned, hand dropping, fingers fisting, nails digging. "Why do you not tell me?"

"Each tablet contains 8.75 grains of corrosive sublimate. One tablet causes violent convulsions, often followed by death. Two tablets inserted into your vagina, mademoiselle, would most certainly bring about your death."

Victoria felt the blood drain out of her face. Dolly had told her to insert both tablets into her body in order to prevent conception.

She had not told her what they were or what they could do.

She had not told her that they would hurt her . . . *kill* her.

"You are lying," Victoria said. And did not believe it for one moment.

The silver-eyed, silver-haired man did not comment.

He did not need to comment.

Dropping the two tablets onto the brown paper, he refolded the whole.

"She said many women use the tablets," Victoria persisted.

"No doubt. However, women who use it once obviously do not do so again. And having survived its use, a woman would certainly not recommend it for contraceptive purposes." He crimped the ends of the paper. Slowly his eyelashes lifted, pinning her with the truth. "Was your friend young and inexperienced, mademoiselle?"

Dolly had been a self-proclaimed, two-pence prostitute who had whored from the time she was ten years old. A woman with graying brown hair and missing front teeth.

She had urged Victoria to crash the opening of the House of Gabriel. No one would notice her, she had declared, in the busy traffic of people.

Only rich, powerful men would be allowed inside, she had added. Men who would pay far, far more for her virginity than men in a brothel or on the street.

And all the time she had plotted Victoria's death.

Hoping, no doubt, to take Victoria's money while her body lay cold in an alley.

All in the name of survival.

The elegant room was too close. The overhead chandelier too bright. The crackling fire too hot. The hair hanging down her back too heavy.

Victoria needed to get away from those piercing silver eyes.

Warily she circled around him and grabbed her cloak off the back of the pale blue leather chair.

She did not need her reticule—he could keep it. The poison. Her toothbrush. Her comb.

The hairpins.

He did not stop her.

The door was constructed of mirror-shiny wood that was neither brown nor yellow, but something in between. The governess inside Victoria identified the wood as satinwood, indigenous to India and Sri Lanka.

The door was not locked.

It did not need to be.

The waiter who had led her to the library stood at attention on the other side. Victoria did not doubt that he, too, wore a pistol underneath his black coat.

"Bring up a tray, Gaston." The all-too-familiar voice skidded down her spine, smoother than satin. "And a pot of tea. Mademoiselle will be staying with us."

"Very well, monsieur."

Gaston gently closed the satinwood door in Victoria's face.

She pivoted, dress tangling about her ankles, hair swinging, heart gorging her throat. "You cannot keep me here against my will."

"*Au contraire.*" Gabriel faced her rather than the desk. "If your life were not dispensable, mademoiselle, you would not be here."

The callous dismissal of her life momentarily took her breath away.

"You don't want me," Victoria said compulsively, gripping her wool cloak as if a lifeline.

"You would be surprised at what I want," he returned cryptically. Watching. Waiting.

As if she were the one who were dangerous and not he.

"You never intended to lie with me," Victoria recklessly accused him.

"No," he agreed. Light and darkness glimmered inside his silver eyes. "I did not intend to lie with you."

"You bade me undress," she said. *Knowing that you would not take me,* she did not need to add.

He had seen her pitiful, makeshift garters and sagging stockings and threadbare drawers and worn shoes.

His silver eyes remained cold. Impervious.

"Why?" Victoria's cry bounced off the ceiling, skirted the pale blue enameled walls. "Why did you lie to me?"

Why had he seduced her with images of entwined bodies dripping with sweat in the aftermath of shared pleasure?

Why had he told her he found her desirable?

"I needed to know," he said simply.

Before, she had mistaken the fleeting shadows inside his eyes as regret; she did not make that mistake again.

"What did you need to know? How far a virgin would go in order to gain money?" Victoria fought to keep the shrillness of fear out of her voice. "You have sold your body. I assure you, sir, I would have gone a lot farther than standing over you with my breasts in your face."

Her jaws snapped shut, hearing the echo of her words.

The pale blue enameled walls shrank until she could feel them pressing against her back, her chest, her sides.

She would have taken him into her mouth.

She would have taken him into any and all of her orifices.

And he knew it.

It was patently clear that her virginity possessed no value to him. But it was all she had left.

He knew that, too.

"I needed to know if you possessed a weapon, mademoiselle," he merely said.

"You bade me remove my drawers"—she gulped air—"to see if I concealed a weapon inside them?"

"Yes."

"Where did you think I would hide this weapon—inside my *vagina?*"

"It is possible."

Victoria stared at him.

"What a dangerous sex we women are, to be sure. And how very fortunate." The bubble of laughter that was trapped inside her chest inched up into her throat. She remembered the older brother of a past charge who had devoured penny dreadful novels depicting the American frontier. "We do not need a holster, we have our vaginas ready for the draw."

The laughter traveling up her throat was not reflected inside his eyes.

"Men, too, have cavities, mademoiselle," he said flatly.

The bubble of laughter burst.

Victoria remembered . . . *Empétarder . . . to receive something through the back.*

Humiliation burned her cheeks. "I hardly think a woman's—or a man's—orifices are designed to accommodate pistols, sir."

"Knives are just as deadly, mademoiselle. And pistols come in varying sizes and designs."

Yes, it was quite fashionable for women to wear necklaces or even earrings of miniaturized pistols with moving parts.

"Do you feel it necessary to search all the women whom you purchase?" she asked tightly.

"I do not purchase women for sex."

Did he purchase women to kill?

"Then I am at a loss as to why you bid on me."

"You have something that I want."

"You have said you do not want my virginity."

"I want the name of the man—or woman—who sent you to me."

Irritation pushed aside her fear. "I told you that no one sent me to the House of Gabriel."

Victoria had freely chosen to sell herself.

"Then tell me the name of the woman who gave you the corrosive sublimate."

There was solid steel behind the silk of his cultured voice.

"And if I do?"

"I will find this person."

"And if I do not?"

"That person will die."

She would *not* give way to hysteria.

"And when you find this person? What would you do to her?"

"Whatever is necessary to gain the information I need."

He would hurt her.

He would—

Victoria's eyes widened in sudden comprehension. "You believe that my . . . friend"—she stumbled over the word—"deliberately sent me here. To you."

He did not respond.

He did not need to respond.

"You believe I came here to harm you," she said incredulously.

His silver gaze did not waver from hers.

"May I remind you, sir, that it was *you* who bid on *me*. Why did you bid on me if you believed I would cause you an injury?"

"If I had not bid on you, mademoiselle, you would die a far worse death than any caused by corrosive sublimate."

Victoria remembered the man who had met her opening price. *I will give you one hundred and five pounds, mademoiselle, for your . . . innocence.*

A cold chill raced down her spine.

Had he intended to purchase her virginity, or her life?

She determinedly swallowed the rising panic that fizzled inside her like seltzer water. "And now?"

"You may still die."

"You threatened to shoot me, sir." She convulsively squeezed the cloak. "I will take my chances with this other man."

His refusal was clear in his eyes.

Victoria could not get enough oxygen into her lungs. "Please let me go."

"Are you begging me, mademoiselle?"

She recoiled. "No."

Never.

His eyelids drooped; jagged shadows marred his marble-smooth cheek. Holding wide the mouth of her reticule, he reached inside.

Victoria's stomach knotted, knowing what he would find. "Let me have my reticule back."

He brought out a bundle of letters.

Every word written within them was imprinted on Victoria's brain. Her skin crawled, first hot, then cold.

He gazed at her through dark lashes. "You have a male admirer, mademoiselle."

No admirer had written those letters.

Victoria's horror that Gabriel read the letters outweighed her fear. She closed the distance between them and held out her hand. "I do not give you leave to read those letters, sir. Please return them. They are private."

"I did not ask your leave"—fully raising his eyelids, he stared down at her and said her name deliberately—"Victoria."

He stood four inches taller than she. Victoria had never before felt so small or helpless.

"Let me go," she repeated.

"I can't do that."

Desperation prodded her.

"You have known hunger," she said rashly.

"There are many types of hunger, mademoiselle."

Hunger of the body. Hunger of the soul.

Hunger of the flesh.

Victoria skittered away from the latter.

He must not read those letters.

"You have lived on the streets."

"I was born in a gutter in Calais."

Calais, France, was directly across the English Channel.

Had his body been sold in France or in England? she wondered. And then, *Were the streets of France safer than those in England?*

"I do not know what crime it is you think I have perpetrated, sir," she said in her most reasonable governess voice. "But London streets will exact a far harsher punishment than you. I am asking you one more time: please let me go."

He cocked his head. The coldness inside his eyes took Victoria's breath away. "You are afraid of what I will find in the letters."

She was afraid of what *she* had found in the letters.

"You do not want me," Victoria repeated.

"But I do, mademoiselle," he returned, silver eyes devoid of desire.

No, he did not want her, but he knew that she wanted him.

Had he known when he stroked the leather wrinkle that she had felt his touch inside her body? she fleetingly wondered.

Immediately she dismissed the notion.

Of course he had known. Every move—every word he spoke—was calculated.

"If you wanted me, sir, you would have taken me."

A familiar stillness settled over Gabriel.

Victoria's face was reflected inside his pupils, two pale orbs surrounded by blackness.

"I cannot take you, mademoiselle," he said finally.

"Why?"

Why rebounded off the pale blue enameled walls.

"Because if I take you, you will die."

You will die raced down her spine.

"I may die if I stay with you; I may die if I leave you." It was not Victoria who spoke, surely, yet it was her voice that rang inside her ears. "It seems to me, sir, that if I am going to die, I would rather it not be as a virgin."

Her brazen words hovered over them.

His eyes burned.

How could silver ice burn? Victoria wondered in that part of her brain that was still capable of wondering.

"I will not let you die," he said.

"But you have already said that you cannot guarantee that," Victoria riposted.

He did not respond.

"If you compel me to stay, sir, I will seduce you," Victoria asserted, pure bravado. She had no notion of how to seduce a man.

"Then you will pay the consequences, mademoiselle." The black of his pupils swallowed the silver of his irises. "As will I."

Darkness closed around her.

"Why do you think I would harm you?" Victoria asked. And could not hide the desperation in her voice.

"Why are you afraid for me to read your letters?" he countered.

"Perhaps, sir, because we both share the same fear."

Silver outlined the black of his pupils.

"What is it that you think I am afraid of, mademoiselle?" he asked politely.

Death lurked in his eyes, his voice.

Victoria had not killed, but this man had. She did not doubt for one second that he would do so again.

"I think that you are afraid of being touched by the opposite sex, sir." Victoria clutched her cloak, inhaling fog, inhaling damp, inhaling the acrid aroma of her fear.

"You think I am afraid of being touched by the opposite sex," he repeated softly, tasting the words for flavor. "You think I am afraid of being touched by women. Are you afraid of being touched by women, mademoiselle?"

Touched by women . . . as he had been touched by men?

Victoria swallowed. "No, I am not afraid of being touched by women."

"Then what are you afraid of, mademoiselle, that we share the same fear?"

"I am afraid of being touched by a man," Victoria said forcefully.

The light rimming his pupils shone brighter than the chandelier above them, a stark, dangerous circle of pure silver.

"I am afraid that I will like being touched by a man," she continued determinedly.

Victoria's heart drummed inside her ears, admitting the truth she had hidden for so long. A truth the letters had forced her to recognize.

"I am afraid that I am a whore in fact as well as in deed."

Chapter

4

Victoria's voice reverberated between them.

The silver-eyed, silver-haired man seemed riveted by her words: *afraid of being touched . . . afraid that I will like being touched . . . afraid that I am a whore in fact as well as in deed.*

Or perhaps Victoria was riveted by the fact that she had uttered such words.

The shame that should arise from her confession did not come.

Victoria tilted her chin, daring him to judge her, he who had sold his body. As she had sold her body.

"The letters inside my reticule made me realize what I am. I *was* wet with desire. Because I *did* want you—a stranger—to touch me."

Pain ripped through her chest.

"It is not the selling of one's body that makes one a whore, is it?" she said lightly; her voice was not light. "It is the enjoyment one derives from the sexual touch. I wanted your touch; therefore, I am a whore.

"I did not think that I would be affected in such a way this night." Victoria blinked back sudden tears. "But I am. Does that warrant my death?"

Seconds spanned a lifetime. Only Gabriel's eyes were alive. Silver beacons shining with need.

To touch . . . to be touched. To hold . . . to be held.

A log collapsed, reality intruding.

He did not want to touch or be touched by her. And he most certainly did not want her to hold him.

"I can't let you go, mademoiselle."

Regret touched his voice, his face. And then it was gone.

His need. His regret.

The longing to touch. To hold.

Once again the man who stood before her was a living, breathing statue, beauty unmarred by emotion.

"Gabriel was God's messenger," Victoria said impulsively.

"Yes. Michael was his chosen," he returned, silver irises eating the black of his pupils.

Victoria braced herself. "What are you going to do with me?"

"I will try to save you."

But she could yet die.

"I hardly think the woman who gave me the—the contraceptive tablets constitutes a dire threat," Victoria said bracingly. "She merely hoped to rob me. I will not now gain enough money for her to trouble herself over."

Nor would Victoria gain enough money to escape.

Hunger. Cold.

The man who had written the letters.

"No, she will not trouble you again," he agreed evenly.

Victoria sighed with relief. "There you are—"

"She will not trouble you again, mademoiselle, because she is dead. Or soon will be."

Dolly had promised to accompany Victoria to the House of Gabriel; Victoria had waited until Big Ben had announced the quarter hour to twelve.

She had not shown up.

Nausea closed Victoria's throat.

"How do you know that?" she managed.

The silver-eyed man pivoted; between one blink and the next he faced Victoria and held out the white silk cloth that had earlier concealed his pistol.

"I know because of this, mademoiselle."

Victoria instinctively reached out; the white cloth dropped into her hand. She blankly examined the square of silk, a napkin, surely—
"Turn it over."

Black ink stained the opposite side of the white silk cloth. Slowly the black blots took form.

They were letters. Bold, black, masculine letters.

A note was scrawled across the silk.

Victoria read the short missive. Once. Twice. Thrice. Each time she lingered over the last sentence:

> You have set the stage, *mon ange,* now I bring you a woman.
> A leading actress, if you will. *Laissez le jeu commencer.*

Let the play begin. . . .

With a calmness she was far from feeling, she carefully folded the napkin and held it out.

Gabriel did not accept it.

Victoria's hand clumsily dropped to her side; the silk crumpled between her fisting fingers. "My . . . The woman who gave me the tablets did not write this."

Even if Dolly could write—and in such a bold, masculine script—she would not be able to quote from Shakespeare.

"No, she did not."

All the world's a stage, and all the men and women merely players.

Victoria had identified the quote in the note, by both author and play. Surely he did not think . . . ?

"I am a governess," she exhorted defensively.

"Yes."

His response was not promising.

"My position requires a certain knowledge of Mr. Shakespeare's works."

He silently watched her flounder.

"I do not . . ." *Know the man who wrote the note.* Victoria licked her lips. "What does it mean, you have 'set the stage'? Who did you set the stage for?"

"A man, mademoiselle."

"The man who wrote this note."

"Yes."

"And you think that this man, that—that it is because of *him* that I am here."

"Yes."

"That's absurd. How could he possibly know—"

Her breath snagged inside her throat.

Six months earlier the husband of her employer had accused Victoria of flirting with him.

Victoria had not.

Her employer had not been interested in the truth. She had dismissed Victoria without so much as a reference.

Three months later the letters had started coming, morning missives slipped underneath the door of her rented room. Letters claiming that someone was watching her. That someone was waiting for her.

Letters that described in detail the pleasures she would soon experience.

From a man's lips. A man's hands.

A man's—

"It's not possible," Victoria said abruptly.

She knew who wrote the letters: they came from her former employer's husband. His handwriting did not match that on the silk napkin.

Unlike the man who had written on the silk napkin, the husband of Victoria's former employer did not frequent places such as the House of Gabriel. If he did, he would have paid for a woman instead of taking away Victoria's reputation and career.

Merely so that he could possess her virginity.

"I will have my reticule now, if you please."

"Soon, mademoiselle."

After he had read the letters, he did not need to say.

"I assure you, sir, I possess no letters which match the handwriting on this napkin."

"Then you have nothing to fear."

The electric light scorched her skin.

"I was not aware of your existence prior to tonight," Victoria reasoned.

"So you said."

"I have no intention of injuring you."

"Nor I you."

"What would be the purpose of this man sending me to you?" Victoria burst out.

She did not know either the man who called himself Gabriel or the man who supposedly sought to kill her.

It was not *rational*.

Lowering his lashes, Gabriel dropped the letters back inside her reticule. Slowly, he raised his eyelashes.

The expression inside his silver gaze snagged her breath: she stared at fear.

If *he* was afraid . . .

"I do not know, mademoiselle." Instantly the fear vanished from his gaze. He dropped her reticule back into the chair. "Your tray will soon be here. Would you care to refresh yourself?"

No.

"Yes, thank you."

Perhaps there was a window in the lavatory by which she could escape.

Silently, he turned.

Victoria resisted the urge to reclaim her reticule.

If she picked it up, he would take it from her.

She did not know what she would do if he used force: scream. Faint.

Fight back.

What Victoria had thought was a satinwood cabinet turned out to be a door.

A door that opened into stark blackness.

Victoria's heart thumped against her ribs.

Light slashed across a bare wooden floor, glinted off a brass bed. The smell of beeswax polish and clean linen enveloped her.

Crushing the silk napkin in her right hand and her cloak in her left, Victoria followed him into the scented darkness.

His footsteps were soft, unobtrusive; Victoria's were loud, invasive.

There were no windows in the bedroom.

The soft snick of a door opening was deafening over the roar of Victoria's heartbeat. Bright light abruptly blinded her.

Gabriel glided back into the shadows, silver hair shining. "You may join me when you are finished, mademoiselle."

Victoria resolutely stepped forward.

The door closed, shutting her inside. Immediately she noticed a large copper bathtub encased in satinwood—tub, front end. A copper-lined hood sealed the three sides.

Victoria had seen combination bathtubs and showers displayed in the Crystal Palace—crafted out of mahogany or walnut wood rather than the more precious satinwood—but she had never before worked in a household furnished with the luxury apparatus.

The hood was seven and one-half feet tall. It was quite impressive.

On the opposite side of the door a satinwood cistern hung over an ivory-tinted porcelain toilet. A box of tissues sat on top of the narrow cabinet that hid the connection of the flush pipe to the toilet.

Etiquette taught that personal tissues were to be hidden from sight at all times, lest one be reminded of what they were used for.

Obviously the man called Gabriel did not adhere to polite niceties.

It was difficult to remember the time when she would have been offended at such a sight.

At the opposite end of the bathroom a woman with a pale face framed by dark, lusterless hair watched her.

Victoria's spark of pleasure at seeing the combination bath and shower quickly died.

The woman she saw was her reflection in the mirror over a gold-veined, white-marble washstand.

One realization followed another: there were no windows in the water closet.

Victoria was trapped.

* * *

Gabriel flipped the electric switch, brass plate cold, wooden knob smooth. Light exploded overhead.

A plain satinwood armoire monopolized the inner wall of the chamber; a brass bed hugged the outer wall. It was covered with a pale blue silk spread.

The French madame had preferred fussiness over simplicity; opulence over elegance.

Perfume over cleanliness.

She would not approve of his house. Did Victoria?

Taking a safety match from the obsidian urn adorning the satinwood mantelpiece, he hunkered down and lit the bed of kindling underneath the layered sticks of wood. Blue and yellow flames leaped to life.

He held the burning match for long seconds, remembering the years he had lived without food. Shelter.

Safety.

Will you beg me, mademoiselle?

No. No, I will not beg you.

And she had not.

Victoria had not begged for food. For money.

She had not begged for her life.

She had not begged him to satisfy the desire she so obviously felt for an untouchable angel.

Instead, she, a virgin, had threatened to seduce him, a man who for twelve years had been the seducer.

Victoria would have taken him into her mouth. She would have taken him every way that Gabriel had ever taken a man or a woman.

She would still take him, knowing what he was.

His cock throbbed, remembering the fresh scent of her desire. It did not slow the thoughts racing through his head.

Six months ago Victoria had been discharged from her position.

Six months ago Gabriel had killed the first man.

. . . Now I bring you a woman.

A woman who had lived long enough on the streets to understand the rules of survival but who had yet to be destroyed by the knowledge.

A woman who did not judge his past.

We do what we must to survive.

Heat licked his skin.

Gabriel glanced down at the match between his thumb and middle finger.

Blue fire skimmed blackened wood.

Victoria's eyes were the same vivid, guileless blue as the fire that burned.

Did the second man hope to distract him with sexual dalliance?

Victoria feared what he would find in her letters.

She had lied about her name. Did she lie about the second man?

Immediately Gabriel remembered the shocked hurt in her eyes when he had told her what corrosive sublimate did to a woman.

A whore would have killed her, and Victoria had still protected her.

Exactly how far would she go to protect a lover? he wondered.

Where had the second man found her?

How had he found her?

Why had he found her?

Tossing the match into the fireplace, Gabriel stood up.

A Colt derringer and a bowie knife occupied the top drawer of the satinwood nightstand.

Instruments of death.

She had come to him with no weapons; she would find no weapons in his suite. Death would come from the second man or it would come from Gabriel: it would not come from a woman.

Scooping up the derringer and knife, he silently padded across the room that for the next few days, weeks or months would serve as Victoria's bedchamber.

The aroma of freshly brewed tea drifted through the gaping bedroom door.

Gabriel halted.

It was not Gaston who waited for him inside his study.

Chapter

5

Michael perched on the edge of the black-marble-topped desk, head bowed, black hair shining with blue highlights. Beside him, a large silver tray abutted his hip; gray steam curled out of a silver teapot. He held a small, brown earthenware pot in one hand and a small crustless sandwich in the other.

Both hands were a solid mass of angry red welts. Fingers. Palms. Backs.

Even as Gabriel watched, Michael dipped the sandwich into the earthenware pot.

It came out covered with chocolate.

The throbbing inside Gabriel's groin spread to his left hand, his right hand, the first gripping the bowie knife, the second holding the Colt derringer.

He was not prepared to deal with Michael. Not when the scent of Victoria's desire lingered in his nostrils and the sound of the second man's voice rang inside his ears.

It did not matter.

Gabriel's desire; Victoria's desire.

Death.

Laissez le jeu commencer. Let the play begin.

Gabriel had set the stage; now he must perform his role.

Silently he padded forward and closed the bedchamber door behind him.

Michael outwardly appeared intent upon his sandwich: he was not. Michael was aware of Gabriel's presence.

Just as he had been aware of the second man in the saloon.

"I told Gaston to evict you, Michael," Gabriel said neutrally.

Michael slowly raised his head, violet eyes coldly calculating. The puckered burns that scored his hands edged his right cheek, a stark contrast to the perfection of his features.

"Did you truly think that I would leave without seeing you, Gabriel?" he queried softly.

Michael's voice had not changed in the six months since Gabriel had last heard it. It was pitched low, sultry and seductive, the voice of a man who has made his fortune through whoring.

No, Gabriel had not expected Michael to walk away from him. But he had wanted him to.

After all these years he still wanted to protect the dark-haired angel with the hungry violet eyes.

Gabriel's gaze glanced off of Michael and settled on the chocolate covered sandwich.

A sharp pang constricted his chest.

Twenty-seven years earlier Michael had been unable to stomach the smell of chocolate, let alone the taste.

"When did you acquire an appetite for *chocolat, mon frère?*" he asked neutrally.

Gabriel knew that his voice bore the same knowledgeable cadence as did Michael's: they had both been trained to entice, to seduce, to gratify.

"Six months ago," Michael said. And popped the chocolate coated sandwich into his mouth.

Gabriel's lips burned in memory: six months earlier he had kissed Michael's scarred cheek. Then he had killed the first man.

How easy it would have been to pull the trigger and kill Michael. Six months earlier.

Tonight . . .

"How is Anne?" Gabriel asked abruptly.

The warmth that welled inside Michael's eyes and the smile that lit his face almost brought Gabriel to his knees.

For one heart-stopping second he did not recognize the man before him.

Gabriel had seen Michael half starved with hunger and fear. He had seen him half mad with pain and grief.

He had never before seen Michael happy. But he did now.

Michael had found what Gabriel would never find: love. Acceptance.

Peace.

All with a woman who preferred violet eyes over gray. A dark-haired angel over a fair-haired one.

A man who valued life instead of a man who had taken life.

Instantly, the light illuminating Michael's face dimmed, violet eyes once again coldly calculating. "Why don't you come visit us and find out for yourself, Gabriel?"

"Do you miss me, *mon frère?*" Gabriel mockingly riposted.

"Yes."

For one unguarded second Michael dropped his mask. There was no deception in his eyes, no artifice in his voice.

An invisible fist clenched inside Gabriel's stomach.

Michael loved him, and Gabriel did not know why.

Michael had never condemned Gabriel for being a nameless bastard or for the choices he had made.

Gabriel wished he had belittled him, judged him.

Gabriel wished he could hate, and know that it was hatred he felt rather than fear in disguise.

He looked away from Michael's violet eyes.

They had not changed in the twenty-seven years Gabriel had known him—they still openly hungered.

Victoria's eyes were also hungry.

Guileless blue eyes that hungered for sex.

For love.

For acceptance.

The second man had sent Victoria to him *because* she hungered. As Michael hungered.

Because she wanted. As Gabriel was incapable of wanting.

But *why?*

"You taught me to read and write," Gabriel said, wanting to understand the second man's motives. Wanting to understand Michael's motives. "Why?"

"You taught me to steal; I thought it a fair exchange." Sharpness spiked Michael's voice. "Who's the second man, Gabriel?"

Gabriel unflinchingly met Michael's gaze.

"You know who he is," he replied imperturbably.

It had been Michael who had found Gabriel chained in an attic like a dog, lying in his own filth, praying for death.

But Michael had not let him die.

Gabriel wished he had.

"You told me he was the second man who raped you," Michael said.

Two men had raped Gabriel; he had killed one, the second man still lived.

Gabriel did not look away from the suspicion that glimmered inside Michael's gaze. "I said there was a second man," he agreed evenly.

"Yet prior to six months ago you never mentioned that there was a second man."

"I did not realize you were interested in details. Forgive me, *mon vieux*," Gabriel said silkily, purposefully goading Michael. "I thought your interests lay elsewhere."

In women instead of men, he implied.

Michael did not rise to the bait.

"What I thought, Gabriel, was that you were the one person in my life whom my past did not destroy." Black lashes veiled Michael's eyes; he sat the earthenware pot of chocolate down on the silver tray.

Pain sliced through Gabriel.

It was inevitable that Michael eventually put together the pieces.

And Gabriel wished he could spare him that, too.

The soft click of glass impacting metal sounded over the drumming of his heart.

Slowly Michael raised his eyelashes, violet pinning silver. "But I was wrong, was I not, *mon frère?*"

"None of us escape the past, Michael," Gabriel said truthfully. And waited. Knowing that there was nothing he could do to stop the coming sequence of events.

Michael soundlessly slid off the desk, violet eyes intent, the scar edging his cheek white with tension.

He took one step forward . . .

"Why did the woman auction off her body inside your house, Gabriel?"

Two steps . . .

"Why does anyone sell their body, Michael?" Gabriel asked ironically.

His heartbeat accelerated.

He wondered how far Michael would push Gabriel in his quest for the truth. He wondered how far the second man would push him in this game of death.

He wondered what he would do if Victoria tried to seduce him.

Three steps . . .

"You never before allowed auctions, *mon ami*," Michael challenged.

Four steps . . .

"Tonight is the grand reopening of my house," Gabriel returned calmly. Choosing the truth and the lies with equal care. "I thought it appropriate."

Five steps . . .

Michael raised an ironical brow. "And did you think it appropriate for the proprietor to outbid his patrons, Gabriel?"

Six steps . . .

"Perhaps I got lonely, Michael," he said quietly. "Perhaps I wanted a woman of my own."

Gabriel did not know if he lied or not.

Seven steps . . .

"And the second man, did he also get lonely?" Michael caustically rejoined, violet eyes implacable in his quest for the truth. "Is that why he bid twice on your woman?"

Your woman rebounded off the white enameled ceiling.

Black, masculine hair turned into dark feminine hair. Victoria's voice rang inside his ears: *I am afraid of being touched by a man . . . I am afraid that I will like being touched by a man . . . I am afraid that I am a whore in fact as well as in deed.*

Instantly, Victoria's dark hair turned into Michael's black hair, a woman's nakedness into a scarred angel's determination.

Gabriel felt the heat of Michael's body, *too close*. He forced himself not to back away from his approach. Just as he had forced himself not to bolt earlier when Victoria had approached him one step at a time, pelvis jutting, hips swaying, breasts bouncing.

She had almost touched him. And for one heart-stopping moment he had almost let her.

Victoria had not known the consequences of touching him; Gabriel did.

Michael did.

"Perhaps," Gabriel said easily, every muscle inside his body throbbing with awareness.

If Michael did not stop . . .

Eight steps . . .

Gabriel stiffened, left palm molding the hilt of the knife, right middle finger curving to cradle a trigger.

Michael halted. Chocolate-scented breath caressed Gabriel's cheek.

Two angels stood eye to eye, one dark-haired, one fair-haired. One trained to please women, the other trained to please men.

"Why didn't you kill him, Gabriel?" Silver eyes reflected inside violet, violet inside silver, two men trapped in a past neither had chosen. "I know he was here. You were prepared to shoot the woman; why not the second man?"

So Michael had seen the blue-plated pistol.

Did he know how close he had come to death?

Did he know how close he *now* was to death?

"Did *you* see him, Michael?" Gabriel returned evenly.

"No, I didn't see him, but you were standing over us, Gabriel. It would have been impossible for you *not* to have seen him."

Gabriel concentrated on the moist scent of chocolate instead of the violet eyes that sucked at his soul and his fingers that independently tightened to protect himself. "Perhaps I do not see as clearly as I would like to believe I do."

Another truth. Gabriel had not planned on an accomplice who entered his house on the pretext of auctioning off her body.

He had not planned on finding a woman who would not judge him. *To make up for everything he endured.*

"Is the woman alive?" Michael asked, eyes sharp.

"When I left her a few minutes ago, yes," Gabriel said.

But for how long?

"Is she a whore?"

Gabriel fought down a spurt of anger. "No."

Victoria was not a whore. Whores did not offer everything, their life, their pain, their pleasure.

"Is she a virgin?"

"Yes." The scent of chocolate coated Gabriel's tongue. "She's a virgin."

"And how would you know that, Gabriel?" whipped the air between them. "Did you touch her?"

Pain . . .

Gabriel did not want to feel pain.

I don't want *to want* . . .

"You know I didn't, Michael," Gabriel said deliberately, calmly, every sense attuned to the woman in the adjoining room and the man who confronted him. "You know exactly how long it's been since I've touched anyone."

Any moment now Victoria would open the door . . .

Would she, too, prefer violet eyes over gray? he wondered remotely.

The jealousy the thought engendered took him by surprise.

The second man had sent her to Gabriel, not Michael. He didn't want her to choose a dark-haired angel over him.

Gabriel wanted what Michael had, a woman who would accept his past and the needs of a male whore.

A muscle ticked inside his jaw, heat building, pressure growing.

If Michael did not step back . . .

Michael did not step back.

"She knows that you were sold for two thousand, six hundred and sixty-four francs," he persisted.

The equivalent to one hundred and five English pounds.

"She knows," Gabriel agreed, muscles coiling tighter. Preparing to act or to react.

To kill or to run.

But there was nowhere to run.

"The second man sent her to you."

Gabriel did not deny the obvious. "Yes."

"Why does he want to kill you, Gabriel?" Michael asked provocatively.

Gabriel knew what Michael was doing: he had used the same pattern on Victoria. Aggression. Seduction.

He held perfectly still, breathing the scent of Michael's breath, caged by the heat of Michael's body.

Trapped by the truth.

"He wants to kill me," Gabriel said coolly, "because he knows that if he doesn't, I will kill him."

The truth but not the whole truth.

"Did the woman touch you, Gabriel?"

Gabriel stiffened, knowing where Michael's questioning was headed, unable to stop it. "No."

"Six months ago you touched me."

Shared memories flickered between them.

Scarred flesh. Cool lips.

Crimson blood.

"What would you do, Gabriel, if *I* touched *you?*" Michael asked softly.

Shatter.

Gabriel would shatter if Michael touched him.

And one of them would die.

Perhaps both of them would die.

Michael had not killed; that did not mean he was not capable of doing so.

"Don't play this game, *mon frère*," Gabriel said tightly.

"But it is a game, *mon ami,*" Michael said caressingly. "You have searched for the second man for almost fifteen years. And in all that time you have not been able to find him. Why would he hunt you down now in fear of his life?"

"Perhaps he is tired of running."

As Gabriel was tired of running.

Time physically ticked away—inside his cheek, inside his hands. Counting down the seconds until the woman barged through the door and chose a dark-haired angel over a fair-haired one.

Until Michael touched Gabriel.

Until Gabriel killed Michael.

And he shattered.

"I don't think so," Michael said gently.

"What don't you think, Michael?" Gabriel asked, suffocating on the scent of chocolate.

"I don't think he's tired of running." The violet eyes were too knowledgeable. "I don't think he's ever run from you, Gabriel."

"Then tell me why you think he came tonight," Gabriel murmured enticingly, playing the game.

It had always been a game: the first man, the second man.

"My uncle destroyed everyone I cared about," Michael said softly, violet eyes intent.

Everyone but Anne.

Another woman.

Another pawn.

"I killed your uncle, Michael."

The first man.

And Gabriel would do it again.

Brief anger flared inside the violet eyes: Michael still had not forgiven Gabriel for killing his uncle so that he would not be tainted with murder. He quickly recovered. "You said my uncle knew the name of the second man who raped you."

"Your uncle knew many things," Gabriel evaded.

"My uncle knew his name, Gabriel," Michael said deliberately, violet gaze inexorable, "because he hired the two men who raped you."

Gabriel fought the never-ending memories of pain that turned into pleasure and pleasure that destroyed the very will to survive.

Michael could *not* know the truth.

"How do you know that, Michael?"

"I know that, Gabriel, because you have hated me ever since you were raped."

Michael's chocolate-scented breath snagged inside Gabriel's throat.

"Restitution," Michael whispered, an echo of Gabriel's voice six months earlier.

For what? Michael had asked.

Pleasure. Pain.

"You wanted to kill me when you held the gun to my temple." Michael's violet eyes were devoid of both pleasure and pain. "You want to kill me now. But not because of the women who chose me over you."

Gabriel looked down on two men, one dark-haired, one fair-haired.

"Wasn't it, Michael?" he asked disinterestedly. Playing the part. Unable to fight. Unable to run.

"You were never jealous of me, *mon frère*," Michael said decisively.

The truth would not be stopped.

"I have *always* been jealous of you, Michael."

Gabriel had envied Michael as a thirteen-year-old boy—he had envied his need to love. Gabriel had begrudged Michael as a man—he had begrudged his courage to love.

The violet eyes did not flicker, reading the truth in Gabriel's gaze. The love. The hatred.

"I didn't understand six months earlier, Gabriel. But you and Anne made me realize the truth. You loved me, and because of that love, you suffered. Out of that love, you protected me. I am certain my uncle derived no end of enjoyment through your nobility and my ignorance." Brief irony colored Michael's voice, instantly faded. "Just as I'm certain that he would have taken great pleasure in arranging your death in the event of his own. For no other reason than to make me suffer. And I assure you, Gabriel, I would suffer if you died."

"So you think that your uncle left instructions for the second man to kill me in the event that he himself was killed"—Gabriel spoke around the ball of chocolate-scented breath lodged inside his throat—"in order to cause you pain?"

"That is exactly what he did, Gabriel," Michael said unshakably.

"If that were the case, Michael, then were I you, I would not leave Anne unprotected. Her death would cause you far greater suffering than that of my own." An image of the earl rose before Gabriel, legs twisted, faded violet eyes malevolent with hatred. "And I assure you, your uncle was very aware of that fact."

Doubt flickered inside Michael's gaze, disappeared. "Anne is not alone. I have guards watching her in addition to the men you've posted."

Gabriel's men were professionals: professional whores, professional thieves, professional cutthroats.

They should have been more efficient at concealing their presence.

"Guards can be bribed," Gabriel said.

As could doormen.

"You won't let anything happen to Anne."

Michael spoke with soft assurance.

Three hours earlier Gabriel had possessed that same assurance. That had been three hours ago.

He had thought the second man would kill a dark-haired angel, but he hadn't. Instead he had sent a fair-haired angel a woman.

A leading actress who was armed with neither weapons nor knowledge nor malice. And Gabriel did not know *why*.

"I may not be able to stop him," Gabriel said truthfully.

"And the woman can?" Michael asked alertly.

"I don't know."

"What will you do with her?"

What would Gabriel do with a woman who desired him—a woman who accepted him?

A woman whom he desired?

"I don't know."

"Will you fuck her?"

How do you want to be taken, mademoiselle?

I want to be taken with respect . . . because *I am a woman.*

The pulsating throb traveled up Gabriel's arms, settled in his chest, his groin, his testicles.

"Will you kill her, Gabriel?" Michael deliberately persisted.

Burning wood collapsed in the fireplace, reality turning into ashes.

Michael had been burned by fire, but he still had not learned . . .

The pulsing increased until Gabriel did not know where it stopped or where it had begun. With a thirteen-year-old boy or with a thirty-four-year-old woman.

"Which would you prefer that I do, Michael?" Gabriel asked tautly. "Fuck her or kill her?"

Michael's pupils dilated until all Gabriel could see inside his eyes was a ring of violet circling a halo of silver hair. "Six months earlier you wanted to help me."

"I did the best that I could."

Another lie cocooned in truth. Gabriel should have killed the first man outright instead of playing his game.

"Let me take the woman."

Six months earlier Gabriel had offered to take Michael's woman. To save her from the first man.

History repeating itself.

"I can't do that, *mon vieux.*" There was no regret in Gabriel's voice, any more than there had been in Michael's voice when he had rejected Gabriel's offer six months past. "She was sent to me, not to you."

A woman for the untouchable angel.

"You've seen this game played out before, Gabriel."

But he hadn't seen this game played out before . . .

"Do you think your uncle arranged a woman to be sent to me in order to lure me to my death?" Gabriel taunted.

It was possible.

The first man could have arranged for Victoria to be dismissed from her position.

He had killed every person Michael had ever loved. Destroying one more life would not matter to a dead man.

"I think you are far more vulnerable than you want to think you are." Violet fire glittered inside Michael's eyes. "And yes, I believe my uncle knew that."

Gabriel did not doubt it in the least.

"Sex was your pleasure, Michael, not mine," he said flatly.

"You're lying, Gabriel."

Gabriel stiffened. It had been a long time since any one had called him a liar to his face.

"I do not advise you to call a man a liar when he has in his possession a gun and a knife," Gabriel said softly, "both of which he is proficient at using."

There was no fear inside Michael's eyes. "Then tell me you don't want, Gabriel."

"I don't want this, Michael." Truth vibrated in Gabriel's voice.

"Tell me you don't remember what it's like to taste a woman. To touch a woman's flesh," Michael said unflinchingly. Still unafraid. *But he should be.* "Tell me you don't want to lose yourself inside a woman's pleasure."

The distant bong of Big Ben penetrated wood and glass.

Gabriel remembered . . . the men he had taken for money. The women he had taken for recompense.

"Tell me you don't want a woman, Gabriel." Gabriel's pain flared in Michael's eyes. "Say it, and make me believe it."

Gabriel couldn't deny it.

But neither could he admit it.

I don't want *to want* . . .

"Go home, Michael," Gabriel said. *Leave before the memories of pleasure overcome the memories of pain.* "Go home to Anne."

Anne with the pale brown hair and pale blue eyes.

Anne who had wished him a woman. *To make up for everything he endured.*

"Why?" Michael challenged.

Prepared to stay. Prepared to die.

All for the love of a man who had twice aimed a pistol at his head.

There was no need for Gabriel to lie. "As long as you stay away, *mon vieux*, I will survive."

And so would Michael.

Neither man blinked, breathed, moved.

The heat of Michael's body and the scent of his chocolate-scented breath washed over Gabriel. If he did not step back . . .

Gabriel balanced the hilt of the knife in his left hand, ivory warming to his flesh, conforming to his needs—

Between one heartbeat and the next, Michael stepped back.

Gabriel breathed deeply, inhaling the scent of freshly brewed tea and wood smoke instead of chocolate.

"Is that why I did not receive an invitation?" Michael asked tersely.

"Perhaps."

Perhaps Gabriel had not been able to pen an invitation requesting Michael attend the opening night of the House of Gabriel, knowing the consequences of his actions. Or perhaps he had known that Michael would be far more suspicious by not receiving an invitation than by receiving one.

Perhaps by not sending him an invitation, he had more surely secured Michael's role in this play of which he had no knowledge.

"Did you restrain the woman?"

Victoria had desired Gabriel, but she did not trust him.

She had thought he would kill her.

And so he should.

"No. I did not restrain her."

Was she even now searching his bedchamber for a weapon to protect herself with?

Gabriel had removed the most obvious ones, but any object could become a weapon. A toothbrush. An urn. A necktie.

He remembered the cane in his armoire. When twisted, the silver knob became the hilt of a short sword.

Michael had a cane with a gold knob instead of silver: both had been custom designed by the same man with the sole purpose of killing.

Falsely, politely, wondering what he would do if Michael accepted, Gabriel invited, "Would you like to meet her?"

Michael saw through Gabriel's pretense. And accepted it. As he had always accepted Gabriel.

His past. His choices . . .

The thirteen-year-old boy he had been; the forty-year-old man he had become.

"I won't let you die, Gabriel," Michael said simply. "Remember that."

Whereas Gabriel had all too willingly endangered Michael's life.

Before Gabriel could respond—with a half-truth or a half lie—Micheal turned. He paused at the desk.

His right elbow bent; at the same time his black dress coat strained across the width of his shoulders.

He could be reaching for a weapon.

Gabriel forced himself not to raise his derringer to fire off the first shot. Knowing he was too close to the edge.

Michael was the only goodness that Gabriel had ever possessed.

A white envelope sliced through the air, landed beside the silver tray on the black marble desktop.

"It's an invitation, Gabriel." Michael did not turn around. He knew the danger that he was in. "Anne and I are getting married."

Michael. Anne.

Married.

For a second, Gabriel could not breathe.

"And what name shall you give her, Michael?" he lashed out. "Shall she be known as Madame des Anges, or Lady Anne Sturges Bourne? Will she be the wife of a whore, or countess to the earl of Granville?"

It was too late to take back the hurtful words.

Michael had not claimed the title that was his by law upon the death of his uncle. He did not deserve Gabriel's vindictiveness.

The words accomplished what Gabriel had earlier been unable to do: they drove Michael from Gabriel's office. Gabriel's house.

Gabriel's life.

The scent and the taste of chocolate lingered in his nostrils and on his tongue.

Michael would survive without Gabriel, but could Gabriel survive without Michael?

His gaze settled on the ragged wool reticule cradled by pale blue leather.

A street person would not bother stealing it. It would be worthless even on St. Giles Street, where the meanest rags were picked apart for salable threads.

There was hunger in Victoria, but there was also pride.

It had taken care and patience to reduce her to the point where she would sell her virginity.

The dismissal from her post could have been engineered by the first man. Or it could have been engineered by the second man.

When she had denied the possibility of a stranger orchestrating the auction of her hymen, the protest had lodged inside her throat.

Her letters would determine if Victoria lied or told the truth.

They would let Gabriel know what to expect when he opened his bedroom door: an actress. Or an assassin.

A woman who would love a male whore. Or a woman who would kill to escape poverty.

They would let him know whether she would live or she would die.

Chapter

6

Victoria did not know what she looked for, she only knew she had to find something: a means to aid in her escape; a weapon to protect herself with.

A key with which to lock the bedroom door.

Gabriel would not leave her alone much longer. Each breath, each heartbeat measured the passing minutes.

Each breath, each heartbeat reminded her that at any moment he would catch her. And there was *nothing* she could do.

Victoria jerked open the bottom drawer in the satinwood chest.

The hair on the back of her neck prickled with sudden awareness.

" 'I know you, Victoria Childers.' "

Victoria froze.

" 'You want what every woman secretly yearns for.' "

The letters.

He had read them.

" 'You want to be kissed and caressed.' " Victoria scooted round, wool-protected knees sliding on polished wood. She slapped her palms onto the floor to keep from falling; her hair swung on either side of her head like twin pendulums.

The man—Gabriel—stood in the doorway, silver eyes gleaming, hair a silver halo. Matching silver glinted in his hands.

She had not heard him open the door. But why should she have? she wondered in that part of her brain that was still capable of reasoning. Victoria had not heard him open it when she stood directly behind him. Now the entire bedchamber separated them.

He made no attempt to conceal the small snub-nosed pistol—the metal was shiny silver instead of dull blue-black—and the lethal-looking knife that he held.

Neither were of a size or shape that could be concealed inside a women's—or a man's—body.

Victoria stared at the knife. The tip was jagged—like the teeth of a saw—the blade long, wide.

She had never seen anything like it.

Her gaze glanced off the knife, focused on the man instead of his weapons.

" 'Your breasts ache to be fondled and suckled by a man,' " he quoted, silver eyes glinting. They were far, far more dangerous than a knife blade. " 'The eternal hunger of a woman.' "

The words were seductive in script; spoken in that silky, caressing voice they were fantasy given speech.

" 'I would soothe your aching flesh,' " he continued. " 'I would satisfy your hunger.' "

Victoria's heartbeat faltered.

The silver-eyed, silver-haired man looked as if he had never ached or hungered in his entire life.

Who was the real Gabriel?

The man who had asked her if she would let him hold her *dripping with sweat*, or the man who effortlessly wielded the deadly knife?

" 'Soon your suffering will cease, and you will know the pleasure to be found in a man's arms,' " Gabriel continued quoting. " 'You will know the pleasure to be found in *my* arms, Victoria Childers. I will care for you, comfort you, rescue you from the burden of your impoverishment . . . All you need do, my very dear governess, is gift me with your maidenhead, and you need not suffer anymore.' "

Memory filled in the missing half sentence:

... I will care for you, comfort you, rescue you from the burden of your impoverishment, an evil which I'm sure you will come to understand as necessary when I have fully satisfied your desires. All you need do, my very dear governess, is gift me with your maidenhead, and you need not suffer anymore.

"You have an excellent memory, sir," she said evenly. Wondering when her self-possession would disappear like the illusion it was.

It should not be possible for a man who moved so leisurely to eat up space so quickly.

"Yes, I do, Victoria Childers." Gabriel stood over her, face pale, expression enigmatic. Holding the knife and the short, snub-nosed pistol out for her inspection, he gently asked, "Were you looking for these?"

He appeared calm: he was not. Victoria could feel the energy radiating from him.

He did not like having his drawers searched: she didn't blame him. He did not like the fact that she would escape him: for that she did blame him.

Would he kill her now, or would he let her live?

Whatever the outcome, she would *not* beg.

"I don't know," she said truthfully.

He stepped to the side of the open drawer. Her face turned upward to his. Warily following him.

Not knowing what to expect.

Not knowing when to expect it.

Gabriel dropped the pistol and the knife.

Instinctively her gaze followed the fall of silver. The two weapons landed inside the bottom drawer on top of a pile of neatly folded, starched shirts.

The dark wooden pistol grip and the leather-bound knife handle sank into the pile of white shirts more deeply than did the silver barrel and blade.

"You did not need to search my bedroom, mademoiselle," he said in that deceptively smooth voice. "There are weapons inside the bathroom."

Victoria did not answer.

"A toothbrush, for example, can pierce the throat if applied with enough force."

Yes, Victoria had seen all manner of death these last six months.

Lifting up her head, she resolutely met his silver gaze; the crackling fire snapped and popped inside her ears. "It does not sound like a very effective weapon."

"Then I would recommend that you use the derringer." Silk whispered, leather boots creaked. One second Gabriel loomed over Victoria, the next second he hunkered down, legs an inviting black V, hands resting lightly on his thighs. "It shoots accurately within a distance of three feet. A knife is certainly sharper than a toothbrush, but it, too, requires a certain amount of force. It also entails a larger degree of risk than does a revolver, especially for a woman. You must get close to your intended victim in order to use it; if the man—or woman—whom you intend to dispatch is stronger, the knife will be taken away and used against you. Unless, of course, you're proficient at throwing a knife, which I doubt you are. But I leave your choice of weapon up to you."

Victoria's eyes widened. "Are you inviting me to kill you, sir?"

"Yes." Picking up the short, snub-nosed pistol, he turned it and held it out grip first. "Take it, mademoiselle."

Take it echoed over the crackling fire.

She had rummaged through his underwear—thin silk socks, embroidered silk handkerchiefs, fine woolen drawers that were softer than down.

This could not be happening.

A man who wore silk socks, embroidered handkerchiefs and fine woolen drawers did not ask a woman to kill him.

Victoria numbly took the proffered pistol; the hard wooden grip was warmed by his hand.

There was neither encouragement nor discouragement in his silver gaze.

Victoria licked her lips, flesh rough and chapped. "If I shoot you, the waiter outside will apprehend me."

Gabriel's lips looked petal soft. "Probably."

The pistol dropped from her nerveless fingers; a muffled impact filled her ears, the collision of the pistol and starched shirts. "Then you will pardon me if I do not accept your invitation."

He leaned forward, reaching . . .

Victoria did not take her gaze from his.

Slowly he lifted the knife in front of her.

Light glinted off the serrated blade. A blade that had been designed for no other purpose than to kill.

To kill while inflicting as much pain as possible.

He knew how to use that knife, Victoria thought with a catch in her breath. For pain.

For death.

Expertly he balanced the ivory grip in the palm of his hand. "But you see, mademoiselle," silver glinted through long, dark eyelashes, "it is not a choice that I offer you."

Slowly his eyelashes lifted, silvery gray eyes gleaming unimpeded. "If you do not kill me, then I will kill you."

Victoria glanced at the snub-nosed pistol half buried inside his pile of starched shirts. She glanced at the knife so casually wielded in his left hand.

The desire to live warred with the desire to survive.

Taking a deep breath, she met his gaze. "In that event, I would prefer that you shoot me, sir. I believe it would be less painful than being killed by a knife. Unless, of course, it is your intention to cause pain."

"This is not a game."

Victoria's heart lurched, sped to make up for the skipped beat. "It is certainly not one that I am familiar with."

"You do not think I will kill you," Gabriel said flatly, expression unreadable.

"On the contrary, sir." Victoria's heart surely could not maintain its current level of activity—she would die of heart failure. "You were generous enough to advise me as to which weapon would be most effective in the hands of a woman. I merely wished to relay my preference as to which weapon I would have used against me."

"Are you afraid to die, mademoiselle?"

Yes.

"I have lived with the thought of death these last six months," Victoria said with a calmness she was far from feeling. "I am tired of being frightened."

"But you are frightened."

"Fear is a natural response to that which is unknown." The serrated teeth glinted hungrily. "I have never before died."

The little death.

The *final* death.

"Desire is natural, also, mademoiselle. Yet you are afraid of that, too."

Anger leaked through Victoria's fear. "I will not become a victim of a man's lust."

"Nor will you beg."

"No." She firmed her lips. "I will not beg."

"A man can make a woman beg, mademoiselle."

For pleasure, he did not need to say.

Scalding blood filled Victoria's cheeks.

"Some women, perhaps." She defiantly tilted her chin. "I am not like that."

"We are all like that."

"Men do not beg for sexual release," Victoria said scornfully.

Her father had taught her that. Women were weak, not men.

Women paid the consequences of their desires, *not men.*

"I have begged for sexual release, mademoiselle."

Victoria stared.

Darkness glittered inside Gabriel's eyes.

She remembered how he had avoided contact with her hand when she had reached for the silk napkin.

If I had not bid on you, mademoiselle, you would die a far worse death than any caused by corrosive sublimate.

Victoria grappled with the truth. "This man whom you believe directed me to the House of—to *your* house—"

Gabriel silently waited for Victoria to complete the connection.

"—it was he who made you beg," she concluded.

"Yes," he said bluntly.

Waiting for Victoria to condemn him.

Perhaps she would have six months earlier.

"And you think that this man would . . . do . . . *things* . . . to make me beg."

"If you leave this house, yes."

"Why?"

Why would a man whom she had had no knowledge of prior to this night wish to harm her?

"Men kill for many reasons. Some men kill for money. Some men kill for sport. And some men, mademoiselle, kill merely because they can."

The blood drained out of her face.

In the last six months she had seen respectable men physically abuse beggars, genteel ladies verbally assault streetwalkers, and children taunt children because they did not have shoes or unfrayed clothing.

Simply because they could.

Victoria rallied. "You said he would kill me, sir, not rape me for his enjoyment."

"What he does has no bearing on pleasure or enjoyment." There was no pleasure or enjoyment in Gabriel's eyes. *What had the man done to him?* "In the end, he would kill you."

"He did not kill *you.*"

"It was not a part of his plan."

Rape. *Death.*

Laissez le jeu commencer.

Let the play begin.

When would it *end?*

Victoria tried to match Gabriel's cold logic. "But my death *would* be a part of this plan."

"Yes."

"Because I am dispensable," she repeated his earlier words.

The serrated silver blade glittered in agreement.

"Yes."

Yellow orange and blue flames leaped inside the satinwood fireplace.

Victoria had never known burning logs could emit so much cold. "Do you plan on killing me, then, to spare me this . . . death?"

"You would thank me in the end."

Anger bubbled up inside Victoria. "The man who wrote those letters said that after I gifted him with my virginity I would understand the 'necessary evil' of losing everything I've ever worked for. Now you claim I would thank you for killing me. You will forgive me, sir, if I do not agree with either of you."

"The man who wrote the letters did not offer you a choice. I do."

"A choice between what?" Hysteria rang in Victoria's voice. "The manner by which you dispatch me?"

"I give you the choice of life, mademoiselle."

First death, now . . .

"And what do I have to do in order to obtain this life you offer me?"

"Be my guest."

"I beg your pardon?"

How many times had Victoria now begged his pardon? she wondered incongruously. Four? Five? More?

"Remain here, in my chambers, until it is safe." Safety—there was no safety inside his eyes. His room. His house. "I have men who will guard you."

"You said earlier that you could not guarantee I would be safe," Victoria retorted.

"Nor can I."

The brass bed gleamed.

There was no invitation in his eyes to share it.

She thought of the streets that awaited her. And contrarily chose them.

"I cannot stay here in your private chambers," she said firmly. Sounding like the thirty-four-year-old spinster governess that she had once been.

"You came here prepared to do more than sleep in my bed, mademoiselle."

The memory of his rejection when she had reached out to touch him chafed.

"But you do not want me . . . in that manner."

Her jaws audibly snapped shut. Why had she said that?

Gabriel had said that if he took her, she would die.

"When this is over, I will pay you two thousand pounds," Gabriel offered.

With two thousand pounds Victoria could live the rest of her life in comfort. Without fear of hunger. Cold.

A man who waited to snatch her virginity . . .

"I have no desire for money that I do not earn."

Victoria cringed. She sounded self-righteous even in her own ears.

"I will find you a position, then," the silver-eyed man calmly rejoined.

"As a governess?" she asked. And wondered why she did not feel more eager to resume her profession.

"Yes."

"I do not think that family men would be eager to hire a governess who has spent time inside the House of Gabriel."

"Mademoiselle, my patrons would far prefer to hire a governess who has been my guest than to have their sexual idiosyncrasies made public."

Victoria should not be surprised. So why was she?

"That's blackmail," she said uncertainly.

"That's the price of sin," he returned implacably.

"You are offering me your protection," she said slowly, trying to understand, to reason, *to not give way to panic.*

"I am offering you my protection."

She felt a leap of relief. And despised herself for it.

She did not want to be dependent upon a man.

Not for food. Not for shelter.

Not for sexual satisfaction.

"For how long?" Victoria asked shortly.

"For however long it takes."

For however long it took to hunt a man down, was what he meant. *And kill him.*

"How do you know that I am not this man's accomplice?"

Horror welled up inside Victoria.

She could not have said what she had just said. *But she had.*

"How do you know that I do not make this offer so that I may kill you when your screams are less likely to disturb my clientele?" he returned reasonably.

Victoria kept her gaze trained on his eyes instead of the knife in his hand.

"Are you?" she asked steadily.

"This is a night house, mademoiselle," he replied matter-of-factly. "If someone heard you scream, they would think you did so in the throes of passion."

The men on the street sometimes grunted when they coupled, like pigs rooting for food; the streetwalkers silently endured.

"Do men . . . and women . . . often scream in your night house, sir?" she asked.

"The walls are designed to afford privacy," Gabriel said politely, deliberately misunderstanding her. "You will not hear them."

"The men and women who . . . couple . . . on the streets—they do not scream in the throes of passion," Victoria said more bluntly.

She saw his past reflected inside his gaze: the hunger.

The cold.

The sex.

The will to survive.

No matter the cost.

What would cause a man such as he to beg?

"The men and women on the street couple like they live, mademoiselle," Gabriel said indifferently. "They steal a few moments of pleasure here, a purse there."

A life in between.

The wool padding of Victoria's dress was wearing thin: her knees ached. The palms of her hands were damp. She rubbed them on her thighs to dry them.

The wool was coarse, abrasive.

"I cannot give you the name of the prostitute," she said.

Victoria could no longer call Dolly friend, but she would not be responsible for the death of another woman.

She, too, had been a victim of circumstance.

"I told you, if she's not yet dead, she soon will be." The knife blade glinted in his hand, his fingers long, elegant. "Her name would be useless."

Victoria averted her gaze.

His silver eyes were waiting for hers.

He did not ask for her help. So why did she feel compelled to give it?

"The man who wrote the letters . . ." Victoria licked her top lip, a rasping flick of her tongue. "He would have no knowledge of the man who . . . abused you."

"How do you know that, mademoiselle?"

Victoria was not fooled by the politeness of Gabriel's tone.

"I know that because he would have no knowledge of *you*, sir."

"Many men have knowledge of me, mademoiselle," Gabriel said cynically.

"If he had knowledge of your house, sir," Victoria retorted, "he would not prey on his children's governess."

Not prey on his children's governess rang inside her ears.

There should not be any more blood left inside Victoria's head to drain from it: there was.

The silver eyes were hard, uncompromising. "You are either a fool, mademoiselle, or a liar."

Victoria glared at him. "I cannot help you, sir."

If she gave him the name of the man who wrote the letters, the silver-eyed, silver-haired man would hunt him down.

Victoria did not want Gabriel to know who her father was.

She did not want him to know about her past.

"I cannot help you," she repeated.

"But I can help you, mademoiselle," he said silkily.

With food. Shelter. A position.

Her choice.

Life.

Death.

But at what price?

Tears pricked her eyes.

Tears of exhaustion, she told herself.

And knew that she lied once again.

"Why do you want to help me knowing that I cannot help you?" she asked evenly.

He stood up, a sudden creak of leather.

Victoria's eyes were on a levee with the juncture of his thighs. There was no mistaking his sex through the tight, black silk trousers.

Are you that large, sir?

I measure over nine inches long.

Victoria threw her head back.

Gabriel's silver eyes glittered.

"Perhaps, mademoiselle, because I, too, once said that I would not beg. Perhaps I would spare you that."

There was too much pain in his eyes. Too much death.

Had he ever laughed, this man who had been born in a gutter in Calais, France?

"Have you ever begged a woman for sexual release?" she asked impulsively.

The heat inside the bedchamber crystallized.

"I am Gabriel, mademoiselle. I whored for men, not women."

"So that you could eat," Victoria said firmly.

"So that I could become rich," Gabriel softly countered. "How do you think I was able to build this house?"

Victoria's father had taught her that sin was ugly.

She had seen ugliness.

There was nothing ugly about Gabriel or his house.

Victoria realized she was in far more danger now than when he had caught her rummaging through his drawers. Gabriel would forgive a trespasser; he would not forgive a woman who pried into his past.

He could kill her with a knife, a gun, a toothbrush . . .

No one would mourn the passing of Victoria Childers, a virgin spinster.

Who would mourn Gabriel?

"You did not answer my question, sir." Victoria's voice sounded as if it came from a long distance away. "If you do not answer my questions, then you cannot expect me to answer yours."

For a second she did not think Gabriel would respond, and then . . .

"No, mademoiselle, I have never begged a woman for release."

"Has a woman ever begged you for release?" she persisted. Heart pounding.

Sex a seductive lure.

"Yes."

"Did you enjoy it?"

"Yes."

"Did you . . . cry out . . . with your pleasure?" Victoria asked. Unable to stop the questions.

Wanting to know more . . .

About sex.

About a man called Gabriel and a woman called Victoria.

She wanted to know why it was she who had been sent to him and not another woman.

Long seconds passed, one heartbeat, three heartbeats, six . . . nine . . .

Victoria strained to hear—the men and women inside the house, a passing carriage outside of the house.

Finally . . .

"No, mademoiselle, I did not cry out with pleasure."

But he had given pleasure.

Pleasure to make up for what he did not receive.

The only sound inside the room was the crackling of the fire and the beating of Victoria's heart and the truth lurking in the shadows.

"Did these women who begged you for release do so before or after you yourself . . . begged . . . for release?"

"Before."

Victoria was riveted by the starkness inside Gabriel's eyes, dull gray now instead of silver.

The truth slowly dawned inside her.

It was too late to stop the questions, but she wished she could.

She had asked for the truth; it looked her in the face.

"It has been fourteen years, eight months, two weeks and six days since I begged for release, mademoiselle." The man behind the marble-perfect mask flared to heated life—a man who desired to touch, to be touched, to hold and to be held; he was instantly locked away behind an alabaster wall of beauty. "I have not touched a woman since."

Chapter

7

"**W**hy?"
Gabriel's voice echoed hollowly inside the empty saloon. Guttering candles fought the darkness.

Reckoning time had come.

The two doormen stood stiffly at attention. Light and shadow played across their faces; golden blond hair alternately turned into wheat, brown hair into fire and bronze.

Neither man met Gabriel's gaze.

Neither man expressed fear or regret.

For a long second Gabriel did not think they would reply. And then . .

"*C'est*—it was her eyes, monsieur."

Gabriel's head whipped toward Stephen; red fire flamed in his brown hair, died.

I told them I was in need of a protector, Victoria Childers had said.

"You violated my orders because of a pair of *beaux yeux*?" he asked bitingly.

"*Non*, monsieur." Amber eyes unflinchingly met Gabriel's silver ones. "I violated your rules because I remember what it's like to be hungry and to have nothing to sell but oneself."

"Your memory was not so acute six months earlier, Stephen."

Stephen had been in Gabriel's employment for five years. He had not once allowed a streetwalker or dolly mop to cross the threshold.

Until tonight.

But Victoria was neither a streetwalker nor a dolly mop: she was a pawn.

Sent by the second man.

Cerulean blue eyes suddenly locked with Gabriel's. "If we had turned her away, sir, she would not have survived the night."

John was a simple Lancashire boy who had come to London to make his fortune. One of the thousands who annually flocked to the city.

His beauty had been the only quality that had distinguished him from the other boys looking for employment.

John had been raised to be a farmer, simple, honest work. Whoring had gone against his every principle.

But he had done it.

John had been a whore for five years.

It had nearly killed him.

Gabriel had taken John off the streets, fed him, clothed him, employed him, educated him. He had been with Gabriel ten years. Six months earlier Gabriel had trusted him to protect Michael and his woman.

He felt the dawn pressing down on him.

"You know the price for disloyalty, John."

There was no remorse in John's eyes. No protest.

Both John and Stephen had known what their actions would cost them.

Yet they had acted.

Why?

A fleeting smile glimmered in John's cerulean blue eyes, died with a guttering candle. "She was quite splendid, wasn't she, sir?"

In retrospect . . .

"Yes," Gabriel said. "She was quite splendid."

The bloods and the politicians had been aghast that a whore claimed as much self-worth as their wives and daughters and sisters.

"Stephen and I will collect our things and be gone before the house servants rise," John said matter-of-factly.

Gabriel could not afford to keep the two men on, not now that the second man had returned.

John, more than any other of his employees, understood that. More than ever, Gabriel needed men whom he could rely upon.

By allowing the woman inside his house—a woman who could just as easily have been an assassin—they had proven their unreliability.

He could never trust them again.

That knowledge did not ease Gabriel's task.

"Gaston will issue you two months' salary for severance pay," he said neutrally.

Stephen's amber gaze glanced off of Gabriel's silver one. "Thank you, sir." Turning, he walked away, chestnut hair dark and lifeless in shadow.

"John."

John paused mid-turn; gold glimmered in his hair. "Sir?"

Gabriel's eyes narrowed, watching his face and his body for signs of tension.

For signs of betrayal.

"Was there anyone—anyone at all—who accompanied the woman?"

"No, sir." John looked past Gabriel's shoulder. "She came alone."

He could be lying. Or he could be telling the truth.

Gabriel would never know.

John turned, footsteps soundless. He halted.

Gabriel instinctively reached underneath his dress coat, satin lining a warm caress, the grip of the revolver hard and smooth.

John was armed as Gabriel was armed. As were all of Gabriel's waiters and doormen.

The doorman's arms remained straight at his sides.

"The fog was thicker than pea soup, sir," John said evenly. "Truth be, I do not know if the woman came alone or not. There could have been someone with her who waited outside the parameters of the lamp on the door. All I can say for certain is that I did not see anyone with her."

Gabriel's chest tightened.

John told the truth. But had Stephen?

"Why did you do it, John?"

"She reminded me of Mr. Michel."

Hungry eyes.

"And she reminded me of you."

Gabriel's eyes had never been hungry.

"She reminded me of all of us."

Whores. Pimps. Beggars. Cutthroats. Thieves.

All who worked inside the House of Gabriel had survived the streets.

English streets.

French streets.

"I wondered where we would be now," John continued, "had someone given us the opportunity to make enough money, our first time out, to escape the gutters."

John had escaped the gutters long before Gabriel had found him.

"Take your severance pay and buy some land, John," Gabriel said quietly.

"It's too late."

Gabriel thought about Michael. He thought about Anne.

He thought about their upcoming nuptials.

Gabriel's people, Michael dubbed his employees, immigrants and homeless people all.

A picture of the gray-haired man flashed before Gabriel's mind's eye. It was followed by images of the Hundred Guineas Club.

John had escaped the gutters to work inside the homosexual club.

No, he could never go back to being a simple country boy.

"Do you trust Stephen, John?" he asked impulsively.

Hating the plans that were formulating inside his mind. Knowing there was no alternative.

Gabriel would not allow his house to be turned into a killing field, not if he could stop it.

John's back stiffened. "I trust everyone here, sir."

Another sin.

Whores could not afford to trust.

Love.

Hope.

"Do you trust me?" Gabriel asked softly.

"Yes."

In the end, Victoria Childers had also trusted him.

She had eaten his food and now she slept in his bed. Believing she was his guest.

She was not.

Victoria was as much a prisoner as Gabriel was.

"Should I trust you?" Gabriel queried gently.

"I did what I thought was right," John said stiltedly.

And he would do so again.

Perfect prey.

The dawn closed around Gabriel.

He must choose. To let go of John and Stephen—because they did what they thought was right.

Or to keep them—knowing that their humanity would cause more death.

The second man *could* have bribed them.

If they were guilty, the second man would kill them.

If they were innocent, Gabriel's dismissal would kill them.

It would be a far worse death than that which the second man would minister.

All of London would know they had been discharged. No one would hire the untouchable angel's rejects.

John and Stephen would return to whoring.

A far, far better fate than that which would be theirs if Gabriel asked them to stay.

No one had a right to ask a man to do what Gabriel would ask them to do.

"They did not deserve dismissal, monsieur."

Gabriel stared at the wine-stained tablecloth: a woman's delicate profile emerged, nose straight, brow sweeping, chin firm.

Victoria did not believe that she was beautiful: she was.

Gabriel had only ever seen her type of beauty in one other person, and she would soon belong to Michael.

"You warned them that a man would try to kill Monsieur Michel; you did not warn them against a woman," Gaston stiffly protested. "John and Stephen planned no harm when they allowed the woman inside tonight."

Gabriel's decision was made.

He could not afford regret. Indecision.

Compassion.

Immediately Victoria's image blurred; the linear profile of her face became a series of overlapping stains.

"Why do you think my actions were too harsh, Gaston?" Gabriel glanced up from the tablecloth. "They disobeyed my orders. Should I have increased their pay instead of discharging them?"

"They love you, monsieur."

Faint sounds penetrated the empty saloon, a pan clanging, a soft curse.

Pierre was preparing a late breakfast.

Soon the house servants would come and clean up the carnage in the saloon.

Gabriel remembered the occasion and the year in which he had acquired each of their services.

He did not want their love; he wanted their loyalty.

"Love has a price, Gaston," Gabriel said coolly. "It goes to whomever pays the highest salary."

Or fee.

A whore's love changed with every patron.

"The men are uneasy, monsieur."

"Their positions are secure as long as they abide by the rules of the house."

"They thought you died six months ago."

Gabriel stilled.

Not once had Gaston or Gabriel's people discussed the events that had occurred six months earlier.

"As they can see, I am very much alive."

"You burned down the house," Gaston said stonily.

And then Gabriel had rebuilt it.

The first to save an angel; the latter to catch a monster.

"I reimbursed them for the things they lost."

"It is not a matter of possessions, monsieur." The candle on Gaston's right sputtered, died; the right side of Gaston's face darkened in shadow. "You did not trust them with the truth. They no longer know if they can trust you."

Trust.

Truth.

The faint aroma of coffee wafted over the stale odor of wine and cigars.

Whores could not afford to trust.

Gabriel had once thought he knew the truth; the second man had proved him wrong.

"Are you saying, Gaston, that none of my employees can be trusted?" Gabriel asked carefully.

Gaston squared his shoulders. "There is no one in your house who would betray you."

"Yet you did not evict Monsieur Michel per my instructions," Gabriel said sharply. "Some might say that is a form of betrayal."

The past haunted Gaston's eyes. "Monsieur Michel would not let go of your body," he said with unaccustomed emotion.

Gabriel remembered . . .

. . . The echo of gunshot.

. . . The silver mist of breath.

Did you mourn me?

Yes.

"It was not my body," Gabriel said remotely.

Michael had held the burned body of a beggar—not Gabriel.

Gabriel had placed the beggar's corpse in his bed, hoping it would be mistaken for him.

And it had been.

Gabriel had done what was necessary to save Michael. So that he could live a life instead of a nightmare.

Only to discover the nightmare had just begun.

"He thought it was your body, monsieur." The rare burst of emotion illuminated Gaston's face. "He loves you. Monsieur Michel is a part of this family. I will not evict him. *Jamais.* He took care of us when we had no place to go."

Two words struck Gabriel like a fist.

Jamais. Never.

Family.

They were all whores. Pimps. Beggars. Cutthroats. Thieves.

Their past would *never* change. They would none of them be together if they had a *family.*

Gaston stared over Gabriel's head. "Shall I give myself two months' severance pay, monsieur?"

The left corner of Gabriel's mouth kicked up.

Gaston had been with Gabriel for fourteen years. Gabriel had found him beaten to a bloody pulp in an alley in Seven Dials.

The House of Gabriel would not be possible without Gaston. He managed both the house and the people who worked inside it.

"So that you can seek employment with Monsieur Michel?" he asked easily. "*Je ne crois pas, mon ami.* The two of you would open a rival house, and then where would I be?"

Gaston did not relax at Gabriel's sally.

"The men are afraid, monsieur."

All sense of levity abruptly dissipated.

"Pay them extra," Gabriel said tautly.

"They want to know whom they should kill, monsieur, instead of jumping out of their skins like rabbits every time a bottle of champagne is uncorked. *S'il vous plaît.* If you would only describe the man who comes for you . . ."

Victoria had said similar words.

If you do not answer my questions, then you cannot expect me to answer yours.

Gabriel opened his mouth.

It was a reasonable request. Men who placed their lives in jeopardy in order to save the life of another deserved to know what their potential killer looked like.

The words refused to come.

"There was a man here tonight," he said instead.

"There were several hundred men here tonight, monsieur."

Gabriel ignored Gaston's sarcasm.

"The man has gray hair—he's in his mid- to late fifties. His name is Gerald Fitzjohn. I want his London address. Send Jeremy to the library to look it up."

"Jeremy just retired, sir."

"Then I suggest you wake him, Gaston," Gabriel said softly, dangerously.

"Very well, monsieur," Gaston replied woodenly.

"Send Jacques around to the *Times* and the *News*."

They were two of the most popular newspapers in London.

Gaston opened his mouth to protest—Jacques, too, had just retired.

He shut his mouth.

"I want Jacques to check the employment advertisements for the last year and a half." Gabriel remembered Victoria's assertion: *If he had knowledge of your house, sir, he would not prey on his children's governess.* "Tell him to look for repeated advertisements for a governess by the same party. If he finds any, I want him to write the names or addresses down."

Victoria might believe that she was a random victim of her employer; Gabriel knew better. Men who preyed upon women usually had a history of previous victims. The household in which she had been employed probably advertised for governesses on a regular basis.

"*Très bien,*" Gaston said.

"Have David visit the employment agencies." David could charm either man or woman, young or old. "Tell him to say that a governess named Victoria Childers applied for employment, but he misplaced her address."

Gaston's eyes widened, learning the cloaked woman's name and previous profession.

"When Jeremy finds Fitzjohn's address, tell him to search through the archives for the family name of Childers. If he finds a Childers family listing a daughter named Victoria, take down the names and address."

"Très bien."

Very good.

There would be no good from the night.

The killing had begun.

"Gaston."

"Oui?" Gaston asked guardedly.

"I want this information by noon today," Gabriel said softly. "Have a maid wake me when they return."

Gabriel was suddenly dead tired.

The thought of sleeping on a leather couch was not a pleasant one.

Twenty-seven years ago he would have thought it a luxury.

No, he was no longer a boy.

He was a man, and he knew the price of life.

"Très bien, monsieur. I have appointed Evan, Julien and Allen to guard the woman. They will change shifts every eight hours."

"Merci."

Gaston wrung his hands.

Gabriel wondered if the woman slept . . . or if she, too, worried.

No one has ever held me, she had confessed.

But she would have let him hold her . . . drenched with sweat and sex.

"Many men sympathize with the woman's plight," Gaston blurted.

Gabriel felt the hair on the back of his neck prickle.

"I will kill the man who lets her escape," Gabriel said softly. Dangerously. "Tell that to the men who sympathize with her."

"They do not like to think you are punishing her."

"And why would they think that, Gaston?" he asked, the softness in his voice barbed.

"Marcel did not discuss the note he found, monsieur," Gaston said defensively. "But the men, they sense there is something wrong. You could have stopped the auction, yet you did not."

No, Gabriel had not stopped the auction. Instead, he had bid on the woman and now he had the woman.

By noon, word of the cloaked woman who had tempted the untouchable angel would have spread all over London.

"Tell them that the man who wishes to kill me will also kill her." Gabriel let the truth leak into his eyes and his voice. "If she escapes, she's a dead woman."

Gaston's gaze settled on Gabriel's. In his brown eyes was a single question.

Why?

Why had Gabriel built a house where every desire could be fulfilled merely to lure an assassin?

Why would an assassin want to destroy two male whores so badly that he would willingly walk into a trap?

What had the second man done to him—after twelve years of whoring—that Gabriel could not tolerate a simple touch?

Gaston did not ask the questions. But Gabriel knew that Victoria would.

He had told her more than he had ever told anyone.

He had told her that he had begged, but he had not told her what he had begged for.

He knew that she would ask, though. In a day. Or two days.

Victoria would ask what he had begged the second man for. And Gabriel would tell her.

She deserved that much.

"We would die for you, monsieur," Gaston said simply. "No one will go against your wishes."

Yes, men—and women—would die. That was part of the play. Gaston glanced away. "What I said about Monsieur Michel—"

Gabriel remembered his parting words to Michael.

"I don't think we need worry about Monsieur Michel," he interrupted, pushing aside the pain.

He thought of Victoria's worn wool dress, tattered silk drawers and sagging stockings.

My virginity is all I have left, she had said.

But that wasn't all that Victoria had left.

She had passion.

I wanted your touch; therefore, I am a whore, she had told him.

And he had let her believe it.

But it wasn't passion that made a man or a woman a whore—it was performing sex when there was no passion that made one a whore.

Michael had been a prostitute; he had never been a whore.

Unlike Gabriel.

Does that warrant my death?

"Send a message to Madame René," Gabriel said abruptly. "Tell her that we are in need of a seamstress."

Chapter

8

B lackness pressed down on her eyes, *a man's hand*—
Gasping, Victoria fought to sit up, breasts quivering, hair impeding.

Only to discover that the blackness was not a hand.

Victoria had gone to sleep in darkness; she awoke in darkness.

She became aware of the firmness of the mattress beneath her buttocks and the softness of the sheet encircling her.

It was not her bed.

The room Victoria rented was equipped with a sagging mattress; it had no sheets.

No light penetrated a sooty window—neither gray daylight nor golden streetlight.

A rich, sweet flavor lingered in her mouth.

Chocolate.

Memory followed consciousness.

Victoria slept in the silver-eyed, silver-haired man's bedchamber: it did not have a window. And the rich, sweet substance coating her tongue came from the pot *au chocolat* that had been a part of her supper.

A supper she had eaten alone.

Underneath the scent of laundry soap and starch, she could smell a faint whiff of . . . *him:* the musky clean scent of masculine flesh.

Victoria had slept between the sheets that *he* had slept between. A man who called himself Gabriel.

His scent had lulled her to sleep the night before. Or was it still night?

She strained to hear . . .

His breathing.

His presence.

His thoughts.

There was no sense of him.

This is a night house, mademoiselle . . . The walls are designed to afford privacy.

Heat flooded Victoria's body.

The thoughts she had expressed and the questions she had asked the beautiful silver-eyed, silver-haired man the night before flowed through her like an open tap.

Have you ever begged a woman for sexual release? . . .

No, mademoiselle, I have never begged a woman for release.

Has a woman ever begged you for release?

Yes.

Did you enjoy it?

Yes.

Did you . . . cry out . . . with your pleasure?

No, mademoiselle, I did not cry out with pleasure.

Did these women who begged you for release do so before or after you yourself . . . begged . . . for release?

. . . It has been fourteen years, eight months, two weeks and six days since I begged for release, mademoiselle. I have not touched a woman since.

The darkness pressed on Victoria's chest.

She had counted the days, weeks and months since she had been discharged from her position. The losses and the indignities she had suffered paled in comparison to what Gabriel had experienced.

He denied the needs of his flesh, because of an act he had had no control over. And he had counted every minute, every hour of each passing year.

Immediately Victoria remembered the streetwalker called Dolly and the folded paper she had pressed into Victoria's hand. For protection, she had assured Victoria.

A masculine voice laid bare the lie.

Did your friend tell you what this is?

Victoria tried to push aside the truth.

It is corrosive sublimate, mademoiselle. Did your friend tell you how to administer the tablets?

The truth would not be pushed aside.

One tablet causes violent convulsions, often followed by death. Two tablets inserted into your vagina, mademoiselle, would most certainly bring about your death.

The pressure weighting her chest became an anvil—it dropped straight down to her lower abdomen.

Victoria threw back the bedcovers and stood up.

The wooden floor was icy against her bare feet; the air embracing her nakedness, chill.

There were no embers inside the fireplace to provide light. Heat. Safety.

Gabriel, admitted proprietor, whore and murderer, could barge through the door at any moment and turn on the light.

I was *wet with desire. Because I did want you—a stranger—to touch me.*

The shame that had refused to come when she uttered her confession remained curiously absent.

Victoria forcefully turned off the tap of memories.

She could not afford to feel fear. Hope.

Desire.

The eternal hunger of a woman.

Holding out her arms straight in front of her, Victoria walked into black space—and then she walked into a black wall.

The sharp slap of flesh impacting wood exploded the pulse-pounding silence.

Not a wall . . . She had run full-body into the armoire.

Victoria froze, heart palpitating.

Had he heard her?

What if he investigated the noise?

She was naked, without even a pair of stockings to hide behind.

Her dress—where was it?

The bathroom—where was *it?*

Sliding her hands in rhythm with her feet, Victoria found the side of the armoire, the adjoining wall . . . She skimmed the wall with the fingers on her left hand, right hand thrust forward to ward off attacking furniture.

Or an attacking man.

Her fingers stubbed a wooden frame, plunged into empty space. She had found the bathroom.

Reaching through the open doorway, Victoria lightly swept the wall with her fingertips, circling, circling . . . slick enameled paint . . . icy metal . . .

A wooden switch.

Light blinded her. Materializing out of the glare appeared gleaming copper, the combination bath and shower . . . a marble monolith, the wash basin . . . and a naked woman shrouded in dark, tangled hair.

Victoria's gaze skidded away from her mirrored image above the marble basin.

Age-yellowed silk limply covered a wooden towel rack; shapeless flesh-colored tubes hung beside it.

Last night she had washed her drawers and her stockings before retiring, as she did every night.

Had he entered the bedroom and the bathroom while she slept?

Had he seen what no man had a right to see—a woman's futile attempt to remain genteel when gentility was not an option?

Her gaze unerringly returned to the mirror.

The naked, dark-haired woman within boldly stared back at Victoria.

White breasts peeked through twin streamers of dark, snarled hair—a woman stripped of earthy possessions and prideful vanity.

I know you, Victoria Childers, the man who wrote the letters claimed.

But Victoria did not know the woman in the mirror.

She did not know the woman who had undressed in front of a perfect stranger and felt no shame.

Her breasts jutted out from her chest, a proclamation of her sex.

A symbol of weakness and vulnerability.

The sin of a woman.

Desire is a part of all of us, mademoiselle.

Victoria remembered the members of the *ton* who had watched her auction off her virginity.

Men who served in parliament; women who ruled society.

Had they found the passion they sought?

A pale, slender hand rose up in the mirror.

You want to be kissed . . . a familiar masculine voice murmured provocatively.

The woman in the mirror touched reddened lips.

Chapped skin pricked Victoria's fingertips; electric sensation jolted through her.

No man had ever kissed her lips.

Men did not kiss women on the streets; they merely coupled with them.

Now she understood why.

The streetwalkers possessed drawn, chapped lips—like Victoria's lips.

Six months earlier they had been plump and soft.

Had she secretly admired the fullness of her lips and the softness of her skin?

Had her vanity been so obvious?

Your breasts . . . the provocative masculine voice urged.

The pale, slender hand in the mirror slowly descended, trailing down a sharp chin, a corded throat, a pulsing indentation. Warm hair blanketed the backs of the woman's fingers.

Underneath the cover of dark hair, callused skin cupped a round breast. It was soft and plump as the rest of Victoria was not.

A nipple peeked through the cup of her hand and the blanket of tangled hair: a dusky dark rosebud.

It did not feel like a rosebud.

It was hard. Tiny bumps—like goose bumps—pebbled it. On the very tip there was a slight depression.

Before the letters Victoria had never looked at her naked body, had never touched herself save through a washcloth.

Had never recognized the sensuality that had been lying dormant beneath her plain wool dresses, waiting for her to acknowledge it.

Now the silver-eyed, silver-haired man had read the letters. And he knew . . .

You want what every woman secretly yearns for.

But she didn't want to want.

To be kissed.

To be fondled.

To be suckled.

She didn't want to ache.

She didn't want to hunger . . .

For the warmth of a touch.

For the union of penetration.

She didn't want to ache and hunger for a man's fingers . . . a man's penis . . . a man's *tongue*.

Victoria pivoted, hand dropping, hair flying.

The last six months she had squatted over a chipped chamber pot; the luxury of sitting on a smooth wooden toilet seat was a pleasant diversion.

It reminded her of the conveniences she had once taken for granted and the comforts she had been cheated of.

Of the comforts that she might never know again.

Gone.

Everything was gone.

Her china trinkets. The freshwater pearl necklace; the coral earrings she had never dared wear. The engraved silver watch that had been a gift from her first employer. Her clothes.

The room that stank of poverty and despair.

Rent was due and she could not pay it. By now someone else would have rented it.

Would they receive the letters intended for Victoria?

Would they read them and yearn for more, as Victoria had yearned? Victoria reached for the box of tissues behind her.

The cistern flushed with a small gurgle instead of the clamoring belch of the more outdated plumbing her previous employers had utilized.

Her drawers were still damp, her future still undecided.

She could return to bed, or she could get dressed.

She could pretend to be Gabriel's guest . . . or she could be the prisoner she knew that she was.

Her choice . . .

The combination bath and shower beckoned to her.

Victoria tried to remember the last time she had acted for no other reason than for her pleasure.

She could not.

As a child, she had been afraid of her father, fearing he would revile her. And he had.

As a governess, she had been afraid of her employers, fearing they would dismiss her. And they had.

Now she was neither a child nor a governess: she was a woman on her own. Victoria had nothing left to lose.

Neither a father's love nor an employer's salary.

Determinedly she padded across the cold tile floor.

Six brass cocks lined the satinwood panel on the combination bath and shower. They were plainly marked "Hot," "Cold," "Supply to Bath," "Needle Spray," "Liver Spray" and "Shower."

Heart in her throat, Victoria turned the "Shower" cock.

Nothing happened.

Quickly, she closed the cock. *Had she broken it?*

Long seconds passed before reason prevailed.

Tentatively she opened the "Cold" cock.

The resulting roar of cascading water did not come from the copper bathtub spout—Victoria tentatively peered underneath the copper hood—nor did it come from the large, round, perforated copper disk above.

A small thermometer above the six copper cocks caught her attention.

It dawned on her that the cold water was going into a mixing chamber.

She opened the hot water cock.

The thermometer instantly registered an increase in temperature. Beside the thermometer, a meter gauged the fullness of the mixing chamber. One quarter full, two quarters full, three quarters full . . . *Full.*

Victoria hastily closed the hot and cold water cocks.

Excitement quickened her blood.

There was no lock on the bathroom door. The thought did not dampen her excitement.

Stepping into the copper tub—toes curling at the icy metal—she cautiously walked underneath the copper hood.

Immediately, Victoria was enclosed front, sides and overhead—it was like stepping into a copper grotto. Two smaller copper disks on either side of her were bent downward—they were hip high. A copper pipe blended into each of the four corners; they were perforated top to bottom.

A copper-skinned woman mirrored Victoria's movements—head turning when Victoria's head turned, breasts thrusting forward when Victoria's breasts thrust forward, arm raising . . .

Victoria opened the "Needle" cock.

Instantly, warm water assaulted her—breasts, buttocks, left hip, right ankle, face, stomach, back. There was no place on her body that the water jetting through the four perforated pipes did not target.

Her hair stuck to her shoulders and her spine; steam filled her lungs.

She turned off the "Needle" cock—the water immediately stopped. Daringly she opened the "Shower" cock.

And was immediately rained upon.

Victoria had never felt anything like it. The force of the water pounding down on her head and shoulders both stung and caressed.

It was like being caught naked in a summer shower.

She instinctively turned into the rain and the heat.

A recessed copper shelf contained a bar of soap and a bottle of— Victoria investigated—shampoo. The labeling was blurred by steam. She recognized the soap by its smell—it was *his* soap. *His* shampoo.

The man who had promised to protect her. *If* he could.

Victoria used Gabriel's soap. And then she used Gabriel's shampoo.

And then she turned her face up into the summer shower until she used up all of the water in the mixing chamber.

For a few brief moments she recaptured the joy that comes with innocence. And then that, too, was gone.

Her joy.

Her innocence.

Victoria opened her eyes and stared at the copper-skinned woman with dark, slicked-back hair.

The copper panels were beaded with water, like a window pelted by rain.

Silver water slowly streamed down the copper-skinned woman's body in slow, sinuous rivulets; her features were blurred, surreal, unashamedly sensuous.

Woman before the condemnation of man.

It was strangely empowering, gazing at the copper-skinned woman. The illusion of power did not dissipate when Victoria stepped out of the copper grotto.

The pale blue towel draped over the wooden rail beside the bathtub was soft, thick, luxurious.

Victoria used Gabriel's towel.

The mirror above the marble basin was fogged with steam. There was no pale-skinned, dark-haired reflection to replace the copper image inside the shower.

Victoria Childers, for a few moments, did not exist.

A silver-blond hair was trapped between the teeth of an ivory comb.

A sharp pang stabbed through her chest.

You don't want me, she had accused Gabriel.

You would be surprised at what I want, mademoiselle, he had replied.

Victoria used Gabriel's comb. Considerably more strands of water-blackened hair joined the single silver-blond strand.

Scalding tears stung her eyes.

Determinedly clinging to the illusion of control, Victoria opened the top drawer underneath the marble wash basin. She gazed at an ivory-handled toothbrush.

Gabriel's toothbrush.

Her own wooden toothbrush was inside her reticule, with the letters and her small, snaggle-toothed comb.

There had been two pots *au chocolat* on the dinner tray the night before. Had he returned after Victoria had retired?

Had he eaten the pot *au chocolat?*

Exactly what had the man done to Gabriel that he would not touch a woman?

Rummaging through the satinwood drawer, Victoria found another toothbrush: it was identical to Gabriel's ivory-handled one. It appeared to be unused.

She used it. And then she used Gabriel's tooth glass beside the water basin to rinse out her mouth.

Victoria was clean as she had not been in many months. It was exhilarating.

Her drawers were still damp. There was nothing to do but to wait for them to dry. And to don a dress that was not clean, no matter how hard Victoria worked to keep it so.

Suddenly shivering from the cold and the slick wet hair clinging to her back and her buttocks, she opened the bathroom door.

It was not night.

Bright electric light flooded the bedchamber.

A small woman with flaming red hair stood by the valet chair where Victoria had draped her dress the night before. A small blue hat with a jaunty peacock feather perched on top of the petite woman's elegantly coifed hair. Behind her, a petite woman with flaming red hair and a matching blue hat and peacock feather was reflected inside the cheval mirror.

Both images disdainfully held Victoria's brown wool dress away from them—as if afraid of vermin. The slender back of the red-haired woman was stiff; the expression on her rouged and wrinkled face was one of disgust.

No sooner had the intruder's presence registered in Victoria's brain, than the older woman glanced up. They stared at each other in silence: one through shocked eyes, the other through critical ones.

The red-haired woman summed Victoria up like the men and women who had witnessed her auction.

Shock gave way to rousing anger.

The woman had no right to judge Victoria—either her actions or her clothing.

A pearl collar gleamed about her throat. The sale of that pearl collar would feed every single homeless person in London.

Victoria had the choice of hiding inside the bathroom or hiding behind her hands.

Or of taking back what was hers.

Pride.

Dignity.

Her dress.

She strode toward the older woman and jerked the brown wool dress out of unresisting hands.

The woman was short, no more than five feet tall; Victoria had to bend her head to gaze down at her from her own height of five feet eight inches.

Clutching the dress against her breasts so that brown wool concealed her body shoulder to feet, Victoria stepped back, dignity regained.

"I'm afraid you have come to the wrong bedchamber, madam," she said frigidly.

"*Madame*," the older woman imperiously corrected her. "I am Madame René."

She spoke as if she were French royalty, or at the very least, as if Victoria should recognize her name.

"Nevertheless, *madame*," Victoria bit out, "you are in my bedchamber. Be so good as to leave."

"This *chambre de coucher*, mademoiselle, belongs to Monsieur Gabriel, not you. We are not in the habit of making house visits. *Vite* . . . there is no time to waste. I have clients waiting for me."

Clients . . . *men?* . . . *waiting* for her?

Was the older woman a *prostitute?*

Hands far stronger than Victoria's yanked the wool away from her.

For a second Victoria wondered if Gabriel had sneaked up behind her and grabbed the dress. But there were only the two of them inside the bedchamber: an elegant, petite old woman of indeterminate age dressed in the height of fashion, and a thirty-four-year-old woman who wore nothing more than clinging wet hair.

The woman who called herself Madame René circled around Victoria.

Victoria pivoted, intent upon reclaiming her dress.

Two warm hands cupped her breasts, simultaneously lifting them up and squeezing them together.

"You have passable breasts, mademoiselle"—instantly, Victoria's breasts sprang free. Madame René reached inside a side pocket and retrieved a rolled-up tape. She pulled a short strip out, stretched it taut between small, slender hands. A pigeon egg–sized diamond ring flashed on the forefinger of her right hand—"but you have no hips or derriere. We will design dresses to emphasize your bosom, *oui?* And then we will add padding to the hips and the derriere."

Victoria gaped down at the woman. Men mauled women's breasts; women did *not* maul other women.

The wool dress lay on the floor between them.

Victoria forgot about dignity.

She had stood naked in front of Gabriel; she *would* not parade around nude in front of a woman who manhandled her breasts.

Victoria dove for her dress.

A small, leather-shod foot kicked the dress away. It skidded across mirror-shiny wood.

"You are in my charge now, mademoiselle." Years of authority rang in the older woman's voice. "I will not abide a woman of mine to dress in rags."

In my charge . . . a woman of mine.

Did Gabriel think to find Victoria a new position by training her to be a prostitute?

Acutely aware of her dangling breasts that were mirrored by the polished wooden floor, Victoria straightened. An icy rivulet of water trickled down the crevice between her buttocks.

She clenched her chapped hands into fists.

"Madame René, I am not in need of a bawd."

The older woman drew herself to her full height. "I am a *couturière*, mademoiselle."

A modiste.

Gabriel had said his house was not a brothel. Why would a modiste visit it?

"Madame, obviously there has been a mistake." Victoria's nipples stabbed the air between them. "I did not send for a . . . a *couturière.*"

The bright tawny eyes narrowed with speculation.

"C'est vrai," she said.

"What is true?" Victoria asked sharply, arms digging into her sides rather than moving to cover up private places as they seemed to independently want to do.

"Monsieur Gabriel, he cannot—how do you English say it—get erect for a woman."

A picture of Gabriel's black silk trousers as he stood over her the night before flashed before Victoria's eyes. It was followed by the echo of her words, *his words.*

It had hurt him to tell her the truth. But he had.

How dare this woman judge him?

The surge of anger was stemmed by the sharp acuity behind the woman's tawny stare.

There was only one reason that the autocratic woman would be here. *This* chambre de coucher . . . *belongs to Monsieur Gabriel,* she had said.

"Monsieur Gabriel sent for you," Victoria shrewdly asserted.

The older woman perched her head to one side. "He sent for one of my seamstresses, *oui.*"

But he had not directly sent for Madame René.

"And so you yourself came because you wanted to see the woman whom he bid on," Victoria surmised.

"All of London wants to see the woman whom Monsieur Gabriel bid on, mademoiselle."

So they could judge him. As he had already judged himself.

"You have accomplished your goal, Madame René," Victoria bit out. "Now please leave. You may inform your clients that Mr. Gabriel has no difficulty in getting erect for a woman."

And that Victoria had a passable bosom but no hips or *derriere*.

Inquisitiveness shone in the older woman's tawny eyes. "You are angry."

Victoria did not deny it.

"I do not enjoy gossip, madame."

Lies had lost Victoria her job. And now possibly they would cost her her life.

"Gossip cannot hurt someone who has no name, mademoiselle," Madame René said dismissively.

Victoria had long ago accustomed herself to such snobbery.

"But Mr. Gabriel *does* have a name," she said pointedly.

The modiste, with her head cocked to the side, all at once reminded Victoria of a bright, inquisitive bird . . . of prey.

"And you think that he would be hurt by this gossip?" Madame René asked curiously.

" I should think, madame," Victoria's voice did not invite further conversation, "that any man would be distressed at having his private life bandied about."

"*Mais* Monsieur Gabriel is not just any man, *est-il?*"

"No, he is not," Victoria agreed coldly, voice matching the temperature of her naked skin. "If he were, he would not still be alive."

Madame René straightened her head; the peacock feather waved.

"No, he would not," the modiste briskly concurred.

Victoria blinked.

For one fleeting second approval shone in the older woman's tawny eyes; immediately it was replaced with smug condescension.

"You are fortunate, mademoiselle. Monsieur Gabriel is *très riche.* Not just anyone can afford my dresses."

Dresses . . .

Gabriel had hired a seamstress to make her dresses.

Victoria pictured a feminine, frivolous concoction of silk and satin. The stab of desire to own a new dress was a physical pain.

Immediately the image was supplanted by the brown wool gown crumpled on the floor.

She did not want charity.

"I do not need additional dresses, thank you, Madame René," Victoria said coolly. "If you will pardon me . . ."

The tawny eyes glittered craftily. "If you send me away, mademoiselle, you will only increase speculation about Monsieur Gabriel's abilities."

Victoria hardened her heart against the modiste's manipulation. Blackmail was the price of sin, Gabriel had said.

"Are you blackmailing me, Madame René?"

"You are still a virgin, mademoiselle," the modiste pronounced.

The muscles inside Victoria's vagina clenched.

"You are mistaken, *madame.*"

"Mademoiselle, had Monsieur Gabriel taken you, your eyes would shine with satisfaction and your mouth and your breasts and your sex lips would be swollen. I assure you, he has not touched you."

Sex lips reverberated inside Victoria's ears. She felt the peal of *swollen* all the way between her thighs.

Victoria instinctively squeezed her legs together; her arms compressed her ribs.

"And you will, of course, report these observations," she said cuttingly.

"He was *un prostituée,* mademoiselle."

For men rather than women, she did not need to add.

"I am aware of what Monsieur Gabriel was," Victoria icily retorted.

"But are you aware of what he is now?" the modiste inquired.

How much longer must she stand before this woman with her every flaw visible underneath the harsh electric light?

"He is the proprietor of this house," she said stiffly.

"He is the untouchable angel, mademoiselle," Madame René corrected her. "And he employs our kind. Not all of us are successful."

Our kind.

Victoria instinctively glanced at the pearl collar that concealed the modiste's throat.

"But you were successful," she said impetuously.

"*Oui,* I was *très* successful. Most prostitutes, mademoiselle, die from disease or poverty. You have seen poverty; it is in your eyes. Very few men—or women—pay the amount of money that you were paid last night."

But Gabriel had not bid two thousand pounds so that he might engage in sexual congress with her.

The coldness that suddenly permeated Victoria had nothing to do with the lack of fire in the satinwood fireplace or the wet hair that plastered her back.

Had the man who bid one hundred and five pounds and then one thousand pounds wanted her virginity . . . or had he wanted her life?

"Did women also purchase Monsieur Gabriel's . . . services?" Victoria asked compulsively.

The question came unbidden.

"*Oui.*" Memory glowed inside Madame René's eyes. "He and Monsieur Michel were the toast of London. *Les deux anges.*"

The two angels.

Michel in English was Michael.

Gabriel was God's messenger, Victoria had said.

Michael was his chosen, Gabriel had countered.

Was he the man who had hurt Gabriel?

Had Michael been the man who had bid one hundred and five pounds and then one thousand pounds? . . .

"This Monsieur Michel . . . were he and Gabriel . . . rivals?"

"They were friends."

"And now?"

"There are bonds, mademoiselle," the modiste said cryptically, "that nothing can sever."

Except death.

Victoria recoiled.

"You have seen me, *madame*." Sharp irony laced Victoria's voice. "You may now leave."

Else she would expire from the cold and the strain of holding her arms at her sides instead of hiding behind them as she had hidden behind wool dresses and other women's children.

Madame René did not leave.

"You disappoint me, mademoiselle."

Her chest ached—from the pressure of her arms. There was no reason why Victoria should care one way or another about what the *couturière* felt.

"I beg your pardon," she said rigidly.

"I thought you were a brave woman."

"History has often mistaken desperation for heroism."

"It would take a brave woman to love a man such as Gabriel."

What if I wanted more than your virginity?

Victoria didn't have anything else to offer a man.

"Then it is as well that Monsieur Gabriel did not purchase me to love him," she rejoined.

Madame René's eyes narrowed. The diamond on her forefinger flashed disapproval.

"Monsieur Michel is named because of his ability to pleasure women."

Victoria's heart skipped a beat.

"How can a man be named because of his ability to pleasure women?" she countered politely.

"He is known as Michel des Anges."

Michael of the angels.

"Angels do not engage in sexual congress, *madame*."

Madame René was not deterred by Victoria's cynicism.

"We French refer to an orgasm as *voir les anges*, to see angels."

Gabriel had referred to an orgasm as *la petite mort*, the little death.

The eye of the peacock feather and the modiste's stare were equally unblinking. Both searching for . . . *what?*

"Some women, mademoiselle," the modiste said deliberately,

"claim that Monsieur Gabriel's expertise is superior to that of his friend."

The cold enveloping Victoria was chased away by blazing heat.

"Madame, you will forgive me, but I am not in the way of holding a conversation without clothing."

Madame René shrugged. "We are women, mademoiselle. And Monsieur Gabriel is not offended by a woman's body."

"Monsieur Gabriel has not been with a woman in some time."

Now why had Victoria said that?

"*Oui.*"

"I do not know how to seduce a man."

I do not know how to seduce a man reverberated inside the chill bedchamber.

Satisfaction shone in Madame René's tawny eyes.

"*Tournez autour,* mademoiselle, *et je vous montrerai comment séduire un homme.*"

Victoria automatically translated the older woman's French: Turn around . . . and I will show you how to seduce a man.

Apprehension danced inside her stomach.

The older woman's gaze silently dared Victoria to be a woman.

To love a man who spurned love.

Victoria turned around and gazed in the cheval mirror.

Silver eyes stared back at her.

Chapter

9

Victoria had not heard Gabriel come into his bedchamber. But there he stood.

She had not felt Gabriel's presence. Now she felt it in every part of her body: her breasts that were passable, her hips and derriere that were not . . .

Three people watched Victoria: Madame René, cobalt blue dress and flaming red hair topped by a hat with a bobbing peacock feather; Victoria, water-blackened hair glued to her naked body, and Gabriel, alabaster face dark with shadow, white shirt open at the throat.

Madame René waited to see just how brave Victoria was.

Victoria waited to be struck down with mortification.

What did Gabriel wait for?

"Lift your arms, mademoiselle, so that I may take your measurement."

Madame René's voice came from a long distance. Her intentions were all too clear.

She wanted Victoria to posture before Gabriel.

She wanted Victoria to seduce a man who was renown for seduction—a man who had not touched a woman in *fourteen years, eight months, two weeks and six days.*

Victoria thought of the years she had lived in other women's houses caring for other women's children, paid by other women's husbands.

She had no home, no children, no husband.

Gabriel's home was a tavern, he employed prostitutes who were less fortunate than he, and he had no one to hold him.

The dark-haired woman in the cheval mirror lifted her arms; Victoria the woman felt her breasts lift and her nipples harden.

Passable breasts, the modiste had said.

The silver eyes in the mirror tested Victoria's breasts, gauging their roundness, their fullness.

Their desirability.

Did he, too, find them passable?

Madame René stepped forward. Cobalt blue-covered arms reached around Victoria's chest.

Encircling her.

Touching her.

The measuring tape cinched her breasts while heat and light scaled up and down her skin.

Victoria's heightened awareness was reflected inside Gabriel's eyes.

How long had he stood in the doorway—listening, watching? Victoria wondered breathlessly.

Why hadn't he made his presence known?

Why hadn't he protested at being the topic of discussion?

Victoria took a calming breath.

She had never been brave.

Perhaps with this man Victoria could be what she had never before been.

"Madame René. You said if Mr. Gabriel had taken me, that my mouth and my breasts and my"—Victoria faltered, gained courage from the sudden stillness in those watching silver eyes—"my sex lips would be swollen."

The measuring tape dropped; Victoria's nipples popped up. The scratch of a lead pencil scribbling on paper raced up and down her spine.

"Have you seen . . . women . . . like this . . . naked . . . after they spent the night with him?"

The body-warmed metal tab dug into Victoria's left armpit.

The silver gaze inside the mirror focused on Victoria's left armpit.

"I have, mademoiselle."

The tape extended to Victoria's wrist, smoothed by deft fingers. The silver gaze followed Madame René's hand.

The breasts of the naked woman in the mirror rose and fell; Victoria's lungs alternately inflated and deflated.

"Is he . . . was he . . . gentle with the women?" Victoria asked.

She did not recognize her voice.

It was husky with desire.

Or perhaps it was fear that made it husky.

Both tape and metal tab dropped.

The silver gaze snapped up to Victoria's waiting eyes.

"*Un prostituée*, mademoiselle," Madame René said, voice unnaturally businesslike in this most unbusinesslike situation, "is as gentle or as rough as a patron wishes."

More hurried scribbling.

Victoria felt rather than saw Madame René circle behind her back to her right side; all of her attention was directed on those silver eyes.

The hard tab dug into her right armpit.

The silver eyes bore into Victoria's tender skin and the dark tuft of hair that resided there.

Victoria licked her lips—lips that were rough and chapped.

Reality jarred through her.

What was she doing? . . .

"Surely a woman . . . a woman does not enjoy it when a man is rough with her," Victoria said unevenly, breath rasping her throat.

The silver gaze prodded the pulse that rapidly beat at the base of her neck.

"When aroused, mademoiselle, we do not want gentleness." One second the tab was digging into Victoria's skin—almost painful, but not quite—the next second it was replaced by chill relief. "An experienced man—or woman—knows when *une petite* pain will heighten the pleasure."

Pain. Pleasure.

There is always pain in pleasure, mademoiselle.

"And Monsieur Gabriel . . . he knows when a little pain will heighten a woman's . . . pleasure?" Victoria asked.

"He knows, mademoiselle."

The silver eyes neither confirmed nor denied Madame René's assertion.

Victoria's throat inexplicably tightened.

Had the man who raped Gabriel also known when pain could bring pleasure?

"You may lower your arms, mademoiselle."

Victoria lowered her arms.

The silver eyes in the mirror measured the shift of her breasts.

Suddenly, Madame René stepped between the woman in the mirror and the woman who was Victoria, and then the elegant, red-haired modiste disappeared.

A swish of silk was followed by a soft thud.

Victoria stared down.

Madame René knelt on her knees before Victoria. Her face was on a level with the tightly curled hair that marked the juncture of Victoria's thighs.

The peacock feather danced.

"Spread your legs, mademoiselle."

Victoria gazed into silver eyes and found the courage she needed: she spread her legs.

Frigid air invaded her.

Something more substantial than air feathered her stomach—the peacock feather. At the same time, a metal tab imprinted the juncture of her right thigh—close, too close to the feminine flesh that was suddenly, painfully swollen.

Victoria involuntarily started.

Warm fingers firmly held the metal tab in position. Or perhaps it was the silver eyes in the mirror which held it in position.

Gabriel's gaze burned . . . Victoria's mouth, Victoria's breasts, Victoria's *sex lips.*

"What type of"—forcefully Victoria concentrated on forming a sentence instead of on drowning inside those silver eyes and the debilitating heat they engendered—"of woman did Monsieur Gabriel prefer?" she asked, sandwiched between the man behind her and the woman who knelt on the floor before her.

"Monsieur Gabriel prefers"—deft fingers lightly traced the measuring tape down Victoria's inner thigh—she sucked in cold air— down the curve of her calf, pressed her ankle—"what any man prefers, mademoiselle," Madame René said in a deceptively distracted voice.

Madame René was not distracted either by the measurement she was taking or the conversation in which she was engaging. She knew *exactly* what she was doing. To Victoria.

To Gabriel.

The encroaching fingers abruptly withdrew—from the juncture of Victoria's thigh . . . from the inner curve of her ankle. The scratch of a pencil scribbling across paper grated across her skin.

The silver eyes inside the mirror dared Victoria to continue.

How far will you carry this game, mademoiselle? he had asked.

Farther than this, Victoria thought.

"And what is it that men prefer, Madame René?" Victoria asked unsteadily.

The hurried scribbling stopped; it continued to echo inside Victoria's ears.

A metal tab dug into the juncture of her left leg. It was icy.

"Men want to be wanted"—the silver eyes in the mirror followed Madame René's busy fingers: they mapped Victoria's inner thigh, the curve of her calf—"for who they are as well as for their sex. Men, mademoiselle, want to be loved. Just as we women want to be loved, *oui?*"

Madame René rose as quickly as she had dropped down.

"Maintenant, pull your hair up off of your back, *s'il vous plaît."*

Victoria slowly lifted her arms, high, higher, at the same time reaching back with her hands and piling her hair up on top of her head.

It was cold and heavy and wet.

Her breasts were cold and heavy and swollen.

The eyes watching her were cold and deadly and intense.

He was the proprietor, they said. He was a whore, they warned. He was a killer, they threatened.

Victoria saw an untouchable angel.

"How does a woman love a man, *madame?*"

Tape stretched across Victoria's shoulder blades.

"Does she kiss him, to show him that she desires him?"

Electricity sparked the air.

"Does she suckle his nipples, to give him pleasure?" Madame René's fingers pressed the metal tab on Victoria's left shoulder, the measuring tape on her right.

"Does she take him into her body to show him that neither she nor he need be alone?"

Madame René's fingers withdrew.

"A man's body is not so different from that of a woman, mademoiselle. They desire the same attention that we ourselves crave."

More scribbling. Less oxygen.

"A woman, mademoiselle, is not afraid to explore a man's body to find out what it is that pleases him."

Michael and Gabriel had been friends.

The key to Gabriel, Victoria thought, lay inside that friendship.

"Is Monsieur Michel as well endowed as Gabriel?" Victoria asked recklessly.

Danger charged the erotic tension.

She was going too far, those silver eyes said.

Every nerve inside Victoria's body agreed.

The metal tape dug into Victoria's right shoulder. "They are both reputed to be built like *des étalons*"—the measuring tape crawled down her spine to her waist, was held firmly in place—"like stallions."

The heat of madame's fingers dissipated; it was replaced by the scribble of figures.

Victoria's breasts shimmied with the force of her pounding heart.

There was nothing Gabriel could not see in her position: the lift of her breasts, her unprotected armpits, the ribs that stuck out too sharply, the protruding bones of her hips, the dark triangle of hair between her thighs.

The dusky rose lips that peeked below.

What had been dormant before was now swollen with desire.

Did he see her?

Had the modiste seen her?

"Is it necessary for a man to be large in order to satisfy a woman?" Victoria asked, heart inside her throat.

"*Non*. But a man who is *un prostituée* is not expected to be an ordinary man. Women do not want to pay for *une bitte* that is no longer than their own fingers, mademoiselle."

Une bitte.

Victoria had no problem identifying the modiste's French.

Did Gabriel refer to his member as *une bitte*?

Had he spoke French to the women who had purchased him . . . or English?

"How large does a man have to be, *madame*, in order to be compared to a . . . a stallion?"

The metal tab dug into Victoria's left shoulder. Madame René's fingernails traced the tape, imprinting the inches into Victoria's back while she audibly counted.

"One inch . . . two inches . . . three inches . . . four inches . . . five inches . . ." The sharp fingernails trailed over her shoulder bones. Victoria felt the measurements deep inside her vagina. "Six inches . . . seven inches . . . eight inches . . . nine inches . . ."

Victoria couldn't breathe. The silver eyes inside the mirror were overlaid by the vision of a man's member—of *Gabriel's member*—eight inches long, *nine inches long* . . .

"A man must have at least nine inches to be compared to *un étalon*, mademoiselle," Madame René said decisively. Her measuring fingers suddenly skimmed down Victoria's back and pressed the tape into her waist. And then they withdrew—the vision of a man's burgeoning member, madame's fingers, the measuring tape.

The silver eyes did not withdraw.

The manual measurement of Victoria's flesh was reflected in his gaze.

Gabriel had said that he was more than nine inches.

How much more? she wondered.

"Has a man ever begged you for release, *madame?*" Victoria asked, body so brittle that it felt like it would crack.

Gabriel's molten gaze froze into silver ice.

"That is what *un prostituée* does, mademoiselle—give pleasure." The modiste scribbled down measurements, seemingly impervious to the significance of Victoria's question. "*Le plus* pleasure, the better, *oui?*"

The more pleasure, the better. *Yes.*

"Has a . . . a patron ever caused you to beg, madame?"

A garrote closed around Victoria's neck.

"*Non, non,* do not move, mademoiselle. I must take this final measurement. *Voilà.*"

Victoria stood still.

The measuring tape tightened about her throat—

"When there is mutual respect and affection"—warm breath tickled Victoria's back—"there are a thousand methods by which a man and a woman can make each other cry out with pleasure."

—and then Victoria was free.

The modiste made a notation, a quick grating of lead on paper.

The silver eyes inside the mirror held Victoria's gaze.

"And when there is no respect . . ." Victoria dryly swallowed, "or affection?"

"It is a rape of the senses."

Madame René stepped back.

"Whereas seduction, mademoiselle, is a teasing of the senses. It is painting naked images with words. It is creating the anticipation of . . . *un baiser,* a kiss . . . *une caresse,* a caress . . . *un embrassement,* an embrace . . . That is the art of seduction, *n'est-il pas,* Monsieur Gabriel?"

"*Oui,* Madame René," Gabriel agreed neutrally.

Beneath the coldness inside his eyes was the imagery the modiste had deliberately implanted. *Un baiser,* a kiss. *Une caresse,* a caress. *Un embrassement,* an embrace.

Victoria imagined Gabriel's masculine flesh—his *bitte*—kissing her, caressing her, penetrating her. Eight inches, *nine* inches . . . Gabriel imagined Victoria's feminine flesh embracing his, inch by inch by inch.

The modiste had skillfully forced them to confront their desires.

"I will send clothes for mademoiselle *immédiatement,* monsieur," Madame René said with satisfaction. "*Au revoir,* mademoiselle."

In the mirror Victoria watched the back of Madame René's tasseled bustle saucily sway, recede.

Gabriel suddenly stepped out of Victoria's sight; the French modiste disappeared through the doorway. Leaving behind her a fully clothed man who denied his desires and a naked woman who had openly revealed her wantonness.

Victoria dropped her arms. Cold, damp hair tumbled down her back.

She pivoted, hair pitching over her naked shoulders.

Gabriel stood beside the door. The shadow that had enveloped his face in the mirror was nothing more than the dark stubble of beard. His facial hair was the same color as his eyebrows—brown instead of blond.

He wore the white silk shirt he had worn the night before. It was minus a collar. Cuffs. Studs.

The shirt was rumpled, as if he had slept in it. Dark hair the color of his eyebrows and beard stubble curled through the open V of the white silk.

Victoria stared at the dark curls of hair. They would tickle a woman's breasts, surely.

Without warning, a picture of the combination bath and shower flashed before her eyes. The two sprays that had been angled downward had been hip high. Had they been lifted, and the cock turned, water would have sprayed directly between her thighs.

Her clitoris throbbed in sudden comprehension.

Victoria's head jerked up.

Gabriel's silver gaze waited for her.

"The Liver Spray . . . It is not positioned to massage the liver," she said inanely.

He did not pretend to misunderstand her.

"No."

Victoria thought of the staid, respectable people who viewed the combination bath and showers at the Crystal Palace. Did they know that a spray that was advertised to massage the liver, was in fact used for so-called self-abuse?

Her gaze instinctively dropped down to Gabriel's thighs.

"Is the spray stimulating for men?"

The black silk throbbed in time to the pulsations beating through her own body.

"Not to the extent that it is for women."

His voice was cool and composed.

Victoria's gaze snapped back up to meet his.

"Yet your shower has that accessory."

"It came equipped with it."

"Was Michael the man whom you outbid?"

Victoria's hair stood on end at the electric tension that emanated from Gabriel.

"No," he said politely. "The man who bid on you was not Michael."

"But Michael was there in the saloon," Victoria persisted.

"Michael was in the saloon," Gabriel agreed lightly.

There was no lightness inside his eyes.

Les deux anges. The two angels.

They are rivals, Victoria had said.

They are friends, Madame René had corrected her.

"The man whom you outbid . . . Is he the one whom you thought sent me to you?"

"Yes."

If I had not bid on you, mademoiselle, you would die a far worse death than any caused by corrosive sublimate.

Victoria's rapidly rising and falling breasts belied her outward calmness.

"Is he the one whom you think will kill me?" she asked evenly.

"If I do not keep you safe, yes."

But he did not know if he could keep her safe.

"How long did you eavesdrop?" Victoria asked before she shattered with the brittleness of danger and desire.

"Long enough, mademoiselle."

Long enough for what?

"Do men want to be loved?"

"I would not know, mademoiselle," he politely evaded.

Neither did Victoria.

"Do you refer to your . . . male member . . . as a *bitte?*"

The electric light was too bright.

"No, mademoiselle." He did not acknowledge her impertinence by so much as a flicker of an eyelash. "I refer to it as my cock."

"Do you get erect when you are with women?"

"I have not been with a woman in over fourteen years," he said flatly.

"I am not ignorant, sir." Victoria's nails dug into her palms. Pleasure. *Pain.* "I am fully aware that a man does not need to have sexual intercourse with a woman in order to get erect."

"Perhaps you should rather ask, mademoiselle," Gabriel said, voice suddenly, dangerously, provocative, "if I get erect when I am with men."

The coldness inside his eyes took Victoria's breath away.

She took her life in her hands. "Do you?"

Gabriel strode toward her.

Victoria's heart leaped up inside her throat.

Gabriel halted in front of the satinwood fireplace.

Hunkering down, he grabbed the black-iron shovel from the bronze poker stand and pushed aside the ashes from the night's previous fire. Leaning over, he grabbed one stick of wood from the wood bucket, two sticks, three, shirt alternately stretching—revealing the corded play of muscles—and then bunching.

He was hiding.

Victoria knew that because she had spent her entire life hiding.

"Why is it, Mr. Gabriel, that Madame René refers to an orgasm as *voir les anges*, yet you refer to it as *la petite mort?*"

Gabriel abruptly rose and reached inside the obsidian urn on top of the satinwood mantel. Squatting back down, his knees yawned widely.

The taut globes of his buttocks were clearly delineated inside the black silk trousers.

A safety match ignited; sulfur fumes burned her nose. A tiny yellow flame nibbled on a log, spread in a sheet of blazing blue and orange fire.

Victoria did now know how much longer she could stand naked in his presence. And then she did know.

She could not stand before him naked one second longer.

Victoria pivoted on bare toes that stuck to the wooden floor. Righting herself, she stepped toward the lifeless brown wool dress.

"If you pick up that worthless rag, mademoiselle, I will take it from you."

She halted, buttocks tensed.

The silver eyes reflected inside the mirror were above her own: Gabriel had soundlessly stood up.

"You wanted to know if I get erect when I'm with men."

There was no emotion in his voice; so why did pain suddenly squeeze the breath out of her lungs?

"Yes," she managed.

"Turn around, mademoiselle, and face me if you want the truth."

Victoria slowly turned, bare toes mashing polished wood. Squaring her shoulders, she met his gaze.

It was as flat as the mirror behind her.

"A man, mademoiselle, does not need to feel desire in order to have sex, all he needs is a stiff prick."

Bitte. Cock. *Prick.*

"I don't"—she tilted her chin—"understand."

"You were aroused by Madame René's touch."

Victoria sucked in air. "How dare y—"

"—because you imagined that it was *I* who touched you."

Yes.

But she did not say it.

"Sexual organs, mademoiselle, are apparatuses." Cynicism tarnished the silver of his eyes. "Like my bath or my shower. If you turn a valve cock"—he paused, allowing the double entendre to sink in, valve cock, *cock*—"it releases water. It does not care whether it is a man or a woman who turns it."

If that were the case, then why were his eyes so bleak?

"You are saying that there need not be emotion, or feeling, in order for a man to . . ." Victoria struggled to find the words, she, a governess who had never even heard the word *cock* until six months earlier, "to sexually perform—"

"That is correct."

"—and that the . . . that copulation is merely a reflexive response, a matter of cause and effect."

"Yes."

She would *not* look away from his gaze.

"Are you saying, then, that you did not orgasm when you were with . . . a patron?"

"No, mademoiselle, I am not saying that," he said frankly.

And when there is no respect . . . or affection?

It is a rape of the senses.

"You do not enjoy sex," Victoria said.

Gabriel did not deny it.

"If your cock, sir, were no different than a mechanical apparatus, you wouldn't be afraid to touch a woman. Yet you are."

Darkness glittered inside his eyes.

There was only one thing that could have put that darkness there.

If Victoria continued, there would be no going back.

He could kill her for what she was about to say. Victoria would not blame him.

But there were worse things than death.

Living without the comfort of touch was far, far worse than death.

Victoria knew that because she had denied herself that simple comfort for over eighteen years.

She said what had to be said.

"The man who raped you"—the warning inside Gabriel's gaze

stabbed through Victoria's heart; it did not stop her—"he gave you pleasure."

Victoria was vaguely surprised that the crackling flames inside the fireplace did not freeze.

"He knew how to make pain pleasurable."

Darkness obliterated the silver of Gabriel's irises.

"He made you enjoy sex."

Chapter

10

66 **A** nd you will never forgive yourself for it."
Victoria's voice rang out with feminine conviction.
Jamais. Never.

Gabriel timed her breathing with the rise and fall of her breasts rather than the memories her words evoked.

He could kill her. And she knew it.

Or he could let the second man kill her. And she knew that, too.

She was afraid. But she did not hide behind her fear.

She was the one woman who dared confront his past.

How had the second man found her?

Gabriel padded toward Victoria with calculated intent. She did not back away.

Purposefully he circled her.

Her hair the night before had been dull and lustreless—like her cloak. It now shone underneath the electric light—a cold, wet, slick shield.

Victoria turned with Gabriel.

He could feel the heat of her nakedness. See his reflection inside her blue eyes, clouded with fear one moment and glowing with desire the next. He could smell his soap and his shampoo on her skin and hair, masculine scents femininized by the sweetness of her sex.

Stooping, Gabriel grabbed up her dress.

His gaze was on a level with her pelvis.

Victoria's pubic hair was dark and curly. The lips of her sex were dark rose, like her nipples.

They were moist with arousal. Swollen with desire.

And he had not even touched her.

Damn Madame René to hell.

Victoria's curiosity would build. As would Gabriel's.

She would wonder how it would feel, to take a man one inch at a time. He would wonder how Victoria would feel, slick wet flesh stretching one inch . . . two inches . . . five inches . . . seven inches . . . nine inches . . .

He would wonder what she sounded like when she cried out, first with the pain of losing her virginity, then with the pleasure of obtaining her first climax with a man.

He would wonder what it would take to make Victoria beg.

Gabriel straightened.

"Yes, Mademoiselle Childers, he made me enjoy the rape," he said coldly, deliberately. "Just as you enjoyed reading the letters written by a man who terrorizes you."

Gabriel turned his back on her—he could not remember the last time he had turned his back on either a man or a woman—and threw her dress into the fireplace.

Black smoke curled up the chimney.

Gabriel tensed.

If Victoria tried to save the wool dress, he would stop her.

He didn't want to hurt her. But he would.

"You have no right to destroy my clothing," Victoria said tightly.

She did not try to salvage her dress. She, too, knew that he would hurt her if she interfered.

Right.

Whores did not have rights.

Blue fire skimmed a brown wool sleeve, died.

"You have lived on the streets long enough to know that might is right," he said bluntly.

"And your might is greater than mine."

Anger laced Victoria's voice.

She did not like having to rely upon a man.

Gabriel knew too well what it was like being powerless.

"Yes, Mademoiselle Childers," he turned back toward her, "my might is greater than yours."

The stench of smoldering wool permeated the bedroom.

Victoria's blue eyes sparked fire. "I do not have any more clothes."

Gabriel could give her that much.

"Madame René will send clothes shortly."

Velvet. Silk. Satin.

Clothes of beauty as well as practicality.

Gabriel would do everything within his power in order to give her a life in which to enjoy them.

Victoria tilted her chin, lips chapped, cheekbones too sharp, the line of her jaw too vulnerable. "I do not want your charity."

No, a woman such as she would not want charity.

"What do you want?" Gabriel asked softly. Knowing the answer.

She wanted the pleasure an angel could bring. *Voir les anges.* But did she want the pain an angel could bring? *La petite mort?*

"You said you would assist me in obtaining a position as governess," Victoria returned stubbornly.

Gabriel did not reply.

He did not want to see her working in another man's house, supervised by another man's wife, caring for another man's children.

Tension coiled about them.

Fear. Desire.

A drying strand of dark hair glinted auburn underneath the overhead electric light. "I do not think the clothes that Madame René creates are designed to be worn by a governess."

Gabriel wanted to reach out and touch Victoria's hair, to feel the outward chill and the warmth of her skin underneath.

She would not survive the streets, let alone the second man.

Would she survive Gabriel?

It was time to find out.

"But you are not a governess, Mademoiselle Childers." Gabriel held her gaze. "Are you?"

Victoria read the truth in his eyes.

She squared her shoulders; fleeting regret streaked through Gabriel that her nipples were no longer hard. "How did you discover who my father is?"

"Libraries are wonderful institutions, mademoiselle," Gabriel said politely. "The births and deaths of the members of the ton are meticulously recorded for the good of the general public."

She stiffly walked toward him, breasts lightly bouncing. She stiffly walked past him, buttocks gently swaying.

Gabriel watched her through narrowed eyes.

Victoria jerked the pale blue silk spread off the bed and clumsily wrapped it about her.

She was hiding from a past that she did not want to admit.

Gabriel listened to the rustle of silk, the pop of an ember, waiting for her to regain her courage.

It did not take her long.

Slowly, pale blue silk clutched in a knot above her breasts, Victoria Childers—daughter of Sir Reginald Fitzgerald, one of the richest men in England—turned to face him.

"My father will not pay to have me returned," she said with quiet dignity.

Gabriel believed her.

"I do not plan on returning you to him," he said truthfully.

"Nor will he pay you to keep silent about my . . . my lapse of respectability."

A pulse throbbed in the base of Victoria's throat.

She had a beautiful throat. Long. Slender.

It would bruise easily.

"I do not need more money."

Gabriel had more money than he could spend in two lifetimes.

Victoria did not believe him.

"Then why did you go to the effort of digging up my parentage if you do not plan on blackmailing me?" she asked tightly. "Blackmail is the price of sin, is it not?"

His cynical words, coming out of her mouth, momentarily jarred Gabriel. It did not deter him.

"Have you sinned, mademoiselle?" he gently taunted.

Victoria looked him squarely in the eyes. "Not yet."

Gabriel's testicles tightened.

With anger. With desire.

He could not touch her. He would not let another man touch her. Not as long as she remained in his protection.

"Your father could be indirectly involved with the man who sent you here," he suggested.

A swift intake of air was his answer. It was followed by quick denial. "You don't believe that."

"Don't I?"

Gabriel no longer knew what he believed.

I think you are far more vulnerable than you want to think you are, Michael had told him. *And yes, I believe my uncle knew that.*

But did the second man know it?

"No, you do not," Victoria said emphatically.

The fear and the desire and the anger pulsing through Gabriel's veins found an outlet.

He did not want to want this woman. But he did.

And yes, his desire did make him vulnerable.

"Then tell me, mademoiselle," he said ruthlessly, "what I am supposed to think about a man—a wealthy man, a man of reputation—who allows his only daughter to sell herself so that she might have food and shelter."

And never once caring if she were killed or hurt.

Emotion flickered inside Victoria's blue eyes—eyes that had seen too much, felt too much, wanted too much. "He does not know that I am here."

"Are you so certain of that?" Gabriel bit out.

"Yes, I am certain of that." Her knuckles clamping the pale blue silk coverlet about her breasts whitened. "My father has no use of a daughter."

The registrar had listed a son, Daniel Childers. Victoria had a brother four years younger than herself.

In a society that passed wealth and title through male progeny, it was not uncommon for men to favor sons over daughters.

Gabriel wanted to spare Victoria; he could not.

Secrets killed.

Men. Women.

Whores.

"Why is that, Mademoiselle Childers?" he challenged. The stench of burning wool stung his nostrils. "Why would a father allow his daughter to become a prostitute?"

Pain lanced through Gabriel—it came from Victoria.

She did not glance away. "Because my father believes that women are whores, sir."

Victoria had been a governess for eighteen years, she had said. She had become a governess at the age of sixteen.

Either her father had driven her out, or Victoria, in order to escape her father's rule, had chosen to live the life of a servant rather than that of the lady she had been born.

There was an alternative reason: Gabriel did not want to think about that.

He had to think about it.

"He married a woman, mademoiselle," Gabriel goaded her.

"And she was a whore," Victoria returned, chapped lips drawn, chin high.

The registrars had mentioned nothing more than names and ranks.

"Your mother belongs to the untitled aristocracy," Gabriel said sharply.

"My father believes that women are born into sin." The bleakness darkening Victoria's eyes weighted Gabriel's shoulders. "And he was right. My mother left him when I was eleven. For another man. I am like my mother. I am a whore."

Emotion killed. So why couldn't he block this woman's emotions?

Gabriel offered Victoria the only comfort he could. "You are not a whore, mademoiselle."

"If I were not a whore, why did"—Victoria swallowed, holding on to the last of her secrets, her employer's name—"why did he have me dismissed from my post? Why did he write me those letters? Why did I read them? Over and over I read them. Why?"

The second man called to Gabriel.

He was out there, waiting for Gabriel to find him.

For the first time, he had left a trail to follow.

Gabriel couldn't leave Victoria alone. Not like this.

"We all want, Victoria."

The words were ripped out of Gabriel's chest.

Victoria stilled, cloaked in pale blue silk.

His woman, sent to him by the second man.

"When I was a boy, I wanted a bed to sleep in."

The madame had given it to him.

"When I became a whore, I wanted to be successful."

So that he need never go hungry again.

The madame had made it possible.

"When I became a man, I wanted to experience a woman's passion. Just once I wanted to feel the pleasure that I gave."

Time slipped.

Gabriel remembered silky wet flesh weeping for release.

He remembered the taste of a woman; he remembered the scent of a woman.

Silk rustled; it immediately dispelled the memory of other women. It did not dispel the memory of his desire.

After all these years, it still had not died.

Gabriel focused on Victoria's eyes, Victoria's body. Victoria's scent that permeated the room, overpowered now by the stench of burning wool, but there nevertheless.

"Did you?" she asked softly.

"No."

The truth.

Gabriel had never lost himself in a woman's pleasure.

The truth should no longer be capable of hurting; so why did it?

"You asked Madame René how to seduce a man," Gabriel said remotely. "I'll tell you. When he's hungry, feed him. When he hurts, offer him hope. When he has nowhere to go, give him a bed to sleep in. In order to seduce, one must be able to create the illusion of trust.

"The man who wrote the letters made you dependent on him:

you were hungry; he told you he would feed you. You were afraid; he told you he would comfort you. And when you had nowhere to sleep, he said he would share his bed with you.

"You're not a whore. When one has nothing to lose and everything to gain, Victoria, it's very easy to succumb to sex."

The acrid sting of burning wool had brought tears to Victoria's eyes. He should not have burned the dress.

He should not have tried to comfort Victoria; there was no comfort to be had from a man who had killed, and who would kill again.

Gabriel turned his back on Victoria—twice in one day, now—and strode into the bathroom. He softly shut the door behind him. A barrier to reinforce the one that had momentarily slipped inside him.

Gray mist still writhed in the air.

Victoria had used his toilet: Gabriel lifted the wooden lid and used the toilet.

Worn drawers and limp stockings neatly hung over a towel rack.

Victoria's pain-filled cry reverberated through him. *I am as clean as you are.*

Water spotted the marble wash basin.

Gabriel stared into the mirror above it.

Dull gray peered through a fading patch of steam.

For one fleeting second Gabriel stared into the eyes of hope.

It coiled and disappeared like the illusion that it was.

Victoria stared at the closed door, unable to breathe.

A faint splatter penetrated the satinwood.

Hot color surged into her cheeks, identifying the sound.

Even an angel had to relieve himself.

The sense of unreality his confession had created dissipated. And once again she could breathe.

She firmly tucked the silk spread between her breasts. Grabbing the skirt to lift clear of her feet, she gave him privacy.

A silver tray glinted on the black-marble-topped desk. The smell of ham and eggs and coffee filled the air.

Victoria's stomach growled.

When he's hungry, feed him. When he hurts, offer him hope. When he has nowhere to go, give him a bed to sleep in, rang inside her ears.

Gabriel had fed her and he had given up his bed that she might sleep in it.

He had not offered her hope, but he had sought to comfort her.

Seduction.

The illusion of trust.

There was only one cup on the tray.

Victoria did not want to eat alone.

She poured a cup of coffee and inhaled the savory odor. It tasted like pure nectar.

Gray light permeated the library. Gold lettering glittered invitingly.

Victoria knew books; books had been her life for as long as she could remember. She did not know how to comfort an angel.

Idly, she perused the rows and rows of leather-bound books. Straining to hear . . . a whisper of air. A footstep.

Gabriel.

Bold-embossed lettering caught Victoria's eye: one man's name, Jules Verne.

Journey to the Center of the Earth; Voyage au centre de la terre; Twenty Thousand Leagues Under the Sea; Vingt mille lieues sous les mers; The Mysterious Island; L'Ile mystérieuse; Around the World in Eighty Days; Le Tour du monde en quatre-vingts jours . . .

Gabriel possessed many works by Jules Verne, both in English and French.

She more carefully studied other books by Victor Hugo. George Sand . . . the English author Shakespeare . . .

Every title came in both a French volume and an English volume.

Coffee forgotten, Victoria plucked up *L'Ile mystérieuse,* the French edition of *The Mysterious Island* by Jules Verne, and stood beside the one window.

The English version was far less weighty.

Which language did Gabriel prefer to read? she wondered . . . English or French?

Blinding light exploded overhead.

Victoria blinked.

She did not have to see Gabriel to know that it was he who had turned on the chandelier. Every bone inside her body cried out her awareness.

He stood by the blue leather couch, framed by the glittering expanse of setting sun and shimmering blue ocean in the painting behind him. His face was slightly pink; he had shaved. A black wool Derby coat and gray pinstriped wool frock were draped over his right arm. A crimson silk tie was knotted about a starched white collar. The cut of a gray pinstriped waistcoat and trousers expertly fit his body. A silver cane weighted his left hand, a black bowler hat his right.

There was no sign of the man with the beard stubble who had shared his needs with her. In his place was an elegant, freshly shaven man.

Twenty-four hours earlier she would have thought him a pampered gentleman.

Victoria did not make that mistake now.

Gabriel was elegant. Gabriel was beautiful.

Gabriel was dangerous.

"Don't stand in front of the window," he curtly commanded. "And keep the blinds closed."

Victoria did not move away from the window. "No one can see me."

"You will not see the man who has a gun trained on you, mademoiselle," Gabriel said silkily. "Perhaps you will see a flash of light when he releases the trigger, perhaps not. One thing is for certain—you won't hear the gunshot: you'll be dead."

The danger of being shot by a man she had never seen was not real; the man in front of her was.

"You are going out," Victoria said evenly. "Who is going to prevent someone from shooting you?"

Gabriel dropped the two coats, cane and hat onto the pale blue leather couch that had been his bed only short hours earlier.

Leaning down, he retrieved a leather holster. Lifting up a cushion, then, he pulled a pistol out from underneath. "He won't shoot me."

The barrel of the pistol was a dull blue-black.

The smell of ham and eggs cloyed inside her throat.

Victoria recognized that pistol: it was the one he had hidden underneath the white silk napkin the night before. It was the pistol he had been prepared to shoot her with.

Victoria stepped away from the window, legs trembling. *Stomach* trembling.

Bitter coffee rose up inside her throat. "You are going out to look for him."

And kill him.

The unspoken words hovered between them.

"Yes." Gabriel slipped the holster over his right arm and buckled the attached belt around his ribs.

"The . . ."—tears pricked Victoria's eyes; she didn't want to be afraid, for her, for Gabriel—"the prostitute said there was another House of Gabriel prior to the opening of this one. She said that it burned down. Did the man you are looking for burn it down?"

"No." Gabriel adjusted the leather strap looping his shoulder before sliding the revolver inside the holster, his motions sure, practiced, as if he had done so thousands of times. He plucked up the pinstriped gray wool jacket off the couch and faced Victoria. "I burned it down."

Victoria took a deep breath; the silk knotted at her breasts loosened.

Gabriel's silver eyes dared her to ask the question that raced through her head: *why?*

"Your books—you have both English and French editions," she said instead. "Which do you prefer to read?"

"I learned to read English." He did not lie. "Someday I hope to be equally proficient in French."

Her fingers tightened around soft leather. "Who taught you to read English?"

"Michael."

"Michael is English."

"Yes."

The question came unbidden. "My father has never visited your house, has he?"

The shock Victoria had experienced the night before at seeing reputable men and women—men and women who were her father's associates—lingered in her thoughts.

"No, your father has never visited my house."

Victoria believed Gabriel.

"My father would not hurt me," she said firmly.

But to convince whom? Herself?

Or Gabriel?

"Not even to protect his reputation?" Gabriel queried gently.

"I think he might find vindication in the fact that I am where I am," she said matter-of-factly.

For once, truth did not bring pain.

She had known the price of leaving his protection when she had been sixteen. She would never go back, even if he would accept her.

"And what about your brother?"

Gabriel's question knocked the breath out of Victoria's lungs. Her fingers dug into the leather, insensitive to the damage she might cause. "How do you know I have a brother?"

Stupid, stupid question.

The library registrar . . .

"I know that he is thirty years old." There was no mistaking the scorn in his eyes. "I know that he's a man, mademoiselle, well capable of caring for a sister. But he didn't."

Victoria tilted her chin. He had no right to judge her . . . "My brother is not aware of my circumstances."

"Why not?"

"He ran away when he was twelve."

"And he didn't care enough to ever come back and see how his sister fared?"

Victoria was momentarily taken aback at the anger in Gabriel's voice.

Her brother had cared . . . too much.

"My brother ran away because of me." Memory clouded her eyes. "I do not blame him."

But Victoria blamed her father.

She would *always* blame her father.

"Why did he run away, Mademoiselle Childers?"

Revulsion tightened Victoria's stomach.

"My father punished Daniel," she said reluctantly.

The father had often punished Daniel, she did not need to add.

Gabriel would be repulsed, the old Victoria warned.

Gabriel deserved to know the truth, the new Victoria argued.

Gabriel silently waited. Her choice . . .

Victoria looked back . . .

"I heard Daniel crying later that night, so I went into his bed-chamber, and I climbed into his bed, and I held him. To comfort him," she said defensively, hating that she still felt defensive after all these years. "He went to sleep in my arms. I fell asleep, holding him. My father awakened us."

Victoria could not hold back the pain and the anger.

"He accused us of . . . of lying together in sin." She audibly swallowed. "My father does not understand that one can love—and touch—without carnal desire."

"So you became a governess," Gabriel said.

"Yes."

"And you loved other women's children—"

Victoria's lips quirked in wry amusement. "Not all children are lovable—"

"—because you did not trust yourself with men."

Victoria could no longer run from the truth.

"Yes."

Two faint bongs sliced through the tension, Big Ben announcing the hour.

"Desire is natural, mademoiselle." Silver lights danced inside his eyes. "The man who used your desire against you is at fault, not you."

Victoria imagined a boy who wanted a bed to sleep in . . . an adolescent who wanted success so that he would never be poor again . . . a man who wanted to feel the pleasure he created for others.

"The man who used your desire against you was at fault, sir," Victoria said compassionately, "not you."

Gabriel's head jerked back as if Victoria had slapped him.

Victoria waited for Gabriel to accept the truth.

Thrusting his arms into the pinstripe coat, Gabriel turned his back and grabbed up the derby coat, cane and hat.

She glimpsed the dark-haired guard who waited outside the door.

Gabriel did not acknowledge him.

Victoria stared into dark, curious eyes. And then the door closed behind Gabriel.

Leaving Victoria alone.

She was suddenly ravenous.

Sitting down in Gabriel's chair, she laid the French book down for easy access and lifted the silver dome off of the plate.

A blue enameled ring circled the white china.

Victoria ate with pleasure. When she had finished the last bite of ham, the last piece of egg and the last crust of a flaky croissant, she replaced the silver dome and carried it to the door.

The dark-haired man—younger than Gabriel by at least ten years—turned to her with a drawn gun.

She had surprised him.

He had surprised *her.*

"Please tell the chef that breakfast was quite delicious," she said evenly, holding out the tray.

Slowly the man's dark eyes took in the blue silk spread that bared Victoria's shoulders.

A spark of mischief flared inside his gaze.

Apparently, prostitution had taken neither the joy nor the desire out of him.

"Thank you, ma'am." Sliding the pistol underneath his black jacket, he smiled and took the tray. His voice was soft, cultured, the voice of seduction. "Pierre will be pleased."

Her heart skipped a beat. He really was quite handsome.

"Thank you." Victoria hesitated self-consciously. She took a deep breath. There really was no need for self-consiousness—there was nothing she could do to shock anyone in the House of Gabriel. "Please tell Pierre that I would appreciate it if my next meal is served with a tin of condoms. . . ."

Chapter

11

The London air was damp and chill. Yellow fog embraced the city.

Gabriel idly swung the silver cane.

It was hunting time.

He knew the address he sought; he just did not know if the man he wanted would be there.

Gabriel found the town house without mishap. It faced the park.

Childish voices permeated the yellow gloom that blanketed London. The children played London Bridge; their nannies caught up on gossip.

No one would notice two men strolling in the fog. And if they did, no one would be able to identify them.

"Shoeblack fer a penny, guv'nor," a gruff voice offered.

Gabriel stared down into six-year-old eyes that looked like they were sixty-six. He let the shoeblack shine his shoes.

He did not think of his shoes. He did not think of the man he sought.

Gabriel thought of Victoria.

She thought to save an angel.

Gabriel was not an angel.

How does a woman love a man? . . .

Michael loved Gabriel. His love had destroyed Gabriel's life.

Gaston claimed Gabriel's employees loved him. Their love allowed Gabriel to destroy their lives.

No woman had ever loved Gabriel.

He prayed no woman ever did.

The shoeblack sat back on his haunches so Gabriel could inspect his work. Blue glinted in his young-old eyes.

The man who used your desire against you was at fault, sir, not you.

Gabriel jerked his foot off the box and tossed the shoeblack a florin.

The door to the town house opened.

A woman with two young girls—ages eight and ten—stepped out. The woman was dressed in a drab cloak and bonnet; the two girls wore matching fur hats and muffs.

The governess looped a hand through an arm of each of her charges.

Victoria had said not all children were lovable. Had she been fond of the two girls? he fleetingly wondered.

Would she be fond of a bastard's children?

Gabriel waited to see if the two girls and their governess went inside the park.

They did.

The governess shielded the two girls from Gabriel as she herded them through the gate. Fog quickly shrouded them.

A muffin boy hawked his wares.

Victoria had not eaten her breakfast while he was there. Had she eaten after he left?

Gabriel bought a cinnamon muffin. No sooner had he finished it than the town house door opened again.

It was the man Gabriel sought.

He carried a standard mahogany cane in his right hand.

The silver-knobbed cane in Gabriel's left hand was a reminder that nothing was what it seemed.

Gabriel pushed away from the park gate. Idly he crossed the street, deftly stepping over a steaming pile of manure as he wove around a lumbering omnibus and a mule-drawn wagon. He gained the sidewalk.

The man leisurely walked down the steps and turned north, in the opposite direction of the park.

One pair of footsteps rang out in the coiling fog. It was joined by Gabriel's footsteps.

Transferring his cane to his right hand, Gabriel reached inside his coat and pulled out the Adams revolver from the shoulder holster; he kept it hidden underneath his derby jacket.

The man walked a little faster.

A bobby stood on the corner of the street ahead. Fast approaching the man and Gabriel was a hansom cab.

The man raised his arm to hail it.

Gabriel had no choice but to act quickly.

"Sir. Sir!" Gabriel matched his footsteps to those of the man. Keeping his voice soft and unthreatening, he asked, "Are you Mr. Thornton?"

The man paused and peered at Gabriel cautiously, arm still raised. He was dressed conservatively, a middle-aged man with a pale, narrow, freckled face.

He did not look like a man who would terrorize a woman. Whereas Gabriel knew he looked exactly the type of man he was: a man who had killed and would kill again.

"I am," the man said nervously.

His first mistake.

Neither a lone man—nor a lone woman—should ever admit their name to a stranger on a street.

Gabriel ruthlessly took advantage of the man's innocence.

"Your daughter Penelope has met with an accident, sir. The governess, a Miss Abercarthy"—the woman at the employment agency whom David had questioned had been most eager to tell the handsome man whatever he wanted to know—"asked that I fetch you."

The man dropped his arm. The cabby's nag clip-clopped on by.

"Penelope!" Surprise lit the man's face. "Why, whatever has happened to her? Where is she?"

Gabriel did not have to lie.

"She's in the park," he said. Waiting to see if he would have to use force.

The man willingly turned toward the park.

There was a lull in traffic. Gabriel crossed the road easily, quickly, as if in a hurry to return to an accident.

The man hurriedly followed him. Together they stepped through the open gate to the park.

"Where is she?" the man asked anxiously.

Children's voices continued their play. *"London bridge is falling down, falling down, falling down . . ."* overflowed the foggy park.

"Over here," Gabriel said, stepping toward a thicker patch of fog toward the outline of a tree, away from the playing children.

Thornton heedlessly walked into Gabriel's trap.

Gabriel slammed the knob of his cane into the man's chest.

He catapulted into the tree, breath escaping his chest in an audible *whoosh*. His hat toppled forward, blinding one eye; at the same time, his cane flew out of nerveless fingers.

Gabriel pressed the silver knob into the man's windpipe, effectively pinning him against the tree; simultaneously, he shoved the blue-plated pistol into the man's face.

Thornton gasped, visible eye wide with fear.

"I wouldn't shout out if I were you, Thornton." Gabriel's breath shone silver in the yellow fog. He did not relieve the pressure on the man's windpipe. "You wouldn't want your two daughters to see you with your face blown off."

"Oh, I say . . ." The man's voice rose to a hysterical pitch, breath commingling with Gabriel's.

"Quietly," Gabriel softly warned him.

"My money—it's in my coat." The white of his right eye showed round like a miniature moon. "I can pay you—I'm a rich man—"

Victoria had thought Gabriel wanted to blackmail her father.

For one second he wished the man in front of him were her father.

He would show him how little money mattered.

"I don't want your money, Thornton."

Thornton's eye bulged. "Please don't kill me."

Victoria had not begged for her life. Had Thornton hoped to make her do so?

Had he hoped to make her beg for pleasure?

Had he stolen into her bedchamber and seen her silk drawers when they were soft and white?

Gabriel held on to his anger.

"I won't shoot you if you tell me what I want to know," he said caressingly.

Gabriel didn't lie.

A gunshot would attract attention; a crushed windpipe wouldn't.

"Anything, sir," the man babbled. He had no pride, no dignity, just the title gentleman that was a product of breeding and wealth. "I'll tell you anything you want to know."

Gabriel didn't doubt it.

"Anything, Thornton?" Gabriel asked softly, seductively.

"Yes . . . Yes!" Thornton said eagerly, hope blazing in the one eye that was visible.

It was his second mistake.

Hope killed.

It was time to end the game.

"Tell me why you're terrorizing Victoria Childers."

The man blinked. "Victoria Child—why, she is no longer employed in my household."

"Why not?" Gabriel asked silkily.

The man's eyes rolled nervously. "She—she—my wife dismissed her."

"Now, why would she do that?"

"She—she—Victoria Childers—she flirted with me—"

It was Thornton's third mistake.

A man did not lie when confronted by death.

"Victoria Childers is not a flirtatious woman." Gabriel delicately pushed the bore of the pistol into Thornton's right cheek. Bone and metal impacted. "Why did you lie to your wife?"

"Oh, please—"

"The truth, Thornton," Gabriel crooned. "All I ask is the truth."

"I"—the man tried to swallow, could not— "I did not lie to my wife."

"Are you saying Victoria Childers flirted with you, Thornton?" he asked dangerously.

The man did not make a forth mistake.

His eye rolled upward, as if looking for a savior from above. "No, no, I did not say that."

"Then what did you say?"

"My wi-wi-wife"—he stuttered—"my wife is a jealous woman."

"The employment agency supplies you with a fresh governess every few months, Thornton. Surely you did not think that your scheme would go unnoticed."

"I do not—I do not know what you are talking about." The bore pushed the inner flesh of his cheek between his teeth so he could not completely close his mouth. His vowels broadened. "It is my wife 'oo employs and discharges the governesses."

His wife . . .

"You must have quite a harem by now."

Thornton was beginning to realize how dangerous Gabriel was. "Plese don't 'urt me," he begged.

"You don't think you deserve to be hurt?" Gabriel asked gently.

Wondering what Thornton had planned to do with Victoria if she had come to him.

Wondering what he would have done to Victoria after he had finished with her.

Would he have given her to the second man before or after he had used her?

"I have done nuthing, I tell you," the man said painfully.

"Yet Victoria Childers was discharged. Without a reference. Governesses who do not have references cannot gain reputable employment. You really leave your women no choice, do you, Thornton, but to come to you?"

For food. For shelter. For sex . . .

"I don't know what you are talking about. I don't have women. I have my wife. My wife would know where the gov'r'nesses go.

They don't come to me. No one comes to me. I don't know what you are asking me. I have done nuthing, I tell you."

A discordant peal of truth rang inside the man's voice.

Gabriel ground the bore of the gun harder into his face. The man would have a bruised cheek come the morrow. It would match his bruised throat.

"Oh, please, sir, please put the pistol away."

The man's breath smelled of coffee; the acrid aroma of ammonia wafted upward.

In his fear, Thornton had urinated in his trousers.

A child's giggle drifted through the air. A distant reminder of innocence.

Victoria had said her employer had lied. To get her discharged.

She had said her former employer had written the letters. To seduce her.

Do you think your uncle arranged a woman to be sent to me in order to lure me to my death? Gabriel had taunted Michael.

"Where were you going when you left your house?" Gabriel asked sharply.

"To my"—the man's distorted voice wavered—"club."

Doubt crawled up Gabriel's spine.

The man had admitted Victoria had been employed. *By his wife.*

If he was not the man . . .

"If you don't have a fountain pen, Thornton, I'm going to kill you," Gabriel said deliberately.

"Oh, I have a foun'n pen, sir!" the man said eagerly. "Inside my 'rock here! See!"

It could be a ruse.

The man could have a gun inside his frock instead of a fountain pen.

There was only one way Gabriel would ever know the truth.

"Get the pen out of your frock," Gabriel ordered.

"I ca-ca-can't. My co-co-coat is buttoned."

"Unbutton it."

"I ca-ca-can't with th' pistol in my cheek, sir."

Cynicism twisted Gabriel's mouth.

"You would be surprised at what a man can do, Thornton." A man could kill. Or a man could grant life. "Unbutton your coat."

The man fumbled with the buttons. Some seconds later his coat fell open.

"Now reach inside your frock. Slowly."

Thornton reached inside his frock. Slowly.

Gabriel's thumb cocked the hammer of his revolver, a deadly click that echoed in the fog.

If Thornton produced a pistol, he was a dead man, the click said.

Sweat dripped down Thornton's cheek, glistened on the blue-plated muzzle. He carefully pulled out a thick bronze fountain pen.

It uncontrollably waved back and forth.

Had Victoria trembled in her fear? he wondered.

"I want you to write something," Gabriel said brusquely.

It was time to find out who the real letter writer was.

"I do not—I do not 'ave any paper."

"Remove your left cuff."

Gabriel stepped back far enough to allow Thornton to bring his hands in front of him.

He read Thornton's intentions before the man had time to carry them out: he was going to run.

"Do you know what a bullet does to a man's face at this range?" Gabriel asked softly.

Thornton ripped off his left cuff.

Carefully, Gabriel eased back the pistol. A round white pressure spot indented the man's right cheek.

"If you yell, I will kill you," he said clearly. "If you run, I will kill you. Do you understand me?"

"Yes." Thornton breathed in short quips of air. "Yes, I understand you, sir."

"*Bon.* I want you to write on the cuff."

"What? What do you want me to write? I'll write anything you want. Anything. Just tell me what to write . . ."

Gabriel quickly thought. "Write, 'The eternal hunger of a woman.' "

There was no recognition on Thornton's face, only the fear of dying and the willingness to do anything at all to escape death.

Using his mouth to uncap the fountain pen and his left palm as a desktop, Thornton hurriedly scribbled the words down on the stiff white cuff, breath steaming the air.

Finished, he looked up eagerly, a child waiting for approval.

"Hold up the cuff so I can read it," Gabriel ordered.

Thornton held up the cuff, bronze cap plugging his mouth, hand visibly shaking, cuff weaving back and forth, black script dancing.

Gabriel snatched the cuff out of Thornton's hand.

The black script did not match that in Victoria's letters.

His guts knotted with realization.

Thornton was not the man who had written Victoria Childers's letters.

Chapter

12

A stiff white cloth floated down onto the linen sheet that Victoria tucked underneath the mattress.

Puzzled, she picked it up.

It was a man's cuff. Black ink slashed across it.

Victoria turned the cuff right side up.

The eternal hunger of a woman slapped her in the face.

Her heart slammed against her ribs. Victoria dropped the cuff; at the same time she jerked upright.

The cuff spiraled downward. Warm breath tickled the back of her neck.

She pivoted around.

Gabriel stood only inches away from her. He smelled of cold air and London fog.

The eggs and ham and croissant Victoria had earlier devoured rose up into her throat.

"I met your former employer, Mademoiselle Childers."

Met her former employer . . .

"The man who wrote that note on the cuff was not my employer," she said stiffly.

"*Au contraire*, mademoiselle." Gabriel's breath smelled faintly of cinnamon. "Peter Thornton was very much your employer."

Was her employer?

Did Gabriel infer that Peter Thornton was her former employer? Or that he was the *former* Peter Thornton?

Had Gabriel killed him?

Victoria brought her hand up to her throat. Her pulse throbbed a warning against her fingers: *death, danger, desire.* "How do you know that Peter Thornton is the name of my former employer?"

"I sent one of my men around to the various employment agencies." The warmth of Gabriel's breath was a sharp contrast to the coldness in his eyes. "He told them that he had interviewed a governess named Victoria Childers whom he wished to employ, but he had misplaced her address. The West Agency found your file. They did not have your current address, but they hoped that your former employer would."

Admiration vied with Victoria's resentment. "You are very thorough, sir."

Frighteningly so.

The man who had written the letters could take lessons from him.

"Ignorance kills, mademoiselle," Gabriel said softly. "So do secrets."

He knew about her father. Her brother.

Victoria did not have any more secrets.

One thought rapidly followed the next.

Victoria had never seen Peter Thornton's handwriting, but if it was not he who wrote the letters, who did? At the same time it dawned on her that she had never before seen the handwriting of the silver-eyed, silver-haired man before her.

Laissez le jeu commencer.

Let the play begin.

But who were the players?

Unexpected hurt squeezed Victoria's chest.

Gabriel did not trust her. But she had trusted him.

She *would not* be afraid.

Dropping her hand, Victoria squared her shoulders; her breasts strained against the knotted silk. "And so you once again believe that I am in league with this—this man whom you claim is after you."

Hot breath seared her cheek.

"Aren't you?" Gabriel asked lightly.

She tasted cinnamon.

Gabriel's eyelashes were too long, too thick. His face too beautiful. Too remote.

The smell of burned wool lingered in the air.

Victoria wore the cover to his bed. Even if she had a safe place to run to, she couldn't. He had burned her dress.

She was trapped. With only the truth as her savior.

Truth had not saved her position six months earlier.

"No." Victoria gritted her teeth. "I am not."

"The man who wrote the letters knew you wore silk drawers, mademoiselle."

Peter Thornton had been the only man she knew who had had access to her bedchamber and intimate apparel.

Who else would know—

"I sold all but one pair of my drawers on St. Giles Street." Victoria did not look away from those dangerous silver eyes. "Anyone who followed me could have went into the store after I did and purchased whatever I'd sold."

The thought that a stranger had dogged her footsteps did not comfort Victoria.

"It's possible," Gabriel admitted.

But not likely, his silver eyes said.

She would not beg. Cry.

She would not be hurt because an untouchable angel did not believe her.

Victoria notched her chin up higher. "I will not be a victim."

The black of his pupils devoured the silver of his irises. "You already are, Victoria Childers."

Awareness of her bare chest and shoulders above the pale blue silk spread and of her nakedness underneath it inched over Victoria's skin.

He was too close, the heat emanating from his body too hot.

How could he doubt her?

He had *talked* to her. . . . He had told her his needs. . . .

"And whose victim am I, sir?" Victoria challenged. "You say there is a man who would hurt me; I have not seen this man. You claim you will protect me; it is you who are threatening me. Whose victim am I?"

Her hurt was briefly reflected inside his gaze. It was replaced by cold calculation.

"A man is terrorizing you, mademoiselle." Cinnamon-flavored heat feathered her lips. "Yet you won't give me his name. Why is that?"

"I don't know his name," Victoria repeated stubbornly. There was no disguising the desperation in her voice.

"You said it was Thornton."

"Yes," she bit out.

"Why didn't you give me his name?"

She licked her lips, tasting cinnamon, tasting Gabriel's breath. "Because I was afraid."

She was *still* afraid.

"Of what, mademoiselle?"

Both his voice and his breath were a caress. The coldness inside his eyes froze her eyelashes.

"I was afraid that you would find him," Victoria said.

"But I did find him."

"I was afraid you would talk to him."

"I did talk to him."

Black specks dotted Victoria's vision. "I was afraid he would tell you who I am."

"I know who you are."

"You do not know who I am!" she lashed out.

He did not blink an eyelash at her outburst—an outburst that proved anew Victoria was not the woman she had always thought herself to be.

Calm. Rational.

Above the desires of the flesh.

Dark knowledge glimmered inside Gabriel's eyes. "I know you, Victoria."

He had seen her naked body, his eyes said.

Gabriel knew the size of her breasts, the narrowness of her hips, the curve of her buttocks. But he did not know *her.*

"What do you know of me?"

"I know that you enjoy the feel of silk against your skin." His gaze flicked over her naked shoulders, toyed with the silk tucked between her breasts. "I know that you're courageous. I know that you're loyal."

His eyelashes lifted, silver gaze pinning hers. "I know that you're going to get me killed."

Victoria's breath caught in her throat—or perhaps it was his breath that snagged inside her throat. "I would never hurt you."

"I know that, too."

"How do you know that?"

"Because of your eyes." Gabriel's eyes darkened, silver becoming gray. "You're here because of your eyes."

She must not have heard him correctly. "I beg your pardon?"

"Madame René told you that Michael and I are friends."

It took a second for Victoria's thoughts to switch from one subject to another.

"Yes. She said that there are bonds between you that could never be broken."

Except through death . . .

"When we were thirteen, a madame in Paris took us in." The past crowded Gabriel's gaze. "She trained us to be whores."

Six months earlier Victoria would have been horrified. In the last six months she had seen far younger boys and girls on the streets pandering their flesh.

"Michael." Victoria carefully phrased her next question, afraid of upsetting the precarious balance that flowed afresh between them. "Was he also trained to please . . . men?"

Gabriel's face remained impassive. *"Non."*

Victoria tried to imagine the sort of friendship that would grow between two boys trained so differently.

"Do not pity me, mademoiselle," Gabriel said sharply.

"I do not." Victoria's throat tightened. "I think you are fortunate to have a friend like Michael."

A friend who would understand the boy Gabriel had been and the man he had grown up to be.

A muscle ticked inside Gabriel's left cheek. "You are here because you have Michael's eyes."

Victoria blinked in confusion. "Your friend has blue eyes?"

"Michael has hungry eyes, mademoiselle. The color doesn't matter."

Hungry eyes . . .

Heat coursed through Victoria. "I do not . . . *flirt.*"

She *had not* invited the last six months . . .

"You want to be loved, mademoiselle."

The five years Victoria had lived under her father's care after her mother had left crashed down on top of her. He had forbade emotional expression, physical contact, endearments.

A woman's need to love, he had repeatedly said, was a woman's sin.

"And is that so wrong?" Victoria asked, her voice echoing a young girl's cry. "Is it a sin to need love?"

"Whores can't afford to love."

"Why not? Why should anybody be deprived of simple affection?"

Cinnamon-flavored regret flickered inside Gabriel's eyes, silver to gray, gray to silver. "I am not capable of loving a woman, mademoiselle."

Victoria stood to her full height. "I did not ask for your love, sir."

"I have shared with you more than I have ever shared with anybody else—"

"Thank you—"

"—but trust comes at a price."

It always came back to one man.

Victoria could not keep the anger out of her voice. "I do not know who the man is that you seek."

"I know that."

Then why did he keep questioning her?

"I don't know who wrote the letters."

Cinnamon burst over her cheek and her lips. "Then tell me something that you do know, mademoiselle."

Victoria did not know how to love a man. She did not know how to *seduce* a man.

"I cannot imagine knowing anything that would be of interest to you, sir," she said. "I am a governess, not a—a—"

Victoria floundered.

"Whore?" Gabriel supplied cynically.

"I did not say that," she retorted.

"You defended me to Madame René," he said unexpectedly. Wariness tinged his voice, shadowed his eyes. "Why?"

Why had Victoria defended a man who had by turns seduced her and threatened her?

"Because you want," Victoria said.

Despite his past. Or because of it.

Gabriel did not deny his wants.

Regret glimmered inside his eyes. "If you could, mademoiselle, would you help me?"

Help an untouchable angel . . .

"Yes."

Victoria would help him.

"You have information that I need."

There he went again—

Victoria opened her mouth.

"I want to know the interior layout of the Thornton house," Gabriel said.

Her mouth snapped shut. "What?"

"I want to know what room Mrs. Peter Thornton sleeps in," he said, as if it were the most common thing in the world for a man to ask a woman whom he had praised for courage and loyalty to give him information about another woman's sleeping quarters. "Regardless of whether you give me that information or not, I will seek her out. With that information, however, I will be less likely to accidentally surprise someone."

And kill them.

"Did you . . . *injure* Mr. Thornton?" Victoria asked compulsively.

"He is alive, mademoiselle."

For now.

Seduction.

The illusion of trust.

Victoria's mouth tightened. "You are seducing me into providing you private information."

"No, mademoiselle, I am asking you to trust me. As I trust you."

Every breath Victoria drew was warmed by Gabriel's breath.

"Why do you wish to visit Mrs. Thornton in her bedchamber? Why not take tea with her?" Victoria reasoned. "I'm certain she would find you quite charming."

Victoria was horrified to hear the jealousy in her voice.

Mrs. Thornton was a beautiful woman. Her pale blond hair was glossy with health, her lips and her hands were not chapped from cold or exposure.

"She employed you," Gabriel said enigmatically.

"Yes," Victoria said curtly. "It is not unusual for the woman of the house to oversee the employment of "—Victoria had long ago become used to referring to herself as a servant, so why did she balk now?—"servants."

"What is the average stay for a governess?"

Victoria frowned. "That depends upon the needs of a household and the competence of a governess."

"Mrs. Thornton employs—and discharges—two and three governesses a year." Gabriel paused, monitoring her reaction. "*Every* year."

Two and three governesses . . . *Every year.*

Gabriel could not be suggesting what Victoria thought he was.

"That's . . . Her children are spoiled." Penelope, the eldest, loved to tattle; no doubt it had cost many servants their position. "Governesses often seek other employment."

Gabriel's gaze was relentless; his breath was warmly enticing. "You did not seek other employment, mademoiselle."

And how did he know that?

"I was making inquiries."

The truth.

"Did Mrs. Thornton know that you were making inquiries?"

"I . . ." Victoria remembered Mrs. Thornton barging into her bedroom unannounced one evening shortly before dismissing her. Victoria had been poring over a newspaper. "Perhaps."

"Many governesses do not have homes or family."

There could be no mistaking Gabriel's implications.

"And because many of us are homeless, you think that Mrs. Thornton is employing—and discharging—governesses for some nefarious purpose?"

"Yes," he said bluntly, watching her . . .

"You think that those other governesses were subjected to the same treatment that I received?"

"It is possible," Gabriel said.

But if that was the case . . .

"You think that the man who wrote the letters to me also wrote letters to the other governesses."

Gabriel did not respond.

He did not have to respond. The answer was in his silver eyes.

Victoria's skin felt like it was trying to independently crawl away.

"You think those other governesses are dead," she said in dawning horror.

While Victoria was still alive. Saved by stubborn independence.

He unwaveringly gauged her reactions; his body heat did not warm her.

"Surely Mr. Thornton would know if his wife were an accessory to"—Victoria fought down her panic—"to murder."

"It pleases him to believe his wife is a jealous woman."

Victoria had never seen Mrs. Thornton display any signs of jealousy.

"Why would she . . . What pleasure would a woman gain in—I have seen Mrs. Thornton's handwriting." Victoria's floundering voice found reason. "It was not she who wrote those notes."

Warm cinnamon breath licked her face. "Then we must discover who did write them."

Victoria could trust Gabriel. Or she could distrust him.

Her choice . . .

"How do I know the writing on the cuff isn't your handwriting?"

"That is easily proven."

As was Mrs. Thornton's involvement with the man who waited for Victoria to come to him for food. Shelter. Pleasure.

"You will not hurt Mrs. Thornton," Victoria said. But to convince whom?

"I will not kill her," Gabriel agreed.

"How did you . . . persuade Mr. Thornton to meet with you?"

"I met him in the park outside his home."

Yes, the park shrouded in fog would be private.

"Mrs. Thornton shops in the mornings," Victoria hurriedly suggested. "Perhaps you could catch her then . . ."

"I saw the governess they replaced you with, mademoiselle," Gabriel said with calm deliberation. "Perhaps they will lose patience with you and concentrate on her."

And another woman would fall victim to the pattern. Dismissal without a reference. Dying a little every day with poverty and despair.

Receiving letters promising pleasure and safety.

"Very well," Victoria said decisively. "I will help you."

"*Merci,* mademoiselle."

Without warning, Gabriel stepped back.

"Trust, mademoiselle." The warm cinnamon breath was replaced with the acrid odor of burnt wool. "We must both trust."

Victoria would not allow him to lie to her. "Yet you do not trust me, sir."

A drop of London fog glittered on his shoulder. "Perhaps it is myself that I do not trust."

"Don't."

The objection was out before Victoria could stop it.

An ember popped in the fireplace.

"Don't what?" Gabriel asked softly.

"Don't seduce me with an illusion of trust."

Victoria wanted to believe that the beautiful man in front of her found her attractive. She wanted to believe that she could trust an untouchable angel.

She wanted to believe that he would not seduce her with words merely to gain her trust.

Victoria knew better than to believe simply because she wanted to.

"You think the man who wrote the letters can lead you to the man you want." She held his gaze with resolve. "Perhaps he can. I have told you I will help you, so please don't lie to me."

"I do not lie."

He did not like having his drawers pilfered; he did not like being called a liar . . .

"There are many different types of lies, sir." Victoria tilted her chin in challenge. "Omission is as much a lie as prevarication."

"I always pay my debts, mademoiselle."

It was not the response she had expected.

"Do you think that you owe me a debt?" Victoria swallowed. "And that you can repay it by telling me what you believe I want to hear?"

"Yes," he said. "I believe I owe you a debt, Victoria Childers."

"Why?"

"I loved a man, mademoiselle. If I had not loved him, you would not be here."

Michael. The chosen angel.

"You loved him . . . as a friend?"

"I loved him as a brother."

Victoria had loved David as a brother. Her father had twisted her innocent love and defiled it.

"There is no sin in love," she protested involuntarily.

"No, mademoiselle, there is no sin in love," Gabriel said unflinchingly. "The sin is in loving."

A man such as he should not feel so much pain.

A woman such as she should not care.

"I wish I had never read the letters," Victoria said quietly. "I wish I had never learned that aspect of my character."

Gabriel did not move; he suddenly felt miles away. "You wish that you did not desire an angel?"

There was no hiding from the truth.

"No." For better or for worse, Victoria did desire Gabriel. "No, I do not wish that."

She did not have the courage to ask Gabriel if he regretted bidding on her.

"Madame René delivered some clothes to you," Gabriel said abruptly, silver eyes guarded.

Clothes.

Madame René.

Victoria took a deep breath.

It had been a scant few hours since Victoria had stood naked before Gabriel while Madame René measured her. It seemed like a few years had passed.

Gabriel was prepared for her to reject his clothes. His person. His past.

Choices . . .

"Did you bring these clothes up with you?" Victoria asked briskly.

"No."

She stared. "Then how do you know they are here?"

"Gaston told me they had arrived when I returned. I told him to bring them up. I heard the door open and close a few minutes ago."

And had not told her.

Gabriel's omission did not curtail a spark of anticipation. Grasping handfuls of silk in both hands, Victoria preceded him out of the bedroom.

An assortment of white boxes were piled high on the pale blue leather couch—three long dress boxes, shorter rectangular boxes, three hat boxes. Four shoe boxes. The boxes were all stamped with rose petals.

Victoria had not had a new dress in over a year. She had never owned a custom-made dress.

It was unseemly to take frivolous pleasure in expensive clothing when there were so many on the streets who had so little.

"There are too many boxes," she said repressively.

"Madame René has assured me that women never have too many clothes."

Was that a smile in Gabriel's voice?

Victoria quickly glanced up—she had seen cynicism twist his mouth, but she had never seen him smile.

And he did not now. But there was a smile in his eyes.

Beautiful silver eyes . . .

"I will pay you back," she said hurriedly.

His voice was a light caress. "Perhaps, mademoiselle, seeing your pleasure is payment enough."

Her stomach somersaulted. "Are you flirting with me, sir?"

"No, mademoiselle." The smile left his eyes. "I do not flirt."

"But you know how?" she asked breathlessly.

"Yes, I know how."

To flirt. To kiss. To give pleasure.

But he did not know how to receive pleasure.

"What shall I open first?" she asked. And knew that she sounded like a child at Christmas.

Faint memories stirred. Of a loving voice and warm laughter . . .

Sounds familiar to an eleven-year-old girl, not to a thirty-four-year-old woman.

The memories were gone as quickly as they had come.

Gabriel gestured toward the couch. "Whichever box you prefer, mademoiselle."

Victoria tentatively sat down; leather squeaked, silk swished. Carefully she picked up a rose petal–imprinted box.

It was surprisingly heavy.

She curiously lifted the lid.

It was a box full of gloves—wool gloves, leather gloves, white silk gloves, long silk evening gloves. They were stained with red.

Someone had spilled ink on them.

Victoria frowned.

Two of the black leather gloves had mannequin hands stuffed inside them, as if they had been plucked out of a showcase.

Slowly it dawned on Victoria that the hands inside the black leather gloves were not carved out of wood: they were made out of flesh and bones.

The hands were human hands. And the red ink that stained the gloves was human blood.

Chapter

13

"Dear God," echoed in Victoria's ears.

It was a woman's voice, but it didn't sound like Victoria's voice. It came from far, far away.

Too far away to have come from Victoria.

One second the box laid on her lap, the next second it was gone.

Numbly holding the lid between her fingers, Victoria glanced up.

Gabriel's face was dizzily close.

He had fine pores, she thought. His skin was baby-smooth.

Silver eyes captured her gaze.

A silky masculine voice bolted through her memory . . . *If she's not yet dead, she soon will be.*

"It's the prostitute's"—Victoria could not bring herself to vocalize the body parts that had been amputated—"it's her."

"Possibly."

Gabriel straightened, face shooting back. He held the box between long white fingers.

Victoria dropped the lid. "It's not Madame—"

"No, it's not Madame René." There was no emotion inside Gabriel's eyes—no pleasure, no horror. "Her hands are smaller."

Victoria had never before fainted. She had never before *wanted* to faint.

She did now.

Victoria abruptly realized there had been one other person who would have known about her personal artifacts.

"Dolly knew that I wore silk drawers," she whispered.

And now Dolly was dead. As Gabriel had predicted.

Victoria convulsively swallowed.

The room tilted.

"Put your head between your legs," a sharp voice rang out.

Victoria looked at the other boxes—the three dress boxes were long enough to hold a torso. The three round hatboxes were deep enough to hold a head—

The eggs and ham and croissant she had eaten earlier rushed up into her throat.

She lurched up, feet tangling. The silk tucked between her breasts slipped free, slithered down her body.

Victoria ran for the bathroom.

Gabriel had spoken of death, but it had not been real; it was all too real now.

Victoria wondered if Madame René would be disappointed in her weak stomach. And then she didn't wonder anything.

She dropped down on her knees before the porcelain toilet. And remembered more words—hers, Gabriel's.

Do you plan on killing me, then, to spare me this . . . death?

You would thank me in the end.

Perhaps she would.

Gabriel opened up a hatbox. A crimson-stained hat cradled a woman's head.

Death had erased Dolly's pain and horror.

Gabriel opened the second hatbox. A smart Windsor hat with a short black veil resided within.

No death there.

Gabriel opened the third hatbox. The frivolous feathered confection inside held a man's head, gray hair smeared with dark crimson. Gerald Fitzjohn's face was lax.

He saw Victoria's pleasure. He saw Victoria's horror.

For a brief moment he had shared her pleasure. He did not share her horror: Gabriel had lived on the streets too long to be repulsed by faces of death.

Dolly and Fitzjohn had been slated to die; they had died.

The price of sin: blackmail. Death.

Have you sinned, mademoiselle?

Not yet.

Gabriel replaced the three lids. Straightening, he rounded his desk and pressed the buzzer underneath the black marble top. Striding across the carpet, he flung open the satinwood door.

A man with rich mahogany-colored hair jumped to attention. "Mr. Gabriel, sir!"

"Remove the boxes on the couch, Evan," Gabriel calmly ordered while rage rose within him.

He would have spared Victoria the reality of death. The second man obviously did not want her to be spared.

Green eyes stoically met silver ones.

"Yes, sir," Evan said.

Gabriel wondered if Evan sympathized with Victoria's plight. He wondered if he would try to set her free.

Gabriel stepped aside for Evan to enter.

Evan stooped to pick up a box.

"Evan."

Evan paused.

"There are human remains in some of the other boxes."

Perhaps there were remains in all of the other boxes, although Gabriel doubted it. The weight of the boxes combined would have raised questions when they were brought up.

Evan stiffened in horror, proof that not all men who had lived on the streets had lost the ability to be repulsed by death.

"Take the body parts and dump them into the Thames," Gabriel ordered flatly. "Burn the clothes and the boxes."

Many people disappeared into the Thames. Gabriel did not want slivers of human bone inside his furnace.

Evan did not question Gabriel. He picked up a weighted hatbox.

"Evan."

"Yes, sir?" Evan's voice was subdued.

He *had* been a sympathizer.

"Gaston did warn you to guard Mademoiselle Childers well, did he not?"

Evan did not turn around. "Yes, sir."

"Tell Julien and Allen what is in the hatbox you hold," Gabriel ordered blandly. "Tell Julien and Allen that it could just as easily have been Mademoiselle Childers's head if we had not protected her."

Gaston came just as Evan left with the first load of boxes.

"What is wrong, monsieur?" he asked, puzzled. "Did not mademoiselle care for the clothes?"

Gabriel held out the glove box.

Gaston's olive-brown face turned gray.

"When did the clothes arrive, Gaston?" Gabriel asked calmly.

"They arrived just before you did, monsieur."

"Who delivered them?"

"*Je ne sais pas.* A man. Just"—horror momentarily creased his face—"the boxes were from Madame René. I did not know, monsieur."

Gabriel believed him.

He could warn Gaston to check any more boxes that were delivered to the house. There was no need to.

The second man would not repeat a trick.

He wanted to tell Gaston what to look out for in the future. But Gabriel did not know what the second man would do next.

He did not know who he would kill next: a man or a woman.

A friend or a foe.

"Give this to Evan," Gabriel said instead. "And have Julien guard the door in Evan's place."

"*Très bein*, monsieur." Gaston turned around.

"And Gaston."

Gaston paused.

Gabriel glanced at the pale blue silk spread lying across the carpet where it had slid off of Victoria's body.

"Take the silk bedcover with you."

Gabriel silently padded across his office, his bedroom, halted in front of the massive armoire. Opening the door, he rifled through coats, trousers . . . He grabbed a royal blue silk robe. It clung to his fingers like a woman's hair.

Victoria sat on the cold tile in front of the toilet, spine erect, face drained of color. Her hair fell over her right shoulder.

She had dark brunette hair that shimmered with red and copper highlights.

Beautiful hair.

"Her name was Dolly," Victoria said dully.

Gabriel's hand fisted the silk robe.

There was nothing he could do to comfort her. But he wanted to.

The anger inside him kicked up another notch.

The second man had planned everything. And there was nothing he could do to halt the game.

But he wanted to.

"Three months ago a man tried to rape me," Victoria continued in the same shock-dulled voice. "It was raining. Dolly helped me. Everyone else just walked by, umbrellas lowered so they wouldn't see what was happening."

Gabriel tensed; a pulse suddenly pounded inside his left temple.

He knew who had accosted Victoria—he knew everything about him save his name and the extent he would go to fulfill a dead man's will.

"What did the man look like?" he asked, voice deceptively calm.

Victoria was not deceived. Realization flowed across her drawn features.

"The man you are looking for," she visibly swallowed, "he paid Dolly to save me that night."

And then he had killed Dolly. Just as he would kill Victoria.

She read the truth in Gabriel's eyes.

"I found the first letter underneath my door the next morning," Victoria said convulsively.

Gabriel waited for her to piece together the puzzle.

Comprehension sparked inside her shock-dulled eyes; the spark left, leaving behind the comprehension.

"I'm sorry," she said with the calm that only comes after witnessing violent death. There was no hunger inside her eyes, no desire for an angel's touch. "He grabbed me from behind. I never saw his face. But it doesn't matter, does it? He will kill me. That is why he gave Dolly the tablets for me to use, is it not? He will kill anyone who comes into contact with him. Won't he?"

Gabriel wouldn't lie. "Yes."

"You talked to Mr. Thornton today."

"Yes."

Gabriel's muscles coiled tighter, knowing the course of her thoughts, knowing there was only one conclusion she could draw.

"Mr. Thornton was alive."

Victoria voiced Gabriel's fears.

"But if he or his wife were associated with this man you are seeking, they would be dead, wouldn't they?"

But if they weren't associated with the second man, then Victoria was being pursued by two men, her eyes said.

The second man wanted to kill her. What did the other man want?

"Fear," Victoria whispered.

Gabriel strained to hear her, to comfort her. "What?"

"You said he sent me to you because of my eyes."

Hungry eyes.

Sharp pain twisted inside Gabriel's gut. "Yes."

"No." Victoria stared down into the porcelain bowl; Gabriel stared down at her bowed head. "He didn't choose me because of my eyes."

Gabriel fought to distance himself.

You don't know me, Victoria had accused him.

But he did know her. He knew her, and he wanted her.

"Then why do you think he chose you?" Gabriel asked, voice strained.

Victoria raised her head and met his gaze. "He chose me because I was afraid. And because you were afraid."

They were still afraid.

Awareness glimmered underneath the fear and the shock inside Victoria's eyes. "You said fear is a powerful aphrodisiac."

The wire inside Gabriel coiled tighter.

Sex. Murder.

Fear *was* an aphrodisiac. Through sex, men and women had the power to create new life. A final victory over death.

"I'm cold," Victoria said suddenly.

Her breasts quivered.

She was trembling.

Thornton had trembled in his fear; Gabriel had felt only contempt. Victoria trembled in her fear; Gabriel wanted to weep for the pain he had brought her.

He did not weep.

Angels didn't cry.

Her bottom lip quavered. "I don't think I will ever be warm again."

Gabriel had the power to warm her.

Knees trembling, he entered the bathroom.

Copper gleamed; the mirror sparkled.

The walls closed around him.

Victoria stared up at him. Not expecting warmth. Comfort.

Gabriel stepped behind her, unable to look into her eyes.

Victoria didn't blame him for the whore he had been. The danger he had placed her in. The carnal comfort he didn't give her.

Gabriel wished that she did blame him.

He hunkered down, knees spread wide on either side of her back; her hair glistened like a dark waterfall. Slowly, carefully, he draped the silk robe over her shoulders. Feeling her warmth and fragility; inhaling her femininity and her vulnerability.

Almost touching, not quite daring.

"I won't let him hurt you," he murmured.

They both knew he lied.

Gabriel couldn't stop the second man. All he could do was try to find the second man before he found a way to get Victoria.

Chapter

14

Yellow fog embraced London like the arms of a possessive lover. A hansom cab cautiously maneuvered through the coal smoke–induced haze that was the price of human life.

They would be dead, wouldn't they? the horse's hooves clacked. *They would be dead, wouldn't they?*

And they would be dead, *if* they were associated with the second man.

But the Thorntons weren't dead.

And Gabriel didn't know why.

Dull light shone through the sulfur-laden night like warning beacons.

Gabriel had not needed Victoria to describe the interior layout of the Thornton house; Peter Thornton had done so in great detail. What Gabriel had needed to know was if he could trust Victoria.

She could be trusted, unlike Gabriel.

He leaned against the metal park gate, watching the town house windows that were brighter than the fog. And thought of Victoria.

She had lived with the Thorntons as their servant. She had tended their children as their governess.

A downstairs window dimmed, was swallowed by the yellow mist. Another missing piece.

Fear.

He didn't choose me because of my eyes . . . He chose me because I was afraid. And because you were afraid. Fear is a powerful aphrodisiac.

An upstairs window suddenly lit up the fog, a revelation.

Victoria did not want to desire a man's touch. Yet she did.

Gabriel did not want to desire a woman's touch. Yet he did.

It was his desire that warranted Victoria's death, not hers.

The golden eye that was the porch light dimmed, died.

Gabriel motionlessly watched the upstairs window. Time crawled on its belly.

Was Victoria asleep? Gabriel wondered. Was she warm?

Did she still desire to be touched by an angel?

Why were the Thorntons still alive?

The upstairs window dimmed, disappeared into the fog and the night. The last member of the Thornton household had retired.

Gabriel waited until Big Ben pealed twelve times. Silently he crossed the street to the Thornton town house.

The front door opened soundlessly.

Thornton had upheld his part of the bargain.

In the end it had not been violence that had persuaded Peter Thornton to assist Gabriel; it had been the fear of scandal. He had threatened to send the information about the governesses to *The London Times.*

Gabriel allowed his eyes time to adjust to the darkness inside the town house. Furniture loomed like silent sentries: a table, a chair . . . There was a doorway on the right; on the left . . . there were the stairs . . .

A step sharply creaked.

Yellow-tinged darkness yawned before him.

Gabriel froze, breath arrested, left hand gripping the knob of his cane.

He did not want to kill, but he would.

He did not want to take Victoria, and he knew he would do that, too.

No one stirred.

More carefully, Gabriel stole up the remaining steps. He turned left into more darkness.

A wool runner muffled his footsteps.

He could feel Thornton in his bedchamber at the end of the hallway; the man tensely wondered when Gabriel would enter. He did not realize that Gabriel was only thirty feet away.

Gabriel could feel nothing from Mary Thornton—no fear, no challenge.

No awareness.

Silently he opened a wooden door blackened by night.

The room smelled of coal smoke and a woman's expensive perfume. Red embers glowed inside a white marble fireplace; white and blue flames danced over ash-whitened coals.

Thornton's wife slept undisturbed inside a canopied bed.

A brass lamp gleamed on the nightstand; beside it, liquid sparkled inside a crystal carafe. A small bottle, more shadow than substance, sat beside an empty water glass.

Gabriel silently cursed.

The woman's sleep was laudanum-induced. Had Thornton warned her? . . .

Gabriel remembered the man's eager betrayal and the ammonia smell of urine.

Peter Thornton cared more for his reputation than his family. He would not have warned his wife.

He gently closed the door behind him; a soft click sounded over the hungry snap of burning coals.

Mary Thornton slept in a silk and lace negligee. Shadow-darkened blond hair trailed across a stark white pillowcase.

The darkness did not hide the fact that Mary Thornton was an attractive woman. Gabriel was not attracted to her.

Slowly he pulled the bedcovers up to her shoulders and stealthily tucked the sides underneath the mattress. He followed the bed rail along the side, the foot. Soundlessly padding around the bed, he pulled the covers up to the height of the pillow and tucked them tightly underneath the mattress from head to foot.

Pulling off his wool knitted cap, he stuffed it into his coat pocket. Twisting the silver knob on his cane, he pulled out the short sword.

Razor sharp steel glinted in the firelight.

Kneeling by the bed beside the head of Thornton's wife, Gabriel gently laid the scabbard on the floor to free his right hand.

"Mary," he whispered seductively. "Mary, wake up."

Strawberry red highlights glinted off her blond hair. She did not respond.

It would take more than whispers to wake her.

Gabriel raised his right hand to his mouth; teeth sinking into his leather glove, he slid his hand free and pocketed the glove. Standing, he picked up the crystal carafe off the nightstand and poured water into the empty glass. Sitting down on the bed, thigh securing the covers holding down her shoulders, he dipped his fingers into the glass. Slowly he dribbled water onto her face.

"Mary," he crooned. "Wake up, Mary."

She turned her face away from him to escape the dripping water. "Hmm . . ."

Gabriel once again dipped his fingers into the glass.

"Mary, wake up." A silver drop of water splattered her cheek; she instinctively turned back toward him. Gently he positioned the edge of the blade against her throat while he continued to dribble water onto her face. "Wake up, Mary . . ."

Delicate eyelids fluttered open.

Mary stared blankly up at him.

Gabriel knew what she saw: she saw an angel with a halo of silver hair.

She saw an assassin.

He pressed the sword edge so that she could feel the prick of cold steel.

Her eyes widened. Realization glittered inside them.

Her body was trapped beneath the covers; she could not move. She opened her mouth to scream.

Gabriel grabbed the pillow beside her.

He could stifle her screams. Or he could suffocate her.

And there was nothing she could do.

Mary knew it. Gabriel knew it.

"I know what you've done, Mary," he murmured softly. "Do you think it's wise to scream?"

For long seconds she stared up at him, mouth open. Her jaw audibly clamped shut.

"Who are you?" she snapped.

There was no recognition in her eyes. No knowledge of the untouchable angel.

"I am a man who can slit your throat and leave you to die." He allowed the truth of his words to sink into her consciousness. "Or I can let you live."

Anger. Fear.

Gabriel waited to see which emotion was the stronger in Mary Thornton.

"How did you get inside?" she whispered angrily.

"Your husband let me in." There was no need to lie. "It was easier that way."

Mary Thornton did not seem surprised at her husband's betrayal. "What do you want?"

"I want," Gabriel murmured provocatively, "your blood"—he nicked her slender white throat; liquid black shadows beaded in the firelight—"but I will settle for information. Who do you pander for, Mary?"

Mary did not move. Her very stillness screamed her guilt.

"If you hurt me, my husband will go to the police."

"Then I will kill him, too," Gabriel said playfully. The fear and the anger crowding him grew.

Mary Thornton was alive.

But she shouldn't *be* alive.

"I do not pander for anyone," Mary denied.

Unlike Peter Thornton, she would not beg.

Unlike Victoria Childers, her bravado did not inspire Gabriel's admiration.

Mary Thornton was a society whore who preyed on the weaknesses of those less fortunate than herself.

She had preyed on Victoria Childers.

"Tell me who wrote the letters, Mary."

"I don't know." Mary Thornton convulsively wriggled to break free of the imprisoning covers; she couldn't. "Let me up this instant!"

"I know you're lying, Mary." Gabriel's eyes were cold and deadly; his voice was deceptively seductive. "Tell me who wrote the letters and I'll let you up. Was it a lover?"

Mary stilled. "I do not have a lover."

"My condolences," Gabriel said sympathetically.

Mary was not fooled either by his seductiveness or his sympathy. "Why are you here?"

"You have been careless, *madame*. You shouldn't have hired so many governesses through West Employment Agency."

The lingering horror of waking at knifepoint mutated to genuine fear.

"I don't know what you are talking about," Mary lied.

Women like Mary Thornton played with death, but there were worse things than death to women like Mary Thornton.

"Imagine if there were an investigation," Gabriel said lightly. "So many governesses for so few children. What would the investigation yield, I wonder? Pandering. Prostitution. Murder . . ."

"We did not murder . . ."

Mary realized her mistake the moment the words were out of her mouth.

Gabriel smiled. There was no pleasure in it.

Had Victoria known how much pleasure he had derived from her unabashed eagerness over the new clothing?

Had she known that he had ached for her innocence, that she could still be horrified by death?

"Who is *we*, Mary?" Gabriel asked caressingly. "A lover?"

"We have hurt no one," Mary Thornton said angrily.

"I'm sure others would feel differently. Take Victoria Childers, for example. She feels that she has been hurt . . ."

"We did not hurt her," the woman repeated stubbornly.

But she would have.

"Who do you pander for, Mary?" *The man who wrote the letters? The second man?* "I think seeing your name in *The Times* would hurt you more than if I slit your throat. Shall I go to the papers?"

Mary's ruination flashed through her eyes.

Society would shun her. Friends would snub her. Banks could foreclose on mortgages. Business acquaintances could call in IOUs.

"Will your lover help you, Mary?" Gabriel crooned.

In the end her husband would have no choice but to divorce her.

"Will your husband keep you?"

No and *no*, her eyes said.

She would lose her lover.

She would lose her reputation.

Mary Thornton would lose everything that made life worthwhile to a woman such as her.

"What is worth more, Mary? This"—he rubbed the silk pillow against her cheek—"or your lover?"

He was not surprised at the answer in her eyes.

Gabriel had fucked women like Mary. She was loyal to herself alone.

He had never fucked a woman like Victoria. She had protected a prostitute who would have killed her, a father who had emotionally abused her, and a brother who had abandoned her.

Defeat danced in Mary Thornton's eyes like flame skimming over burning coals.

"His name is Mitchell," she said bitterly. "Mitchell Delaney."

Gabriel had never heard of the man. But he knew the type.

Some men preyed on fear. Some men preyed on innocence.

Some men hunted to kill. Some men hunted to fuck.

Men like the second man preyed on both fear and innocence; hunted to kill and to fuck. Did Mitchell Delaney?

A picture of Victoria Childers flashed through his mind's eye.

She was alone. She was afraid.

Victoria was not an idle woman. She would seek distraction.

Mary Thornton's expensive perfume engulfed him.

Gabriel suddenly knew where Victoria would seek distraction. And he knew that she would find it.

She would find the transparent mirrors.

Sex. Murder.

Act two was about to be played out.

Fear accelerated Gabriel's heartbeat. It was not fear that hardened his body.

He stared down at Mary Thornton and the steel that caressed her throat.

She saw the rage. She saw the desire.

Her eyes widened until they were twin pools of white terror.

Victoria stared at the ceiling. Crimson blood superimposed the white enamel paint.

She closed her eyelids.

Crimson blood stained the darkness behind her lids. It was punctuated with dialogue.

You won't see the man who has a gun trained on you . . . Perhaps you'll see a flash of light when he releases the trigger, perhaps not. One thing is for certain—you won't hear the gunshot: you'll be dead.

Victoria's eyelids flew open.

She did not want to die.

The scent of Gabriel engulfed her. It came from his sheets, his robe.

I will not be a victim.

You already are.

An image of the silk napkin slashed with bold black ink flashed before her eyes.

. . . I bring you a woman.

A leading actress for a man who avoided men, women, love, pleasure.

I learned to read English. Someday I hope to be equally proficient in French.

Michael had taught Gabriel to read.

Les deux anges. The two angels.

I loved a man, mademoiselle. If I had not loved him, you would not be here.

Was Michael an actor in this unscripted play?

The sin is in loving, Gabriel had said.

He had been hurt through the love he bore his friend.

But loving was not a sin.

When I became a man, I wanted to experience a woman's passion. I wanted to feel the pleasure that I gave. Just once.

She had breathed in the heat of Gabriel's body. Had tasted his breath.

Victoria didn't know the touch of his skin.

She didn't want to die without knowing if Gabriel's touch was worth dying for.

Fear was a powerful aphrodisiac: the void it created demanded to be filled.

By knowledge.

By action.

By Gabriel.

Laissez le jeu commencer.

Flinging back the covers, Victora slid out of bed.

A metal tin gleamed on the nightstand. It was filled with condoms. Flat rubber sheaths that were rolled onto a man's erect penis.

The seduction of an angel . . .

Dolly had told her that a man would not seek to protect himself with a virgin, and then she had given Victoria the corrosive sublimate tablets.

Now Dolly was dead and Victoria was alive.

Gabriel's silk robe clung to her breasts and her buttocks. It was floor-length. It would reach Gabriel's calves.

Were they covered with the same dark hair that matted his chest, she wondered, or were they covered with the silver-blond hair that capped his head?

Cap . . . *Hats.*

Victoria hurriedly stepped into the . . . study, he had called it. A library by any other name.

Ridiculous disappointment sliced through her. She had known he was not in his suite merely from the throbbing emptiness inside her.

Victoria perused the gold-embossed books—and did not see one single title or author.

She saw blood. She saw Mary Thornton.

She saw Gabriel.

Victoria wondered what he was doing—waiting in the night, breaking into the Thornton's town house, or returning to his own house.

Victoria wondered if he would learn that the Thorntons were associated with the man he sought, or if he would learn that they worked independently to destroy women's lives.

Gabriel had said that he did not fear a bullet. He had also said he did not know what to expect.

Victoria wondered if Gabriel was still alive.

Victoria wondered how long she would live.

Gabriel had burned down the former House of Gabriel. Why? So many whys . . .

Vigorously she prowled Gabriel's study, steering clear of the pale blue leather couch.

The lone boatman riding the shimmering sunset and the glittering blue water silently watched her from the safety of the painting.

A cabinet proved not to be a cabinet, but a door similar to the one leading to the bedroom. Victoria pushed it open.

The plush maroon carpet inside Gabriel's office gave way to flat, dark wool carpet. Dim electric light illuminated a hallway.

Freedom.

Victoria stepped inside the narrow corridor.

The door swished closed behind her.

Gasping, she whirled around, images of the glove box filling her head.

The door had not locked behind her.

Victoria's heartbeat did not slow down.

There was danger in the corridor.

There was danger in Gabriel's suite.

Victoria faced the corridor and the danger.

The hallway was short, only forty or so feet long. Reflected light shone at the end. It was brighter than the dim light that lit the corridor.

She realized another corridor intersected the short, narrow hallway. A corridor with windows of light.

Heartbeat outracing her feet, Victoria cautiously walked toward the lit corridor.

She reached the end of the hallway.

A long corridor ran diagonal to the short hallway. Light splashed the outer wall at regular intervals.

The light was not caused by windows.

Windows adjoined outer walls; the lit portals came from an inside wall.

There was no reason for the wave of fear that crashed over Victoria or the undercurrent of longing that tugged her forward.

Pulses pounding inside her ears, she stepped up to the first portal.

Brilliant light illuminated a plush red bedchamber. The bedchamber was not empty.

She stepped up to the second window; the bedchamber on the other side was a lush green instead of red. It was not empty, either.

The third bedchamber was decorated in gold; the fourth in blue . . .

Victoria saw men; Victoria saw women.

Victoria saw the world that Michael and Gabriel had ruled. A world where no touch was forbidden and pleasure was the price of desire.

Victoria saw naked need in all of its guises . . .

Chapter

15

Victoria knew the moment Gabriel stepped inside the corridor. She felt him through the silk of his robe and through the thin covering of her own skin: a burning awareness of what the French madame had made him, and of what the man he sought had taken away from him.

They were two reflections in the glass, a dark-haired woman who had been taught that touch was morally reprehensible and a silver-haired man who had indulged in the pleasures of the flesh without ever once experiencing its beauty.

The man and the woman on the other side of the glass experienced both the pleasure and the beauty.

They touched, feminine hands skimming hard masculine flesh; masculine hands skimming soft feminine flesh. They kissed, lips brushing, clinging, devouring. They embraced, breasts to chest, stomach to stomach, thighs to thighs.

He was young, handsome; she was neither young nor handsome.

They were oblivious to the difference in their ages and their outward attractiveness. Passion made them partners; need made them equals.

"Can they see us?" Victoria asked softly.

"No." Gabriel's voice was curiously taut. "They see a mirror."

While Victoria and Gabriel saw a window. And inside that window, the man and the woman that neither Gabriel nor Victoria dared to be.

"How is it that we see them but they see a mirror?"

"The mirror is only half silvered." Gabriel's gaze did not waver from the man and the woman. "Strong light reflects off the silver, like in a regular mirror, so that a person will see their image instead of glass, but if strong light were shone behind the glass as well as in front of it, it would become transparent."

Victoria had never before heard of transparent mirrors.

"Can they hear us?" she asked softly.

"Not if we speak quietly."

The man and the woman parted. She spoke; he responded.

Victoria could see their lips move, but she could not hear what either said. She could only watch them. And imagine the words they murmured.

Words praising a woman's passion.

Words venerating a man's need.

Words Victoria had never heard or spoken but would like to hear and speak before she died.

The man strode toward a mahogany nightstand—erect manhood fencing the air, twin leathery pouches bouncing below—and picked up a squat white jar.

Victoria had seen men flash their appendages on the street; she had never before seen a man fully naked. Buttocks sculpted, muscles delineated. Body studded with hair.

The sight was breathtaking.

"Do they know that the mirror isn't a . . . mirror?" Victoria asked.

She sounded breathless.

She *was* breathless.

The letters had spoken of many of the things she had witnessed this night; seeing was far more compelling than reading.

"The man knows," Gabriel said.

The man was a prostitute, he did not need to say.

"But the woman doesn't?"

"He might have told her." Superimposed over the man and the

woman on the other side of the mirror was Gabriel's silver eyes.

"She came to the old house once a month."

The house that he had burned.

But she didn't want to think of fire. Destruction.

Death.

"With the same man?" Victoria queried, mouth dry, skin flushed.

"Yes."

"You've seen them together before."

"I've seen them occasionally."

She watched his reflection. "You watch people when they engage in sexual congress."

"The House of Gabriel is a business, mademoiselle. In this business men and women sometimes die. It is up to me to ensure that no one dies in my house."

Gabriel was not a vain man. Yet he had named his house after himself . . .

"Why did you name it the House of Gabriel?"

"So that the second man would know where to find me."

Victoria swallowed. "Is there a first man?"

"He's dead."

By Gabriel's hand.

Victoria tried to fit this latest piece of the puzzle into the frame of her life.

"You said that you blackmail people."

Now Victoria knew how he got the information with which to blackmail them.

"I merely make recommendations to certain people, mademoiselle," Gabriel returned neutrally.

And he employs our kind, Madame René had said.

Did Gabriel blackmail his patrons to find work for failing prostitutes?

Motion snagged Victoria's attention.

The woman sat down on the bed, back facing the mirror; gray-streaked brown hair brushed the silk sheet.

Her eagerness for the younger man's touch was palpable.

Victoria could identify with her need.

For a second she felt the give of the mattress, heard the squeak of springs. Felt the cool caress of silk.

Impossible.

"Do you get . . . aroused when you watch them?" Victoria asked hurriedly.

The silk robe caressed her nipples with each inhalation, each exhalation; it felt like sandpaper. Her skin felt like overripe fruit about to burst.

"It's business," Gabriel said flatly.

The business of pleasure.

Victoria had entered the business when she auctioned off her virginity.

Would she have had the courage to do so then, knowing what she now knew? she wondered. Would she have sold herself knowing that sexual congress touched the soul as well as the body?

The man unscrewed the squat white jar, sat both the lid and the jar down on the mahogany nightstand.

Victoria fought to control her breathing. "What is in the jar?"

"Lubricating cream."

Lubricating cream pierced her vagina.

She was wet, Victoria realized.

And Gabriel knew it.

Was he erect?

"Are all the bedchambers equipped with jars of . . . of lubricating cream?"

"Yes."

"The man has . . . touched her," Victoria said unevenly. "Surely the woman doesn't need artificial lubrication in order to . . . to accept him."

The silver eyes inside the mirror snared Victoria's attention. "That depends, mademoiselle, upon where he penetrates her. And with what."

Where.

With what.

She did not have to ask about where. But—

"What do you mean, *what* he penetrates her with?" she asked carefully.

Watching the man. Watching the woman.

"Each room is supplied with an assortment of"—he hesitated—"*godemichés.*"

Victoria was captivated by both Gabriel's hesitation and the unfamiliar French term.

"What is a . . . *godemiché?*"

The masculine eyes reflected inside the mirror glinted pure silver. "It is a leather device that is shaped like a penis."

Victoria's vagina involuntarily clenched. She had earlier witnessed a man inserting a penis-shaped device into a woman's body. They had both seemed to derive enjoyment from the act.

"The assortment you supply . . . they come in various sizes?" Victoria asked.

Gabriel's image was transposed over that of the younger man and older woman. His shirt was not buttoned. Shadowy hair showed through the vent. "Yes."

Less than nine inches? More than nine inches?

"With what other devices may a man penetrate a woman?"

"Watch and see, mademoiselle."

The older woman laid back on the silk sheets in a tangle of gray-streaked brown hair. The younger man kneeled between her legs.

Victoria stared.

He was . . . kissing her. There. Between the thighs. On a woman's most sensitive flesh.

Victoria's nether lips throbbed.

"Surely he does not require lubrication in order to kiss her," she said on a sharp intake of breath.

She had witnessed this act over and over during the night; it was far different witnessing a man kiss a woman's privates with Gabriel standing behind her.

"He is preparing her," Gabriel said impassively.

He was not immune to what he witnessed. The intensity of his gaze scorched her skin.

"What is he preparing her for?" Victoria insisted.

The woman's legs came up; her heels notched the edge of the bed. She reached for the man's head, to hold him in place.

Victoria clenched her fingers.

The younger man eluded the older woman. Reaching for the squat white jar on the nightstand, he scooped the fingers of his right hand into it.

Gabriel was left-handed.

The thought came from nowhere.

The man brought his lubricated hand between the woman's splayed legs.

Victoria squeezed her thighs together.

The woman threw her head back, face contorted with ecstasy. Or perhaps it was contorted with agony.

"What is he doing?" Victoria breathed.

"He's stretching her."

Victoria felt the woman's penetration all the way up to her throat. Her breath caught in her throat. "With his whole hand?"

"He will start out with one or two fingers."

Victoria remembered Gabriel's fingers.

They were long. White.

The young man leaned over and kissed the older woman between her thighs. He did not remove his hand.

Victoria did not have to see what he did in order to feel it.

She trembled . . . with desire. Earlier she had trembled with fear.

"What does a woman feel like, when a man has his fingers inside her?"

Even Victoria's voice shook.

"Like hot, wet silk."

The anger in Gabriel's voice took her by surprise.

His eyes in the mirror were not looking at Victoria's reflection; they stared through the window. Gazing into his past and seeing the women he had been with.

The women who had begged him for their pleasure and who had then begged him for release.

But he had not begged them.

Gabriel had only begged for release once in his life. A rape of the senses.

Victoria saw the pleasure Gabriel had given women in the twist of his mouth. In the silver eyes she saw Gabriel's pain.

The older woman on the other side of the glass tossed her head back and forth, silk sliding, hair tangling. Her breasts quivered, as if she ran a race.

A race to completion.

Gabriel ran with her.

The woman's mouth opened—to take in air or to cry out, Victoria did not know which.

Gabriel was lost—in the memories of pleasure or in the memories of pain, she did not know which.

"What do you feel?" she asked Gabriel. Aching with pleasure. Aching with pain. "How many fingers do you have inside her? One or two?"

"Five," Gabriel said raggedly.

Victoria couldn't breathe.

Five fingers jabbed deep inside her.

"I want to feel her pleasure," he rasped. "I want to be a part of her pleasure—just once, and not apart from it. I want to be a part of a woman that I am pleasuring."

And not apart from her.

It should not be possible to splinter with pain at the same time that one swelled with desire: it was.

"This woman. Does she"—Victoria marshaled her voice—"does she enjoy having five of your fingers inside her?"

A drop of moisture beaded on Gabriel's forehead; it sparkled like a diamond in the dim light. "A woman's vagina is created to stretch."

But surely not to accommodate an entire hand.

So why did Victoria's body yawn to accept it?

"How did you . . . penetrate her with five fingers?"

"One finger at a time." The drop of sweat disappeared inside Gabriel's eyebrow. "I spent three hours preparing her body."

Victoria imagined receiving one finger, two, three, four, five. A finger at a time. Hour after hour. Panting breath ticking off the min-utes . . . body opening . . . lubricated hand slipping . . . entering through the ring of her portal.

Pleasure building.

Ecstasy. Agony.

"Tell me," Victoria said, breathing in time to the rise and fall of the older woman's breasts. "Tell me what you feel."

Silver lights glittered inside Gabriel's reflected gaze.

"I feel a woman's clitoris against my tongue."

Victoria's clitoris swelled to the point of pain.

"It's so hard it feels like it will split open with her need to or-gasm." Gabriel's voice scraped Victoria's skin. "My fingers are fluted, my thumb tucked into them. The woman's vagina is so hot it burns. I can feel her flesh stretch—taking my fingertips . . . my fin-gers . . . first knuckle deep . . . second knuckle deep . . . the width of my palm. The walls of her vagina are forcing my fingers to curl into a fist. All I can see and smell and hear and feel is her. The smell of a woman's need. The suction of a woman's flesh. The sight of a woman's stomach tightening."

Victoria felt Gabriel's fingertips slide into her . . . first knuckle deep . . . second knuckle deep . . . the width of his palm. Her stom-ach tightened, filled with an angel . . .

The body of the woman on the other side of the mirror bowed until only her head and her heels supported her weight. Her mouth opened wide in a guttural cry.

"I feel her orgasm bursting over me," Gabriel said, breath harsh in the narrow corridor. "It clenches around my wrist and squeezes my fist until there is only her pleasure."

Slowly the older woman's body sank down to the bed, body lax.

The younger man raised his head: his features were strained with his need.

Victoria had seen many different types of need this night. She had seen the need for intimacy, the need for sexual gratification, and occasionally, in the eyes of both patron and prostitute, the simple need for human contact.

The younger man's need was reflected in Gabriel's face. "But it was her pleasure that milked my hand—"

Suddenly the silver eyes reflected in the glass pinned Victoria. She returned his stare unflinchingly.

"—not mine."

Vaguely she noted that the man behind the glass wiped his hand on the sheet beside the woman and reached for a small flat tin beside the squat jar of cream. It was identical to the tin of condoms that had come with her dinner tray.

The younger man jerkily stood up and then he was standing between the older woman's legs and she was raising her arms and her body to take him while the man behind Victoria stood apart from their passion. Apart from Victoria's passion.

Apart from his own passion.

"This is what he wants," Victoria suddenly realized.

Gabriel's nostrils flared. "What?"

"He wants you to hurt."

But Victoria didn't want Gabriel to hurt.

She took both of their lives in her hand. She turned and faced their desire.

"You want to touch me," she said. Praying that it was true.

The truth shone in his eyes. "Yes."

Victoria's chest constricted at the need in his eyes. "But you're afraid."

"Yes."

Of touching. Of being touched.

Victoria gambled. "I want you to touch me."

Gray. Silver.

Fear. Passion.

"I know you do," Gabriel said.

He did not touch her.

"I want you to feel my pleasure," Victoria said baldly. "I want to lie down on your bed, naked. Like the woman behind the mirror. Like the woman you remembered. I want you to prepare my body. I want you to give me the pleasure you gave her. And I want to share it with you."

Gabriel sucked in his breath. "You're a virgin."

If Victoria looked away from the naked need inside those silver eyes, she would run.

Victoria didn't look away. "You bought my virginity."

The air pulsed around them.

"I don't know what I would do, Victoria, if you touched me." Gabriel's voice was taut.

Pain. Pleasure.

They clawed at her chest.

"Then I won't touch you," Victoria assured him.

"But you would let me . . . touch you. In whatever way I wished."

Empétarder . . . *Would you grant me access there, mademoiselle?*

Victoria struggled to breathe. "Yes."

"You would let me do anything . . ."

You would let me hold you when both of our bodies are dripping with sweat and the scent of our sex fills our lungs.

"Yes."

"And you won't touch me." Gabriel's gaze was stark with need. "Regardless of the pain or the pleasure that I bring you."

Victoria was suffocating—from Gabriel's robe, Gabriel's scent. Gabriel's words . . . *pain . . . pleasure . . .*

"I won't touch you," she promised.

He reached out . . . and touched her, a butterfly touch, a rasp of callused fingertips across chapped lips.

Erotic sensation bolted through Victoria.

"I'm sorry." She flinched. "My lips are not . . . soft."

Whereas his lips looked softer than a rose petal.

Gabriel would not let her turn away from him: his gaze held her; his finger electrified her.

He lightly strummed her bottom lip. "Open your mouth."

Victoria's bottom lip quivered.

Silver fire blazed in his eyes; a dark flush edged his cheeks. He rested his finger against the seam of her lips.

Gabriel trembled.

With fear. With need.

Of her. For her.

Victoria opened her mouth.

"Suck my finger," he said hoarsely.

Blue eyes locked with silver, Victoria took Gabriel's forefinger into her mouth, a preliminary penetration.

An invisible finger stabbed up her vagina.

She tasted him, a quick swipe of her tongue.

Gabriel's head slammed back, as if in pain. *"Dieu."*

Victoria stared at the corded muscles of his throat. A pulse pounded and throbbed, there above the vent of his white shirt and the whirls of wiry hair.

His fingertip was callused; it tasted salty.

She suckled him, as if he were a sweet. And felt the laving of her tongue between her thighs, lips wet, finger hard . . .

Gabriel slowly lowered his head.

There was no question of what had dragged out the agonized *Dieu:* it was pleasure. A pleasure so intense it was pain.

Victoria felt his pleasure, her pleasure; his pain, her pain . . .

One second she was suckling his fingertip, the next second her mouth was empty and his saliva-slickened finger smoothed the inner edges of her chapped lips.

He kissed her. Silver eyes staring into hers; finger pressing open the corner of her mouth.

Warm breath filled her lungs, searing heat glided the path his finger had traced.

Gabriel soothed Victoria's chapped lips with his tongue.

Hot. Wet. His tongue. His lips. A taste; a tease. A commingling of breath and saliva.

Of Gabriel and Victoria.

It was Victoria's first kiss. She wanted more: more breath, more tongue.

More Gabriel.

Victoria curved her fingers to cradle his head and take more.

Gabriel watched the need build inside her eyes . . . and she knew this was what he waited for: he waited for her to touch him.

But she couldn't touch him.

Victoria closed her eyes and clenched her fists.

His tongue instantly filled her: deeper than his finger. Hotter. Wetter.

The second penetration.

Vaguely she was aware of his saliva-slickened finger that trailed up her cheek, joined by more fingers. He lightly cupped her face while his tongue stroked and stroked . . . the top of her tongue . . . underneath her tongue . . . the roof of her mouth.

Oh . . . dear . . . *God.*

Victoria sucked in cool air.

Her eyelids snapped open.

Gabriel's tongue and fingers and breath were no longer a part of her. He stood back, watching her, waiting for her to reach for him.

Victoria did not reach for him.

But she wanted to. *Please* don't let him turn away from her . . .

She needed him.

She needed to be loved.

For the first time in her life she would not deny her need.

Gabriel's gaze glanced past her shoulder—fleetingly calling to Victoria's mind the man and woman behind the mirror—and returned to her face. "I've trusted one person in my life."

Michael.

And Gabriel had been hurt.

"I won't touch you, Gabriel," Victoria said unevenly.

"God help you if you do, Victoria." Finality weighted Gabriel's voice. *"Puisque je ne puis pas."*

Because I cannot.

Chapter

16

Gabriel stepped aside for Victoria to precede him down the corridor. She looked neither left nor right, every sense focused on the man behind her.

The electric chandelier inside the study was blinding; she stumbled.

Gabriel did not catch her.

They must trust one another, he had said.

She must trust that he would give her pleasure.

He must trust that she would not touch him.

The light in Gabriel's bedroom was only marginally dimmer than the one in his study.

Victoria paused by the bed, fingers worrying the blue silk sash cinched around her waist. "I . . . am thinner than I used to be."

The women behind the transparent mirrors had come in varied sizes; none had possessed ribs that ridged their sides.

Gabriel's face hardened. "I won't turn out the light, Victoria."

Her heart skipped a beat. "I don't want you to be . . . put off by my appearance."

Shadow darkened his face. "I have seen you, mademoiselle, and I assure you, I was not put off by your appearance."

How ridiculous she was being. Victoria had undressed for him the very first time they met. She had stood naked in front of him while Madame René had measured her and Victoria asked how to seduce a man.

How to love a man.

She squared her shoulders. Gabriel's gaze dropped to her breasts. Victoria did not have to glance down to know that her nipples stabbed the thin silk.

She notched her chin higher. "I would enjoy seeing you."

"I'm not an angel, Victoria."

A smile was surprised out of her. "I assure *you*, sir, I have no expectations of finding wings underneath your garments."

Gabriel did not return her smile. "But you expect a miracle."

Gabriel was God's messenger, Victoria had said.

Michael was his chosen, Gabriel had returned.

For better or for worse, the lives of two boys had been forever altered by a French madame. The cost of survival.

Victoria had once believed in fairy tales, but . . .

"I have never believed in miracles, Gabriel."

"I will try not to hurt you."

Trust.

But Gabriel still did not trust her.

He didn't trust her to touch him.

He didn't trust her to see him naked.

But she trusted him.

"I know you will," Victoria said shakily. She dropped the robe.

Gabriel weighed her breasts with his eyes. And then Gabriel weighed them with his hands.

Victoria stiffened her knees to prevent them from buckling at the lightning sensation that shot through her.

"You have beautiful breasts, Victoria," he said hoarsely, calluses rough, the heat of his skin scorching hot.

She forced air into her lungs to speak. "Thank you."

He traced her right rib cage, a raspy trail of pleasure, smoothed her waist. "Women wear corsets to have waists like yours—"

"Thank you—"

His gaze snared hers. "I know what it's like to go hungry. You have no need to apologize for your appearance. Not to me. *Jamais.*"

Never.

The heat of his hand and his gaze scorched her skin.

"I don't have any cream," she said breathlessly.

"You won't need it."

She sucked in air. "But you said—"

"Sit down, Victoria."

Victoria sat on the edge of the bed.

Her gaze unerringly rested on gray wool trousers. They were tented.

"You are erect," Victoria's voice was hushed.

"I have been erect ever since you walked into my study."

Harsh truth rang inside Gabriel's voice.

It seemed a lifetime ago when she had walked into his study. But it had only been a day and a night . . .

She had witnessed death. And in the last few hours, she had witnessed the need that drove every man and woman.

Victoria had seen other men naked. She dug her nails into the palms of her hands to stop them from reaching out and unbuttoning Gabriel's trousers.

She gazed up. "I want you to feel pleasure, too, Gabriel."

"Then lie down, Victoria, and let me touch you."

Fully clothed. While she bared her all.

Victoria lay back.

Immediately, hard hands dug underneath her buttocks. She was bodily dragged across the bed.

Victoria clutched the bedcovers.

Her buttocks were poised on the edge of the bed. Her legs fell apart.

Hard hands were instantly there, gently pushing them farther apart.

The cold, invasive air was promptly replaced by the heat of silver eyes.

Gabriel audibly sucked in air.

He touched her.

Victoria audibly sucked in air.

"You're wet, Victoria."

Yes.

His finger throbbed, there where no one had ever touched her. She had not touched herself there until six months earlier.

Victoria stared up at the white enameled ceiling and clung to two fistfuls of velvet.

If he touched her clitoris . . .

Hard, callused heat glided up the slippery lips of her sex and pressed her clitoris.

Victoria gasped. And climaxed. While electric light pounded her face and the pressure of his finger pierced her soul.

"You orgasmed."

Gabriel's voice grated in her ears.

She gulped air. Electric tingles continued to surge from his finger into her clitoris. "Yes."

"What did you see?"

Victoria squirmed to escape his finger. He did not let her escape. He continued to press her, lightly, pulse throbbing and pounding.

"Light," she said.

Just when she thought she was going to explode again, that enervating fingertip glided back down the slippery lips of her sex.

He gently probed.

Her muscles contracted.

Victoria bit her lip. "What do you see when you orgasm?"

"Darkness," Gabriel gritted.

Darkness. Death.

"What do you see now?" she hurriedly asked.

"I see you, Victoria, your lips red and swollen and glistening. I see my finger, swirling in your desire. Your *portail* is a darker red. I see my finger sinking into your *portail* . . ."

Oh . . .

It burned.

Victoria jackknifed upward, legs snapping together.

His hand was buried between her thighs.

Victoria jerked her gaze away from the white cuff and shirtsleeve that stuck up above a thatch of dark pubic hair.

Silver eyes were waiting for hers.

And you won't touch me . . . regardless of the pain or pleasure that I bring you, rang inside her ears.

I won't touch you, she had promised.

Victoria fought the bed to find a grip, arms stiffly holding up her weight.

His hand was buried between her thighs. It felt as if it penetrated her with a burning poker.

Slowly, slowly Victoria unclenched her muscles and accepted his finger.

Relief flickered inside Gabriel's eyes. Or perhaps it was the overhead light that flickered. Victoria was not familiar enough with either Gabriel or electric light to judge.

"Open your legs for me," Gabriel murmured, "and I'll tell you what I see."

He had said he had penetrated a woman with his entire hand. Victoria did not know if she could take another finger.

She licked her lips. "What is . . . *portail?*"

Gabriel's finger continued to burn and throb. "Portail. It is a French term for a woman's vagina."

Victoria's body had a will of its own. It bore down, taking more of his finger.

Gabriel's face hardened.

In desire? Disgust?

"Do you always refer to a woman's anatomy in French?"

"No."

"What word do you use?"

"Cunt."

An English street term.

"But you don't use that term now."

"*Non.*" There was nothing soft about the French negative.

Her vagina clenched and unclenched about his finger, as if milking it.

She struggled to understand. "Why?"

For a second Victoria did not think Gabriel was going to answer her. "I spoke French before I spoke English."

Before he became a whore.

Before the man had taken away the control he had valued so much.

Before Gabriel's need had been turned against him.

Victoria opened her legs.

Dark eyelashes shielded his eyes.

Victoria followed his gaze. All she could see was her dark pubic hair and the white cuff marking the hand that was between her thighs.

"I see . . . my finger appearing . . . It's wet and slippery . . ."

Victoria felt Gabriel's finger easing out of her . . . slowly. . . . In her mind's eye, she visualized it . . . long, pale, slippery wet . . .

Contrarily, her body clenched to keep it inside her.

"*Calme-toi,*" he murmured huskily.

Relax.

"I remember the first time I saw a woman like this."

Gabriel's gaze was intent on Victoria.

"How old were you?"

"I was thirteen."

The same age he had been when the madame had sold his services.

Gabriel's finger reversed its journey, slowly . . . slowly . . . sinking inside her until it filled her.

"What did you think, when you saw her . . . like this?" Victoria managed.

"I thought that if a man had a soul, it existed inside a woman."

Victoria's chest constricted; then her vagina constricted.

One finger became two.

Stretching her. Opening her.

She sharply inhaled. "Gabriel . . ."

His dark lashes slowly lifted. "I like the way you say my name."

Slowly his two fingers slid out of her while he watched her face for signs of pain . . . pleasure.

"How is that?" she asked, voice catching.

"As if you believe I have a soul."

He curved his fingers, as if they were a hook, and gently raked the inner wall of her vagina. "Come for me, Victoria. You said you'd share your pleasure with me. Share it."

He held her gaze, hooked fingers sliding, twisting, searching . . . Electricity shot through her body.

It felt as if she had a second clitoris inside her vagina, or as if her clitoris were accessible from within.

Gabriel stroked. Fingers hooked. Holding her gaze.

Fire raced through Victoria's veins, shimmied down her spine.

There was no fire inside his eyes, just calculated intent.

She wanted more than his expertise.

"I can't," she choked.

A smile flitted across his face. "You can. You will . . . You are."

Victoria's body bore down. She exploded. Voice crying out.

When her gaze focused, Gabriel waited for her. "What did you see?"

"Light," she panted.

Shaking. Inside. Outside.

Two fingers became three.

Her body was wide open; she could not squeeze him out. Victoria's orgasm fluttered around him—*three fingers.*

"I feel it," she gasped. "I feel myself . . . fluttering around your fingers . . ."

"Yes." A curious expression crossed his face. "I feel it."

Victoria couldn't draw in enough oxygen. "I said I wouldn't touch you."

His gaze sharpened. "Yes."

"But I didn't say I wouldn't tell you what I want."

"What do you want, Victoria?" Gabriel asked, sudden remoteness coming into his eyes.

How many had told him what they wanted . . . and never asked him what he wanted?

"I want you to taste me. I want you to remember my taste."

Not a rape of the senses . . .

"And then I want you to do what you want. Anything. Everything."

His dark lashes blocked her gaze.

She could feel moisture oozing out from her vagina. Did he see it?

Perhaps he did not like the taste of sex . . .

Gabriel sank down between her thighs. Three fingers sliding . . . out . . . in . . . out . . . in. Deep. Hard.

Riding out one orgasm. Creating the need for another.

Silvery-blond hair merged with dark pubic hair.

When Gabriel's breath whispered across her vulva, Victoria thought she would die. When Gabriel's lips closed around her, she knew she would die.

When Gabriel's tongue touched the hard tip of her clitoris, Victoria did die.

There is always pain in pleasure, Gabriel had said.

Darkness glittered inside the light, but still, only, light.

Victoria opened her eyes. And stared up at white enamel.

She did not remember closing her eyes; she did not remember lying down.

All she could feel was the emptiness inside her body and the tiny aftershocks that continued to dance on her clitoris.

The dull clang of metal impacting wood penetrated her consciousness.

"What did you see, Victoria?"

Victoria had seen . . . "Light."

She sluggishly turned her head toward Gabriel and the dull clang.

Gabriel reached into an open tin. His mouth was wet and shiny. From her.

"What I wanted, Victoria," he grated tautly.

It took Victoria several seconds to remember what was inside the tin . . . It took her several more seconds to realize what Gabriel was doing.

A silver drop of moisture glimmered on the tip of the large, plum-shaped crown . . . *bite*, Madame René had called it. Pinstriped wool framed a bush of dark blond pubic hair. Smearing the silver drop of moisture over the purple-hued head, he expertly smoothed up a rubber sheath, one inch, three inches, five inches, seven inches, nine inches . . .

Her stomach convulsively tightened.

Victoria's gaze jerked up to Gabriel's face.

She did not recognize it. His lips were drawn, skin darkly flushed, eyes silver shards of light.

"You said anything and everything I wanted."

Yes.

"This is what I want," he rasped. "I want to bury myself inside you, and then I want you to come until you make me come."

Gabriel looked as though he expected her to object.

Victoria fought for air. For one paralyzing second she did want to object.

"That sounds"—terrifying, exhilerating—"heavenly."

His sheathed manhood jutted out from the pinstriped wool trousers. "There is no heaven, Victoria, but I can show you hell."

Victoria did not doubt it.

Gabriel knelt on the floor. He bowed his head, silver hair sweeping his forehead.

Wool scratched her inner thighs. Rubber prodded ungiving flesh.

Victoria edged back on the bed.

The rubber was far, far thicker than had been his fingers.

A finger lightly pressed her clitoris.

Victoria's breath caught in her throat. She was riveted by silver eyes.

"Take me, Victoria," he said rawly. "I took your hymen with my fingers. Now take me . . ."

"You're larger than your fingers . . ."

But smaller than his hand . . .

Gabriel circled her clitoris, lightly, beguilingly. *Her choice* . . .

Victoria's muscles unclenched.

A fist . . .

It felt like a fist prodded her, impossibly large . . . and then it was impossibly lodged inside her.

He circled her clitoris, light, hard, slow, sure . . . Pain. *Pleasure* . . . Victoria's body opened, impossibly, for more. More pain. More pleasure . . .

The pain stilled; the pleasure did not.

A heartbeat throbbed inside her.

Harsh breath filled the room. "Come for me, Victoria, and I'll give you another inch."

The fist lodged inside her portal remained steadfast; the finger circling her did not. It slipped down . . . tested the tightness of the thin ring of flesh circling him, glided back up, slippery wet . . . circling round, and round, and round, lacking depth; she needed him deeper . . .

Victoria cried out. And convulsed. "God!"

The large fist-shaped crown that stretched her beyond bearing sank inside . . . two inches deep.

"What did you see?" he grated.

Light. Darkness.

Silver. Gray.

"Light . . ."

Circling. Circling.

"Gabriel . . ."

Victoria's body yawned independently. Jagged sensation ripped through her.

He sank inside her another inch . . . three inches deep.

Victoria panted for air.

One inch per orgasm . . . Six more to go . . .

"What did you see, Victoria?"

She throbbed. He throbbed.

The bedcovers clenched inside her fists throbbed.

"What did you see, Victoria?" he repeated tensely.

"Light," she said stubbornly. There was no darkness in pleasure . . . *No sin in loving* . . . "Oh, God"—the sound ripped out of her throat— "Gabriel . . . I can't . . . Gabriel . . ."

"What, Victoria?" Sweat dripped like tears down Gabriel's face. "What can't you do?"

Or not do . . .

He wanted her to stop him.

Victoria did not stop him.

"I need . . ." she gasped, the light of pending orgasm circling before her eyes, his finger circling her clitoris.

"What do you need?" Gabriel crooned. Holding himself back from the pleasure.

Anger tore through Victoria.

He must feel it. How could he not feel her flesh caressing him, milking him?

Gulping him?

"I need to have another orgasm."

Gabriel gave her another orgasm. And then he gave her another inch.

She couldn't breathe past the fist that lodged inside her vagina.

"What do you see, Victoria?"

"Light."

Another orgasm. Another inch.

Five inches . . .

"What do you see?" he repeated. Wanting her to see the darkness that he saw.

"Light," she gasped. Silver strands of hair haloed his head. "I see light."

Victoria could no longer differentiate between pain and pleasure. She pushed up for another orgasm, another inch of Gabriel.

Six inches . . . seven inches . . . eight inches. . . .

"What do you see, Victoria?" Agony laced Gabriel's voice.

His white linen shirt clung to his chest. The sweat-soaked linen revealed his every inhalation, his every exhalation. His breath timed to the pulse that drummed inside her vagina and against her clitoris.

Victoria with difficulty focused on him and not the fading orgasm that fluttered into the need for another. There was no room inside her body for breath, thought.

The fist inside her plugged her every sense.

Gabriel's body. Gabriel's need.

She would die if he did not stop; she would die if he did.

An angel's pleasure . . .

Gabriel's circling finger would not give Victoria respite.

What did she see . . . ?

"I see you, Gabriel," Victoria gasped. "When I come, I see you."

Pain.

The pain on his glistening face sealed the air inside her lungs. The impact of his body knocked it out.

Gabriel slammed into her, against her, flesh, hair, wool trousers, past, present. At the same time another orgasm slammed through her body.

A voice cried out. Victoria did not know who it belonged to, her or Gabriel. His heartbeat was hers, her flesh was his, the orgasm that ripped through them was theirs.

Victoria knew that Gabriel had felt her pleasure. She knew it because he left her. Body. Soul.

Her fists clenched in the mangled covers.

She had not touched his body, but she had touched an angel.

Victoria did not know if Gabriel would forgive her.

She squeezed her eyelids shut and stared at darkness, listening to the soft click of his boots, crossing the bedroom floor, entering the bathroom . . .

Her body counted the passing minutes. She felt hollow inside, as if he had created a tunnel inside her.

The faint sound of plumbing vibrated in the air: Gabriel had flushed the toilet. A soft click penetrated the stillness, a door opening.

She could feel his stare; it was as palpable as the throb deep inside her womb.

"Mary Thornton cooperated," he said flatly. Tension throbbed inside his voice. "The man who wrote the letters is Mitchell Delaney."

She would not cry.

The darkness behind her eyelids writhed. "I do not know a Mitchell Delaney."

"He knows you, mademoiselle."

"My name is Victoria," Victoria said. And she enjoyed the way Gabriel said it, the "V" a soft caress.

Yes, the man who wrote the letters knew that she wore silk drawers instead of wool. He knew that women had the same sexual needs as did men.

He did not know the woman who was Victoria Childers. But Gabriel knew her.

He had touched the very heart of her soul.

Gabriel turned around and walked away.

Chapter

17

G abriel walked the streets, turning, twisting, slipping through an alley, waiting on the other side, breath misting the yellow fog, heartbeat measuring the silence, silver sword raised in welcome.

No one followed him.

He wished someone had.

Gabriel wanted to kill.

Gabriel wanted to escape the scent and the feel of Victoria.

Gabriel wanted to deny the pleasure she had given him.

I see you, Gabriel. When I come, I see you.

For a second—with the head of his cock pulsing against the mouth of her womb—he had almost believed that he had a soul.

Forcibly, Gabriel concentrated on the night.

No one had followed him to the Thornton town house, either by day or by night. Yet someone had watched Madame René enter his house.

Someone had intercepted the boxes of clothing she had sent to Victoria.

A dull clip-clop interrupted Gabriel's thoughts, the hooves of a solitary horse. Heartbeat accelerating, he eased back inside the mouth of the alley.

Approaching light materialized into carriage lamps. A hansom cab rattled by.

The driver could be headed to the stables. Or the driver could be following Gabriel.

It disappeared into the fog.

Gabriel maneuvered three more streets. Several more hansom cabs meandered through the early morning fog. He hailed the third one by stepping out in front of the passing horse and grabbing the leather halter.

The horse shied; the cabbie cursed.

"Git yer 'ands off me 'orse, ye—"

"I will give you two gold sovereigns if you take me up," Gabriel said softly.

The average cab fare was sixpence per mile; a sovereign was equivalent to two hundred and forty pence. Gabriel did not have to clearly see the cabbie's face in order to see the calculation in his eyes: he would have to travel eighty miles to earn two sovereigns.

Gabriel understood the streets: he understood the men and the women who worked them.

He did not understand Victoria.

"Where'd ye be wantin' to go?" the cabbie asked cautiously. "I need to be gittin' back to th' stables."

"Not far," Gabriel said pleasantly, aching from sex, aching for more sex. "I want to go to the Hundred Guineas Club. I want you to slowly circle the block until I pound on the roof. When I pound on the roof, I want you to stop. Another man will join me. He will then tell you where to take us."

The cabbie did not have to ask directions to the Hundred Guineas Club. Like the House of Gabriel, it was known wide and far.

"I'll do it if I gits th' gold boys up front," the cabbie said craftily.

The horse nervously sidestepped, narrowly missed Gabriel's foot.

Gabriel quickly calmed the sweaty horse, gloved hand firmly sweeping its neck. Remembering the feel of Victoria's pain, taking his fingers and then his cock; remembering her pleasure, taking the orgasms he forced upon her and asking for more.

He knew what the cabbie thought: he thought Gabriel trolled for a male whore.

Unaccustomed anger shot through him; he tamped it down.

Thoughts did not kill; the second man did.

"I will give you one sovereign now and one when the ride is over," Gabriel said easily.

Greed surpassed the cabbie's moral scruples.

" 'Op in, guv'nor."

The cab stank of stale cigar smoke, cheap gin, old perfume and sweat.

Gabriel stared out the window. Streetlights battled the fog, winning on one street, losing on another. Men, women and children wove in and out of the yellow mist.

He thought of Victoria, walking the streets, alone. Living on the streets. Alone.

Quickly he squelched the image.

She would not live on the streets. Gabriel would make sure of that.

A stream of cabs clogged the street in front of the Hundred Guineas Club.

Gabriel pulled a heavy silver watch out of his pocket: it was not yet time.

The cab slowly circled the block four times. On the fifth circle a tall blond-haired woman wearing a crimson velvet cloak stepped toward the cab stand.

Gabriel thrust his cane up, knob first, and sharply rapped on the roof three times.

The cab pulled over.

Scooting across the leather seat, Gabriel kicked the door open, keeping as far away from the window facing the sidewalk as he could.

The woman hesitated.

Gabriel thrust the head of his cane through the open door, silver shining in the yellow fog.

The woman approached, paused to give the cabbie her address. The front of the cab dipped, wood protesting; seconds later the woman sank into the seat, worn leather creaking, velvet rustling.

A hip pressed Gabriel's hip: he gritted his teeth. Cloying perfume drowned out the various other stenches.

Leaning forward, the woman grasped the door handle. The darkness that closed around Gabriel had nothing to do with the slamming door, and everything to do with the shoulder that suddenly rubbed his shoulder.

There was no room to move, no space in which the side of the cab or another human body did not block him.

The cab lurched forward.

Gabriel turned his head and stared at the blond head beside his while every muscle inside his body coiled to kick open the door so that he could escape.

Back to Victoria. Back to the hope she promised.

"Did you discover anything?" he asked neutrally.

"Yes."

The voice was not feminine; it was masculine.

Self-disgust resonated inside the cab.

A hand fisted inside Gabriel's chest. He had done this to the man sitting beside him—he and the second man.

"I told you that you did not have to do this, John," Gabriel said quietly, fighting the sway of the cab and the fear he had lived with for almost fifteen years.

"I have done nothing this night that I have not done thousands of times before," John said tonelessly.

Ten years earlier, John had whored to survive; this night he had done it for Gabriel. John would never forgive either Gabriel or himself.

Gabriel did not blame him.

Reaching up, John ripped the blond wig off his head.

"You did not have to take me in ten years ago." John's hair briefly shone gold in the light of a passing street lamp; it was immediately dulled by shadowy fog. "I would still be there if it were not for you."

They both knew better. John would not be a whore at the Hundred Guineas Club; he would be dead.

"I did not see Stephen," he said instead.

"You are not supposed to see him." John continued to stare at the cab door. "Stephen is surveying the club, as you instructed."

Whereas Gabriel had instructed John to play the whore.

John slowly turned his head; his eyes gleamed in the darkness. "They use feminine names. I could not directly ask about Gerald Fitzjohn."

John did not tell Gabriel anything that he did not already know. But Gabriel had information to relay to John.

"Fitzjohn is dead," Gabriel said remotely. And then, remembering Evan and Gaston's horror, added, "He was decapitated."

John showed neither surprise nor horror. This night he had endured far worse than death. "A man said that Geraldine had stood him up."

Geraldine was the feminine version of Gerald.

Gabriel tensed.

Gerald Fitzjohn could go under the name Geraldine. But then again, he could use another name.

The cab rounded a corner. Gabriel grabbed the overhead strap. "What was the name of the man?"

"He called himself Francine."

Francine . . . Frances.

Viscount Riley bore the name of Frances. He was a crony of the Duke of Clarence, the heir to the throne of England.

The royal duke signed in the club register with his mother's name: Victoria.

"He said the night before that Lenora stood both Geraldine and himself up," John continued unemotionally, "and that he had not seen Lenora since."

Lenora . . . Leonard.

Gabriel did not know offhand of a member of the ton or a parliament member who was named Leonard.

Did the second man?

Had the second man killed the man who called himself Lenora as he had killed Gerald Fitzjohn?

The questions rose with the throbbing pressure of John's hip and shoulder.

Why had not someone followed Gabriel?

Why were the Thorntons still alive?

"Do you know of a man named Mitchell Delaney?" Gabriel asked, control slowly eroding from the cloying smell of perfume and the closeness of John and the pleasure that continued to throb inside his groin. Victoria's pleasure.

What did the second man plan? For Michael? For Gabriel? For Victoria?

"No." John shifted in the darkness; he created as much space between them as he could, whether because he could not bear the touch of another man after the night or to give Gabriel a reprieve, Gabriel did not know. "Does he belong to the club?"

"I don't know," Gabriel said. The carriage wheels echoed his apprehension.

Gabriel was not a fool.

There were men who were more adept at hunting than he.

The men who guarded Michael and Anne *could* be bribed or killed.

A man *could* have followed Gabriel without his knowledge.

Any moment, now, the cab would stop.

Men *could* be waiting in front of John's door. Men *could* kill John and take Gabriel.

The cab jerked to a halt.

John stuffed on his wig; his thigh and hip and elbow and shoulder unavoidably crowded Gabriel's thigh and hip and arm and shoulder.

"The woman who owns the flat does not know what I am," he said stiffly by way of apology. "I would rather she think a woman came to visit me."

"You know the landlady?" Gabriel asked, hoping for John's sake that he knew her carnally.

Hoping for John's sake that he could find the solace the second man had deprived Gabriel of.

"She's a widow. We occasionally take comfort in each other."

"Take comfort in her tonight, John."

John did not respond. Leaning forward, he pushed open the cab door and stood up.

Back bowed, he abruptly spoke: "It is said you have not had a woman in almost fifteen years."

"So it is said," Gabriel agreed.

A brief smile quirked his lips. What did his employees think now that Victoria had requested a tin of condoms?

"Who will you take comfort in tonight, Gabriel?" John asked.

Gabriel could not block the images of Victoria that flashed before his eyes. Victoria watching the male whore and the woman through the transparent mirror. Victoria offering to let Gabriel touch her.

Victoria's breasts flushed with pleasure as her stomach tightened in preparation for orgasm and her splayed legs pushed up for more: more fingers, more Gabriel.

"There is no comfort for some men," he said shortly.

Yet Gabriel had been comforted.

The thought of the second man sent a chill down his spine. If he touched him now . . .

"I did what I did tonight willingly, Gabriel." Flickering gaslight silhouetted John's head. "Do not blame yourself."

Gabriel wondered exactly how far John had gone to help him. He offered the only solace he could. "I will increase your salary."

"There's no need." Gabriel could not see John's expression; he did not need to. "When you have the man you seek, I'm buying a farm. I discovered tonight that in the last ten years you gave me back my humanity. For that, I thank you."

And for asking him to pose as the whore he used to be inside the club he used to work, John would never forgive Gabriel.

Gabriel had given John his humanity back, only to snatch it away.

The cab dipped; the door closed.

Gabriel was alone, as he preferred to be alone. There was no reason for the darkness to press on his chest.

There was no reason to feel the loss of an employee.

Gabriel purposefully helped men and women who had no other

choice but to steal or whore to find occupations better suited to their needs. He would promote another man from within his ranks and hire a replacement.

He should be glad at John's departure: Gabriel wasn't.

The second man was systematically destroying Gabriel's new life, just as he had destroyed his old one.

But he had given him a woman. And Gabriel still did not know *why*.

Chapter

18

Victoria blindly watched Gabriel open the armoire, seeing in her mind's eye what she heard. Silence popped inside her ears. A drawer opened, closed. A second drawer opened, closed. A third drawer opened.

She envisioned the contents of each drawer.

She had seen his underclothes, touched his wool drawers—fine wool as soft as silk—watched a gun and a knife sink into his pile of starched white linen shirts.

The third drawer closed.

Victoria saw Gabriel leave in the whispered closure of a door.

She wondered what time it was.

She wondered when Gabriel would forgive her. And instantly realized he would not forgive her until he forgave himself.

Victoria had wondered what she would feel like after losing her virginity; now she knew. She felt empty.

She opened her eyes and stared at the black pit that was the ceiling: in her mind's eye she saw again the brilliance of white enameled paint and the sweat that had poured down Gabriel's face like tears.

Victoria had known Gabriel's touch. She would never be complete without it.

Swinging her legs over the bed, she sat up.

She winced.

It felt like she had been reamed out with a stovepipe.

It felt like her heart was being ripped out of her chest.

She had not asked for this . . . the letters. The pain.

The pleasure.

Victoria stepped into the bathroom. And remembered . . .

I'm cold. I don't think I'll ever be warm again.

Gabriel had warmed her, first with a robe, and then with his finger, his lips, his tongue, his *bitte*.

Victoria stepped into the copper tub. And remembered . . .

The Liver Spray . . . It is not positioned to message the liver.

No.

Is the spray stimulating for men?

Not to the extent that it is for women.

Victoria showered in stinging hot water. And remembered . . .

I remember the first time I saw a woman like this.

What did you think, when you saw her? . . .

I thought that if a man had a soul, it existed inside a woman.

Victoria soaped herself. And remembered . . . every place Gabriel had touched her. Her lips. Her tongue. Her cheek. Her breasts.

Her clitoris . . .

Victoria's clitoris throbbed in memory.

Did Gabriel throb in memory?

Her vulva was swollen; it radiated heat. He had called her vagina a *portail*.

I like the way you say my name.

How is that?

As if I have a soul.

Victoria quickly rinsed the soap away and toweled herself dry.

Gabriel's brush possessed neither dark nor pale hair. All evidence of their joining destroyed.

His toothbrush was damp. Averting her gaze from the dark-haired woman in the mirror, she brushed her teeth.

Victoria still had no clothes.

The silk robe was in the bedroom, on the floor where she had dropped it. Feeling unexpectedly shy, Victoria wrapped the damp bath towel about her body.

She should not have been surprised to find that Gabriel's bedchamber was occupied: she was.

Victoria clutched the knotted towel between her breasts. At the same time, a brown-haired man looked up. He looked to be in his midthirties, and did not appear at all chagrined to see a woman wearing nothing but a towel.

She immediately recognized him as the man who had led her to Gabriel the night she had sold her virginity. *Gaston,* Gabriel had called him.

Scrambled thoughts flitted through her head. He would know of the condoms that she had requested. Would he now apprise the servants of her scrawniness?

Victoria took a fortifying breath. She had stood naked in front of Madame René without running for cover; she could at least stand before Gaston covered in a towel without collapsing into hysterics.

"May I help you, sir?" she asked icily in the voice that had occasionally quelled rambunctious charges.

Gaston smiled, brown eyes warm. *"Mais non,* mademoiselle. I merely brought you these boxes."

The white boxes he held out were stamped with red rose petals. Victoria shrank back.

"Non, non, mademoiselle," Gaston said quickly. "I delivered these myself from Madame René. See?"

Gaston set the boxes onto the rumpled bed.

Heat surged through Victoria; it was not sexual in nature.

A large stain blotched the corner of the sheet where she had lain, body leaking her pleasure. A metal lid lay on the satinwood nightstand; there was no mistaking the rolled sheaths that lay inside the small tin beside it.

Gaston did not seem to notice. Or perhaps, employed in the House of Gabriel, he no longer paid attention to the physical realities of sexual union. He lifted the lid off of a rectangular box.

Victoria steeled herself, remembering blood, remembering Dolly's ha—

The box contained a black satin corset.

Apprehension turned into feminine curiosity.

"Voilà." Gaston turned to Victoria and flashed her a smile. He had perfect white teeth. "It is merely a pretty corset, mademoiselle."

The heat surging through Victoria's body did not diminish at Gaston's reassurance, a carryover from the years spent pretending to be a paragon of virtue. It did not matter that her pleasure stained the sheets or that an open tin of condoms sat on the nightstand. Men *did not* discuss—or flaunt—women's underwear.

Gaston was impervious to the restrictions imposed by society. He proceeded to open each box, describing the softness of silk chemises, holding up a pair of drawers adorned with blue ribbons so that she could admire the paper-thin silk, proudly displaying garter belts, silk stockings, fine silk gloves, a bustle that looked more like an apron than the wire cage Victoria had worn for years.

Approval glinted in Gaston's brown eyes. "It is *très* fashionable— Monsieur Gabriel picked it out."

While Victoria pondered the thought that Gabriel had personally chosen intimate apparel for her, Gaston—like a magician pulling a rabbit out of a hat—held up a golden brown colored silk reception dress that should have looked tawdry with its garniture of wine-colored velvet and lampas underskirt of cream with green, yellow and dull red figures; it was beautiful.

She involuntarily reached out. Corded silk clung to her fingertips.

It was far softer than the cheap silk drawers she used to purchase—only not so cheap on a governess's salary.

"Mademoiselle will need help with her dress," Gaston said with obvious anticipation.

Victoria snatched her hand back, abruptly, achingly aware of the towel that draped her body and the bare flesh it did little to hide. She would *not* allow another man to see her naked. "I assure you, sir, I am capable of dressing myself."

Gaston really did have a disarming smile. She remembered the smile in Gabriel's eyes when yesterday she had reprimanded him over the number of boxes stacked on the couch.

And now he had picked out underwear for her.

"*Non, non,* mademoiselle, you misunderstand me," Gaston said hurriedly. "I do not offer my services; Monsieur Gabriel employs maids. I will send one of them to you."

Victoria had dressed herself ever since leaving her father's house.

"Thank you, but that is not necessary."

"*Mais oui,* it is necessary, mademoiselle," Gaston adjured. "Monsieur Gabriel has instructed that we care for your every need."

There was no stopping the blistering heat that surged into Victoria's cheeks. "I assure you, sir, my every need has been attended to."

"*C'est très bon*—it is good that you have come." The knowing gleam inside Gaston's brown eyes was unmistakable. "Monsieur Gabriel, he has been alone too long."

Gabriel had referred to an orgasm as *come.* Surely Gaston did not—

"He will not allow me to touch him," Victoria said.

She bit her lips—too late, the words rang out.

Gaston's brown eyes did not condemn her. "But he has touched you, *n'est-pas?*"

There was no mistaking the evidence of his touch.

Her lips were swollen, her eyes shadowed.

"Yes." Victoria squared her shoulders. "He has touched me."

Gaston slowly refolded the dress. "Monsieur Gabriel has not touched a woman—or a man—in all the time I have been with him, mademoiselle."

Victoria's throat tightened. "How long have you been with him?"

The brown-haired Frenchman neatly tucked the beautiful golden-brown dress back into the box. "I have been with Monsieur Gabriel for fourteen years."

"You are his friend?"

The rose-petal stamped lid closed over the crimson silk dress.

"We at *le* Maison de Gabriel—the House of Gabriel—are not his friends, mademoiselle."

Victoria's eyes widened in surprise.

Dress safely boxed, Gaston's thick dark lashes slowly lifted. Victoria looked into Gabriel's eyes, brown instead of silver.

"We are his family," Gaston said flatly. "In this house we are all family to each other."

Gaston, too, had survived the streets.

"Are you a . . . *une prostituée?*" she asked impulsively.

Gaston's gaze did not waver. "*Oui*, mademoiselle, I was *une prostituée*, if there were clients who wanted me. When there were not, I was—as you English say, a pickpocket and a cutthroat."

A cutthroat . . .

Victoria took a deep breath. "I take it you are no longer engaged in your former occupations."

Suddenly the cold flatness of the streets left Gaston's eyes. They twinkled engagingly. "*Non*, mademoiselle, I am no longer engaged as a pickpocket or a cutthtroat. Monsieur Gabriel would not like it if we stole from or killed his clients. I manage Monsieur Gabriel and his house."

And the employees who worked in the House of Gabriel.

A family of prostitutes, thieves and cutthroats.

Victoria squared her shoulders. "I am relieved to hear that, sir."

"*Pas du tout*—not at all, mademoiselle." There was admiration as well as humor in Gaston's brown eyes. "Your breakfast is in the study. You may eat it now or wait until a maid has helped you to dress."

As a governess, Victoria had eaten with the servants. She was not used to being fussed over. The lingering heat of embarrassment dissipated at the novelty of being pampered.

"Truly, monsieur, I do not need the services of a maid. But thank you. I will enjoy breakfast—and the clothes. They are very beautiful."

Gaston looked pleased at her praise. "If there is anything you need, you must feel free to ask."

She needed to heal an angel.

There was only one way to do so.

Victoria looked into Gaston's kind brown eyes and asked for what she needed.

For what Gabriel needed.

Chapter

19

A shadow covered Victoria. Gabriel's image lay heavily on her eyelids, her breasts, her stomach, her thighs.

Instantly, she awakened, heart pounding, breath catching.

The bathroom door gently swung closed. A thin line of white light flooded the crack between floor and door.

Gabriel had returned.

Throwing back the bedcovers, she slid out from between the linen sheets.

Her nipples hardened. From cold, she told herself.

And knew that it was from fear.

Victoria was not looking forward to the part she must play this night, but she would play it. She would free an angel.

Orange and blue flames licked blackened wood.

The fire was dying from lack of care.

Victoria had been dying ever since her mother had left her with a cold, unloving father. Gabriel had died a little every time he gave pleasure but did not receive it in return.

The squat white jar on the satinwood nightstand was a pale blur in the feeble light.

It was all the light Victoria needed.

She reached out, fingers grasping—

Metal.

The silver tin of condoms.

Letting go of the metal, she grasped the glass jar that Gaston had earlier delivered. Fingers trembling, Victoria unscrewed the lid and carefully laid it on the nightstand.

Metal impacting metal shot down her spine.

Victoria had placed the lid on top of the small tin. She could only hope that her decision was better planned than her coordination.

The smooth wooden floor was cold, hard. Her breasts—passable breasts, Madame René had said; symbols of a woman's sin, her father had claimed—stabbed the air.

Gabriel had seen Victoria's breasts; she had not seen him.

Gabriel had touched Victoria; Victoria had not touched Gabriel. *Yet.*

God help her if she did, Gabriel had said. Because he couldn't. Or wouldn't.

Victoria opened the bathroom door.

She could sense Gabriel's awareness the moment she stepped inside.

A long, elegant hand reached out from the depths of the shower and turned a cock. Water sprayed in the silence; steam billowed out of the wood casing.

Strangling the glass jar of lubricant she had asked Gaston for, Victoria stepped forward.

Gabriel's face was turned up into the shower spray, hair sleek and dark. Water sluiced down his muscled back, tight buttocks, and long, long legs.

He was beautiful. Far, far more beautiful than any other man she had ever seen.

Gabriel knew Victoria had entered the bathroom. He knew Victoria watched him.

He knew what Victoria intended to do.

Slowly he lowered his head. Water-darkened hair hugged the back of his head, shaped the nape of his neck.

"I will kill you if you touch me, Victoria."

Gabriel's voice was distant; tension penetrated the water and the building steam.

"I would not be here, Gabriel, if you did not want me to touch you," Victoria returned calmly. And knew that it was true.

The man who was responsible for being at the House of Gabriel had known Gabriel's needs. He had provided Victoria to fulfill them.

"My name is not Gabriel."

Victoria steeled herself for the truths she would learn this night.

"What is it, then?"

"*Garçon. Con. Fumier.*"

Victoria knew that *garçon* was the French word for boy. *Con* and *fumier* were not a part of her French vocabulary. Any more than had been *portail*, a woman's vagina, and *godèmiche*, a leather phallus.

"We are not responsible for what other people call us," she returned evenly.

"Do you know what *con* is, mademoiselle?"

Gabriel's voice echoed hollowly in the copper grotto over the steady spray of water.

"No," Victoria said truthfully.

"It's bastard. Do you know what *fumier* means?"

"No." But she had no doubt that Gabriel was going to instruct her. "I do not."

"*Fumier* means a piece of shit. Gutters are filled with sewage; I was born in a gutter. I lived in a gutter. A nameless bastard. It wasn't whoring that made me what I am," Gabriel said into the thickening steam while the water washed over hm, "it was living."

The price of survival.

"There is no sin in living, Gabriel."

No sin in living. No sin in loving.

Victoria knew that it would take far more than words to convince Gabriel of the truth of her statement.

"I once saw a stained glass window in a cathedral. There were two angels in it; I didn't know they were angels. One had dark hair, the other had fair hair. An old woman sat on the church steps, what you English would call a crawler, a woman who begs from beggars. I asked her who *les deux hommes*—the two men—were. She said they were angels. She said the fair-haired angel was Gabriel, God's messenger. Michael, the dark-haired angel, was God's chosen. She said there was no hunger in heaven, and that angels didn't beg. Michael and Gabriel, she said, were God's favorite angels."

Steam billowed out of the copper grotto, clogged inside Victoria's nose and chest.

"When I saw Michael in Calais, he was a half-starved boy with hungry eyes who wouldn't beg and didn't know how to steal. He reminded me of the dark-haired angel in the window. I wanted to be like him; I wanted to have eyes that hungered for more than a crust of bread and a warm, dry place to sleep. I wanted to be an angel, so I took an angel's name. When the French madame gave me the opportunity to escape poverty, I took that, too. I would take it again, given the choice. Make no mistake, I am a bastard. If you touch me, I will hurt you. And I assure you, Victoria, I can hurt you in ways you've never dreamed of."

Emotion squeezed Victoria's chest until she could not breathe over the pressure and the steam. Fear was all too recognizable, but something else superseded the fear.

Gabriel hurt.

She had the power to stop his hurt. *If* she had the courage.

"We do what we must in order to survive," Victoria said quietly. Hearing the echo of her earlier words, hers, his . . .

I am sorry that you were sold against your will.

But it was not against my will, mademoiselle.

"Do we, Victoria?" Gabriel asked incuriously. Water pouring over him.

"Yes," Victoria said decisively, "We do."

Else she would not have auctioned off her virginity at the House of Gabriel. And she would never have met a fair-haired angel who yearned for love.

Gabriel pivoted so quickly, the motion stole Victoria's breath. Or perhaps it was seeing him fully naked for the first time that stole her breath.

Water spiked his eyelashes, sluiced down his chin, splattered onto the slick brown-blond hair that covered his chest and arrowed down his groin.

Victoria stared.

He was erect. Water streamed off the bulbous tip of his engorged sex.

The muscles inside her vagina clenched with desire.

She had seen Gabriel briefly the night before, while he covered himself with a condom, and even more briefly, when he had walked toward her with his rubber-sheathed manhood jutting out from the vent in his gray wool trousers.

This was a man unashamedly exposed, blue veins pulsing, every gradation of color revealed—pale flesh, dark flesh, purple-tinted flesh. Two tight, leathery mounds swung below a thatch of water-darkened hair.

There was no question whatsoever inside Victoria's mind that Gabriel could hurt her in unimaginable ways. Just as he had been hurt.

Just as he would go on hurting.

Her choice . . .

Slowly Victoria raised her eyelashes.

Through the coiling tendrils of gray steam Gabriel's gaze was flat and uncompromising. The eyes of a boy who had wanted to be an angel and a man who had lost the promise of paradise.

For the first time Victoria was glad of the six months that had deprived her of food and clothing and ultimately shelter. Glad, even, of her bones that were too sharp and her flesh too tightly stretched across them.

Victoria knew what it was like to be cold and hungry. She knew what it was like to sell the hope of love for food and shelter.

Madame René had said that seduction consisted of painting naked images with words. *Creating the anticipation of . . . a kiss . . . a caress . . . an embrace.*

"My father forbade kissing," Victoria said deliberately. "I would like to kiss you."

The only sound in the bathroom was the pounding of water and the drumming of Victoria's heart. Slowly she sat the glass jar down onto the wooden cabinet encasing the tub, breasts dangling, head lifting to hold Gabriel' s gaze.

"My father forbade embracing." She straightened up, breasts and vertebrae settling. "I would like to embrace your body with mine."

Carefully she stepped into the copper tub.

"My father forbade touching." Hot water misted her face, lapped her right foot, her left foot. "I would like to touch you, Gabriel."

For one long second Gabriel could not breathe, locked inside hungry blue eyes while hot water needled his head and shoulders. It streamed down his back, his chest, his groin, his buttocks.

Every inch of his body cried out a warning. If Victoria touched him—

Cool fingers enclosed Gabriel's erect flesh.

Electric need.

Blinding anger.

He did not want this.

But Victoria had not given him a choice. Just as the second man had not given him a choice.

Grabbing Victoria's wrist, Gabriel jerked her underneath the shower spray; at the same time he swung her around and slammed the front of her body against the copper-lined shower.

Victoria's hands slapped against the wall.

"You promised," he gritted, water filling his mouth, burning his eyes, his chest, his thighs, every inch of his flesh that touched Victoria. "You promised not to touch me."

But she had touched him.

She had opened her body and taken his fingers and his cock until the darkness of pending orgasm disappeared inside the blinding flash of her pleasure.

"I promised I wouldn't touch you last night," Victoria gasped into the pounding water, bracing herself against the copper wall, "and I didn't. I kept my promise to you, Gabriel."

But she hadn't kept her promise. She had touched him with her passion and her pleasure.

I see you, Gabriel . . .

But she hadn't seen him.

She hadn't seen the boy who had begged beggars or the whore who had begged a man.

Gabriel could feel Victoria's fear, smell it over her desire—she had been afraid when she stepped into the bathroom. It had been her fear that had told him what she planned.

She planned on freeing an angel. But he wasn't an angel.

He was a nameless piece of shit that had wanted more, dared more, and had paid the price.

Gabriel pressed against Victoria, fingers circling the softness of her upper arms, thighs cupping her buttocks, the length of his cock sandwiched between her crevice, hair clinging to them both, hers, his. He let her feel his hardness, his strength.

Her vulnerability.

"Is this what you want, Victoria?" he crooned. The shower scourging his skin.

Victoria turned her face in profile, right cheek riding slippery copper. Water streamed off his face, coursed down her left cheek, plastered her hair to her scalp, a shell-like ear, a fragile neck.

"Yes," she said. Still not giving in to her fear. "I want you to touch me."

He had touched her last night, but it hadn't been enough.

For her. For him.

"How do you want me to touch you, Victoria?" he murmured seductively. Knowing how to please; knowing how to hurt. He did not know how to love. Whores didn't love. "Do you want me to touch you like I touched a woman, or do you want me to touch you like I touched a man?"

Water spiked Victoria's lashes, rained down her cheek. "Is there a difference?"

Steam twined around them.

Evocative. Provocative.

"Women are softer." Gabriel brushed Victoria's ear with his lips— she had a small ear, dainty, infinitely vulnerable. It scorched his lips; the crevice between her buttocks squeezed the length of his cock. "They bruise more easily."

Victoria stiffened at the light kiss, suspicious of his gentleness. An angel bearing gifts . . .

"Men are harder, more muscled." Gabriel delicately tasted the rim of her ear, the core of her ear, a hot plunge of his tongue. Water coursed down his face, his chin, dribbled onto her shoulder. "They like it rougher. Shall I be rough with you, Victoria?"

"Was the man who made you beg rough with you, Gabriel?" Victoria challenged, water-blackened hair clinging to his lips.

Gabriel gritted his teeth in memory.

The second man had not been rough, but his accomplice had been. Gabriel had welcomed the pain.

Victoria would not welcome pain.

But that was all Gabriel could give her.

"Does the thought of men fucking men excite you?" he asked softly, deliberately crude.

It had excited the women Gabriel had been with in the past. They had sought a fair-haired angel to compare with a dark-haired angel.

But Michael was the angel; only he could show a woman angels. Gabriel had shown them the darkness of desire.

"He raped you," Victoria insisted to the steam and the streaming water.

Innocent. As Michael was innocent.

Hungry. As Gabriel could never be.

"Two men raped me," he rejoined silkily, nuzzling her cheek, heartbeat pounding in his fingers that banded her arms, his chest that cradled her narrow spine, the length of his cock that rode the crevice between her buttocks.

"But one man gave you pleasure," Victoria doggedly persisted.

Damn her.

"Yes," Gabriel agreed softly.

One man had brought him pain; the second man had brought him pleasure.

He could have withstood the pain. He had not withstood the pleasure. It would taint Gabriel forever.

And she knew it, this woman who had been sent by the man who one by one had peeled away the layers of an angel until there had been nothing left.

Angels did not beg, but he had made Gabriel beg.

Victoria strained against Gabriel—to see him, to touch him, to be a part of him, he who had fought so long to remain apart from anyone. "I want to know!"

Gabriel had wanted to know . . . what a full stomach felt like, so that he could hunger for more than food. He had wanted to know what it felt like to be warm, so that he could covet more than shoes and clothing. He had wanted to know what it felt like to have a home, a place he wouldn't have to fight other beggars over.

Curiosity killed: love. Hope . . .

Gabriel contoured Victoria's ear with the tip of his tongue; the length of his cock was snug between the cheeks of her buttocks. The tears he could not cry leaked from the tip of his crown. "What do you want to know, Victoria?"

"I want to know what he did to you."

Memory slashed through the heat of the water pounding his body and the softness of Victoria's skin.

Pain. Pleasure.

"You saw men fucking men through the transparent mirrors, Victoria." Gabriel filled her ear with his breath. "Do you want me to tell you what it's like to be fucked in the ass? Or do you want me to tell you what it's like to be raped?"

Water-beaded copper framed Victoria's chin. "I know what it's like to want to be a part of someone, Gabriel."

Last night she had been a part of him, as he had been a part of her.

The darkness of the truth lapped at Gabriel until he felt he would explode.

"I was not apart from one man," he said seductively.

He had never been apart from one man.

Michael. Michel.

For a while, Gabriel had thought he, too, could be an angel.

The second man had shown him what he was.

Con. Fumier.

"He hurt you, Gabriel." Steam blurred Victoria's face. "I want to take away the hurt."

Had the man or men who had taken John hurt his body as well as his soul? Gabriel wondered.

Would his widow take away his pain?

Had Anne taken away Michael's pain?

Who will you take comfort in . . . Gabriel?

No one. *Jamias.*

Never.

Gabriel did not deserve comfort.

"And you think you can take away my hurt by doing . . . what, Victoria?" Gabriel queried lightly, sharing his breath, his heat, the water that deluged his body. "By letting me rape you?"

"I want you to show me what he did to you."

Water dribbled off Gabriel's nose onto Victoria's cheek; it crawled between their bodies and danced on the tip of his cock, washing away his tears. "Which man, Victoria, do you want to know about?"

"I want to know what the man who hurt you did to you," Victoria's voice echoed inside the copper hood, goading him, galvanizing him. "And then I want you to show me what the man who made you beg for pleasure did to you. I want you to make me beg, Gabriel."

Gabriel had not begged for pleasure—he had begged for release. And then he had begged for death.

He did not want Victoria to beg—not Victoria with her hungry blue eyes.

"Do you know where men are raped, Victoria?" Gabriel murmured provocatively. Erect flesh nestled between the crevice of her buttocks. Chest cradling the narrowness of her shoulders and her spine. The crown of his cock throbbing with each breath, each heartbeat. Water buffeting them both.

It would be so easy to kill her . . .

"Yes, I know where men are raped," Victoria said through the pounding of the shower.

But she didn't know. Men weren't raped through their bodies; men were raped through their minds.

Twisting his torso, Gabriel reached back and jabbed his fingers into the jar of cream Victoria had set on top of the cabinet encasing the tub. They came out coated with thick white cream.

Water beaded on his fingers, pearled on the cream.

A part of him yet apart from him.

But he didn't want to be apart from one woman.

"Do you want to know what I felt, Victoria?" he goaded her. Killing her. Killing himself. "Do you want to know what it's like to be fucked in the ass?"

"Yes." Victoria threw her head back, swallowing water, swallowing fear. Her hands remained flat on the copper wall, a willing sacrifice. "I want to know what you felt."

But it wasn't what Gabriel wanted.

He didn't want a woman to know what he felt.

He didn't want anyone to ever know what he had felt.

Easing back, Gabriel brought his hand between their bodies. He smeared himself with cold, slick cream—the crown, the shaft; Victoria's buttocks teased the back of his hand and his knuckles.

Firmly grasping himself, he encircled her with the lubricated head of his penis . . . slipping, sliding, enticing, beguiling. "Is this what you want, Victoria?" he crooned. A whore by nature as well as by training.

Victoria tensed, unprepared for either pleasure or pain.

Last night he had breached her virginity, a thin layer of flesh that he had gradually peeled back to allow one finger, two fingers, three.

He had not ruptured it, neither with his fingers nor his cock.

A clever whore would repair the hymen and sell it again.

But Victoria wasn't a whore.

Her virginity could be reclaimed. If he took Victoria now, she would never be able to claim innocence again. She couldn't heal Gabriel; but she could be destroyed by him.

He didn't want to hurt her.

What Gabriel wanted hadn't stopped him in the past . . . From whoring. From killing.

He knew it wouldn't stop him now.

Circling, circling, Gabriel pressed inward. And almost collapsed at the pleasure that shot through his testicles.

But he didn't want the pleasure.

Victoria instinctively arched her body. Even in this she accepted him. She who had never known the pain that men could give women. The pain that men could give men.

"Is it?" Gabriel whispered invitingly into Victoria's hair, and her water-slickened cheek. Circling, pressing, circling, pressing harder, circling, pressing harder still, wooing her body into accepting his as he had been trained to do twenty-seven years earlier. "Is this what you want, Mademoiselle Childers?"

"Yes." Victoria squeezed her eyelids together and turned her head into his lips, seeking solace in the man she had invited to rape her.

So that *he* might not hurt.

But he would never be free of the hurt.

"Tell me, Victoria, is this what you want?" he crooned, chest cradling her back while her hands flattened against the copper wall tried to hold back her pleasure and her pain. But she couldn't hold them back. Experienced whore that Gabriel had been, even he had not been able to hold them back. "All you have to do is tell me to stop, and I'll stop. Tell me, Victoria. Tell me to stop."

Or he would die. And take her with him.

Victoria took the sloping tip of his penis into her body. And gasped her death sentence. "Don't stop!"

Past echoes screamed inside his skull.

Stop . . . Stop . . . Stop . . .

They were followed by: *N'arrête pas . . . N'arrête pas . . . N'arrête pas . . .*

Don't stop . . . Don't stop . . . Don't stop . . .

Gabriel's muscles bunched inside his thighs and his buttocks. Left hand sliding down Victoria's arm—a woman's arm, soft, slender, so easily bruised or broken—he smoothed her waist and cupped her hip.

He didn't stop.

Victoria's outspread fingers clenched into fists. She milked his flesh, frantically trying to adjust to the alien invasion.

Her pain vibrated in the hot mist.

Gabriel buried his face in her wet hair.

He didn't want this.

The shower relentlessly pounded down on them, a man and a woman who had been brought together because of their fear and their desire.

"Tell me to stop, Victoria," Gabriel whispered, drowning in the spraying water and the tight haven of her body, the past he had survived and the future he had been denied.

"Don't stop!" she gasped.

"Tell me to stop, Victoria," he repeated. And withdrew until just the crown of his cock was inside her.

Victoria's muscles convulsed, trying to stop him, trying to pull him back inside.

The pleasure. The pain.

Gabriel didn't want Victoria to see darkness when she reached her climax.

Voir les anges. Le petit morte.

Gabriel wanted Victoria to see angels, not death.

"Don't stop!" she cried, a death knoll.

He eased inside her another inch. "Tell me to stop, Victoria."

"I can feel the head of you" Victoria sucked in hot mist, water streamed into her mouth—"oh, dear God!"

Gabriel could feel Victoria as keenly as she felt him. Flesh slippery inside and out. Pressure growing, building, seeking an outlet.

She had to stop him.

He drove home.

Victoria's pelvis slammed against the copper wall. "Oh my God!" burst out of her throat.

Heat.

Gabriel did not remember a woman being this hot. He could feel the slick wetness of her skin and the slippery heat of her body knotting inside his testicles.

"Tell me to stop, Victoria," he repeated raggedly, slipping, falling into the past.

"Did you tell him to stop?" she gasped, taking into her body the French boy who had wanted to be an angel and the whore who had begged for release.

"Yes!" Gabriel hissed through clenched teeth. And could not stop himself. He eased out of Victoria. For his pleasure, not hers. "I told him to stop."

Victoria bit her bottom lip—she had beautiful lips, bottom lip only marginally fuller than her top lip. Water streamed down her temple. "But he didn't stop."

He didn't stop. He hadn't stopped until the second man had told him to stop.

Then the nightmare had begun.

"Tell me to stop," Gabriel said.

Begging. But angels didn't beg.

Victoria's buttocks clenched. "No."

For a second, Gabriel couldn't breathe for the pain and the pleasure.

"Then beg me not to stop," he said ruthlessly.

"Make me beg, Gabriel," she challenged, a part of him.

But he didn't want her to be a part of him.

"Make you beg . . . how, Victoria?" Gabriel asked, voice dangerously soft, body shaking with need, inside, *outside*. "Do you want me to make you beg for me to stop?"

Pain.

"Yes."

"Or do you want me to make you beg me *not* to stop?"

Pleasure.

"Yes," she repeated, gasping, trembling.

Willing to take both his pain and his pleasure.

But Gabriel didn't want to give Victoria his pain.

He wanted to think, if just for a moment, that he had found a soul, and that the soul's name was Victoria Childers. A woman who saw his face when she exploded with pleasure, the face of a man who had forsaken his namesake.

Gabriel grasped Victoria's left hip. His fingers spanned her hipbone.

His muscles bunched.

He wanted to ram Victoria until she screamed for him to stop. And then he wanted to ram her until she begged him not to stop.

He wanted Victoria to take away the truth and bring back the nameless boy who had thought he could be an angel.

"They chained me," he said into the tumbling steam and the pounding water. "I couldn't move. I couldn't fight."

All he had been able to do was endure until he could endure no more.

Gabriel slowly withdrew his cock until only his heartbeat was lodged inside Victoria.

The truth would not be denied.

"He didn't use a lubricant," he said rawly.

The two men had taken him for no other reason than to hurt him. Because he had loved a black-haired, violet-eyed boy.

A boy who had taught him to read and to write.

A boy whom Gabriel had joined in prostitution rather than be parted from.

Gabriel flexed his hips: Victoria took him. As he had been taken.

The shower relentlessly pounded down on his head. On Victoria's head.

"There is a word." Water coursed down Gabriel's face. "Algolagnia. It is pleasure that is indistinguishable from pain. Do you want to know how pain can become pleasure, Victoria?" he whispered.

Dying inside. Dying outside.

Cock throbbing. Past overcoming the present.

"Yes." Victoria gulped air. Water. His cock. "Yes, I do."

Gabriel had not begged until the pain had turned into pleasure. But Victoria would not understand that until she herself experienced it.

All of a sudden he wanted her to understand. He wanted her to be a part of him.

He wanted her to forgive what he could never forgive.

Grasping her right hip, Gabriel slid his left hand forward, fingers slippery wet with cream and water, searching . . . finding.

Her clitoris pulsed between his thumb and forefinger, a woman's most sensitive flesh, softer than silk.

She was hard—as hard as Gabriel was now. As hard as he had been made to be in the past.

Victoria convulsively jerked, quivered, stilled, realizing how one man could make rape painful while another man made it pleasurable.

"Gabriel," she whispered, water coursing down her cheek.

Last night she had come for him ten times. Each time she had cried out her pleasure, the internal contractions of her *portail* had squeezed his heart.

"Would you cry for an angel, Victoria?" he murmured.

"Yes," she said unsteadily, heart pounding inside her body. Or perhaps it was his heartbeat that pounded inside her body.

The water riveting down Victoria's cheek was salty. Tears for an angel.

Gabriel gently thrust inside Victoria; at the same time he pumped her engorged clitoris, as if it were a miniature penis.

It throbbed. Like he had throbbed.

Wrapping his right arm about her waist, Gabriel held Victoria against him while he squeezed her and pumped her until both her flesh and his flesh swelled beyond endurance. Until the need for orgasm was greater than the need to breathe.

And then he let her go. Hovering on the brink of release. His flesh sliding inside her body, against her body.

And there was nothing she could do to reach climax.

"Would you beg an angel, Victoria?" Gabriel whispered, fingers hovering over her engorged clitoris that screamed to be touched while he filled her so deeply he touched the very core of the woman who was Victoria Childers.

With pain. With pleasure.

A woman whose only sin was in wanting an angel.

"Beg me, Victoria," he said gently.

Like Gabriel had begged in the end.

Fear suddenly contorted her water-sluiced face.

Victoria realized that her body was an apparatus: an object that could be made to feel pleasure whether she wanted to or not. She could never solely claim ownership again.

"No!" she gasped.

Too late.

Her pain and her pleasure wrapped around Gabriel's testicles.

She strained for the release he had not allowed her even as she fought to regain control of her body.

He did not allow her that, either.

Any moment now she would beg, as Gabriel had begged.

And she would never see light again.

Contrarily Gabriel didn't want Victoria to beg. He didn't want her to live with the knowledge of how easily her body could become a weapon.

He didn't want her to see darkness when he touched her.

The second man had given him a woman: if Victoria died because of her desire to touch an angel, he could at least give her pleasure worth dying for.

Stepping, turning, penis slipping and sliding internally—flesh slipping and sliding against flesh externally—Gabriel carefully turned Victoria so that she faced the side of the shower wall. He tightly instructed her, "Turn the Liver Spray cock."

He did not have to tell her why.

Victoria leaned forward.

The pain and the pleasure of her motion squeezed the air out of his lungs. He couldn't stop it: the pain, the pleasure. Gabriel felt each twist of Victoria's wrist, as if she turned his cock instead of the valve cock, slippery penis sliding inside the fist-tight heat of her body a quarter of an inch, outside a half inch, inside a pulse-stopping inch.

A shock of hot water squirted the top of his foot.

"Angle the spray up," Gabriel said raggedly, holding on to her waist and to his sanity.

He did not recognize his voice. Did Victoria?

She clumsily positioned the spray.

Gently Gabriel walked her closer—penis slipping, sliding, her internal muscles caressing, nipping, two bodies acting as one—until her pelvis pressed against the shower spray and water needled her swollen clitoris.

"Oh, my . . . Gabriel!"

Surprise, pleasure, then pending orgasm flavored Victoria's cry. There had been no joy in Gabriel's release.

Squeezing his eyelids shut and throwing his head up into the spray, Gabriel grasped both of Victoria's hips and thrust so far up inside her that her buttocks cushioned his groin and there was no pending death, no lurking memories, no second man. Just two bodies made one.

The shock of his entry was upstaged by the force of Victoria's orgasm. Her muscles clenched about him until Gabriel gritted his teeth, surrounded by hot water, slippery flesh.

A woman's softness.

A man's need.

Gabriel pumped his flesh into Victoria and held her so that she would gain maximum pleasure from both his penetration and the spray of water. He felt her second orgasm before she did.

"Gabriel, please . . . Don't!" Victoria cried.

Gabriel had cried, a twenty-six year old man who had never before cried. *Please. Stop.*

It had not stopped the second man.

He buried his face into the nook of Victoria's neck, seeking solace in the wet slickness of hair and flesh; the back of Victoria's head ground into his shoulder.

"Oh . . . my . . . God!" She gasped in agonized pleasure. "Gabriel. Gabriel. Please . . . don't . . . stop!"

The truth would not be denied.

"I couldn't stop it," Gabriel said, lips sliding against her hair, her neck, cock sliding inside her body.

Crimson stained the darkness behind Gabriel's eyelids.

He had slit the accomplice's throat. His blood had been hot and slippery.

Like the shower water.

Like Victoria's body.

Like sex.

"I couldn't stop it," he repeated.

And pumped his hips in pleasure and pain. Unable to stop the flow of memories.

Of black hair. Of violet eyes.

Of love. Of hatred.

Gabriel's left hand blindly sought comfort, smoothing up Victoria's water-slick waist, over sharp ribs, curving around soft, round flesh, fingers convulsively closing over her left breast. Her heart hammered against his fingers; her nipple stabbed his palm, passion both balm and scourge.

She could so easily be destroyed. By the second man.

By Gabriel.

He pressed his lips behind Victoria's ear. It did not silence the words that erupted inside his chest and exploded out of his mouth. "I . . . couldn't . . . stop it."

Not the pain. Not the pleasure.

Not the loss.

Love was not innocent. No matter how badly Gabriel had wanted it to be.

The second man had taught him that.

A low cry burst out of Victoria's throat. It vibrated against Gabriel's lips. She suddenly strained backward, body opening, grasping, milking his flesh until Gabriel's knees buckled with the truth and he was slipping, falling

Hard copper impacted his knees.

Victoria fell with Gabriel, body gulping an angel's release.

He had not been able to stop it.

Chapter

20

A shock of water blasted Victoria in the face, and then it was gone, the climax that had brought her to her knees, the water that had brought her to orgasm, the internal heartbeat of the man who had taken her into his world and shown her the pain and the pleasure of sex.

I . . . couldn't . . . stop it, reverberated inside the copper grotto. An angel's cry.

The copper was hard; Victoria would have bruises on her kneecaps. Electric aftershocks danced inside her bottom and her pelvis and her breasts. Five fingers seared her stomach; her heartbeat drummed against the palm of a hand.

Gabriel's hand

Her throat tightened, remembering her pleasure, his pain. *They chained me. I couldn't move. I couldn't fight.*

In her eagerness to free an angel, Victoria had deprived Gabriel of the very choice the second man had deprived him of: she had forced him into carnal relations.

An apology rose to her lips; "The water stopped," came out instead.

It was too late for apologies.

"Yes," Gabriel said tonelessly, his voice a fleeting caress against the base of her neck and her shoulder.

Victoria stared at the copper-skinned woman imprisoned inside the shower. Five copper fingers imprinted her stomach; her left breast was protectively cupped by a copper hand. Copper-blond hair blended into water-blackened hair.

Tears stung Victoria's eyes. She had to know.

"What happened when they finished with you?"

"They left me."

But not to die.

Gabriel's words were muffled by Victoria's hair and skin; his implication was not.

They had not wanted Gabriel to die. But he had wanted to.

"Who released you?" she asked, voice unsteady, knowing the answer.

"Michael."

The chosen one.

A boy with hungry eyes who had not begged.

"He's not French." Water crawled down her cheek. "How is it that he was in Calais?"

"He had stowed away on a boat from Dover when we were thirteen." Gabriel's voice was distant; his lips moved against her hair and, beneath that, the crook of her neck. The hair covering his chest and stomach pricked her back; the wiry hair covering his groin tickled her buttocks. "I watched him steal a loaf of bread through a baker's window; it was obvious he had never stolen before. I pounded on the window to distract the baker so he wouldn't get caught; then I followed him. Michael shared the loaf of bread with me on a road to Paris."

And once in Paris they had both been trained to be prostitutes.

Victoria listened to what Gabriel did not say as well as that which he said. If Michael had not known how to steal, then he had not been born on the streets.

Michael was what Gabriel was not, a boy who had not been raised in a gutter and been labeled filth. Gabriel had named himself after an angel in order to be worthy of Michael's friendship.

Long seconds passed; steam dispersed into wispy gray tendrils of mist. Beads of water streamed down the copper man and woman inside the shower grotto.

Her bottom ached from Gabriel the man; her heart ached for the boy who had wanted to be an angel.

Hot breath caressed Victoria's left ear. "I begged Michael to let me die."

But Michael had not let him die.

Gabriel's words seared Victoria's skin with the truth: Michael loved Gabriel, just as Gabriel loved Michael.

He didn't deserve to hurt.

"You killed the first man." Anger suddenly resonated inside the copper grotto. "Why didn't you kill the second man?"

Six months earlier Victoria would have been aghast at her bloodthirstiness. She had not known then how pleasure could become a weapon.

"I couldn't find him."

Victoria's heart pounded against five fingers. A man had destroyed Gabriel, and . . .

She tried to turn her head, to see Gabriel; her hair that was caught between them stayed her. "You did not know his name?"

"No."

"And now?"

"I still don't know his name."

But Gabriel knew something about this man who had systematically hurt him. Something that he was not telling Victoria.

Something that had come between the love two angels bore each other.

Victoria's knees ached; the heat of Gabriel's body bound her.

She wanted to touch him; she was afraid to. She was afraid she would cause him more pain.

"How long have you been a proprietor?" she asked, wanting to distract him, wanting to hold him.

Wanting to give him the comfort he still could not take.

Gabriel shifted. He sat on his heels, pulling Victoria back with him so that she sat on hard, hairy thighs instead of kneeling on hard, ungiving copper.

Equally hard flesh prodded her behind.

Victoria's heartbeat quickened.

Gabriel's breathing deepened. "Fourteen years."

I have not touched a woman in fourteen years, eight months, two weeks and six days, he had told her the night she had auctioned off her virginity.

"You built your first house"—Victoria grappled for the truth—"in order to lure this man?"

"Yes."

But he had not been lured. And Gabriel had burned down his house. Only to rebuild it.

"Why did he come back, after all these years?"

Gabriel released Victoria's breast. "For revenge."

"But it was he who hurt you."

Gabriel released Victoria's waist. "For money."

Blackmail is the price of sin . . .

"Did he try to blackmail you?"

Gabriel lifted Victoria to her knees. "For sport."

Instantly the copper-skinned woman inside the grotto was free and once again Victoria could feel the cold metal tub, the wetness of her flesh, the burning discomfort where Gabriel had penetrated her, the slipperiness of the cream between her buttocks.

The utter aloneness of the man behind her.

She could sense Gabriel standing, a stir of air, a slight pop of a bone. A copper-skinned man towered over Victoria inside the shower grotto.

Gabriel stepped over the tub. Victoria stared at a tautly muscled thigh, a hair-studded testicle, pale marble buttocks.

Silently he padded across blue-veined marble, halted in front of the satinwood cabinet that encased the wash basin. Mist clouded the mirror; all she could see of Gabriel were his strong shoulders slick with water, sleek back, narrow hips, tight buttocks, long, long legs and the dim reflection of his bowed head.

Water splashed; steam roiled. Buttocks tightening, Gabriel thrust his hips forward.

Victoria did not have to see his actions to know that he washed his genitals.

Her bottom burned and throbbed.

Her pain. His pain.

Gabriel grabbed the washcloth off the wooden towel rack and plunged it into the basin.

Planting her hands onto the satinwood cabinet encasing the copper tub, Victoria clumsily pulled herself up to her feet.

Gabriel turned, washcloth in hand. His face was pale, remote. Apart from her instead of a part of her.

"Nothing has changed, Victoria."

Victoria *would not* cry, not for herself, not for a fallen angel.

She stepped over the satinwood cabinet encasing the copper tub, slipped on marble, grabbed satinwood paneling to keep from falling. Cold, wet hair slapped her cheeks.

"The man will try to kill you," Gabriel said tonelessly.

Instantly the heat of humiliation chilled.

Gabriel's voice was closer.

Victoria's head snapped up.

He stood over her, male flesh erect.

A single drop of moisture glistened on the bulbous tip of his manhood.

He had been a part of her—front, back.

She wanted him to be part of her still.

Victoria straightened. Her clitoris that he had gently pumped swelled.

More acutely aware of the slickness between her buttocks and the moisture that pooled between her thighs than she was of her next breath, she riposted, "He will try to kill you, too."

Gabriel did not skirt the truth. "He will try to hurt me by hurting you."

Victoria's heart skipped one beat, two. *Who was this man who hunted Gabriel, even as Gabriel hunted him?* "Would it hurt you . . . if he hurt me?"

"Yes."

Her chest tightened. "Why?"

"Because I want you, Victoria."

Her eyes burned.

"I want you to touch me."

Her breath stopped.

"I want you to love me."

Her heart halted.

"Yes, it would hurt me if you were hurt." Silver light danced in the gray shadows that was Gabriel's past. "It would kill me to see you die, because you have touched *me* and not just my sex. You've touched me with your passion and your honesty.

"You said you didn't want to feel desire; neither do I. But I do feel desire; I need you to share that desire. He showed me that by bringing you here. He will see you in my eyes and smell you on my skin. And he will stop at nothing to kill you. Simply because you touched me."

As he had killed Dolly, the prostitute, simply because she had guided Victoria to the House of Gabriel.

Victoria's bravado haunted her. *If you compel me to stay, sir, I will seduce you,* she had threatened.

Then you will pay the consequences, mademoiselle. As will I.

Gabriel had known the danger of her desire. He had lived with the knowledge of what the second man was for almost fifteen years.

Have you ever loved anyone other than Michael, Gabriel?"

"No."

I loved him as a brother.

Victoria's chest tightened to the point that it was difficult to breathe. "I do not regret touching you."

Gabriel stepped closer, alabaster skin pale, blond hair waterdarkened. Hard flesh prodded her stomach. "You will, Victoria."

She inhaled sharply. "What do you want in a woman, Gabriel?"

Warm breath licked her cheek. "You feel compassion for a thirteen-year-old boy who wanted to be an angel."

It was not a question.

Victoria wouldn't lie. "Yes."

"And when you look at me"—a callused fingertip traced her bottom lip—"you see the face of an angel."

Victoria's bottom lip quivered. "What do you see when you look at me, Gabriel?"

Dark eyelashes veiled Gabriel's eyes. Slowly, he traced a trail of fire up her face: hard flesh cupped Victoria's right cheek. "I told you my name isn't Gabriel."

Victoria moistened her lips, tasting his breath, the lye residue of soap on his finger, the pleasure he had given her. "You said you named yourself after Gabriel, therefore your name *is* Gabriel."

Slowly his eyelashes lifted. "And you still want to touch me."

Victoria could not lie. "Yes."

"I cried, Victoria."

Would you cry for an angel, Victoria?

Tears welled up inside her eyes; a single tear leaked from the hard flesh riding her lower stomach. "There's no sin in crying, Gabriel."

No sin in living.

No sin in loving.

"No, there isn't." Cold, wet cloth abraded Victoria's left cheek; it was instantly warmed by hot, hard skin. Gabriel cradled her cheek as if she were made of precious glass. "Crying is natural. When there are no tears, *Victoire*, there is the danger."

Victoire. French for Victoria.

Victoria held perfectly still underneath Gabriel's touch, breathing his breath, inhaling his scent.

"I sent a man to the Hundred Guineas Club," he murmured, as if the club held some significance.

It didn't.

"What is the Hundred Guineas Club?"

Hot breath scorched her lips. "It's a men's club."

"A club where men congregate."

London abounded with men's clubs.

"It is a club where men assume the personas of women," Gabriel said. Waiting for her shock. "Some of the men dress as women."

Victoria had seen a woman's severed hands stuffed inside leather gloves. She refused to be daunted by a man's choice of clothing. "Why did you send a man to the Hundred Guineas Club?"

Gabriel gently cradled her face between his hands. "I sent a man there to whore for me."

To whore . . . for *Gabriel?*

"Surely he did not have to do so if he did not want to," Victoria replied unevenly, heart pounding inside her body, outside of her body.

"He hated it." Gabriel's breath filled her nostrils and her mouth. "Now he hates me."

Yet Gabriel had sent him to the club, knowing that he would hate it.

Victoria fought to keep her hands at her sides and not to touch his body that was so tantalizingly near.

There was danger in touching an angel.

Gabriel would fight the very love he wanted.

"Why did he . . . prostitute himself . . . if he hated it?"

Gabriel's manhood slickly skidded across her stomach. "He did it out of loyalty."

"You asked him to prostitute himself, knowing that he would hate you for it," she breathed into his mouth.

The washcloth was slightly cooler than Gabriel's hand. Rougher. More abrasive. "Yes."

"Why?"

Why had Gabriel deliberately sent someone into a situation that demeaned him? *Knowing* firsthand what emotional damage it would do?

Gabriel's breath stoppered Victoria's lungs; the head of his manhood stoppered her navel. "The second man was not alone when he bid on you."

Victoria's stomach somersaulted.

The second man killed everyone with whom he came into contact. If he had been with someone that night, perhaps the hands inside the gloves had not been Dolly's . . .

"Was the man he was with dressed as a woman?"

Hot breath seared her lips; equally hot flesh scalded her stomach. Slick fluid threaded down her inner thighs; a matching thread of fluid meandered down her lower abdomen. "No."

"But he was a member of the Hundred Guineas Club."

"Yes."

Victoria's fingernails dug into the palms of her hands. "And now he's dead."

"Yes," Gabriel agreed imperturbably. As if death were an everyday occurrence.

On the streets death *was* an everyday occurrence. The women he had earlier referred to—the crawlers who begged from beggars—sat on the steps of the poorhouses, too weak to walk, waiting for it to release them from poverty.

Gabriel's heartbeat pounded against her cheeks and her stomach, timing the seconds until she understood.

"This man who would kill—" *us* "—you . . . Does he impersonate a woman?" Victoria asked, surrounded by the heat of his body and his breath.

"Sometimes."

Images of the women Victoria had seen during the auction flashed through her mind. She had seen no woman who looked as if she were a man in women's clothing.

London streets were more simple than London clubs. On the streets men fought men to inflict the pain that had been inflicted upon them.

There was no rhyme or reason to the man Gabriel described.

There was no sense in the cold and the heat that alternately pulsed inside her veins.

Fear. Desire.

They should not go hand in hand.

"You said he would hurt me . . . sexually," Victoria said, struggling to understand what Gabriel understood. "He does not prefer men over women, then."

Gabriel lightly kissed her left eyelid, lips like gossamer. "It is the power of sex that he enjoys, not the act of sex."

Victoria blinked, eyelashes fluttering against silky smooth skin, the wet flick of a tongue. "You are saying that he is removed from the act of sexual release."

"Yes."

As Gabriel was removed from the act of sexual release.

She skittered away from the comparison.

"And when he kills?" she asked. "Is it inflicting pain that he enjoys, or the power of being able to inflict pain?"

Gabriel kissed her right eyelid, lightly tasted her lashes, a wet lick of heat. "The power."

"So by sending someone to the Hundred Guineas Club," Victoria calmly reasoned, heart pounding, pulses racing, "you hoped to find a clue to lead you to this man who would kill—us."

Us reverberated between them.

"That is what I planned," Gabriel agreed, a gust of hot breath.

"You sent one of the men who let me inside your house." Dawning comprehension flowed through Victoria. Her right eyelash fluttered against his lips. It did not stop her accusation. "You sent him there to punish him."

"I sent him there because he is a former club member." Gabriel's lips skidded off of her eyelashes; he stared down into Victoria's eyes, firmly cupping her face, forcing her to face the truth. "You asked what I wanted in a woman. I'll tell you what I want, Victoria Childers."

But Victoria suddenly did not want to hear.

"I want a woman to touch me, knowing what I am," he said, a lash of hot air, silver gaze relentless. "I'm a begger, a thief, a whore, and a killer. There's nothing I wouldn't do to get the second man. I want you to want me, knowing what I am. I want you to look into my eyes when you take me into your body, and know what it is that you're taking, a begger, a thief, a whore, a killer. I told you I want you to love me, but I can't promise I can love you in return. I can't promise I can save you. I can't promise you won't die. But I can promise you that I would give my life to save yours. I can promise you that I can satisfy your every desire. There's no sex act I haven't done, no sex act I wouldn't do to please you. You were excited by what you saw through the transparent glass. I won't share you with another man, but I can show you what it would feel like to be with two men. All I ask in return is that you let me touch you, that you let me take care of you. And that you share your pleasure with me. Make me see light when you orgasm, Victoria. It's the only light I'll ever see."

Can't promise I can love you . . . Can't promise I can save you . . . Can't promise you won't die.

Won't share you . . .

Victoria couldn't breathe for Gabriel's breath; couldn't feel for Gabriel's heat; couldn't move for the anchor of his manhood.

He had been a successful prostitute because he had learned as a child to disassociate himself from hunger, from cold, from emotional involvement.

But one man had touched him.

It would take a brave woman to love a man such as Monsieur Gabriel, Madame René had said.

But Victoria wasn't brave.

She had become a governess rather than expose her father as a misogynist who hid his hatred of women behind moral righteousness. She had taken care of other women's children rather than marry and discover she was a whore who lusted for a man's love over the fruit of his seed.

Victoria had come to the House of Gabriel to survive, not to die.

She had not come to the House of Gabriel to learn to accept herself by accepting a fallen angel. But she had.

She was not brave.

"I don't need you to take care of me," she managed.

Victoria didn't want to rely upon a man.

Gabriel's hands tightened, hard flesh squeezing, cold cloth abrading. "You wouldn't survive the streets, Victoria."

"You did," she quickly rejoined.

His silver gaze would not let her escape the truth. "I was born on the streets; you were born a lady."

Victoria's past rose up between them, the head of his manhood pulsing against her stomach an acute reminder of a woman's weakness. "My mother ran off with another man."

"You're mother left your father, just as you did," Gabriel said bluntly. "Just as he forced your brother to leave."

"I don't understand what it is that you want from me."

"I told you what I want from you."

He wanted her to accept him, all of him. Beggar. Thief. Whore. *Killer.* All he asked in return was that she share her pleasure.

Victoria licked her lips, a slick flick of her tongue on chapped lips. "You are asking me to . . . live in your house."

"Yes," he said bluntly. Silver eyes guarded.

"Providing we survive."

"Yes."

But for how long?

How long would Gabriel be alive? How long would *she* be alive? Reality was an unwelcome intruder.

"That is not necessary," she said stiffly, suddenly, painfully self-conscious of her too sharp bones and tautly stretched skin and her breasts that jutted out from her chest. "I gave my virginity willingly."

"I didn't take you because you were a virgin."

How difficult it was to admit the truth.

"You were aroused because I flaunted myself in front of you. You would not have been tempted if I had not paraded in front of you . . . naked. Or propositioned you, in front of the transparent mirror."

"I am nightly surrounded by women who do more than flaunt their nakedness, Victoria."

Uncertainty twisted inside Victoria. "But this is different . . ."

"Yes." Gabriel would not let go of her face, her gaze. "It is."

Victoria did not glance away from the starkness inside Gabriel's gaze. "Are you sorry you bid on me?"

The heartbeat that thrummed inside her backside and her vagina and her stomach drummed inside her ears, waiting for his answer.

"No."

Victoria read the truth inside Gabriel's eyes.

Beautiful eyes.

"I didn't see light when I reached orgasm inside the shower, Gabriel."

Pain.

Victoria had hurt an angel.

Steam aureoled his water-darkened head. "What did you see?"

Victoria looked into Gabriel's silver eyes and saw his face reflected in the shower, copper instead of alabaster. "I saw you."

She had seen his pain. She had seen his pleasure.

Memory flashed through Gabriel's eyes: the circling of his flesh; the blossoming of her flesh. The cry of her pleasure.

The endless orgasms he had given her the night before.

The endless orgasms he would give her this night.

But she had not known last night what she knew tonight.

No man had ever wanted to care for her.

Words rushed up into Victoria's throat. "My hair is wet."

The hands cupping her face tightened. "I'll dry it."

Hot tears pricked her eyes. "It's tangled."

"I'll comb it."

Desire trickled down Victoria's thighs; the slickness between her buttocks reminded her of how intimately this man knew her desires.

"I was a virgin last night."

Victoria swallowed. Now where had that come from?

Carnal knowledge glittered inside his gaze. "I know you were a virgin."

"But I didn't bleed."

Darkness banished the silver light inside his eyes. "I didn't want you to bleed."

Victoria remembered the bulbous crown of his manhood sliding inside her, inch by inch, orgasm by orgasm . . . The rising heat inside her would not be contained. "Did you see light when I reached my first orgasm?"

"Yes."

"But you only put three fingers inside me."

And not the five he had inserted inside the woman whom he had sought to be a part of.

The heat inside Gabriel's gaze took Victoria's breath away. "You're not ready for that kind of penetration."

"But I will be . . . someday?" she asked uncertainly.

If *he* survived.

If *she* survived.

If he wanted her when danger was no longer an aphrodisiac.

"Someday, Victoria, I will give you five fingers." His face was marble-hard. "Someday I will touch you so deeply and fill you so completely that you will never regret touching me."

Victoria fought for oxygen that was not heated by his breath. "You already have, Gabriel."

Heat engulfed her.

She was going to drown in his gaze. "Please let go of me."

The silver fire glittering inside Gabriel's eyes stilled. Warm breath feathered her lips. "Why?"

"Because I think I am going to orgasm," Victoria said frankly, voice ringing in the misty air.

Light and darkness shimmied inside Gabriel's gaze.

The knowledge of her desire. The knowledge to appease her desire.

Lowering his head, Gabriel lightly rimmed her lips; his tongue stabbed through her womb. In the next heartbeat he was gone. While Victoria's body throbbed on the brink of climax.

As it had throbbed inside the shower, his stomach and chest plastered against her back and buttocks, his *bite* buried so deeply inside her they had been one body.

A towel caught up Victoria's hair—Gabriel gently dried it, each sensuous rub a palpable caress. She stood stock still while he dried her buttocks—skimming over the crevice that still bore the remnants of his penetration—patting dry her legs . . .

A dull thump resonated inside her ears. Coldness abruptly abraded the sensitive area between Victoria's buttocks.

Her eyelids shot open—when had she closed them? "What—"

"I hurt you, Victoria." A muscled arm circled her waist, held her securely in position. Gentle, firm pressure washed away the remnants of the cream, circling around and around. "Let me take care of you . . ."

Victoria forcibly relaxed her muscles. "I would prefer that the care be mutual."

Gabriel washed her and washed her until she squirmed for him to stop, and then she squirmed for him to do more than wash her. Victoria reached behind her . . .

Only to grasp empty air.

She fought down a surge of frustration. "Gabriel, I *will* touch you."

Gabriel's voice came from the vicinity of the washbasin. "You already have, Victoria."

Victoria pivoted. Gabriel turned, comb in hand.

"I will touch more than your"—Victoria hesitated briefly, raised her chin a notch, defying the society that forbade women to use anything but the most harmless of platitudes, chicken bosom for chicken breast, gentleman cow for bull, unmentionables for a man's trousers—"your cock."

Silently Gabriel stalked her, an ivory comb in his right hand. Long, pale fingers extended toward her. "Then take my hand, Victoria."

She stared at the long, naked fingers that had been a part of her the night before. She stared at the long, naked penis that had shortly before been a part of her, and would soon be so again. A tiny heartbeat pulsed in the bulbous, purple-hued head.

Gabriel's desire.

Knees suddenly weak, she took his hand.

Victoria opened the bathroom door and stepped ahead of Gabriel into darkness.

Blinding light pierced her.

Victoria blinked.

The solid warmth of Gabriel's fingers disappeared. "Sit down on the bed."

Victoria mutely sat on the edge of the bed, mattress dipping, springs squeaking, feet firmly placed together on the wooden floor.

Her bottom was tender.

Stooping, shoulder muscles flexing, testicles dangling, Gabriel grabbed three logs from the brass scuttle and threw them onto the fire that still miraculously burned. Black ashes and gray smoke billowed up the chimney.

It seemed a lifetime since she had stared at that same fire.

"I will try to let you touch me, Victoria." Gabriel's voice was muffled, words directed at the flame that slowly curled up the fresh logs.

He would try to let her touch him.

He would try not to let her die.

But he could not promise either.

"I would enjoy giving you pleasant memories to replace the painful ones, Gabriel."

Gabriel turned toward her. "Every time you orgasm, you give me another memory."

She *would not* cry.

Victoria watched Gabriel as he silently padded toward her, long legs eating up the distance, engorged *bitte* battling the air. "I had never seen a man prior to my unemployment. Five months ago I saw one on a street corner. I didn't realize his trousers were open. I thought he had a sausage dangling out of his pocket."

Gabriel halted in front of her. There was no mistaking the flesh that stabbed the air in front of her for anything but what it was. "There is a French term called *andouille a col roule.*"

Victoria threw her head back. "What does that mean?"

"Sausage with a rolled down collar," Gabriel said solemnly.

The twin leathery pouches beneath his manhood were tight.

"What are a man's"—Victoria swallowed, recalling English street slang—"a man's ballocks called in French?"

"*Noisettes.*" Hazelnuts. "*Noix.*" Nuts. "*Olives.*" Olives with an accent. "*Petite oignons.*"

Victoria's eyes crinkled in sudden laughter. "Little onions?"

An answering laugh glimmered inside the depths of Gabriel's silver eyes. "*Croquignoles.*"

"Biscuits," she translated.

The laughter abruptly leaked out of his gaze. "*Bonbons.*"

Victoria's glance involuntarily sought out the twin objects of their discussion. "I enjoy the flavor of bonbons."

Tentatively she reached out a curious finger. Gabriel's testicles were ridged, as rough as the hair-studded leather they resembled.

Pure, raw energy slammed into Victoria. It did not come from her.

Slowly Victoria lifted her hand. Holding Gabriel's gaze, she tasted her fingertip, a deliberate swirl of her tongue. "You do not taste like *petite oignons*, sir."

Victoria had never before seen naked need inside a man's eyes; she saw it now, in Gabriel's eyes.

"What do I taste like, Mademoiselle Childers?" he asked hoarsely.

Victoria tasted her finger again. "I would say you taste of . . . *les noix de* Gabriel." The nuts of Gabriel.

The laughter immediately sprang back into his eyes, light dispelling the darkness.

Immediately she dropped her hand, feet primly together on the floor, breasts hot and heavy. "Thank you."

"For what?" Gabriel asked tautly, every muscle inside his body tensing as if to ward off pain.

"For allowing me to be a woman."

And not calling her the whore that every gentleman would have called her.

One second Victoria sat before Gabriel, the next second she was airborne. The squeak of springs surrounded her. A bounce of mattress found her sitting between Gabriel's legs, muscled thighs gripping her hips.

"Don't ever thank me, Victoria."

Gabriel's voice was harsh.

Victoria opened her mouth to retort. Ivory teeth tugged through a knot of tangles.

Deliberately she grasped hard, hairy thighs, fingernails digging into muscled flesh, sharing her pain. The ivory teeth of the comb worked through the knotted tangles.

Victoria did not move, overcome by sudden recall. Her mother had brushed her hair.

But she didn't want to think about her mother.

Heat radiated from the V of Gabriel's legs.

"What are a woman's breasts called in French?" she asked abruptly.

"*Melons.*"

"Melons," Victoria translated. "That's very . . . quaint. Much better than apple dumplings, I'm sure." A popular slang on the streets of London.

Tears abruptly pricked her eyes. The small hurt inflicted by the unknotting of another tangle instantly disappeared in a glide of ivory.

"Miches," Gabriel murmured.

Victoria smiled wryly. "Loaves of bread."

The staple of every diet.

"Ananas."

"What is that?" she asked with a catch in her breath.

"Pineapples."

Victoria's nails dug more deeply into Gabriel's thighs—he did not flinch. "I've never eaten pineapple. Is it sweet?"

"Sweet." The knot in her hair yielded to ivory teeth. "Tart. Prickly on the outside. Juicy on the inside."

The governess in Victoria surfaced. "A woman's breasts are not prickly."

"Your nipples, Victoria, are very hard. They prick my skin."

So, she imagined, did her nails. She unsheathed them.

The comb glided effortlessly through her hair. Victoria's head fell back.

"I used to burn and throb between my legs." She stared up at the white enameled ceiling. "I didn't know that the button of flesh between my thighs was called a clitoris, I only knew that it was wrong to touch myself there. But then, when I had no place to go, I did touch myself. I didn't see light when I touched myself, Gabriel."

Victoria waited for condemnation, confessing what no lady should confess.

"What did you see, Victoria?" Gabriel's voice was hot and moist, there against the side of her head, her ear . . .

"I saw darkness, Gabriel."

The gliding ivory stopped; hard fingers found the top of Victoria's thighs. A single finger worked between her legs, her lips . . .

"I saw cold and hunger and loneliness . . ." Lightning bolted through Victoria's clitoris, the seesaw motion of Gabriel's finger; she bit back a gasp. "But I didn't see any sin."

Prickly skin nuzzled aside her hair—Gabriel's cheek. Scalding heat licked her ear—Gabriel's tongue. "Remember, Victoria."

The bedroom tilted.

Victoria lay on her back, mounded velvet indenting her buttocks, linen sheets smooth against her spine. Brass glinted out of the corner of her eyes, the bed rails.

The mattress shifted; Gabriel reached for the tin on the nightstand, his hip abrading her hip. Metal scraped metal, thudded against wood.

Victoria tensely waited, unable to breathe past the scent of his heat and the closeness of his body.

Mattress dipping, Gabriel straightened, a rolled up sheath of rubber between his thumb and forefinger.

Anticipation squeezed Victoria's lungs.

Dark lashes shielded Gabriel's eyes.

Victoria stared at the jagged shadows gouging his cheeks, at the thick stalk of blue-veined flesh he held in his right hand, glanced back up at the shadow of his face, down again to the engorged purple crown that was swallowed by a cap of rubber. He pinched the tip of the condom. And then there were no blue veins, no gradation of skin color, only a long, thick rubber sheath that ended in a curly thatch of brownish-blond hair. A tiny nipple—the end of the condom—protruded from the bulbous head of his sheathed penis.

Victoria raised her eyelids.

Gabriel was prepared for her. "I am just over nine and one-half inches long when fully erect."

Gabriel read Victoria's thoughts inside her eyes. He waited for her to ask the question.

To pit one angel against another.

Victoria did not ask it. She did not need to know how Gabriel compared to another man. Instead she asked, "Why did you leave space at the end of the condom?"

"For my sperm."

Victoria had felt his seed spurt inside her other orifice, a hot jet of fluid. She wondered what it would feel like spurting inside her vagina, bathing her womb.

Gabriel leaned over her and grasped her hands. "Remember . . ."

Victoria's arms stretched over her head, fingers guided to cold metal. Closing his fingers around hers, Gabriel locked their hands around the brass bed railing.

"Remember, Victoria..." Gabriel murmured, a whisper of breath caressing her cheek, manhood lightly nudging her femininity.

"I remember, Gabriel."

Slowly he sank down on top of her, a prickly blanket of human flesh, chest compressing her breasts, stomach molding her stomach, hips sinking between her thighs.

Victoria remembered ... how cold and barren her life had been. Because of one man's hatred of women.

Victoria remembered ... the pain Gabriel had experienced. Because of one man's ... what?

She did not know why the second man had hurt Gabriel.

She did not know why he had not killed Gabriel when he had been chained and helpless. Begging to die.

She did not know how love turned into hatred. She only knew that it did.

A husband's love for his wife.

A brother's love for his sister.

The love between two angels.

Cold air surrounded her right hand—her knuckles, her palm. With his left hand Gabriel found the core of her vulva. Nippled rubber seared her, stretched her, penetrated her, filled her.

Gasping, Victoria convulsively grasped the brass rails in both hands.

"Don't ever forget what I am"—scorching breath filled her lungs, a scalding tongue rimmed her lips— "or what I can do ..."

Victoria could see every pore in Gabriel's marble-perfect skin, could count every dark, thick eyelash framing his eyes, could feel every nerve inside her body stretched to accommodate the rubber-sheathed penis that pulsed inside her.

A pale circle shone inside his eyes—her face. Did Gabriel see himself inside her eyes? "I remember everything you've ever said, Gabriel."

You have hungry eyes. Like Michael's.

It wasn't whoring that made me what I am, it was loving.

There were two angels . . . I didn't know they were angels.

I wanted to have eyes that hungered . . .

How could Gabriel not see the hunger inside his own eyes?

"And knowing where I came from"—hot breath filled her mouth; her vagina was gorged on his manhood—"knowing what I am, do you want me, Victoria?"

Victoria did not have to pause to think about her answer. "Yes," she said, and cried out at the tunneling flesh that lodged inside her throat and knocked the breath out of her lungs.

Gabriel swallowed Victoria's cry. The mattress dipped, and then his left hand swallowed her right hand and he was sucking her soul into his mouth, groin grinding into her groin, manhood knocking at the very heart of her, mattress a squeaky symphony. He licked her tongue; he nibbled her tongue. He suckled her tongue as if it were all that kept him alive. Gabriel licked and nibbled and suckled Victoria until his breath became her breath, his flesh her flesh, and she didn't care if she died; there was a pleasure beyond death.

A light beyond darkness.

The light was Gabriel—his tongue, his lips, his hands, his manhood that slickly pistoned between the lips of her sex and the walls of her vagina.

Victoria's back bowed, legs climbing hair-studded thighs, vagina yawning wider, taking him deeper . . .

"Look at me, Victoria."

Victoria with difficulty opened her eyes.

Silver eyes were waiting for hers.

Slowly the silver shrank until all Victoria could see was Gabriel and a pale-faced woman reflected inside his eyes. The images exploded in a burst of internal light.

A woman cried out; it was not followed by the cry of a man.

Slowly Gabriel's face swam back into focus. Sweat beaded his face; agony laced his voice. *"J'en vous encore."*

I need more.

Words filled her mouth, her soul. "Give me more, Victoria."
More pleasure. More orgasms.
"Show me the light."
Victoria opened her body and gave Gabriel what he needed.
More pleasure. More orgasms.
Memories to lighten the darkness.

Chapter

21

Gabriel's eyelids snapped open, heart pounding.

Darkness blinded him; it smelled of sex and sweat. Liquid heat pooled on his left thigh.

Instantly he remembered . . . pounding hot water. Suffocating steam. Victoria.

She had touched him.

She touched him still.

Her body lay curled in a ball against his left side, head pillowed on his shoulder, leg riding his thigh. The liquid heat of her satisfaction saturated his leg.

His scalp tightened.

He could feel the second man; smell him over the scent of Victoria.

Gabriel had no weapons in either the nightstand or the armoire; his cane, along with the derringer, bowie knife and Adams revolver were in his study.

He was Victoria's only means of protection. And he was unable to protect her.

Rage chased fear.

Victoria had shown him light again and again; he would not let her die.

Gabriel carefully eased out from underneath Victoria's head and her knee. Cold air evaporated the wet heat that pooled on his left thigh; icy wood impacted his feet.

The darkness was his ally. If Gabriel could not see the second man, then the second man could not see him.

Stealthily, he padded toward the study door.

The sensation of being watched dissipated, as if a door had closed.

Gabriel halted, every sense alert. He filtered out the smell of sex, the soft, rhythmical sound of Victoria's breathing, his heartbeat . . .

There was no one inside the room save for him and Victoria.

Now.

There was no doubt inside his mind that just moments earlier they had not been alone.

Gabriel had designed the bedchamber door to open into the study, so that no one could use the door to hide behind inside the bedchamber. Someone could very well be hiding on the opposite side, however, someone who waited for Gabriel to enter the study.

Someone armed with a knife or a gun.

Gabriel was not afraid to die. But he was suddenly, heart-stoppingly frightened for Victoria.

Inside the shower he had shown her how easy it was to make a woman—or a man—beg for release; he did not want her to learn how easy it was to make a woman—or a man—beg for death.

He flung the bedchamber door back, catching it just before it slammed the wall so as not to awaken Victoria.

There was no one behind the door.

There was no one inside the study.

But there had been. The second man's presence lingered in the air like cheap perfume.

The silver cane leaned against the couch; the Adams revolver and holster were draped over the blue leather couch arm.

They were undisturbed, like Victoria's sleep.

There was only one way to enter—or exit—his suite.

Gabriel yanked the Adams revolver out of the holster and strode across the carpet. He jerked open the satinwood door.

Allen leaned against the wall, black hair gleaming with moon-silver highlights, black eyes alert. Immediately, he straightened.

He was neither surprised nor embarrassed nor alarmed to find his employer standing before him naked with a revolver in his hand: whores, pimps, beggars, cutthroats and thieves were not easily discomfited. Whereas Gabriel was all too aware that Allen wore a holster underneath his black coat.

Had it been Allen instead of the second man who had entered his suite?

"Good afternoon, sir," Allen said politely.

Afternoon.

"What time is it?" Gabriel asked sharply.

"After four, sir."

Gabriel had instructed Gaston to find out everything he could about Mitchell Delaney, and to report to him promptly.

Dread knotted his stomach. The killing would continue as long as the second man lived. "Where is Gaston?"

"He tried waking you earlier, sir," Allen said easily.

Gabriel's eyes narrowed. No one had tried to wake him . . .

Immediately he remembered where he had slept.

Gaston would have knocked on the study door, or perhaps not. But finding the study empty, he would not have entered Victoria's bedchamber.

Had it been Gaston whom Gabriel had sensed in the suite?

"When did Gaston try to wake me?"

"He has been here several times, sir." Allen's black eyes did not waver. "Most recently he was here an hour ago."

So it had not been Gaston who had awakened Gabriel.

Allen outwardly showed no interest in either Gabriel's nakedness or the fact that he came from a woman. But there was no mistaking the smell of sex.

Allen knew he had been with Victoria. Gaston, too, would have known where Gabriel slept, else he would have awakened him.

The rumor that Gabriel had purchased a woman had already spread throughout London. The fact that he had fucked her would spread even more rapidly.

Perhaps it was already spreading.

Gaston was the only other person with a key to his suite.

He could have given it to Allen. Gaston trusted the men and women whom Gabriel employed.

"Were you inside my suite today, Allen?"

Allen did not blink. "No, sir. I do not have a key, sir."

The fewer keys to his suite, the fewer people who could be killed—or bribed—to obtain them. But there had been someone . . .

"How long have you been on guard?" Gabriel asked.

"Since noon, sir."

"Where were you ten minutes earlier?"

"Here, sir."

Gabriel could not afford to trust his employees as Gaston trusted them.

"That is impossible, Allen," Gabriel said silkily, dangerously.

"No, sir, it is not impossible." Allen's gaze did not waver from Gabriel's. "I was here, guarding you and the woman as I was instructed to do."

"Then how do you explain the fact that a man was inside my suite only minutes earlier?"

"I cannot, sir." Anger glimmered inside Allen's black eyes—anger and hurt. "Begging your pardon, sir, but an intruder would have to enter your suite through this door. The only way he could do that was if he killed me. We are loyal to you, sir."

Allen's anger could stem from the fact that Gabriel did not trust him. Or it could stem from the fact that Gabriel had outwardly dismissed John and Stephen—no one knew that they were still in Gabriel's employ, not even Gaston.

Or Allen's anger could stem from the fact that Gabriel had burned down his house six months earlier.

Anger, like a conscience, could be preyed upon.

Fear, too, could be preyed upon.

Gabriel had eaten, slept, pissed and shit these past years for the sole purpose of killing the second man. The smell and the sight of him had tainted Gabriel's every waking thought, his every dream.

The feeling of being watched when he awoke could have stemmed from a dream. The scent of him in the dark bedchamber could have been conjured from memory.

Gabriel's concern for Victoria *could* be making him paranoid.

He could not afford to trust. To feel. To want.

To need.

But he did feel. He did want.

He did need.

History was repeating itself.

Six months earlier Michael had allowed his feelings for a woman to interfere with his judgment. Michael would have been killed if Gabriel had not interfered.

Michael would have died because of a woman.

Michael might still die because of a woman.

Because of Victoria. A woman who had become a servant rather than be dependent upon a man who belittled women; a woman who had sold her virginity rather than succumb to a man who victimized her because of her virginity.

And now she was dependent upon Gabriel; victimized because of a man she had never met.

We do what we must in order to survive.

"Send Gaston up." He hid the fear pumping through his blood behind the mask that was Gabriel. "I will watch over the woman for the time it takes you to get him."

"Yes, sir," Allen said.

Gabriel remembered the feel of Victoria's body pressed against his. She was so thin he could snap her bones like twigs.

"Have Pierre prepare breakfast *à deux*," he said abruptly. *I've never eaten pineapple. Is it sweet?* "Tell him to include fresh pineapple. I will ring when I want the tray sent up."

Gabriel did not wait for Allen to respond. He closed the door.

Victoria drew him toward the bedchamber.

Light from the window in the study sliced across the wooden floor. The scent of sex and sweat and satisfaction permeated the air.

Hers. His.

Gabriel's flesh immediately hardened.

Victoria lay as Gabriel had left her, damp hair spread over the pillow instead of his shoulder; leg sprawled over the sheet instead of his thighs.

He remembered the silk of her skin, slick with water in the shower, slippery with sweat in his bed.

He remembered the wet silk of her hair and the heat of her buttocks between his thighs as he combed through the tangles of their past.

He remembered the touch of Victoria's finger on his testicles. The sight of Victoria tasting her finger flashed through the darkness of his life, dark hair blackened by water, cheeks flushed with excitement, blue eyes glinting in the electric light.

I would say you taste of . . . les noix de *Gabriel.*

No woman had ever played with him. They had climaxed for him, but they had not played with him.

They had not touched him.

They had not loved him.

Victoria's eyelids popped open.

Blue eyes studied silver eyes, color blackened by darkness, need shadowed.

Victoria had witnessed his naked orgasm. And not once had she asked the question he could not answer.

Gabriel had thought himself impervious: to pain, to pleasure. To a woman.

Once again the second man had proven him wrong.

Gabriel tensely waited for Victoria to regret touching a homeless *fumier.*

"I got your pillow wet," Victoria said in a small voice. She sounded far, far younger than the thirty-four-year-old woman Gabriel knew her to be.

"I'm not concerned about my pillow."

"I got you wet."

A sudden smile creased Gabriel's face, secure in the knowledge Victoria couldn't see the smile or the vulnerability that lay behind it.

"Yes, you did," he agreed solemnly.

"I'm wet now," Victoria said guilelessly.

Gabriel had had two orgasms only hours earlier. He should not be hard. He should not want Victoria so badly that his testicles ached.

She was everything he had ever wanted in a woman.

She was death in disguise.

"Show me," Gabriel said silkily, knowing the danger of playing sex games but unable to resist the temptation that was Victoria Childers.

"It's dark," Victoria reasoned. Gabriel pictured her teaching a silver-haired child; she would speak in that same tone of voice. "You can't see."

"I can see."

Gabriel could see the trap that was Victoria.

Gabriel could see that he had seriously underestimated the second man.

Victoria flipped the covers aside, bed squeaking, cloth rustling.

Her skin glowed like pale, polished marble. She had long, slender legs.

Gabriel had felt them wrapped around his waist; he wondered what they would feel like thrown over his shoulders.

He could not help himself. He sat on the bed and touched Victoria, the perfect bait.

The wet heat of her fisted inside his groin.

Her clitoris was swollen with need.

Gently he slipped his finger between her lips and stared at the shadow that was her sex. The lips of her labia furled around his middle finger, as they had furled around his cock only hours earlier.

She was so wet he could drown in her. She was so responsive that he wouldn't mind dying inside her.

But there were more lives at stake than his own.

A tentative hand grasped his penis.

Gabriel stiffened, bracing himself. The expected memories did not come.

Gabriel would pay for the reprieve; he just didn't know how.

He didn't know when the second man would come to take away the gift of Victoria Childers.

A padded thumb swirled around the crown of his penis; the touch vibrated inside Gabriel's chest.

"You're wet, too," Victoria whispered, unable to hide her excitement.

She was too new to sex games to draw out the arousal. Gabriel had been trained in sex games since he was thirteen.

He concentrated on the changes he had created in Victoria's body instead of the vulnerability she inspired.

Her plump flesh was hot and swollen, from both his use and her desire. Her vagina was an open ring instead of a tiny fissure. It easily accepted his finger.

Gabriel was instantly gripped by molten silk.

Victoria drew in a deep breath; at the same time her fingers tightened around his penis.

He hurt her. The ache of his penetration dully throbbed inside Gabriel's chest.

She parted her legs to give him better access. So that she could take away *his* hurt.

Gabriel wanted to reach inside Victoria and feel her womb convulse around his hand; instead, he withdrew his finger. It was coated with slick heat.

The essence of Victoria Childers. A woman who feared passion, only to embrace it.

Just as she would embrace an angel.

Gabriel smeared her essence onto her lips.

Victoria jerked back, "What—"

Gabriel took her lips, her words, her breath, her essence.

He had told Victoria that sharing his pain and his pleasure inside the shower hadn't changed anything. He had lied.

It had changed everything.

The second man had given him Victoria, knowing that Gabriel would want more than an hour or a day or a week with her. He had known Gabriel would die to get more of her.

Victoria tasted of salty-sweet satisfaction.

Using his tongue and his teeth, Gabriel took more from her—a tiny nip of pain, soothing licks of pleasure. He used every ounce of his expertise to take Victoria's soul with his kiss, because that was what he had been trained to do.

Not enough.

Gabriel lifted his head up, lips teasing instead of devouring, and whispered, "Taste yourself, Victoria."

Gabriel did not give her time to agree or to disagree; he licked inside her mouth and transferred her essence onto her tongue.

She held still, unresponsive.

Gabriel made her respond. He licked the roof of her mouth.

Victoria sucked in his breath.

He wanted more.

He had the ability to make her give him more.

Taking her nipple between his fingers, he gently pinched and pulled, knowing that with each pinch, each tug, her womb contracted.

Her fingers that gripped him squeezed and pulled his penis in time to his fingers that squeezed and pulled her nipple. Victoria's tongue gently licked at his tongue, underneath his tongue. Giving as well as taking.

Gabriel squeezed his eyelids shut and concentrated on the feel and the taste of Victoria instead of the rhythmic squeezing and pulling that squeezed and pulled his very testicles.

A soft, short knock interrupted the pounding of his heart.

Gaston had arrived.

Gabriel did not stop pinching and tugging Victoria's nipple. He did not stop licking her.

He did not stop wanting what he could not have.

A home.

A woman.

A soft preorgasmic moan vibrated his tongue.

A sharp preorgasmic tingle shot up his urethra.

The outer door to his suite opened.

It could be Gaston.

Or it could be the second man.

Gabriel imagined Victoria's womb contracting about his hand while he mentally followed the man inside the suite.

A soft thud sounded, leather impacting marble.

Victoria agitatedly moved her head from side to side. Gabriel grasped the nape of her neck with his right hand and ruthlessly followed her, mouth glued to hers, tongue licking, fingers pinching and tugging.

She was almost there.

Victoria squeezed Gabriel harder, taking him with her.

A soft swish erupted through the open bedroom door; the man inside his study had sat down in the leather chair facing Gabriel's desk. At the same time Victoria's body bowed; fingers knotted in Gabriel's hair.

Pain. Pleasure.

Hungry blue and violet exploded the blackness behind Gabriel's eyelids. Victoria's convulsing womb briefly fluttered around his fingers and then he came inside Victoria's hand and the feel of her orgasm was gone, replaced by the presence of the man inside his study and the awareness of the information he possessed.

Slowly Gabriel eased the pinching, tugging rhythm that had for one brief moment become his orgasm. The apparatus that was his cock spurted three times, four times, five times . . .

Victoria collapsed, sobbing for air that he finally allowed her. His erection subsided; his need did not.

Her fingers clutching his hair was an intimacy he had not allowed in almost fifteen years.

Gabriel wanted more Victoria, more intimacy.

Gently he released Victoria's nipple and caressed her cheek, reaching too high. Her eyelids fluttered against his fingertips like the tantalizing flutter of an orgasm.

Cocooning Victoria, Gabriel kissed her eyelid. It fluttered against his lips.

The knot inside his groin spread to his chest.

"You . . ." Victoria gulped air. "My breast . . . it was . . ."

"Shh . . ." Gabriel pressed his lips against hers: he did not want Gaston to overhear how vulnerable Victoria was in her passion. "Go back to sleep, Victoria. I have to go. I'll be back later."

He sat up.

The fingers fisted inside his hair tightened; at the same time Victoria released his quiescent flesh.

Gabriel did not see the hand that reached up until it touched his chin. It was cold and sticky.

Before he could react, warm fingers smeared cold, sticky fluid onto his mouth—his sperm.

Victoria smeared his sperm onto his lips. And then she licked his sperm off his lips.

And then she licked the seam between his lips.

Gabriel didn't want to taste himself. He wanted nothing to do with his body that had betrayed him.

He opened his mouth for Victoria. And did not know why he did so.

Gabriel allowed Victoria to share with him the taste of his seed. And did not know why the mechanical release of a male whore tasted like hope.

The butterfly flutter of Victoria's satisfaction resonated inside his chest.

And Gabriel knew . . .

Slipping out of Victoria's kiss and the fingers that held his hair, Gabriel stood up and flipped the covers up over her naked body, darkly silhouetted against pale sheets. Blindly he grabbed a coat, trousers and a pair of boots from the armoire; he took socks, a shirt and a handkerchief from the chest. From the floor by the bed, he scooped up the used condom.

. . . Gabriel knew that the second man had won. He just did not know at what.

Chapter

22

Victoria listened to familiar sounds, an opening drawer, a drawer closing . . . Gabriel rifling through the armoire.

Silver glinted; Gabriel approached the bed.

Her calming heartbeat accelerated.

Gabriel reached down, quickly straightened, an elongated rubber sheath in his left hand, his clothes bundled up underneath his right arm. He stepped into black shadow. The bathroom door quietly closed behind him.

Victoria's fingers were sticky. Her lips and tongue burned.

She had tasted herself; it had been surprising, certainly, but it had not been revolting. Then she had felt Gabriel's orgasm swell inside her hand as her orgasm had swelled between his fingers.

Faint sounds penetrated the bathroom door—the splatter of water on water, the decided flush of the toilet, water splattering marble, a quick, sharp tap—an ivory toothbrush impacting the edge of the marble basin?

Her chest tightened.

It was endearingly intimate, listening to Gabriel perform his morning toilet.

Victoria reached underneath the covers and touched her left nipple.

It was hard and swollen. As Gabriel's manhood had been hard and swollen.

She had not known that a woman could orgasm by having her nipple squeezed. She had not known how sticky a man's ejaculation would be or how quickly the thick, viscous fluid chilled or how salty it tasted.

She had not known that a woman's body could ache yet be replete with satisfaction.

A soft swish interrupted her thoughts. Gabriel exited the bathroom, silently padded out of the bedchamber.

She bit her lip to keep from calling him back.

He would be back, he had said.

Victoria believed him.

The man who had written the letters, she thought on a note of contempt, was a poor excuse for a man.

Muted voices penetrated the bedroom door. Gabriel had a visitor.

He had told her to go back to sleep. But Victoria didn't want to sleep.

She wanted more of Gabriel.

Victoria threw back the bedcovers. The sheets smelled of Gabriel, of her, of their combined sweat.

The hard wooden floor was an icy awakening.

Gabriel could die.

She could die.

Victoria stepped into the bathroom. And remembered the sight of Gabriel's erection piercing the steam.

Victoria stepped into the copper tub. And remembered how Gabriel had utilized the Liver Spray.

A grin hitched up her lips. Every household should possess a combination shower and bath.

Immediately her thoughts returned to Gabriel.

Was he eating breakfast?

Deftly she twisted off the shower cock. There was no resemblance whatsoever between it and Gabriel. Gabriel, unlike the brass apparatus, felt both pain and pleasure.

He could reject touch, but he had not rejected her touch when she grabbed his hair to pull him closer. He had not rejected her touch when she smeared his sperm onto his lips—petal-soft lips—and tasted him.

He had let her share the taste of his pleasure with him.

Gabriel had hung up the damp towel. Victoria patted herself dry with it.

He had rinsed out the washcloth he had cleansed her with the night before and hung it up to dry beside her worn silk drawers.

There's no sex act I haven't done, no sex act I wouldn't do to please you.

She hadn't told Gabriel that she didn't want another man.

She hadn't told Gabriel . . . so many things.

The comb—it was still in the bedroom. Victoria hurriedly brushed her teeth.

The flip of a wooden switch turned blackness into a lit bed-chamber.

There were the brass rails that Gabriel had laced her fingers around. He had clamped his fingers over hers and held on to her while the bed beneath them shook and quaked.

The logs Gabriel had stacked the fireplace with the night before were a pile of black-and-gray ashes.

Time was slipping away.

Rummaging inside the boxes neatly stacked beside Gabriel's chest, Victoria retrieved silk drawers. A pair of buckled kid slippers. The corset—it had garters sewn into the front and back panels—silk stockings, petticoats, chemise—no, the corset had no whalebones that required protective covering. Putting back the chemise, she lifted up the golden brown dress out of its rose-petal printed coffin.

All the while she strained to hear Gabriel: she did not. Victoria did not have to open the bedchamber door to know that he was not inside his study.

The front of the corded silk dress fastened with tiny eyelets. Victoria's wool gowns had been simple shirtwaists with front buttons. Her fingers were painstakingly slow with the unfamiliar closure. Ruthlessly she combed her hair.

Stockings . . . Stockings . . . What had she done with the stockings?

Brown silk gleamed on the back of the satinwood valet chair.

Securing the stockings to the bottom of the corset took considerably more time than it had to locate them. The elastic clasps weren't as elastic as they should be; or perhaps the stockings were not as long as they should be.

Victoria thought of Gabriel choosing the corset, the stockings, the dimity bustle . . . The garter clasps snapped over the top of the stockings.

The kid slippers, dyed to match the wine-colored garniture on her gown, fit her feet like a glove. Forcibly she thrust aside the cost of such luxury.

Globular stains darkened the edge of the sheet where Gabriel had ejaculated.

She lightly touched the largest stain. It was still damp.

The taste of Gabriel lingered underneath the bite of tooth powder.

Victoria swung open the bedchamber door, silk rustling, air swooshing.

The study was empty.

Like Victoria's body.

The overhead chandelier battled the coming sunset.

Or perhaps the sun had already set. In the winter months it was difficult to tell when foggy day became foggy night.

Gabriel had promised he would die in order to save her life. But Victoria didn't want him to die.

She didn't want fear to diminish the pleasure that still pulsated throughout her entire body.

A silver tray sat on the black-marble-topped desk. Victoria smelled—she picked up the lid—sausage and egg omelet. She did not recognize the thick, meaty slices of fruit in the small, translucent china bowl. She did not need to.

Tears clogged her nose.

Victoria had said she had not tasted pineapple. Gabriel now provided her with the opportunity.

She picked up a yellow slice of the exotic fruit between her thumb and forefinger, juice dripping.

It was tart yet sweet. Exactly as Gabriel had described pineapple. She licked her fingers.

Drowning in silk and satin—how quickly she had become accustomed to nakedness—she sat down in Gabriel's chair.

Victoria remembered the taste of his kiss; she licked a drop of pineapple juice off her lips, and tasted Gabriel. She held up the sausage—it was far smaller than Gabriel—and bit off the end.

Abruptly her appetite perished.

Victoria could die; Gabriel could die.

She pushed away from the desk—she had to grab the edge of the marble top to keep from catapulting into the wall. Gabriel's chair had wheels. Shakily she stood up.

Was Gabriel inside his house, attending business?

A different man guarded the door. He had thick auburn hair that flowed down his back.

Victoria was momentarily taken aback at his exotic beauty.

Was he a prostitute?

Stoically he returned her stare. "May I be of help, ma'am?"

There was no question of his origin: he was English through and through.

Victoria had never before seen anyone like him in England.

She wondered if Mr.—*Monsieur* Gaston had apprised him of the jar of cream she had requested.

Victoria did not doubt for one second that the emerald-eyed man before her was aware of the many purposes for which it could be used.

She squared her shoulders. "I would like to see Mr."—she would not be a hypocrite, no doubt every person inside the House of Gabriel knew of her relationship with its proprietor—"I would like to see Gabriel, please."

There was neither approval nor condemnation inside his green eyes. "Mr. Gabriel is not here."

Victoria's stomach clenched.

He would come back.

The house was Gabriel's home, whether he wanted to accept it or not. And the man before her was a part of Gabriel's family.

Victoria suddenly wanted to see Gabriel's home and visit his family. "The House of Gabriel is very beautiful."

"Yes, ma'am."

"I would enjoy seeing more of it."

The guard's expression did not alter. "That isn't possible, ma'am."

Victoria refused to be intimidated. "Why not?"

Men and women of wealth visited it every night.

"My instructions are to guard this door."

"Your instructions are to protect me," Victoria said firmly.

"Yes, ma'am."

The knowledge of what had happened to one unprotected woman was foremost in both of their thoughts.

Victoria forcefully pushed aside the picture of crimson-stained gloves.

She tilted her chin in challenge. "Which are you instructed to do, sir, to guard this door or to guard me?"

"Both," the auburn-haired guard said flatly.

The streets lurked inside his emerald-green eyes.

Family, Gaston had said.

Whores. Thieves. Cutthroats.

While she had not engaged in the two latter activities, Victoria had certainly embarked on the first profession.

"What is your name?" she asked politely.

The guard did not so much as blink at Victoria's question. "Julien, ma'am."

"Are there guests downstairs?"

"No, ma'am. The House of Gabriel doesn't open its doors until nine o'clock."

Victoria tucked away the knowledge that Gabriel's house had been open only three hours when he had purchased her virginity.

"Monsieur Gaston said you are family," Victoria said impulsively.

The guard blinked. She had surprised him.

"Yes, ma'am," he said in a voice that said nothing at all.

"My family and I are . . . estranged." Victoria fleetingly thought of her father and her mother, both members of the untitled aristocracy. *Your mother left your father, just as you did,* Gabriel had told her.

Just as he forced your brother to leave. "You are very fortunate to be surrounded by people who care about you."

The emerald-green eyes remained distant. "I cannot let you leave this room, ma'am."

"Do you not trust your family, sir?"

Victoria had trusted her family—once.

"Yes, ma'am," the guard said reluctantly, "I trust them."

Victoria pounced on Julien's admission. "Then there is no danger if I leave this suite, is there?"

"That isn't for me to determine, ma'am."

Victoria glanced at his shoulder. He did not openly carry a pistol; he must wear it in a shoulder holster underneath his coat, as did Gabriel.

He would not shoot her; but she was certain that he could stop her.

She remembered the strength of the man who had grabbed her on the street.

The man who would kill her.

"I am aware that I am in danger, sir."

The guard's expression remained impassive. "Yes, ma'am."

"I do not wish to put myself into further jeopardy."

"No, ma'am."

Victoria had had more success in persuading recalcitrant charges to study than she was having with this man Gabriel had assigned as a guard.

"You know that Gabriel purchased my virginity."

There was no way that he could *not* know, working in the House of Gabriel as he did.

The embarrassment burning up Victoria's face was not mirrored by the guard's face. "I am instructed to guard you, ma'am, and I will do so."

The electric light overhead drummed on Victoria's head. "I want to know Gabriel."

"You will not learn to know Mr. Gabriel through his house."

How long ago it seemed since Victoria had followed Monsieur Gaston up the narrow steps behind the guard.

"You are wrong, sir. Everything inside the House of Gabriel is a part of the man who built it."

Victoria had gained the guard's full attention.

"I want to please Gabriel," Victoria said evenly. "I would like to visit the . . . the guest bedchambers to see with what means other women please men."

Objects she might not have noticed through the transparent mirrors.

The smirk she expected to see on the guard's face did not appear.

Emotion flickered inside his emerald-green eyes; disappeared. "Perhaps, ma'am, it is not artificial aids that Mr. Gabriel needs."

"I will use whatever aids are available," she said truthfully.

The guard glanced over her shoulders.

Victoria forcibly tamped down her frustration. She could not condemn an employee for his loyalty.

"How long have you been employed by Gabriel?" she asked politely.

He did not look at her. "Six years."

Whereas Gaston had been employed fourteen years.

"Someone wants to kill him."

The guard's gaze snapped back to Victoria. "No one will harm him in the House of Gabriel." Deadly intent rang inside his voice. "We will protect him."

Family.

"But he is not now in the House of Gabriel," Victoria pointed out.

"No." The frustration Victoria had earlier felt was reflected in the guard's emerald-green eyes. "He is not."

Gabriel fought the love his family felt for him, just as he fought his need for a woman.

"Gabriel could die. If not today, then tomorrow."

Just as she could die. If not today, then tomorrow.

She could die by the hand of the man who would kill Gabriel. Or she could die by the hand of the man who had written the letters.

The guard did not respond.

"He is known as the untouchable angel," Victoria desperately persisted.

Emerald-green eyes froze Victoria in her shoes. "We who are employed at the House of Gabriel know what Mr. Gabriel is."

And would not discuss him with an outsider.

Victoria felt the rebuff all the way down to the soles of her kid slippers.

"I think he deserves to be loved," Victoria said quietly, hiding her pain. They both deserved to be loved before it was too late. "I would like to love him. I would like you to help me."

"I cannot help you, ma'am." The emerald-green eyes flickered. "I would lose my position."

But he wanted to help her.

He wanted Gabriel to find love.

They all wanted Gabriel to find love.

"No one need ever know of this but you and I," Victoria assured him.

"There are no secrets in this house, ma'am."

"There are secrets in every house," she corrected him.

There had been secrets in her father's house, a man renowned for his sterling reputation.

"I do not have a key to Mr. Gabriel's suite; if we leave, you cannot get back inside."

Hope welled up inside Victoria. "Surely someone other than Gabriel must have a key."

"Mr. Gaston does."

Victoria crimped the silk of her skirt in her fist. "I will explain to Mr. Gaston the reason we need to borrow his key."

The guard no longer looked stoic; he looked trapped. Torn between the loyalty to guard the door as he was instructed and torn between his desire to bring his employer some happiness.

His face cleared as suddenly as it had clouded. "Follow me."

Victoria smiled.

For a second, her smile was mirrored in the guard's emerald-green eyes, and then he turned and clomped down the brightly lit, narrow stairway. He halted at the foot of the stairs, hand curving around the brass doorknob.

Victoria remembered the terrified woman who had followed

Gaston up the stairs two nights earlier. That woman had believed she could engage in one night of sexual license and not be affected by it. It was not the same woman who walked down the narrow stairs now to join the waiting guard.

The door opened into the saloon. A maid leaned over a white-silk-covered table inserting a beeswax candlestick into the silver candleholder. Her graying hair was caught up in a black net. She halted at the sight of Victoria.

Victoria had no doubt whatsoever that the maid knew who she was.

The maid smiled, lined face crinkling with warmth. "Evenin', ma'am. Jules."

She spoke with a broad Cockney accent.

The guard nodded, "Evening, Mira," and hurriedly herded Victoria toward the plush red-carpeted stairs that hugged the opposite wall.

The white enameled doors lining the first floor were plainly visible from the saloon. A maid in a large mobcap pushed a wooden cart laden with linen and cleaning supplies down the upstairs hallway, her figure striped from the surrounding banister.

Victoria slowly climbed the stairs, glancing down at the rows and rows of white-silk-covered tables, twisting her head to view the darkly gleaming box where Gabriel had watched her, and from which he had then bid on her.

Victoria had been told that sin was ugly; the House of Gabriel was as beautiful and elegant as its proprietor.

The chandelier at the top of the stairs was electric; thousands of tiny crystals sparkled.

She had thought that the Opera House was the only public building to have electric lighting; she had been wrong. All of Gabriel's house was lit by electricity—the chandeliers, the wall sconces—all save for the candlelit tables in the saloon.

Thick red carpet lined the L-shaped hallway at the top of the steps. At the end of the corridor that veered to her right, a curved staircase leading upward to the second floor was lit by another chandelier. The guard threw open the enameled door nearest the top of the saloon stairs: a gilded, ornate seven numbered it.

The bedchamber had dark green carpeting; the bed was covered with a yellow silk spread. There were no windows.

It was not intended to be seen from the outside. She had seen the bedchamber through the reflective mirror the night before.

And there, directly confronting her, was the transparent mirror. It was gilt-framed, elegant as the room was elegant. Innocuous in appearance as the room was not.

Victoria did not recognize the woman reflected inside the mirror.

The hair on the back of her neck stood on end.

Was someone watching her? . . .

Only two pairs of eyes studied her: one pair belonged to the guard who stood beside her, not behind half-silvered glass; the other pair of eyes belonged to Victoria herself, looking inside the transparent mirror instead of through it.

It wasn't a stranger Victoria looked at; she looked at herself.

The cream-colored lampas underskirt with its green, yellow, and dull red figures added substance to Victoria's hips while the short, golden brown corded silk mandarin collar that plunged into a deep, narrow V subtly emphasized her neck and bosom.

Madame René was a genius.

Acutely aware of the transparent mirror and the watching guard who stood beside her—did Julien know what lay behind the glass?—Victoria stepped into the bedchamber.

A squat white bottle sat on the nightstand alongside a silver tin of condoms. The lid was stamped with the words *The House of Gabriel,* just as the one on the nightstand in Gabriel's bedchamber.

Julien silently watched Victoria's every move from the door. Whereas she could see his every move in the mirror.

Turning her back toward the half-silvered glass, Victoria opened the top drawer. And found the penis-shaped devices that Gabriel had told her about. *Godemichés,* he had called them.

They were . . . very lifelike.

One was small, one was medium, and one—a giggle bubbled up

inside her throat, remembering the Brothers Grimm fairy tale "Goldi-locks and the Three Bears"—was just the right size.

Memory flashed through Victoria's mind, a picture of her mother holding Daniel on her lap. He had been four. Eight-year-old Victoria had sat at their feet while her mother had read a fairy tale to them.

She had possessed a musical voice, Victoria suddenly recalled. But Victoria could not remember the fairy tale her mother had read, only the words, *I know it, said the angel, because . . . I know my own flower well.*

Had her mother found happiness with another man? Victoria wondered.

Was she alive?

Or had loving a man killed her, too?

Victoria touched a hard leather phallus, recalling the length and the girth of Gabriel.

I am just over nine and one-half inches long.

Her body clenched in remembered pleasure. She quickly drew back her hand.

The auburn-haired guard remained impervious. Clearly he would not be shocked by . . . anything at all.

Victoria hurriedly closed the top drawer and opened the second drawer. It contained a variety of silk scarves.

Victoria had seen firsthand the uses to which those silk scarves could be applied.

She imagined Gabriel securing her hands over her head and tying her feet spread-eagled to the wooden bedposts at the foot of the bed.

She imagined securing Gabriel.

The woman in the red bedchamber had secured the man she had been with. Straddling his hips, she had rode him astride like a man riding a horse.

There had been freedom in the woman's abandon, and a child-like trust in the man's bondage.

Victoria had known neither freedom nor trust in her life.

Had Gabriel?

He had said there was no sex act he hadn't performed. Had he ever tied up a woman for her pleasure?

Had he ever allowed himself to be tied up?

Immediately a picture of chains flashed through her mind.

Quietly closing the second drawer, Victoria opened the third and final drawer.

Knotted silk formed a whip. Beside it was a leather quirt.

There were brass hooks on the walls and the ceiling.

Anything . . . everything.

Victoria closed the final drawer.

The auburn-haired guard had been right. There was nothing here to help her please Gabriel.

Straightening, Victoria espied a small tin hidden between the white jar of cream and the silver tin filled with condoms.

A smile broke over her face. It was a tin of peppermints. *Curiously Strong Peppermints* was stamped on the metal, followed by the name ALTOIDS.

Picking up the small rectangular box, Victoria impulsively held it out so the guard could see it. "Someone forgot their lozenges."

"No one forgot them." The guard's face remained stoic, emerald-green eyes impassive. "They are for the guests."

Victoria's smile died.

Mints for halitosis.

"That is very generous of Gabriel," she said somberly, hand lowering. She moved to set the tin back onto the nightstand.

"Take it."

Victoria glanced up in surprise. The guard's face was inscrutable. "I beg your pardon?"

"Take the tin of Altoids with you. The peppermints are stronger than other brands. Eat a lozenge, and take Mr. Gabriel into your mouth. It will please him."

Victoria was surprised that the heat coursing through her body did not melt the peppermints.

The guard stepped back, spine impacting the door, clearly signaling it was time to leave.

Victoria wholeheartedly agreed.

Grabbing the Altoids, she turned around and glanced at the half-silvered glass that when seen by a guest was merely a mirror.

The dark-haired woman reflected inside it was elegant instead of ragged, slender instead of scrawny. Her face was as red as the wine-colored velvet garnering her gown.

The auburn-haired guard was profiled in the mirror, black coat a stark contrast to the golden-brown of Victoria's gown. And then they were gone, the auburn-haired guard in his black coat and the dark-haired woman in her golden brown gown. In their place stood a lone man with black hair.

Victoria's eyes widened. Only to see an auburn-haired man in a black coat standing in profile behind a dark-haired woman wearing a golden brown dress.

The guard and Victoria.

Victoria blinked.

"It's time to go," Julien said.

Victoria could not wait to escape the elegant bedchamber.

Standing in the doorway, heart pounding, she cast a quick glance over her shoulder at the half-silvered glass.

It was a mirror, not a transparent window.

"I saw you staring in the bottom drawer."

Victoria started, head snapping forward and up.

Emerald-green eyes stared down into hers. "You are not used to houses such as this."

There was no need to deny what must be blatantly obvious. "No," Victoria admitted. "I am not used to houses such as these."

"In brothels whip thongs and cat-o'-nine-tails are used instead of knotted silk and quirts."

Victoria did not have to ask Julien how he had gained his knowledge: it was imprinted in his emerald-green eyes.

"The House of Gabriel is not a brothel," Victoria said.

"No, ma'am, it is not." Grim memories filled Julien's eyes. "The House of Gabriel is safer than a brothel. For both patron and prostitute."

Victoria was arrested. Gabriel may think the House of Gabriel a place of sin, but—

"You approve of Mr. Gabriel's house," she said curiously.

"Yes," the auburn-haired guard said baldly.

Warmth filled Victoria's smile. "So do I, Mr. Jules. Shall we find Monsieur Gaston?"

They did not have to search for Gaston. He waited for them at the foot of the steps.

In his eyes was the look of the street man he had once been.

I will lose my position, Julien had said.

Gaston opened his mouth—

"It is entirely my fault, Monsieur Gaston. I wished to visit one of the guest rooms so that I"—Victoria took a deep breath, there was no help for it—"might see if there was a device there that might assist me in pleasing Monsieur Gabriel."

Gaston's mouth audibly snapped shut. He quickly recovered from his shock.

"I hope mademoiselle was not . . . surprised . . . at the devices there."

"*Au contraire,* sir." Victoria held up the tin of peppermints. "Mr. Jules very kindly recommended that I try these."

The crimson heat pulsing inside Victoria's cheeks tinged Gaston's cheeks. "*Merci,* mademoiselle. We will not mention this incident to Monsieur Gabriel lest we spoil the surprise of your gift."

Victoria's auburn haired guard marginally relaxed.

Victoria smiled. "Thank you, Mr. Gaston."

"You must not tire yourself, mademoiselle. See mademoiselle back to Monsieur Gabriel's suite, Jules."

The suite.

The door leading to the gallery of transparent windows was in Gabriel's study.

Victoria opened her mouth to tell Gaston and Jules about the man she had seen through the transparent mirror.

She closed her mouth.

What had she seen, really? Just a brief image . . . with black hair.

Her hair, under the right conditions, looked black.

Jules had said no one other than Gaston and Gabriel possessed a key to the suite. The aberration inside the mirror could only have been a trick of light.

"Thank you, Mr. Gaston You are quite right"—Victoria would need all of her strength for the night—"I must not tire myself out."

Gaston preceded Victoria up the private stairs leading to Gabriel's suite. Jules followed behind Victoria. She was sandwiched between two able men.

So why didn't she feel safe?

At the top of the stairs Gaston produced a shiny brass key and unlocked the door.

Victoria stepped inside, feet sinking in the plush maroon carpeting.

Gabriel's study was empty.

How silly of her to hope that Gabriel had returned.

Gaston crossed the carpet to the black-marble-topped desk and swept up the silver tray bearing her half-empty plates.

"Mademoiselle should eat more. Perhaps the food was not to your liking."

Victoria stiffened. Surely he was not mocking her thinness.

"The food was excellent. Pray conduct my compliments to the cook. I will eat with Gabriel when he returns."

Gaston paused at the door, tray expertly balanced on one hand. "Mademoiselle."

Victoria braced herself. "Yes?"

Gaston did not face her. "The Altoids work most effectively when they are allowed to slowly dissolve in the mouth while at the same time tasting a man's *bitte*. This is best accomplished by holding a lozenge inside your cheek rather than on your tongue."

The door softly closed.

Victoria held her hands to her cheeks. The tin and her hands quickly warmed; they did not cool off her face.

"Mademoiselle."

For a second Victoria thought Gaston called through the door. He did not.

Heart slamming against her ribs, Victoria swirled about.

A black-haired man stood only inches away from her. He held a blue silk scarf between long, elegant hands.

"Hello, Mademoiselle Childers." Warm breath fanned her face. "It's so good to meet you again."

Chapter

23

"Mr. Delaney is not at home," the frozen-faced butler informed Gabriel.

"But Mrs. Thornton told me he was here." Gabriel smiled disarmingly; behind his charm he plotted how to best disarm the butler. He was a few years older than Gabriel and slightly shorter, but he was heavier and larger boned. Behind the butler Gabriel could see that a staircase adjoined the foyer; a polished wooden banister and a narrow green carpet climbed upward out of sight. There was no one on the stairs or in the gas-lit hallway dissecting the town house. "I'm certain he would want to see me."

"I'm sorry, sir." There was no regret in the butler's voice. "Mr. Delaney is not at home."

He could be telling the truth. Or he could be lying.

His face was severely marked from smallpox. Many households would not hire a man with a face such as his.

A butler such as he would tolerate many idiosyncrasies in an employer. Perhaps he even benefited from Delaney's hobby of preying on destitute governesses.

There were women, even whores, who would not bed a man who was disfigured.

Perhaps Delaney provided the butler with his castoff governesses.

Yellow fog wafted through the open door.

"This is a matter of urgency," Gabriel said pleasantly. Leaning on his cane to hold it upright, he unscrewed the silver knob by slowly rotating the palm of his left hand. "If you will tell me where I may find Mr. Delaney, much unpleasantness can be avoided."

It was the only warning Gabriel would give.

"I do not know where Mr. Delaney is." The butler was impervious to danger. "If you will leave your card, I will give it to him."

Gabriel's smile did not alter. Reaching up with his right hand as if to pick off a piece of lint from his wool coat, he grabbed instead the butler's throat. At the same time the short sword and the hollow cane separated.

He shoved the butler back inside the foyer.

Delaney could be upstairs, or he could be downstairs.

Or he could be out, as the butler claimed.

Gabriel would soon find out.

The butler was no Peter Thornton. The butler struck out.

Gabriel could not block the first hit; it impacted his jaw. He slammed the butler against a wall of family photos.

Glass cracked, splattered; a silver-framed picture fell to the floor. Glass crunched underneath the butler's foot.

Gabriel dug the tip of the short sword into the butler's throat just above his bobbing Adam's apple; below the sword point, Gabriel squeezed his throat between black leather encased fingers.

Three nights ago he would not have touched the man; now he would touch anyone, do anything, to keep Victoria safe.

Pupils dilating with fear, the butler stilled. Heavy breathing superimposed the echo of shattered lives.

"As I said," Gabriel purred, "Much unpleasantness can be avoided."

Muffled footsteps sped down the carpeted stairs.

"What is the meaning of this?"

Gabriel froze.

The voice coming from above him was neither servile nor masculine.

Gabriel did not take his gaze off of the butler.

"Ring for help, Mrs. Collins!" Sweat poured off the butler's forehead; blood beaded on Gabriel's black leather glove. "Please!"

The butler would not beg an accomplice to ring for the police; he would plead for more immediate assistance.

Gabriel could hold the butler or he could stop the woman. He could not do both at the same time.

He gambled.

"Mrs. Collins, if you move, I will pierce this man's windpipe," Gabriel swiftly rejoined. "It will be many minutes before he dies, but I assure you, he will die. You can prevent his death."

And her own, he did not need to add.

Gabriel could feel the woman's indecision. She wanted to help the butler; pulsing just as strongly through her veins was the instinct to survive.

The woman neither aided the butler nor ran, immobilized by her fear.

It was obvious she had never before encountered violence or death.

Gabriel played on her innocence. "If you help me, Mrs. Collins, no one need die."

"I . . . what . . ." Her voice shook. "What do you want? My jewels are . . . I am a guest. This is my brother's home. I only have my pearls and—"

"Where is Mitchell Delaney, Mrs. Collins?" Gabriel interrupted.

The butler's muscles bunched.

Gabriel's fingers tightened around his throat, at the same time he pressed the tip of the sword into his throat with deadly intent.

"Make no mistake, I *will* kill you," he murmured brutally. And then more loudly, voice kinder, gentler. "I don't want your jewels, Mrs. Collins. I simply want to speak to your brother."

And then he wanted to kill him.

"Mitch . . . my brother is not at home."

Mrs. Collins's voice held the ring of truth.

The butler wheezed for air.

"Who are you?" Mrs. Collins ordered, imperiousness winning over fear. "I demand that you release Keanon."

Gabriel did not want to have to hurt the woman. But he would. "Do you have a governess, Mrs. Collins?" he asked, intently watching the butler.

The pockmarks stood out on his livid face.

Keanon was afraid. He knew about Mitchell Delaney's collection of governesses.

"Yes, of course, but I hardly see what that has to do with—"

"Your brother likes governesses." Gabriel pressed the sword tip more deeply into Keanon's throat, blood spurted; at the same time he loosened his fingers from around the butler's windpipe. "Tell her how Delaney likes governesses, Keanon."

The butler read his death inside Gabriel's gaze.

"He . . ." Keanon croaked; blood dripped down his throat. "I didn't have anything to do with it, Mrs. Collins."

Not good enough.

"Tell Mrs. Collins exactly what it is that you didn't have anything to do with," Gabriel softly ordered.

The butler hesitated: he was afraid Delaney would dismiss him or he was afraid Delaney would kill him.

The more immediate threat to his life won out.

"Mr. Delaney, he . . . he has a special place prepared in the attic." Crimson red stained the butler's starched white shirt collar. "He brings women there . . ."

"My brother is a bachelor." Moral outrage spiced Mrs. Collins's voice. "It is none of our business what women he brings into his home."

Victoria had spent eighteen years at the mercy of women such as Mrs. Collins, women who hid behind their virtue in order to be comfortable with their lives and their men.

Never again.

"Your brother terrorized my woman, *madame*," Gabriel said softly. "It *is* my business."

The butler's eyes widened in shock. The women whom he and his employer preyed upon were not supposed to have men to protect them. To care for them.

To love them.

The approaching clip-clop of a lone horse's hooves sounded out over the butler's labored breathing. All Delaney's sister would have to do was scream . . .

"If my brother is guilty of nefarious practices, these women should have informed the police."

Mrs. Collins continued to hide behind her wealth and her virtue. The governesses were poor; Delaney was rich.

No bobby would arrest him.

"Do you love your brother, Mrs. Collins?" Gabriel asked impersonally.

The lone horse was even with the house; the faint grind of carriage wheels sang out through the evening fog.

"Of course I love my brother!" Mrs. Collins exclaimed. "It is a virtuous woman's duty to love her family." *No matter their faults.*

But she wouldn't admit that, let alone confess it.

Gabriel wondered how Victoria, at the age of sixteen, had gained the courage to walk away from her father.

The grinding echo of the carriage was obliterated by fog and distance; the horse's hooves faded to a dying echo.

"Then you don't want your brother to be killed," Gabriel said flatly.

"Of course not," Delaney's sister said on a loud intake of air. Unaware of the passing carriage that could have been her salvation.

"But he is going to be killed—"

Mrs. Collins gasped; yellow fog curled around the butler's livid face.

"—if I do not reach him before another man does."

Gabriel lied. Or perhaps he did not lie.

He did not know if Delaney worked with the second man. Gabriel would not know until he found Delaney.

Either way he was a dead man.

"My brother did not . . . he did not tell me where he went."

Mrs. Collins spoke the truth again.

Knowledge glittered inside the butler's eyes. Pale green ringed his dilated pupils.

"You know where he is, Keanon," Gabriel said silkily.

The twin rings of pale green vanished; the butler's eyes transformed into two black holes of fear.

"I don't know," he gasped.

Was Delaney a killer? Gabriel speculated. Who was Keanon more afraid of, Gabriel or Delaney?

"You do, Keanon," Gabriel crooned. "But if you don't, then there really is no reason why I shouldn't kill you, is there?"

"I don't know!" Shrillness laced the butler's voice.

Only cartilage separated the tip of Gabriel's sword and the butler's windpipe.

"Take a deep breath, Keanon," Gabriel said gently. "It's going to be your last."

The last of Keanon's loyalty dissipated in a surge of terror.

"He said he was going to get the governess!" the butler babbled. "That's all I know! I swear, that's all I know!"

Ice raced through Gabriel's veins.

Victoria was at Gabriel's house. But did Delaney know that?

Or did he plan to collect her at the cheap room that had been her home?

"How does he know where she is?" Gabriel gritted.

"I don't know! I don't know! I swear to God I don't know!"

So many people who *didn't know*.

"Are there women up in the attic now, Keanon?"

"No! No! Not now."

But the attic was prepared for a woman.

It was prepared for Victoria.

"Do you watch while he rapes the women?" Gabriel asked softly. Time ticking, pulses beating.

"Mrs. Thornton—she watches!"

There were women as well as men who derived pleasure out of another's subjugation. Gabriel could very easily imagine Mary Thornton as being one of those women.

"Does Delaney give the women to you when they finish with them?" he asked.

"No—" Keanon thought better of lying. "Yes. But I don't hurt them. I swear I don't hurt them."

Sweat poured down the butler's pockmarked face; ice spread up Gabriel's spine.

Wounds healed; memories did not.

But perhaps the governesses were deprived even of those . . .

"Do you kill the women for Delaney and Mary Thornton?"

"No, no!" The butler's bulging eyes rolled round in their sockets. "Mr. Delaney gives them money to live in the country. I put them on the train. I swear it. I can tell you where they bought tickets to . . ."

Keanon's head slammed against the wall; a half dozen silver-and-glass picture frames crashed to the floor.

Gabriel stared down at the photograph of a man who stood by a tree; he had an arm about a woman.

He stood in shadow, she in light.

His features were blurred; his hair looked black in the shadow. The woman's features were clear; her hair was hidden underneath a straw hat.

Was the man in the photograph Mitchell Delaney?

Did Delaney have black hair?

Was *Delaney* the second man?

Pivoting, Gabriel gazed up.

Delaney's sister stood on the eighth step.

She was the woman in the photograph, an icon of English mother-hood. In her early thirties, she had pale brown hair secured on top of her head in a loose knot. Her white blouse and dark green wool skirt were expertly tailored to square her shoulders, flatter an artificially narrowed waist, and to maximize full hips.

There was nothing artificial about her shocked expression.

Mrs. Collins had just learned that every family has a secret. The skeleton in her closet was her brother.

Gabriel turned his back and walked out of Delaney's house.

He remembered Victoria and the slick lick of her tongue as she shared with him the taste of his seed. He remembered the letters that Delaney had written, seductive missives promising pleasure and protection.

The handwriting had not belonged to the same man who had

written on the silk napkin. But the writing on the napkin may not have belonged to the second man.

Gerald Fitzjohn had sat at his table.

Gerald Fitzjohn could have written the note on the silk napkin.

It did not matter.

Delaney. The second man.

A man was going to get the governess.

A man was going to get Victoria. *Tonight.*

Twin lamps shone through the yellow fog.

Gabriel sharply called out to the passing hansom cab.

The ride through the fog-shrouded streets was endless. *He said he was going to get the governess,* the cab wheels sang.

I wanted your touch . . . Does that warrant my death?

Gabriel jumped out of the cab the moment it stopped.

"Hey, guv'nor!" the cabby shouted. "Ye owes me two shillin's!"

Gabriel did not stop to pay the cabby.

Eight distant bongs dully penetrated the blanket of fog, Big Ben announcing the hour. The house doors opened in another hour.

Using his private key, Gabriel quickly let himself inside. Yellow tendrils of fog writhed in the darkness. He followed the wafting trail of beeswax polish, roast lamb and danger.

The crystal chandelier at the top of the guest stairs forged jagged shadows in the dark cavern that was the saloon. White silk tablecloths shone like sleeping ghosts. A single candle illuminated a black-haired man who sat at a back table. A black wool coat framed a satinwood chair; a black silk dress coat framed the man's white waistcoat. He tilted a brandy snifter, long scarred fingers cradling the warmed crystal, both human flesh and glass tempered by fire.

Gabriel felt all the old emotions that Victoria had briefly stemmed rise to the surface.

Love. Hate.

The desire to be an angel. The need to protect an angel.

The knowledge that he could never be an angel, beggar that he was.

With emotion came the memories of hunger that hollowed the

stomach, cold that numbed the skin. Poverty that eroded social barriers. Lust that never burned.

Sex had been Michael's salvation; a violet-eyed, black-haired boy had been Gabriel's deliverance.

Silently Gabriel crossed the thick wool carpet, crimson dye blackened by flickering darkness.

A feminine giggle drifted up the kitchen steps, a housemaid flirting with a waiter.

Michael sat alone, as he had sat alone on the dock in Calais.

Regret washed over Gabriel for the twenty-seven years that yawned between two thirteen-year-old boys and two forty-year-old men. He paused outside the circle of the single candle flame. "I thought I told you not to come here again, Michael."

His voice was a hollow echo inside the cavernous saloon. A reminder of other houses, other saloons.

In another hour the House of Gabriel would be overflowing with patrons and prostitutes. Tobacco smoke and expensive perfume would camouflage the aroma of beeswax polish and roast lamb and turn the smells of a home into that of a tavern.

Briefly, Gabriel envisioned Michael's country estate and town house. They smelled of roses, lilacs and hyacinth, living floral scents to camouflage a past riddled with death.

Michael swallowed a sip of brandy before lowering the crystal snifter. "You didn't read the newspaper today, Gabriel."

"Forgive me, *mon vieux*," Gabriel said ironically. "I have been busy."

Downstairs his people were finishing off their supper, some preparing to end the day, some preparing to start it.

Was Victoria still sleeping?

Would she welcome him back to her bed?

How did Delaney plan to take her?

Violet eyes calmly assessed Gabriel. "You were in a fight."

"The streets are dangerous," Gabriel evaded. His cheek throbbed from the butler's fist. He lightly gripped the silver handle to the cane that was no cane. "There is always someone trying to take that which does not belong to them."

Amber brandy sloshed the sides of the crystal snifter; scarring had not impeded the adeptness of Michael's hands or his ability to please women. "Who is he, Gabriel?"

Fear leaped inside Gabriel like a caged animal.

Michael would not stop until he had the truth.

The second man would not stop until two angels were dead.

But there was only one angel among them: Michael.

Victoria was the only living person who knew that truth.

Both Michael and Gabriel's lives were in her hands.

"He's the second man who raped me, Michael," Gabriel replied, playing the game, dying a little with each passing second.

If he went upstairs to Victoria now, Michael would follow him, and the truth would come out.

Gabriel couldn't kill Michael, but the truth would kill Gabriel.

A masculine laugh wafted up from the kitchens.

Amber brandy swirled and swirled inside the crystal snifter. "She touched you, Gabriel."

Gabriel remembered Victoria's wet hair glued to her body, Victoria's clear blue eyes glowing with passion, Victoria's smile at the French euphemisms for a man's testicles.

Victoria's hand reaching out to take his.

"She touched me, Michael," Gabriel said neutrally.

He would kill for the pleasure of Victoria's touch.

Yellow fire spat upward.

Michael's eyes glinted violet in the flare of light. "An article on the front page of *The Times* detailed a suicide and a murder."

Gabriel did not have to ask who the victims had been. The second man had dispatched the Thorntons.

Locks were easily picked.

Either Delaney or the second man could have entered the house while the servants were otherwise occupied.

"There are always articles detailing murders and suicides in the papers," Gabriel fenced. "If there weren't, people wouldn't buy them."

"Sir Neville Jamieson was shot through the head."

Surprise raced down Gabriel's spine. Neville Jamieson was a squire in his late sixties. He had never visited Gabriel's house.

Gabriel shrugged, pretending an indifference he did not feel. "That is unfortunate."

Michael continued swirling brandy inside his snifter, violet eyes assessing, crystal glinting, amber liquor sloshing. "He owns an estate in Dover."

Gabriel froze.

Twenty-nine years earlier the nightmare had started in Dover. Two years later Michael had run away and stowed on the boat that had docked in Calais.

If Michael had not run away, Gabriel would never have met him. If he had not met Michael, Gabriel would never have met the second man. And he would have died from starvation and disease, or he would have died from a knife or a bludgeon.

Gabriel owed everything to Michael.

"I don't know Neville Jamieson," Gabriel said truthfully.

Michael's violet eyes were alert, seeking to pierce Gabriel's shell. "Jamieson was an associate of my uncle's."

An associate . . .

"How do you know that?" Gabriel asked sharply, aloofness pierced.

"Anne read the paper." Candlelight flickering, amber swirled, violet glinted. "Anne told me."

Anne Aimes's estate was in Dover, as had been that of Michael's uncle. She would know.

Gabriel struggled to piece together the play the second man had set into motion.

He had killed a Dover squire. But why?

"Who was the man who reportedly killed Jamieson?" Gabriel asked tautly.

"Leonard Forester."

Leonard Forester was the name of the architect who had redesigned the House of Gabriel.

The fear coursing through Gabriel's veins knotted his stomach.

The paper was wrong. Forester hadn't committed suicide; he had been murdered.

The two men were both connected to the second man. *But how?*

"Why did he kill Jamieson?"

"Leonard Forester is an architect," Michael said, watching Gabriel for a reaction. Both men tied to his past. "Jamieson owns the firm where Forester is employed."

Gabriel remembered . . . the watching eyes that had awoken him. The scent that had lingered in his suite.

John's report on what he had learned at the Hundred Guineas Club. . . . *Lenora stood both Geraldine and himself up, and that he had not seen Lenora since.*

Lenora . . . *Leonard.*

Leonard Forester had rebuilt the House of Gabriel. He had built a secret passage for the second man.

And now he was dead.

The second man *had* been inside his suite earlier that day.

Delaney. The second man.

It didn't matter by what name he called himself. He was inside the House of Gabriel.

He had Victoria.

Gabriel raced through the tables, pushing aside a chair, table tilting, silver candleholder flying.

"Gabriel!"

Michael's voice echoed dully inside Gabriel's ears, no time to worry about the truth.

He took the narrow stairs three at a time.

Julien was slumped in front of the satinwood door, auburn hair spilling around him like a silk scarf. Crimson blood dripped over the wooden lip of the landing.

His throat had been slit.

Gabriel knew what Julien had last seen: he could feel the lingering surprise that survived death like the residue of erased chalk on a board.

Julien had not expected to die inside the House of Gabriel; he had not expected to be killed by a man whom he thought was a friend.

There was no time for regrets now.

Later.

Later Gabriel would mourn the death of another homeless brother. But not now.

Victoria needed him.

Gabriel fumbled in the pocket of his trousers for the key to the door—*merde*—where was the fucking key? Vaguely he was aware of footsteps pounding up the stairs behind him.

It was too late to protect Michael.

Too late to save Julien . . . Julien who had trusted too much and paid with the skin off his back.

Now he was dead.

Another casualty in a twenty-nine-year-old nightmare.

Finding the brass key, Gabriel thrust it home. The door was impeded by the bulk of Julien's body; Gabriel wrenched it open, dragging Julien forward in a slick slide of blood. He squeezed through the opening crack.

Chalk gritted underneath the soles of his boots. More white nodules were scattered over the maroon carpet.

It was not that which held his attention.

The mystery of Delancy and the second man was a mystery no more.

Chapter

24

"Gabriel." The second man perched on the black-marble-topped desk, black hair blue in the light of the chandelier, violet eyes gleaming. A familiar smile spread over his face. *"Mon ange."*

My angel grated across Gabriel's skin.

The second man's voice bore the same knowledgeable cadence as did that of Michael and Gabriel: the voice of a man who had been trained to entice, to seduce, to gratify.

Victoria stood between his splayed legs, golden brown silk dress with its wine-colored velvet lapels and cream-colored panels splashed with green, yellow and dull-red dye a sharp contrast to the stark black silk of a dress coat and trousers.

A fist clenched inside Gabriel's guts, recognizing Madame René's creation. It squeezed his chest, seeing the blue silk scarf that gagged her mouth and the green silk scarf knotted about her hands.

The second man caressed her cheek with a serrated Bowie knife.

It was Gabriel's knife.

A knife whose sole purpose was to kill.

No doubt it had killed Julien.

A blue-plated pistol barrel toyed with the wine-colored velvet bow on Victoria's left shoulder; long, tapered fingers lightly grasped the double-action Colt revolver. It was cocked to fire a single bullet.

The violet gaze slipped past Gabriel.

"Michael." The second man's smile widened. "How nice of you to join us."

Michael's and Victoria's shock was palpable.

In looking at the second man, Michael gazed at himself as he had been before scarred by fire; in looking at Michael, Victoria realized that the man who held her was not the man named for his ability to please women.

Gabriel was neither surprised nor shocked at the man's visage. There should be satisfaction in confronting him again: there was not.

"Close the door, *s'il vous plaît*," the second man invited, pleased with the reaction of his audience. "We do not want Mademoiselle Childers to catch her death."

Amusement at his cleverness sparkled inside the violet eyes.

It would not be cold air that would kill Victoria. If Michael ran for help, the second man warned, he would kill the woman who had touched Gabriel. *Now*.

With a knife. Or a single bullet.

And there would be nothing that Gabriel could do to stop it.

The soft snick of a closing door bolted down Gabriel's spine.

"I believe introductions are in order." The second man spoke with charming courtesy; he had spoken with the same beguiling courtesy when Gabriel had been chained, unable to fight either himself or the man who looked like Michael but who had none of Michael's humanity. "Gabriel, no doubt you recognize Delaney; he bears a marked resemblance to his sister, does he not? Mademoiselle Childers, may I present to you Michel des Anges, the man named for his ability to please women. Michael, allow me to introduce you to Mademoiselle Childers, the woman who sold her virginity to Gabriel. Delaney, no doubt you've heard of Gabriel and Michel, *les deux anges;* they really are quite beautiful, aren't they? Although Michael is unfortunately scarred now."

The book-lined study shrank to a narrow attic room, gold-embossed leather to dull gray chains.

Delaney's gaze nervously darted from man to man, woman to man, a pearl-handled pistol clenched inside his right fist. His hair was black and greasy with macassar oil; his narrow mustache curled in a perpetual smile. Unlike the second man, he hadn't expected two angels.

Behind him, Gabriel could feel Michael's circling thoughts. He knew the exact moment when Michael realized the second man's identity.

"You have guessed who my father is, *mon cousin*," the second man said with unfeigned delight.

"William Sturges Bourne," Michael said flatly.

The Earl of Granville.

Gabriel had killed him six months earlier.

"Your uncle," the second man agreed smugly.

Michael's uncle had been the first man; the son of his uncle—Michael's cousin—was the second man.

The uncle had destroyed Michael's life, then he had sent his son to destroy Gabriel's life. All because of the innocent love two thirteen-year-old boys had borne one another.

Violet eyes clashed with violet eyes.

"I do not claim William Sturges Bourne as a relative," Michael said contemptuously.

A log collapsed in the fireplace; sparks shot up the chimney.

The smile did not fade from the face that was a slightly younger, unscarred rendition of Michael's. "And yet you have inherited his title, the Earl of Granville."

A title Michael had not claimed.

Gabriel's fingers tightened about the silver knob of his cane.

Violet eyes suddenly pinned Gabriel. "Drop the cane, Gabriel, or I will carve your initials into Mademoiselle Childers's cheek. A 'g' for *garçon*. A 'c' for *con*. An 'f' for *fumier*."

Boy. Bastard. Piece of shit.

Victoria's gaze sought Gabriel's.

Thoughts flowed between them: the pounding of water, the slap of driving flesh. The echo of Gabriel's confession.

The knowledge that the second man had heard their every discussion and witnessed their every intimacy. Her cries of pain, her cries of pleasure.

The needs of a male whore.

He had demanded that she share the light of her pleasure, and he had brought her to this.

A dark line of blood welled on Victoria's cheek, a small warning nick of the Bowie knife.

Victoria held perfectly still, unable to escape the consequences of touching an angel.

The second man would give no other warning.

Gabriel had promised he would give up his life in order to keep her alive. And he would.

He dropped the cane.

"Very good, *mon ange*." The second man smiled, white teeth flashing. "Now kick it across the room toward me."

Gabriel kicked the cane toward the black-marble-topped desk; it collided with a small red and white tin stamped with ALTOIDS, struck a satinwood leg.

It dawned on Gabriel that the gritty substance underneath the sole of his boot and the white nodules scattered over the maroon carpeting were mints.

Anger pricked the hair on the back of his neck.

"You said you wouldn't hurt her, Yves," Delaney burst out; glaring light glinted off his greasy hair. "You said you would kill Gabriel, and then we would take her. You didn't tell me there would be another man. This is not what we planned."

Yves.

It could be the second man's name. Or it could be an assumed name.

It didn't matter.

After fourteen years, eight months, three weeks and one day Gabriel could associate a name other than Michael to his face.

"Delaney, you must learn to be more considerate, old chap," Yves said, gaze never leaving Gabriel's. The serrated knife caressed instead of cut, smearing a line of crimson blood across Victoria's paper-white cheek. "Gabriel quite likes Mademoiselle Childers, don't you, Gabriel?"

A pulse throbbed at the base of Victoria's throat; the V of her bodice revealed a hint of shadow, the valley between her breasts.

The Adams revolver weighted Gabriel's shoulder.

He remembered the taste of her cry as he brought her to orgasm just scant hours earlier.

"Yes," he said in an emotionless voice that belonged to neither a boy who had wanted to be an angel nor a man who had wanted to be a part of a woman. "I like Victoria."

Laughter crinkled the violet eyes. "Gabriel, you think I brought the mints. I'm sorry to disappoint you, but they belong to Mademoiselle Childers. I believe she intended to use them on you, but dropped them in her excitement when she saw me. It was quite amusing, *mon ange*, watching the two of you, a governess who had never touched a man sparring with a whore who was afraid to be touched. You were both so very eager to be seduced."

Relief coursed through Gabriel, that Victoria had not been forced to perform fellatio. It was followed by anger.

For the first time in almost fifteen years, he had taken what he wanted. Now it was time to pay the price.

"You said he couldn't fuck a woman," Delaney protested, pearl-handled pistol belligerently pointed at Gabriel. Clearly he was not a stranger to the weapon; he expertly held it between short, effeminate fingers. "You said she would still be a virgin."

Fuck a woman raced up Gabriel's spine; it was chased by *still be a virgin*.

Would Victoria be safe if she were still a virgin?

"Now, now, old chap." Yves did not spare Delaney a glance. "Think how much more amusing it will be to fuck an angel's woman. Although, Mademoiselle Childers, I do apologize: I sincerely doubt if Delaney here is quite *l'etalon*—the stallion—that our two angels here are."

Delaney glared at Gabriel, his mouth petulant underneath the perpetually smiling mustache.

He was a jealous man, and he was a frightened man.

Both emotions were useful.

"How long have you lived within my walls?" Gabriel asked of the second man.

"Forester was quite clever, was he not?" Yves preened; his violet eyes were cold and calculating. "I do not like the English climate, but I confess, watching you plan to entrap me these last months has provided no end of entertainment. Come now, Gabriel, did you not feel my presence just once?"

Yes.

Gabriel had felt his presence every waking and sleeping moment for the last fourteen years, eight months, three weeks and one day.

He had felt it when he woke this day.

Gabriel glanced away from the violet eyes, needing to know . . .

"Who wrote the letters, Delaney?"

Delaney's chest swelled with pride. "Mary and I. It is a part of our game."

A game to systematically destroy women's lives.

"Why are you here?"

Delaney's pride gave way to apprehension. He nervously shifted his feet.

Michael stepped sideways, synchronizing his footsteps to those of Delaney's.

Did he realize the truth yet?

"I came to collect what is mine," Delaney said with the aggression that comes with fear.

"But who suggested you come here tonight, Delaney?" Gabriel prodded, planting the seeds of dissent. "Was it you, or Yves?"

"It doesn't matter."

But it mattered very much when a man was a pawn and didn't realize it. Such men did not survive in games of power.

"You'll never have Mademoiselle Childers," Gabriel said gently.

Victoria had been chosen for Gabriel.

"And who's going to stop me?" Delaney sneered. "You are not in a position to stop your betters, my good man."

"I will stop you," the second man said suddenly. "Your role is over, Delaney. You have played it aptly; now it is time to take your bow."

"I say—"

Between one heartbeat and the next, the second man swung his arm away from Victoria's shoulder, sighted the Colt revolver, and pulled the trigger.

Delaney slammed against the open door behind him; a round hole appeared in his forehead. At the same time the explosion of gunfire ripped through the air.

A look of supreme surprise suffused Delaney's face; his mouth beneath the smiling mustache was a round O. He crumpled to the floor.

The stench of evacuation was immediate.

Victoria's pupils dilated in black shock.

"Michael, if you take one more step, I will have to decide who to kill next," the second man said pleasantly "That is not a part of the play."

Michael paused.

"What is a part of the play?" Gabriel asked carefully.

Every pulse inside his body beat a warning.

Yves had brought Delaney to show Gabriel that he had written the letters and not Yves; when Delaney had no longer served a purpose, Yves had dispatched him.

Yves had sent Victoria to Gabriel; at what point would she no longer serve a purpose?

"Soon, *mon ange*," Yves murmured. "But first you will give me the Adams revolver you are wearing underneath your jacket."

Gabriel instinctively reached inside his overcoat and the wool day coat underneath; the silk lining caressed his knuckles.

The butt of the rosewood pistol was a familiar grip. The weight a comforting burden.

He slipped it out of the holster. His middle finger automatically curled around the trigger.

"I could kill you," Gabriel said provocatively.

Gabriel had waited almost fifteen years to do so.

The second man made no move either to defend himself or to fire the first shot. "But you won't, Gabriel, will you? By the time the bullet reaches me, Mademoiselle Childers will be dead."

The invisible hand wrapped about Gabriel's heart fisted.

"You think that her life is worth more to me than your death?" Gabriel asked, outwardly indifferent.

"Shall we find out, Gabriel?" Bright crimson blood dribbled down Victoria's cheek, the knife cutting instead of nicking. "Shall we show Michael and Mademoiselle Childers how little the touch of a woman means to you?"

Victoria's pain took Gabriel's breath away.

If he admitted how deeply Victoria had affected him, she was dead. If he denied it, she was dead.

The second man smiled smugly. "I thought so. It took Dolly three months to find a woman for you, *mon ange*. I would have preferred that Mademoiselle Childers had pale blue eyes and mousy brown hair—you were quite taken with Michael's woman, were you not?"— out of the corner of his eye Gabriel saw Michael stiffen at mention of Anne Aimes—"but the darker blue of Mademoiselle Childers's eyes is rather splendid, and her hair quite magnificent when properly cleaned. She's intelligent—you would quickly be bored with a woman who was not—so that was a prerequisite. And her eyes, regardless of their color, fairly beg you to fuck her, don't they? That was far more important than their color. It was necessary, Gabriel, to find you a woman who hungered for a man's touch. But you also needed a woman who had just enough knowledge of the streets to make her sympathetic to your past, but not so much that she would become inured to the story of a beggar boy who wanted to be an angel."

Victoria defensively stiffened at Yves's words; Gabriel prayed she would remain still.

He wouldn't let her die. But he couldn't stop the second man from killing her.

He wouldn't let Michael die. But he didn't know if he could stop his death, either.

"How do you know that I'm fond of Michael's woman?" Gabriel challenged, buying Victoria time, buying Michael time. Knowing that his time had run out.

Yves briefly nuzzled Victoria's hair; Victoria's gaze remained locked onto Gabriel. "She smells of you, Gabriel. Your soap. Your desire."

Gabriel's finger tightened around the trigger. All it would take was one bullet . . .

Would Victoria die before or after the second man?

Yves lifted his head. "I know you had a yen for Mademoiselle Aimes, Gabriel, because I followed you. I followed you when you watched over Michael; I followed you when you took Mademoiselle Aimes to that cheap pastry shop. I was in my father's house when you killed him. Now, Michael sensed me that night, didn't you, Michael?"

Prey and predator.

Gabriel did not have to see Michael's scars to know they would be white with tension. "I didn't know it was you."

"No, of course not, how could you, *mon cousin?*" Yves reasoned. "You didn't know I existed. Gabriel couldn't very well tell you, now could he? You thought it was because my father hired a man to rape Gabriel that he hated you; it wasn't. My father actually hired me to kill Gabriel; that would have hurt you, Michael, and that really was all that my father lived for, to hurt you. Understandably. After all, he was crippled because of you. However, I couldn't resist Gabriel, so perfect, so beautiful, so hungry for love. It was I who raped him, Michael. Gabriel hated you because every time he looked at you, he saw me. And he remembered that he begged me . . . *n'arête pas* . . . not to stop.

"Now empty the cartridge chamber, Gabriel, *mon ange,* and gently toss the pistol in my direction or I will proceed to carve the letter 'b' on Mademoiselle Childers's cheek—'b' because I made you beg."

Blue eyes locked with silver eyes as Victoria digested the past of the man whom she had sought to redeem.

Gabriel couldn't breathe.

He had thought the truth would kill him, and it had.

Gabriel emptied the chamber; bullets rained onto the carpet. "Toss the gun at my feet."

Gabriel's fingers clenched about the rosewood grip.

"Gently, Gabriel."

Fresh blood dripped down Victoria's cheek. Her eyes were stricken with the knowledge of the weapon that she had become.

Or perhaps she was stricken because of the man that he was.

Gabriel tossed the pistol; it bounced on the carpet, slid past the silver-handled cane, the white and red tin of mints, disappeared underneath the desk.

"What do you want?" he asked tightly.

What could he possibly want from two angels to have made such elaborate plans?

"I want you to tell Michael why you hate him," Yves said.

The tension stretching between Gabriel's shoulders tightened.

He could not tell Michael. Even to save him, Gabriel could not tell him.

He could not tell the boy he had loved as a brother that Gabriel's body had betrayed him. He could not tell Michael that he had looked into Yves's violet eyes—Michael's eyes—and had been made to feel desire.

And there had been *nothing* Gabriel could do to stop it.

"I want you to tell Michael that you stole the name of an angel."

Gabriel blindly stared into black-fringed violet eyes.

"I want you to tell Michael whose name you cried out when you came, Gabriel."

Gabriel remembered . . . crying out for the innocence that had been his for a brief time when Michael had shared the loaf of stolen bread.

A harsh voice grated, "Don't."

In that one word Michael conveyed the knowledge and the pain that Gabriel had tried to hide from him for almost fifteen years.

Violet eyes appraised violet eyes. "You love Gabriel, Michael."

Michael did not flinch from the innuendo in his voice. Gabriel did. "I have always loved him."

"Gabriel killed my father for you, Michael." Silver light glanced off the serrated bowie knife; blue light glanced off the second man's hair. "What would you do for him?"

There was no pretense inside Michael's eyes or voice. "I would do anything for Gabriel."

"Would you kiss him, Michael?"

"Yes."

"Would you suck his cock?"

Michael didn't hesitate. "To save him, yes."

"Kiss him, Michael, like a lover, and I'll let the woman live. Suck his cock, and I'll let all of you live."

Time froze: Gabriel's breath. The crackling flame inside the fireplace.

Gabriel finally understood.

. . . Now I bring you a woman. A leading actress, if you will.

Laissez le jeu commencer.

Let the play begin.

"There is another choice, Gabriel."

Gabriel knew what the man who went by the name Yves was going to say.

"Tell me to kill Mademoiselle Childers, and I will let Michael live," the second man said lightly. Death glittered inside his violet eyes. "Or tell me to kill Michael, and I will let Mademoiselle Childers live."

Gabriel had not known that he had a soul; he did. "Why?" was wrenched from the very depths of him.

"Why?" the second man asked mockingly. "My father fucked an Algerian whore in 1849. Nineteen years later a man approached me in a brothel and asked if I would like to travel to England and meet my father."

Michael and Gabriel had come to England in 1868.

"He said my father needed me." The blue-plated pistol barrel toying with the wine-colored velvet bow on Victoria's shoulder was suddenly, dangerously still. "He said my father was rich. He said my father would make me rich.

"I came to England. I discovered my father had always known of my existence. He reputedly sent for me because an agent had reported that I looked like him. I didn't know that you existed, Michael; I didn't know that it was because I looked like *you* that my father sent for me. I learned how to speak English. I learned how to be a gentleman. I learned how to be *you*, Michael. So that I might better destroy you. Slowly. Systematically.

"But when I saw *les deux anges,* the two angels who were the toast of both England and France, it was you, Gabriel, whom I was most intrigued by. You were what I was: a homeless beggar—although I, at least, had been given a name by my whore of a mother—a thief, a killer, a whore. But you didn't enjoy the wealth and the sex, yet you pursued it.

"I wondered why.

"In France I located women you had serviced, Michael. I learned to kiss the way you kissed. I learned to fuck the way you fucked. I learned that because I wanted to see what it would take to destroy a fair-haired angel. My father thought it was a splendid plan; he thought he could use you in the future, Gabriel. He believed to the end that I had succeeded in destroying the—shall we say, brotherhood—that had grown between two whores. Of course, you proved him wrong, didn't you, Gabriel? As Madame René said, some bonds can't be destroyed.

"My father sent me back to Algiers with a handsome settlement. He summoned me again six months ago. You were to kill Michael, Gabriel, and I was to kill you. Or perhaps not. Perhaps my father would have turned me over to you. That was what he promised, was it not?" Yves shrugged, a sketch of movement; the serrated knife blade skidded across Victoria's bloody cheek. *"C'est la vie.* My father left a letter with his solicitor. He was aware that he was dying, you see, and had made provisions. In the event that he should die—shall we say, prematurely—he promised me a very impressive fortune if I killed the two of you."

"I have more money than my uncle ever did," Michael stated, bribe implicit.

He would give his wealth for three lives.

It was Michael's innocence that prompted him to make the offer.

Gabriel knew better.

Low laughter ruffled Victoria's copper-tinted hair. "And of course, with Mademoiselle Aimes's money soon to be at your disposal, you would not miss it at all, would you, *mon cousin*?"

The laughter bled from the second man's voice and eyes. "My father taught me many valuable lessons, Michael. I learned under his tutelage that a bullet can kill, but the death is not nearly as satisfying as that death which comes from destroying the soul. Wealth simply cannot compare. I derived tremendous satisfaction from you, Gabriel, far more than I did from the money my father paid me. I knew that the desire I made you feel would eat at you, you who had never really felt desire. You have always been so untouchable, *mon ange*, yet I touched you. And now this woman has touched you.

"What would it be like, I wonder, if Michael touched you? Would you grow hard, like you grew hard with me? Would you cry out, like you cried out with me?

"You want to know why I'm giving you a choice, Gabriel? I'll tell you why. There is a core inside you that has never been touched, not by me, not by Michael, not by Mademoiselle Childers. I want to see what it will take to break into that core. I want to see it now.

"The choice is yours, Gabriel. If you do not make a decision by the time I count to three, I will decide for you. One . . ."

Gabriel could sense movement; he couldn't take his gaze off of Victoria and the end he had brought her to.

"Two . . ."

She didn't deserve to die for touching an angel.

He hadn't deserved being raped because of his love for a violet-eyed boy.

Michael hadn't deserved the uncle who had killed everyone he had ever loved.

"Three . . ."

Gabriel felt rather than saw Michael step toward him.

He stood beside Gabriel, as he had always stood beside him.

A half-starved thirteen-year-old boy who had shared his loaf of bread.

A twenty-six-year-old man who had refused to let him die.

A forty-year-old man who did not judge him, knowing what he was.

Violet eyes replaced blue eyes clouded with the knowledge of death.

Michael stood in front of him. He had made the decision that Gabriel could not.

"Gabriel, *mon ami*," Michael said gently, brandy-scented breath a warm caress.

Scarred fingers cupped Gabriel's cheeks; burned thumbs smeared scalding liquid from underneath Gabriel's eyes.

A dead man's eyes.

But dead men didn't cry.

"*Il est bien*, Gabriel," Michael whispered, brandy-scented breath stoppering his lungs. "It's all right, my friend."

Emotion flickered in Michael's violet eyes: regret for the woman he would marry in two days' time; compassion for Gabriel and the choice he could not make: the love of a friend or the love of a woman.

A miniature face obliterated the regret, the compassion, the love.

Gabriel's face. Michael's eyes.

Petal-soft lips touched petal-soft lips.

The kiss of an angel.

Chapter

25

Pain. Fear.
Anger.

Sorrow.

The conflicting emotions welled up inside Victoria until there was no room for anything but rage.

She would not let that monster destroy Gabriel.

She would not let Gabriel die.

And he would die.

If Michael did to him what the second man—Yves—had done to him, he would die.

And there would be no way of ever again reaching the boy who had wanted to be an angel.

"No!" The scarf ate her protest.

Victoria threw her head back and slammed into the face of the man who held her. Bone impacting bone cracked the air. At the same time Gabriel catapulted across the study and crashed into a pale blue enameled wall.

Sharp pain sliced across Victoria's cheek and exploded inside her head; "Michael!" filled her ears, Gabriel's cry.

It was filled with pain. Fear. Rage.

Desperation.

Michael turned, right hand raised; a revolver protruded from the fingers that were covered in angry red welts.

The second man was not prepared for Michael. He reflexively raised his own revolver.

Victoria staggered, crashed forward in a puddle of silk, scarf-bound hands automatically reaching out to catch herself.

Like dominoes the second man tumbled backward over the desk, black coattails flying; his fall was punctuated by the sharp report of Michael's pistol.

Michael lurched, as if he had been kicked in the chest. A second shot exploded Gabriel's world.

Victoria saw the crimson rose blossom on the white waistcoat of the man who was known as Michel des Anges.

Michael, the dark-haired angel, had taken a bullet for Gabriel, the fair-haired angel.

Victoria, as if caught inside a magic lantern that moved one frame at a time, lifted herself up off the maroon carpet.

Gabriel, too, was caught inside the magic lantern. He ran, one foot at a time, feet dragging through the plush wool bog that sucked at Victoria's body. And then he was catching Michael. Holding Michael. Falling beneath the weight of Michael's body. Calling out Michael's name while bright crimson red blood dyed Michael's white silk waistcoat and shirt.

Michael did not respond.

Rage overwhelmed Victoria.

It could not end this way. *She would not let it end this way.*

Victoria fought silk and more silk to stand up. Her bound hands would not turn. Using the thumb and forefinger of her right hand, chin stabbing her left wrist, she dug the silk scarf out of her mouth.

There was no time to savor the flow of saliva that soothed her parched mouth. The blood that dribbled down her cheek was a vivid reminder of what could still happen if the man—Yves—lived.

Victoria darted around the desk. The drawer that he had earlier forced open yielded Gabriel's derringer.

She would kill him. If he was not dead she would kill him.

She would kill him for the love Michael had borne a silver-haired angel.

She would kill him for the grief that had felled Gabriel and sucked the very oxygen from the air.

Hands trembling, Victoria pointed the snub-barreled derringer at the man on the floor.

Glazed violet eyes blindly stared up at the ceiling. A thin line of crimson oozed from the nose she had broken.

He was dead.

And Gabriel . . . Gabriel cradled Michael, silver hair comingling with black hair. He rocked Michael back and forth in a silent litany of grief.

Victoria dropped the derringer. "Gabriel," she croaked.

He did not hear her.

Yves had wanted to strip away the inner core that had allowed Gabriel to survive poverty, prostitution, and rape: he had succeeded.

Victoria knelt beside Gabriel.

Michael's face was pale underneath the olive tint of his skin, the ridged scars edging his right cheek lax. Thick black lashes darkened his cheeks.

Victoria reached out, wanting to hold Gabriel, to love Gabriel, to comfort Gabriel. "Gabriel . . ."

A crimson fountain caught her attention.

Blood pumped out of Michael's chest.

Victoria the governess kicked in.

Blood did not pump out of a corpse. Pumping blood required a pumping heart.

"He's alive, Gabriel!" Victoria grabbed Gabriel's hand and pressed it against Michael's chest to stop the bleeding. "Gabriel, help me."

Hot blood bubbled up through their fingers.

Gabriel lifted his head, his life flowing through his and Victoria's fingers; his eyes were black with shock.

"Don't," he said flatly, voice remote, eyes dead. "Let me hold him."

Victoria would *not* cry for an angel. Not now.

"Keep your hand over his chest, Gabriel," she said furiously. "He's alive. If you move your hand away, he'll die. Now hold your bloody bleedin' hand there!"

The street cant worked.

Gabriel's silver eyes focused: on Victoria . . . on Michael.

On the blood bubbling up through their fingers.

On life instead of death.

"I'll be back with a doctor," she said.

The door would not open.

Victoria pushed with a strength she had not known she possessed; it opened.

Dark liquid pooled on the top of the landing, dripped down the wooden stairs.

Blood.

Julien's blood.

Bile rose inside her throat; she convulsively swallowed.

There was nothing she could do to help Julien; there was something she could yet do to help a fallen angel.

Victoria stepped in blood, slipped on blood, reached the bottom stairs. The door there was already open.

Candlelight flames lit the labrynth of tables, silver candlesticks gleaming, yellow flame dancing. A waiter wearing a short black coat paused at sight of her, the crimson sash around his waist bloodred against the white of his waistcoat, match hovering over an unlit candle.

Victoria recognized him: he was the black-haired guard who had taken her breakfast tray two days earlier.

"Jeremy!" he shouted. "David! Patrick! Charlie! *A moi!*"

To me.

Suddenly men were racing toward Victoria, hands reaching inside their short black coats; they raced past Victoria, blue-plated pistols drawn.

She incongruously wondered what they would think when they saw the second man.

What had Julien thought when he stared into violet eyes?

He had called out in surprise, "Mr. Michel," when Yves had opened the door, and then there had been a gurgle of watery breath and a dull thud of body impacting wood. Yves had shut the door, smiling in triumph.

"What is it?"

Gaston suddenly stood in front of Victoria, knife drawn, blade winking in the candlelight.

A cutthroat instead of a manager.

Victoria shrank back.

Gaston grasped her bound hands and cut through the silk knotted about them.

She licked her lips. "They're dead."

Gaston's brown eyes widened. "Messieurs Gabriel and Michel?"

"No. Julien." Tears filled her eyes. "Julien and . . . two other men. But not . . . Gabriel. Michel is hurt." For Gabriel's sake, Michael could not die. "He needs a doctor."

"Andy!" Victoria noticed a young boy peering over a table. He could have been five, or he could have been fifteen—some of the children born on the streets never gained full growth. "Bring *Docteur* François. Tell Peter to fetch Mademoiselle Aimes."

Mademoiselle Aimes. Michael's woman. The woman whom Gabriel had liked and whom the second man had tried to find a look-alike for.

Instead, he had found Victoria.

Andy skipped away to do Gaston's bidding.

With difficulty Victoria pushed aside the pain and horror of the last few hours. "The police should be summoned—"

"There will be no police, mademoiselle." Gaston's face was shuttered. "Mira, take Mademoiselle Childers to the kitchen. Pierre will care for your wound, mademoiselle."

And then Gaston was gone.

Mira stared at Victoria with hard, bright eyes, the friendly warmth that had been in her eyes just hours earlier replaced with the knowledge of cold and hunger and death.

Victoria wondered where Mira had come from—the kitchen? She had not been in the saloon, and then she was there. There was no doubt inside Victoria's mind that she had once lived on the streets.

Had she been a beggar, a prostitute, a thief, a cutthroat? And then, incongruously, she wondered how old Mira was. Her face was set with wrinkles that could have come from age or they could have come from deprivation. Only her eyes—the color of perfect blue sapphires—were bright and vivid.

"I didn't"—Victoria swallowed, *hurt him,* she had wanted to say, but she knew that she had hurt Gabriel merely by coming to his house; she had hurt Julien by not mentioning what she had seen in the transparent mirror—"I have to go to Gabriel. He needs me."

And she knew that she lied.

Gabriel did not need Victoria; he needed a miracle.

"Mr. Gabriel's not 'urt?" Mira asked sharply.

"No, he's not hurt." Hurt was not a word Victoria would use to describe Gabriel. "Mr.—Jules is dead." Tears scalded her eyes. "I couldn't call out to him."

The second man had stuffed the scarf into her mouth at the same time he had grabbed Victoria, knocking the tin of mints out of her hand.

Julien had loved Gabriel. And now he was dead.

Sorrow dulled Mira's brilliant sapphire blue eyes. "Aye, we knew there be trouble. Ye'd best come wi' me, then. Ye ain't lookin' so good."

"I'm"—Victoria bit her lip—"I'm quite all right, thank you."

Victoria wondered if anything would ever be all right again.

Would Michael?

Would Gabriel?

"Is 'e dead?"

Victoria's stomach surged at the bloodthirstiness in the woman's eyes that were suddenly clear and bright. "I beg your pardon?"

"Th' man Mr. Gabriel was needin' to kill—is 'e dead?"

"Yes." Satisfaction rang inside Victoria's voice. "Mr. Michel killed him."

"If ye take one, ye take 'em both." Mira's sapphire blue eyes were unnaturally canny. "Cain't turn yer nose up at Mr. Michel's scars."

Victoria bit back a nervous laugh.

Hysteria.

Immediately she pictured Julien, his beautiful auburn hair gleaming in the glare of the overhead hallway light while his blood turned thick and black on the steps.

All desire to laugh died. "I assure you, Miss Mira, I do not turn my nose up at Mr. Michel's scars."

Mira grunted. "Best you sit down, then, an' wait till Mr. Gabriel takes care o' things."

A protest rose up in Victoria's throat. *Gabriel might not be able to take care of "things" this time.* She swallowed it.

"I am so sorry that Jules died." Victoria swallowed a hiccup. "I liked him."

Mira's lined face softened. "Aye, we all liked Mr. Jules. Sit yerself down afore ye fall down, Ms. Victoria. Ye don't look like th' bubbly type. I'll git ye a drop o' gin."

Victoria sat down and numbly waited.

The waiting was no better in the candlelit saloon than it had been inside Gabriel's suite ablaze with electric light.

Three lives had ended this night. How many had died in the past because of the Earl of Granville and his son?

She tried to tell herself they had been insane.

There had been no insanity in the violet eyes of the man who had deliberately pitted two angels against one another.

Burning pain sliced through Victoria's right cheek. She jerked her head back, heartbeat slamming against her ribs.

Sapphire blue eyes peered down at Victoria. Mira held a red-stained washcloth. " 'Old still. Mr. Gabriel wouldn' like it none if we didn' take care o' 'is woman."

"My name is Victoria," Victoria said quietly. "Victoria Childers."

The maid with the wrinkled face and ageless eyes did not recognize the name Childers. And why should she?

Childers was a common name.

It was only when a "Mr." or a "Sir" or an "Honorable" or a "Lord" preceded a name that it took on significance.

My name is Gabriel, reverberated inside her ears.

Gabriel had never pretended to be anything other than what he was. And Michael denied his claim to the world he had been born into.

"Don't need no last name in the 'Ouse o' Gabriel." Mira dipped the washcloth into the water; steam rose from the gray metal basin. "Don't most o' us 'ave one."

Mira was an unusual name for a woman born on the streets. Had she named herself?

"The cut ain't deep on yer cheek, won't be needin' no stitches." A stream of water cascaded into the metal pan. Mira held out the washcloth. " 'Ere ye be, Miss. Victoria, wash yer 'ands now while I dab a little o' somethin' on yer cheek so it don't fester."

Dipping her fingers into the tall glass filled with clear liquor, Mira dabbed gin onto her cheek.

Biting back a gasp, Victoria concentrated on removing the blood from her fingers instead of the pain that sliced through skin and bone.

The gin hurt far, far worse than had the wound.

"Ye drinks yer gin there, now." The washcloth was plucked from between Victoria's fingers. Crimson dyed the water inside the gray metal pan. "I gots t' 'eat water fer Mr. Michel an' the doc."

The candles flickered and flamed while Victoria waited alone, the glass of gin sitting untouched before her. A lifetime passed before Andy returned; a tall, thin man wearing a black wool coat, a tall black bowler hat and carrying a black leather bag trailed after him.

The *docteur.*

The man with the black leather bag disappeared inside the door leading up to Gabriel's suite; Andy sidled close to Victoria, young-old eyes peering up into her face. He pointed to the glass of gin. "Ye drinkin' this?"

"No." Victoria numbly pushed it toward him. If gin increased the pain of external wounds, she didn't want to know what it did to internal wounds.

Two lifetimes passed before the guards appeared: they carried Michael on a satinwood door. Without a word they climbed up the plush red carpeted stairs that edged the far wall into a blaze of electric light. The doctor followed them.

Andy sat across from Victoria, sipping the gin. "They wouldn't be takin' 'im up, if he wus dead," he said kindly. But to cheer up whom?

Three lifetimes passed before Gabriel appeared.

Victoria stood up, heart in her throat.

Gabriel didn't meet her gaze. He followed Michael and the doctor upstairs.

Victoria sat back down, feet primly together. A lady by birth if not by nature.

The men in their crimson silk sashes and short black coats silently descended the guest stairs, carrying with them the satinwood door. They disappeared through the entrance to Gabriel's suite.

A cold blast of air sent the candle flames dancing.

Victoria glanced up. She didn't need an introduction to know the name of the woman who followed behind a boy that was only marginally taller than Andy.

Peter had fetched Mademoiselle Aimes.

Andy slipped out of his chair and skipped toward them. Immediately he raced up the stairs, the woman and the taller boy in hot pursuit.

Tears burned Victoria's eyes, the outsider without a family. Without thinking, she reached over and plucked up the finger-smeared glass that Andy had vacated. There was a swallow of gin left inside it.

Victoria swallowed the clear liquor.

Tears flooded her eyes; for long seconds she couldn't breathe. Immediately a soft glow infused the saloon.

Neither the soft glow nor the burning ball of liquor stopped the loneliness. Nor did they stop the thoughts that flitted around and around inside her head.

She wondered what the older woman who had purchased a younger man's expertise did.

She wondered if Michael lived.

She wondered if Yves had broken the bond that linked two angels.

Faces a mask in the flickering light and shadow, two men in crimson silk sashes and short black cloaks stepped through the doorway leading to Gabriel's suite. They carried the satinwood door between them; auburn hair trailed over the edge.

Julien, who had approved of Gabriel's house and who had been posted to protect Victoria but who had died himself.

Gaston and another man—a waiter, judging by his crimson sash and short black coat—carried a man-sized bundle between them.

Victoria did not have to ask what was inside it.

Immediately following Gaston came two more waiters; they, too, carried a man-sized bundle between them.

Men and women raced up and down the guest stairs, Gabriel's private stairs, traffic gradually slowing, finally stopping altogether while Victoria sat and watched, as she had sat and watched other people live their lives these past eighteen years.

Hours passed. Victoria knew that because the guttering candles spat and sputtered.

She reviewed her life.

Out of the memories of her father's cold judgment came her mother's voice.

A mother who had loved her two children. A mother who had read them fairy tales.

A mother who had withered and died without the love she needed.

I know it, said the angel, because . . . I know my own flower well.

Victoria slowly stood up and climbed the plush red-carpeted stairs, silk and satin rustling, skirt tail dragging.

The room to which Michael had been moved was unmistakable: pails of crimson-stained water and a pile of bloody sheets sat outside the door. The number seven gleamed gold against the white enameled door.

Victoria had visited the room just hours earlier.

Could she have stopped Julien's death if she had told him and Gaston what she had briefly glimpsed inside the transparent mirror?

She would never know.

Quietly Victoria turned the gilded doorknob.

The acrid smell of carbolic acid burned her nostrils.

A dark-haired man and a woman with pale brown hair were reflected inside the transparent mirror on the opposite wall. He lay supine underneath a yellow silk spread, she sat beside the bed in a green-velvet armchair, hatless, hair twisted in an elegant chignon, her peacock blue gown a blatant cry of Madame René's artistry.

Victoria judged the woman to be in her middle thirties, thirty-five or thirty-six to Victoria's thirty-four years.

Pale blue eyes abruptly met shock-dulled blue eyes.

Mademoiselle Aimes unblinkingly studied the standing woman who wore a corded golden brown silk dress embellished with wine-colored velvet and green, yellow and red figured lampas, also of Madame René's artistry.

"She said I had passable legs, but that my breasts were too small and my waist too thick."

Victoria blinked. Michael's woman spoke like a lady: voice low, husky, cultured. English as Victoria was English.

"Madame René said that my breasts were passable, but that my hips and my derriere are too scrawny," Victoria quietly returned. "She said padding would alleviate the problem."

The pale blue eyes in the mirror alertly watched Victoria. "But Gabriel did not find you lacking."

"No, Gabriel did not find me lacking." Victoria rapidly blinked away the gritty exhaustion that blurred her vision. "Is"—what did she call the man on the bed, Michel or Michael? He was the Earl of Granville. Did she address him as Mr. or Lord?—"is he going to be all right?"

Victoria blinked again at the blinding beauty that became the woman's unassuming face. "Yes. Thank you. The doctor gave him a sleeping draught. In the morning I will take him home. Thank you for saving his life."

"How do you know? . . ." Victoria involuntarily glanced at Michael's sleeping face. The scars ridging his right cheek were smooth in repose, as they had been when in Gabriel's study, unconscious instead of sleeping.

"Gabriel told me," Anne Aimes said calmly.

Gabriel had talked to Miss Aimes, but he had not talked to Victoria.

She would *not* be hurt.

"I couldn't let him die," Victoria said truthfully.

Relief flickered inside the woman's pale blue eyes. "Michael and Gabriel are very special."

"Yes."

There was no question inside Victoria's mind at all that they were indeed two very special men.

"My name is Anne," the woman proffered.

Michael slept undisturbed.

"My name is Victoria."

Was Gabriel sleeping?

Or was he hurting because of a past that he could not change?

The pale blue eyes accessed Victoria. "Gabriel purchased your virginity."

Heat burned Victoria's cheeks at the unexpected confrontation. She squared her shoulders, prepared for condemnation. "Yes."

"I purchased Michael to take my virginity."

Victoria stared. Surely she could not have heard Anne Aimes correctly.

Taking a deep breath, Victoria carefully asked, "Did he?"

"All three." Anne's gaze did not waver. "So you see, we none of us can judge the other. We are all of us here because we need physical intimacy."

The echo of *all three* was replaced by *we are all of us here because we need physical intimacy.*

"Yes." The second man—Yves—had chosen her because of her need for physical intimacy. "Where did you meet . . . Michael?"

"Here." Soft husky laughter permeated the bedroom. "Well, not here. I rendezvoused with Michael at Gabriel's previous house. I always wondered what the bedrooms were like there."

Anne Aimes had surprised Victoria again. "You didn't know?"

"No." Annie sounded slightly disappointed. "Michael took me to his town house."

Black hair flashed inside the mirror where Victoria's face should be, was instantly gone. Truly her imagination.

Or was it?

Would she ever again feel comfortable in front of a mirror?

"The mirrors aren't . . . mirrors," Victoria said. And immediately bit her lip.

Anne curiously studied the full-length gilded mirror. "Really."

"They're called transparent mirrors. As long as the light is brighter on one side, a person can look through the mirror and . . . watch."

The lingering image of black hair was suddenly replaced by an image of an older woman with a younger man. Equal in their passion.

Anne's eyes widened. "Have you . . . watched?"

Victoria would not lie. "Once." And then, defensively, "I do not find physical intimacy repellent."

"Neither do I, Victoria." There was no censure in Anne's eyes. "Michael and I are getting married. He would be . . . hurt, if Gabriel did not attend."

Anne Aimes . . . and Michael.

Did Gabriel know they were getting married?

How much did Anne know of the night's events?

How much did she know about Gabriel?

"I can't promise what Gabriel will do or not do," Victoria said truthfully.

She could not guarantee that Gabriel still wanted her. All she could do was hope.

Anne abruptly stood up. The oak nightstand was her goal.

Victoria joined her. She towered over Anne by three inches.

Silver and gold shone in Anne's hair. She held up the silver tin of condoms. "There is a better prophylactic than condoms."

Victoria remembered the corrosive sublimate tablets Dolly had pressed upon her. Surely Anne Aimes did not—

"It is called a diaphragm," Anne said, no knowledge inside her eyes of a prophylactic that killed. "It is a rubber cap that fits over a woman's cervix." Pale pink tinted her cheeks; her gaze did not falter. "Diaphragms are more enjoyable for both a man and a woman, as it allows for maximum stimulation, but they are available by prescription only. I can give you the name of a gynecologist, if you like."

Victoria imagined what Gabriel would feel like without rubber sheathing his manhood. Wet flesh sliding into wet flesh.

The heat coloring Anne's cheeks leaped into her own. "Thank you. I would like that."

Victoria remembered the tin of mints Julien had urged her to take from the nightstand. It had not been replaced.

Impulsively she opened the top drawer, wanting to share the wonders of the House of Gabriel with this woman who had possessed the courage to pursue her passion rather than be victimized by it.

Anne stared down at the row of artificial phalluses for long seconds.

"They are called *godemichés*," Victoria said evenly.

Lightly Anne touched the smallest . . . "And Goldilocks said this one is too small . . ." Anne touched a second *godemiché*, "And this one is too big . . ." Anne did not touch the third *godemiché*, "And this one is just right."

Victoria raised startled eyes to Anne's.

Laughter danced inside the pale blue eyes.

A giggle rose up inside Victoria's chest; it was stalled by the memory of Gabriel's face. His eyes had been dull gray instead of glittering silver. "I have to go."

Compassion shouldn't hurt; it ripped Victoria apart, seeing it in Anne's eyes. "We all need to be loved, Victoria."

We all need physical intimacy . . . We all need to be loved.

It was little wonder Gabriel liked Anne Aimes. Victoria liked her, too.

She swallowed. "I don't know where he is."

There was no need for Anne to say Gabriel's name; he was foremost in both of their minds.

"He's in the adjoining room."

Victoria wanted to hug Anne; hugging had not been a part of her curriculum. Gabriel was the only adult she had ever expressed affection to. "Thank you," she said awkwardly.

For not judging Victoria. For not judging Gabriel.

For loving an angel.

Gabriel lay on top of a blue silk spread, left arm thrown over his face.

There was dried blood on his shirtsleeve; it crusted the front of his shirt, brown instead of crimson.

Victoria leaned against the oak door, heart inside her throat.

Gabriel was not asleep; tension corded his every muscle.

"You didn't lock the door," she said. And turned the lock, a quiet click of finality.

Gabriel didn't remove his arm, his voice was muffled. "You know what I am, Victoria."

Tension danced in the air.

Gabriel was wounded.

Gabriel was dangerous.

She pushed away from the door and reached for the tiny eyelet hooks fastening her dress. "I know what you are, Gabriel, and I will never forget."

The tiny report of metal hooks unsnapping charged the air, each release a miniature gunshot.

One second she stared at a bloodstained sleeve; the next she stared into dull gray eyes. "I'm not an angel."

Cool air gushed inside the widening vent of corded silk. "I think, Gabriel, that angels aren't who we think they are."

A muscle beside the left corner of his mouth pulsed in time to her heartbeat.

"I think angels must know hunger, or they couldn't be an angel."

Victoria shrugged out of her dress. Padded silk slid over the satin corset, briefly caught on the ruffled bustle, slithered over silk petticoats. "I think angels must know desire, or they could not know love."

The heavy silk dress puddled around her feet, a far cry from the worn wool gown she had previously shed for him. *She* was a far cry from the Victoria Childers who had previously undressed for him.

Victoria was a woman now, and she would not deny her needs.

Gabriel's nostrils flared, recognizing the transformation.

Victoria reached for the laces tying the dimity bustle.

Gabriel's face hardened. "Ask me, Victoria."

The ruffled, apronlike bustle dropped to the floor, a muted swish.

Victoria reached for the laces of a petticoat. "Ask you what, Gabriel?"

"Ask me if I desire Michael."

A white silk petticoat frothed over the golden brown dress. She reached for the lace of the second petticoat. "Do you?"

Unforgiving electric light danced on Gabriel's hair; darkness danced inside his eyes, still no silver. "What if I said I did?"

White silk puddled atop more white silk.

Gabriel instinctively followed the fall of the petticoat, stared at the silk drawers that clung to her hips. Immediately his head snapped up, gaze snagging hers. "I don't know."

The cry of an angel.

The pain in Gabriel's voice crushed Victoria's heart. She unbuttoned the two small ivory buttons fastening the band of her drawers, gaze holding his. "Michael kissed you."

Gabriel audibly sucked in air.

"Did you desire him then, Gabriel?" Victoria pursued.

The drawers slipped over her hips, down her thighs, dropped onto a mound of silk.

Gabriel's body was rigid with hurt. Hurt that *she* had inflicted, *but she didn't want to hurt him.* "Why don't you tell me, Victoria," he said rawly.

The pile of silk was perilously high; the pale blue carpeting dangerously thick. Victoria carefully crossed the divide that separated them, bare thighs rubbing, silk stockings swishing, no longer a virgin but a woman who knew well the pain and the pleasure of loving an angel. "I can tell you, Gabriel, that I am just as guilty of Julien's death as you are."

Gabriel mutely stared up at her. His pain fisted inside her stomach.

She had told Julien she would not tell Gabriel that he had allowed her out of the room; Victoria didn't think Julien would mind that she rescinded on her promise.

"I told Julien I wanted to visit a guest room in the hope that I would find something there to give you pleasure. I saw a man with dark hair in the mirror, or I thought I saw a man. But he was gone so quickly I thought it was my imagination. Gaston let me back into your suite. I didn't tell either Julien or Gaston what I saw. If I had, Julien might still be alive."

Denial flashed inside his eyes, a hint of silver. "He would have investigated the corridor. He would have died there."

Surrounded by mirrors that were not mirrors instead of the wooden confines of a stair landing.

"Perhaps," Victoria agreed. "But I will never know, will I? I will never know if my silence killed him."

Her pain shone inside his eyes. "Don't."

"But I have to, Gabriel." Victoria reached down to unfasten his blood-encrusted shirt, to free him from the past. "I have to touch you."

Hard hands cuffed her wrists. "If you touch me, Victoria, I will take you."

Victoria did not flinch from the strength of Gabriel's hold. She would have bruises come the morrow. "That is the idea, sir."

He wanted her to reject him; he wanted her to hold him.

His two disparate needs were ripping him apart.

She would not let him hurt anymore.

"You know what I am," Gabriel said starkly.

"You are Gabriel," Victoria steadily returned.

A man who made it possible for others to survive.

Puzzled frustration shone in his eyes, still more gray than silver. "You've never held my past against me."

Ten fingers pulsed against Victoria's skin; she counted them one by one, five around her left wrist, five around her right wrist . . .

"I'm selfish, Gabriel."

The truth popped out of Victoria's mouth unbidden.

It wasn't the response Gabriel expected.

"You said you wouldn't change the past; neither would I. I met Anne Aimes. She said that she paid Michael to take her virginity. I wish I had possessed the money and the courage to come to your house and proposition you."

He wanted to believe her; he was afraid to believe her.

"Anne prefers violet eyes."

The eyes of a man who had been born with the name of an angel.

"I prefer silver ones." The eyes of a man who had wanted to be an angel. She locked her knees to prevent them from buckling, asking the question that must be asked. "Whose do your prefer? Pale blue eyes or darker blue eyes?"

Gabriel did not pretend to misunderstand her. "Yours, Victoria."

Locked, her knees still almost collapsed with relief.

"I'm hungry, *Victoire*," Gabriel said deliberately. "Can you feed me?"

Two words simultaneously registered with Victoria. Her French name *Victoire*, and *hungry*.

Her pupils dilated with sudden recall.

How to seduce a man . . .

When he's hungry, feed him.

But she hadn't brought up any food.

She looked down into Gabriel's eyes and realized it wasn't food he desired.

"I only have . . . *ananas*, I'm afraid."

Pineapples. A French term for a woman's breasts.

Gabriel released her wrists and sat up, mattress shifting, springs squeaking, knees bumping her thighs, wool-trousered legs spreading, gripping her. "Feed me."

Hands shaking with sudden need, Victoria reached into the plunging black satin corset and lifted her breast. Her nipple was hard.

Leaning over, she offered it to Gabriel, her breast, her nipple, her passion rather than her virtue.

Dark lashes shielding his eyes, Gabriel nuzzled her, cheeks slightly prickly, hair softer than silk.

Every time Victoria orgasmed, she created another memory for him, he had said. Victoria would always remember the texture and the scent and the taste of the man who had named himself after an angel.

A tongue licked her, tasted her, texture wet and scratchy.

Victoria shuddered at the near-painful sensation that stabbed through her womb. She could not help herself—she cupped the back of his head with her left hand, her breast heavy in her right hand, his hair clinging to her fingers. And hoped that Gabriel would not pull away.

He did not.

Hands grasping the tops of Victoria's thighs, Gabriel pulled her closer and took her breast into his mouth and suckled her as if he fed on her flesh instead of her desire.

It took Victoria long seconds to realize that his fingers worked against her thighs to unfasten the garter clasps on her corset even as his mouth and tongue and teeth worked against her breast.

No sooner did Victoria's stockings slip down her thighs than Gabriel tackled her corset, fingers tugging, mouth tugging. A familiar pressure tugged at her womb.

Victoria's corset slipped over her shoulders . . .

Gabriel freed her nipple with a slight slurping sound. His cheeks were flushed, his mouth wet. The gaze looking up at hers was silver with need. "Tell me about angels, Victoria."

When he hurts, offer him hope.

But she didn't know about angels, she only knew about Gabriel. She didn't know the words to give him hope.

The story her mother had read to Victoria the child reverberated inside her ears. And suddenly she did know the words to give Gabriel hope.

I know it because . . . I know my own flower well.

"Whenever a good child dies," Victoria the woman stepped back and slid the corset over her arms; her stockings pooled around her ankles, "an angel comes down from heaven and takes the child into his arms."

Gabriel reached for the top button on his bloodstained shirt, a man, not a child. His silver gaze clung to her every word.

Wanting to hope. Wanting to be loved.

"The angel spreads out great white wings," Victoria dropped the corset, a soft swish of satin impacting wool carpet, "and flies the child over all the places he loved during his life."

With a quick jerk, mattress squeaking, Gabriel pulled his shirt over his head. Dark blond hair curled around a dark pap.

Gabriel's nipples were hard, as Victoria's nipples were hard.

She reached out and lightly touched him.

Gabriel flinched, but did not jerk away.

Victoria straightened, breath coming more quickly. She drew upon all the discipline it had required teaching other women's children, hoping it would be enough to get her through the coming minutes, hours, lifetime . . .

"The angel explains to the child as he flies him about that he gathers up flowers to take to heaven so that they may bloom more brightly in heaven than they do on earth."

Gabriel stood up and unfastened his trouser buttons.

He did not wear drawers.

Victoria licked lips that suddenly felt thicker, fuller. " 'The Almighty,' he says," Victoria said, " 'presses the flowers to His heart, but He kisses the flower that pleases Him best, and it receives a voice, and is able to join the song of the chorus of bliss . . .' "

Dark blond hair filled the widening vent.

Victoria jerked her head up. Only to stare at the top of Gabriel's bowed head as he jerked his trousers down.

" 'These words were spoken by the angel, as he carried the child up to heaven . . ."

Straightening, Gabriel kicked off his trousers.

He was naked with no stockings snagged at his ankles or slippers hiding his feet.

He had beautiful feet.

Between one heartbeat and another he dropped down onto his knees before Victoria, moist breath scorching her stomach. He tugged her left foot up.

Victoria floundered, falling, hands grabbing a head, hair silky soft, no purchase there; hands grabbing shoulders, instead, muscles tensed beneath smooth skin . . .

Gabriel's naked skin pulsed beneath her fingertips. He reared his head back. His breath kissed her lips. "Tell me more, Victoria."

Tell him how a child's fairy tale could help a man who had never been told fairy tales as a child.

Victoria stared into Gabriel's eyes and tasted Gabriel's breath. Leaning over him. Caught by his need and her position.

She told him more. "The angel and the child passed over well-known spots,"—Gabriel pulled off her left slipper, her left stocking, fingertips indescribably erotic, smoothing over her ankle, the top of her foot . . . Victoria caught her breath—"places where the child had often played, and through gardens full of beautiful flowers."

Gabriel released Victoria's left foot, tugged at her right, momentarily pitching her off balance.

Victoria's fingers dug into the knotted muscles that were his shoulders. "The angel asked the child,"—she tried to regulate her breathing, failed—"which flowers shall we take with us to heaven to be transplanted there?"

Gabriel straightened; perforce Victoria straightened.

The room tilted; in one motion Gabriel swept her up into his arms and set her onto her knees in the center of the bed, mattress rolling, springs creaking.

Gabriel reached for the silver tin of condoms on the oak nightstand, long eyelashes gouging dark shadows into his cheeks. "Which flower did the child choose?"

Expecting the obvious: only the most beautiful flowers were worthy of heaven.

"There was a"—Gabriel rolled up a sheath onto his manhood, brown rubber devouring the purple head of his crown . . . the bulging blue veins—"a slender, beautiful rosebush, but someone had broken the stem so that"—the sheath disappeared into the thick blond hair curling around the base of his penis—"that the half-opened rosebuds were faded and withered."

Had there been roses in Calais? she fleetingly wondered.

Gabriel lifted his left knee onto the bed, mattress dipping—he grabbed Victoria to hold her flailing body upright; she simultaneously grabbed him—right knee joining so that he knelt in front of her.

Breast to chest. Stomach to stomach. Groin to groin.

Gabriel did not move, caught in his need to be touched and his need to be free.

The nippled condom prodded her clitoris.

She carefully gripped his waist. There were bunched muscles there, too.

Pain darkened the silver of his eyes.

Gabriel did not pull away. He cupped Victoria's face, hands hard, eyes intent, breath scorching her lips. "Put me inside you, Victoria."

Put him inside her . . . while she . . . ?

She moistened her lips, tasting his breath. "Shall I . . . finish the story first?"

"No." His breath licked her upper lips, his penis licked her nether lips. "When I'm inside you, then I want you to finish it. I need to feel you, Victoria. I need to feel you holding me inside and out. I need you to make me believe . . ."

That a thirteen-year-old boy born in a gutter could be an angel.

Gabriel filled her hand with hot, rubber-sheathed flesh; he overflowed her hand with hot, rubber-sheathed flesh.

Gabriel did not fit into the tight space between her thighs.

Hot breath filled Victoria's lungs; hard flesh seesawed between her nether lips, sliding with each breath, each adjustment of the mattress.

Equally hard hands slid down her face, her neck, her shoulders, her arms . . . he firmly grasped her hips. "Lift your right knee and put your foot on the bed, leg splayed."

"What then?" she breathed.

This was awkward; this was reality.

This was a man and a woman sharing comfort as well as pleasure.

"Then you put me inside you," he murmured, as if in pain, words hot and moist, "and lower your knee so that you squeeze my cock and there is no place that we don't touch."

Inside. Outside.

Victoria raised her knee, leg splayed, and rested her foot flat onto giving silk. Nippled rubber notched her portal.

"Take me, Victoria." Flyaway hair haloed Gabriel's head. "Take me into your body and make me feel like an angel."

Victoria took Gabriel into her body, fingers guiding his flesh, slipping on her flesh, nipples prodding his chest, wiry hair prickling her breasts, elastic portal suddenly opening and swallowing him, the bulbous crown, the thick stalk . . .

Victoria gasped. Gabriel's eyes closed, as if he, too, could not bear the pressure.

Hardly daring to breathe, she lowered her leg. Air locked inside her chest. Gabriel filled her completely, vagina, lungs . . .

His eyelashes snapped open. "Tell me about the rosebush."

Rosebush? . . .

Victoria desperately grasped Gabriel's shoulders, thoughts circling, floundering—where had she left off in the story? "The child—the child wanted to take the hurt rosebush so that it would— it would bloom above in heaven."

With each word Victoria could feel Gabriel vibrate inside her vagina and slide between the lips of her labia.

"When the angel took the rosebush, he kissed the child's eyes open to keep him awake, because he was sleepy." Hot, moist lips kissed Victoria's left eyelid. Tears pooled in her eyes, leaked from her vagina. "And then the angel gathered some beautiful flowers and some plain buttercups and heartsease."

Gabriel kissed Victoria's right eyelid, eyelashes fluttering, his lips petal-smooth. The kiss rocketed down to her vagina.

"The child said"—Victoria squeezed her thighs together; Gabriel's breath plummeted through her—"the child said, 'We have enough flowers,' but the angel only nodded; he did not fly upward to heaven. Gabriel—"

Pleasure robbed her breath.

The agony in Gabriel's eyes gave it back.

"It was dark and still in the big town." She sank her nails into his shoulders, forcibly concentrating on the story and not the agonizing pleasure that was Gabriel. "The angel hovered over a small, narrow street. But the child could only see . . . a heap of straw . . . some broken plates . . . pieces of plaster, rags, old hats, and . . . other rubbish."

The French gutter Gabriel had been raised in suddenly reflected inside his eyes. *Straw . . . Offal . . . Broken glass . . . Rags . . . Rubbish.*

Victoria found the strength to continue the story of an angel instead of bursting like a helium-filled balloon. "The angel pointed to a broken flowerpot . . . 'and to a lump of dirt which had fallen out of it.' The flower had been thrown out into the rubbish."

Like Gabriel had been forced to live in rubbish.

Con. Fumier.

Gabriel's chest rose and fell, nipples rubbing her nipples, the wiry hair matting his chest prickling her breasts.

Victoria ached for Gabriel; Victoria ached from Gabriel.

"The angel said, 'We will take this with us.' " Her throat and vagina tightened, voice and sex strained past bearing. "But the child . . . couldn't understand why."

Did Gabriel understand? Victoria fleetingly wondered.

"The angel . . . he said that . . . a . . . a sick boy with crutches had lived there in a cellar . . . a boy who . . . who was poor . . . and who could not . . . could not go out to . . . see the flowers."

Gabriel bleakly stared into his past, anchored to the present by Victoria's body and her words.

"In the summer"—Victoria's nails gouged crescent moons into his flesh—he did not flinch, flesh turned into marble while hers cried out her need—"beams of sun would lie on the floor for . . . for a half an hour and he would . . . he would sit in the sunshine . . . and he would say he had been outside."

Gabriel's childhood dreams shone on his face. How often had he pretended that he had what passing children had—shoes, clothes that hid elbows and knees . . .

How much longer could Victoria concentrate on a story she had not heard in twenty-three years instead of the thick flesh that nudged her womb and slid on her clitoris every time she breathed, every time she *spoke*? . . .

"One day a . . . a neighbor's son brought him some . . . some field flowers. One of them . . . had a . . . a root. He planted the flower, and it grew."

It had survived, as Gabriel had survived.

Flyaway hair haloed the head of the man who still did not recognize his worth.

Victoria's body greedily clutched Gabriel as she fought to continue an angel's story. "Every year the flower—" she breathed more deeply—"bloomed. It was the boy's . . . own flower garden. He gave it water . . . and made certain it got . . . all the sunbeams. He dreamed about . . . his flower. He turned to the flower . . . for comfort . . . even when he . . . even when he died. But when the . . . the boy died . . . no one was there . . . to take care of his flower. And it was . . . tossed out.

Into the rubbish.

"And that is why, the angel said"—Victoria could feel her body swelling—"they were taking the flower to . . . to heaven . . . because it gave more *real* joy, the angel said, than the most . . . the most beautiful flower in a . . . queen's garden."

Victoria had seen many gardens—flowers planted to blossom in fashionable patterns. They had none of them imparted any joy.

" 'But how do you know all this?' asked the child," Victoria said, voice stronger. " 'I know it,' said the angel, 'because I myself was the . . . boy who walked upon crutches, and I know my own flower well.' "

Gabriel suddenly focused on Victoria instead of his past. "And who am I, Victoria? The boy who died or the angel who's carrying him?"

Victoria fought for control, won. "The angel, Gabriel."

Gabriel's face spasmed, marble splintering into flesh. "Why?"

"Your house is your garden, Gabriel. You take broken people and give them new lives." Victoria remembered the older woman and the younger man, sharing their passion; she remembered Julien, defending the House of Gabriel. "Take joy in your garden."

A harsh, strangled sound escaped Gabriel's throat—he threw his head back, eyes closed, dark lashes spiked. Victoria did not mistake the clear liquid crawling down his cheeks for sweat—they were the tears of an angel.

Gabriel silently climaxed, fingers digging into her hips, hands dragging her forward until Victoria's face pressed into his throat and her arms had nowhere to go but around his shoulders. She held him. Sharing his tears. And then she shared his orgasm.

Chapter

26

The white enamel-painted door swung open.

Gabriel froze, right hand raised to grasp the brass knocker.

Anemic sunlight turned brown eyes into amber. There was no emotion in their reflective depths.

Gabriel would recognize those eyes anywhere: they were the eyes of cold and hunger.

The echoing clip-clop of four hooves trodding a cobbled street rang out behind him.

"Monsieur Gabriel." The butler stepped back; silver threaded his thick chestnut-brown hair. He inclined his head. "Mademoiselle Childers."

Gabriel instinctively sought the small of Victoria's back; his leather gloves and her clothing blocked her flesh but not the healing comfort of touch. He fought the urge to turn around and hail the departing cab; instead, he urged Victoria forward into the small foyer of the brick town house.

Three figures were reflected inside mirror-shiny oak paneling: the chestnut-haired butler, black coat ending in twin tails; a man—taller than the butler—who wore a double-breasted gray wool coat and black bowler hat; and a woman who was the same height as the butler, hair hidden by a black Windsor hat, body shielded by a dark blue cloak.

Victoria reached up and pushed back the black half veil on her Windsor hat.

Even in the oak paneling her skin glowed.

Gabriel's guts twisted.

He had brought that glow to Victoria, a man who demanded her love but who wouldn't promise to return it. And now he saw the past through her eyes.

The small parlor had not changed in the seven months since he had last seen it. The variegated blue blooms of a hyacinth plant and a small, silver tray shone in the polished surface of a small oak side table. A mirror-shiny oak floor stretched out beyond the foyer. Flanked by wrought iron balustrades, a marble staircase marched upward.

"They are expecting you, *monsieur, madame.*" The butler extended a white-gloved hand. "If I may have your cane, sir . . ."

Gabriel's left hand involuntarily clenched the handle of his silver-headed cane. He did not know what to expect . . . from the people who waited.

Victoria caught his gaze. Her blue eyes were clear and calm.

It was his choice, they said.

He could continue living in the darkness of the past or he could step into the brightness of a future.

Gabriel gave the silver-handled cane that was no cane to the butler.

Reaching for Victoria, he held her thick, blue wool cloak while she slipped out of first one sleeve and then the next. Efficiently the butler took the cloak, gloved fingers deftly avoiding Gabriel.

Gabriel peeled off his black leather gloves; Victoria reached up, copper silk bodice straining across her breasts—she had sensitive breasts, beautiful breasts, breasts that even now he hungered to feed off of—and slid out the hat pin securing her hat. Her copper-tinted brown hair was secured in a French twist; he would free it when they got home. Her gown molded her waist; he would remove it in the privacy of his suite.

Or perhaps he wouldn't wait.

Perhaps he would introduce her to the pleasure to be had while straddling his hips inside a moving carriage, the bump and grind of the wheels carrying them both to orgasm.

Taking off his bowler hat, Gabriel dropped his black leather gloves inside the satin-lined felt. The butler silently accepted the hat, fingers skirting Gabriel's.

Gabriel did not wait for the butler's assistance in helping him out of his reefer coat; nor did the butler expect him to.

He held out his left hand for Victoria.

The more she touched him, the more he craved her touch.

Peeling off her gloves, Victoria thrust them into the reticule looped over her wrist. Heat shot through his testicles: the pleasure of naked flesh embracing naked flesh.

Antoine did not need to show Gabriel the way. The sharp click of Victoria's heels rang out; they were accompanied by the softer pad of his own leather boots.

"Monsieur Gabriel."

Gabriel paused, left foot on a marble step. Victoria paused at his side. "Yes?"

"Je suis heureux que vous soyez venus."

I am happy that you came.

It was not a butler who spoke, it was the man who had waited upon tables and clients inside Gabriel's old house; he had eagerly jumped at the opportunity to become a butler seven months earlier.

His hand convulsively tightened around Victoria's fingers. *"Suis ainsi je*, Antoine."

Gabriel lied.

He did not know if he was glad or not.

Echoing steps spiraled upward, the past approaching, the future at his side.

An oak floor ran the length of the upstairs hallway. Gabriel silently traversed the distance . . . remembering . . . trying not to re-member . . .

The door at the end of the hallway was open, revealing a glimpse of pale blue silk-covered walls . . . more oak floor . . . the sweet pun-gency of roses.

I know my flower well . . .

Taking a deep breath, Gabriel released Victoria's hand and sought the heat in the small of her back. She stepped over the threshold, Gabriel following.

Violet eyes locked with silver eyes.

Inside Michael's gaze Gabriel saw the eyes of the thirteen-year-old boy who had taught him to read and to play the gentleman in exchange for lessons on how to fight, to steal, and to kill.

But Gabriel had never wanted Michael to kill.

And now he had killed for Gabriel.

The voice of the second man—Yves—rang inside his ears. *You love Gabriel, Michael.*

I have always loved him.

But Michael had thought his name was Gabriel; now he knew differently.

Michael had thought he was invulnerable; he now knew that was false, too.

Gabriel waited; dimly he was aware of a low, feminine voice— Anne. It stopped midsentence.

"Miss Aimes?" an unfamiliar masculine voice demanded.

Gabriel did not look at the stranger: he knew what the man's profession was, if not who the man himself actually was.

"Is this the man and woman whom you are waiting for?" The stranger sounded slightly garrulous.

The minister had been kept waiting by an angel.

Michael's violet eyes reflected the irony.

Suddenly Anne stood before Victoria. Elegant in a sky blue silk gown.

She was three inches shorter than Victoria.

A spinster and a governess.

Two women who had never known love but who now glowed from the love of a man.

Victoria solemnly pulled out a rectangular silk-wrapped box from her reticule. "I brought you and Michael a wedding gift."

Anne's pale blue eyes reflected Gabriel's surprise. Hurt slashed through him, that Victoria had felt it necessary to keep her gift a secret.

Flushing with pleasure, Anne accepted the silk-wrapped box. "There was no need. You and Gabriel are all that we wished for." A darker flush reddened Victoria's cheeks. "It is nothing, really. Just something that you admired."

Anne stilled. "A *godemiché*."

"Just the right size," Victoria returned evenly.

Laughter.

It boiled up inside Gabriel's chest until it ripped out of his throat. And with the laughter came the need for Victoria.

Hands blindly reaching, Gabriel pulled her back against his chest. Victoria stiffened in surprise, spine rigid, buttocks fitting into the niche of his groin. He wrapped his arms around the woman who had brought him the gift of touch and who now gave him the gift of laughter. Instantly Victoria melted, her bones becoming his bones, her flesh becoming his flesh.

Violet eyes caught his gaze.

And Gabriel remembered . . .

Il est bien, Gabriel . . . It's all right, my friend.

The laughter died as quickly as it had stopped.

It *was* all right.

Turning his face into the warm fragrance of her skin, Gabriel whispered the words he could no longer hold inside, *"Je t'aime, Victoire."*